Craig ... mavens ... was Ge... DeMott ... to grace ...

of Jan. 2... ... was "virtually the only woman" of what the magazine deemed a distinctively American genre, "apt to mix the pleasures of the wake and the moment in a combination of hard drink, hilarity and homicide." This Rice did in high-spirited, Chicago-based spoofs like *8 Faces at 3* (1939), *The Big Midget Murders* (1942) and *Knocked for a Loop* (1957).

Her life was less a laughing matter. The Dorothy Parker of detective fiction, Rice wrote the binge but lived the hangover. Rice's father was a painter, her mother a "cosmopolite"; while her parents sojourned in Europe, divorced, married and remarried, Georgiana was raised by an aunt and uncle. She ran away from Miss Ransome's School in Piedmont, California, to become a "Bohemienne" in Chicago. There she went through a succession of five marriages of her own, providing two daughters and a son.

When *Time* got hold of her, Rice was living in Santa Monica and had written 15 books, including mysteries under the pseudonyms Michael Venning and Daphne Sanders. She would ghostwrite for stripper Gypsy Rose Lee and actor George Sanders. She scripted two entries in the *Falcon* film series and other creditable B movies.

She was deaf in one ear, blind in one eye and threatened with glaucoma in the other. In 1949 she was committed to Camarillo State Hospital for chronic alcoholism. Rice twice threatened suicide.

She was found dead in her Los Angeles apartment on Aug. 28, 1957, "apparently," reported *Newsweek*, "from natural causes."

Rice was 49.

—William Ruehlmann
Series Consultant

Novels by CRAIG RICE
available in a Crime Classics® edition:

featuring Malone and the Justuses
8 FACES AT 3
THE CORPSE STEPS OUT
THE WRONG MURDER
THE RIGHT MURDER
TRIAL BY FURY
THE BIG MIDGET MURDERS
HAVING WONDERFUL CRIME
THE LUCKY STIFF*
THE FOURTH POSTMAN*
MY KINGDOM FOR A HEARSE*

attributed to Craig Rice
CRIME ON MY HANDS by George Sanders

by Stuart Palmer and Craig Rice
PEOPLE VS. WITHERS AND MALONE

forthcoming
Series Consultant: William Ruehlmann

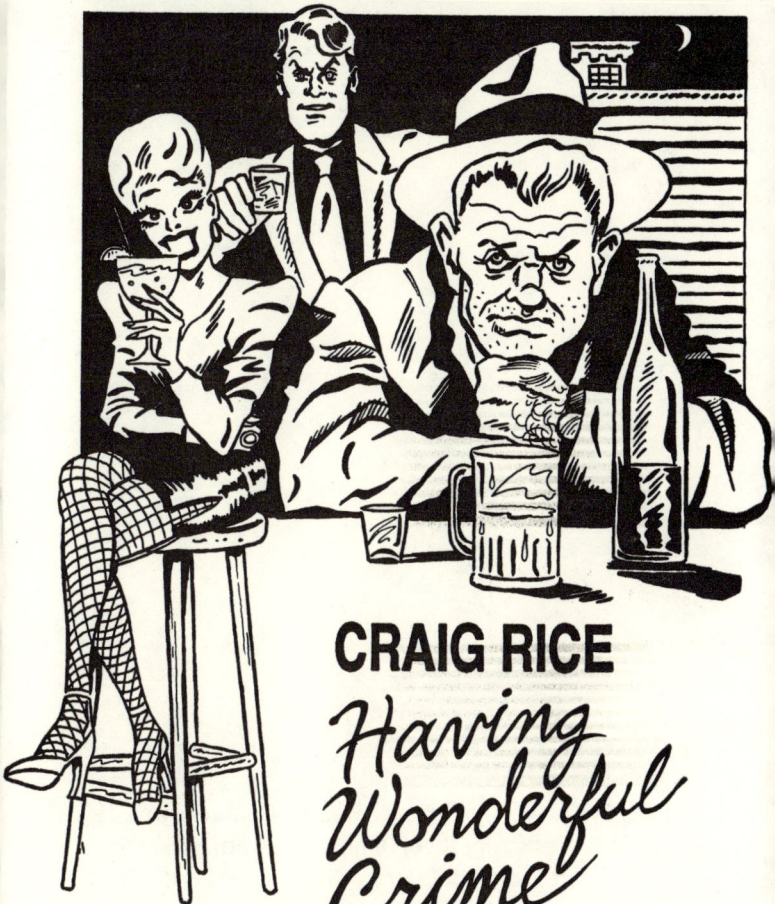

CRAIG RICE

Having Wonderful Crime

LIBRARY OF CRIME CLASSICS·
MISTER E'S™

INTERNATIONAL POLYGONICS, LTD.
NEW YORK CITY

HAVING WONDERFUL CRIME

Library of Congress Card Catalog No. 92-70421
ISBN 1-55882-125-2

Printed and manufactured in the United States of America.
First IPL printing June 1992.
10 9 8 7 6 5 4 3 2 1

TO PHOEBE GODWIN, my favorite reader, with heartfelt thanks for the most wonderful suggestion I've ever received.   C. R.

Chapter One

THERE was always one hour of the day when he believed, acutely, in hell. It came very early in the morning, just before sunrise.

It was a time of torment, of fears, apprehensions, and occasional regrets, of tortured half-waking, half-sleeping dreams, memories he'd tried over and over to bury, and premonitions of a future he didn't like to face.

Then, too, there was a persistent, throbbing pain in his head, and a burning, terrible thirst.

He'd learned that if he could only get back to sleep, and stay asleep for a few more hours, he'd wake feeling himself again, a little on edge, perhaps, and with no appetite for breakfast, but himself. After those few hours he could go out into the world again, the charming, amusing young man who did, occasionally, get a trifle high at parties (but not often, nor objectionably) and did, now and then, win or lose at poker games (but only once in a while, and never too much).

So there would always be the desperate struggle to get back to sleep again, closing his eyes and burying his face in the pillow. Sometimes an aspirin and a glass of milk would do the trick, when he could goad himself into getting out of bed and going to the refrigerator. Or, a bottle of cold beer would invariably work, though that was likely to leave him with an unpleasant, crawling sensation in his stomach when he woke later.

In that hour of awful waking, though, his desire to sleep again had little to do with how he would feel and act when he got out of bed, two or three hours later. Rather it was a desperate need to escape from the things that plagued his mind.

This morning, though, was going to be the last. He turned over in bed, his eyes still closed, and put one arm across his face to shut out the light. Beginning today, from this morning, this moment on, he was on the wagon, and completely on the wagon, a drinker of tomato juice and ginger ale.

It wasn't an ordinary hangover resolution, to be broken by eleven in the morning. He'd never made any of those since he was nineteen, being enough of a realist to know how little they meant. No, he was becoming a teetotaler from pure necessity. After yesterday, he had to.

He'd gone on last night's bender for the same reason. He had to.

He took the arm away from his face and slowly and uncomfortably opened his eyes.

This wasn't his own bed he was in. This wasn't his room. It was a place he'd never seen before.

It wasn't his room, but it was a gorgeous one. Even in his present state of mind and body, he could appreciate it. It was obviously a hotel room, in one of the best and most expensive hotels. The furniture was handsome and re-strained. The walls and draperies were pleasantly unob-trusive. The pictures were tactfully chosen. The bed was swell.

Obviously, he'd fallen in with very charming people last night—not that he could have felt any worse right now if he'd fallen in with bums and wakened with his face on the wet paving of an alley.

One of the charming people was a woman. The mauve

satin-covered down comforter didn't belong to the hotel, nor did the monogrammed pillow slips. A woman of taste and refinement and wealth, who carried her personal linens and comforters with her when she traveled.

He wondered if she was beautiful and susceptible and unmarried, and then reminded himself that it wouldn't matter to him any more, not after yesterday.

He closed his eyes again and reminded himself that he had to sleep, trying to pretend that it was still dark. Sleep, beautiful sleep, dreamless and inviolate, sleep like death, that was the thing. He tried thinking of everything that was darkness, black velvet, a black cat, ebony, the bottom of a mine. He tried to pretend that he was on a fine private yacht, preferably his own, bound for Havana, and that he could hear the soft lapping of waves. He tried to pretend that he was in a hospital room—with nothing serious, of course, a sprained ankle, perhaps—white-walled and hushed, with nurses and doctors to care for him and protect him against the world. He tried to pretend that he was back on Grampa's farm, in the little attic room, that it was just past dusk and that he could hear the crickets under the whispering trees. He tried to do everything but remember the night before. That was always disastrous, in the terrible early morning hour.

But this time, he couldn't help remembering.

This was one morning when he wasn't going to get back to sleep.

With a groan, he pushed himself up in bed and swung his legs over the edge. His hands and feet were cold; for a moment he was trembling and half sick. But his mind was wonderfully clear, now.

The first few steps were always difficult. Then his feet and his mind began to co-ordinate again. He crossed the room and stared at himself in the dressing-table mirror.

He looked like hell. His thin, handsome face was pasty and pale, his dark hair rumpled and greasy. There was a small bruise on his cheek; he must have got that by tripping over some crack in the sidewalk. His protuberant, light-blue eyes were bloodshot and staring.

But his host had excellent taste in pajamas.

His host also had excellent taste in dressing gowns. He picked up the brown brocade one that had been left on the foot of the bed, put it on, and tied the cord. Then he went into the bathroom and splashed cold water on his face and brushed back his hair. He felt a little wobbly, but he was good-looking again.

There was coffee in the next room. He could smell it.

He pushed open the door into the next room and stood for a moment, looking, trying to remember when and where and how he'd met its occupants.

The most beautiful blonde girl he'd ever seen was stretched out on one end of the sofa, sipping at a cup of steaming coffee. Her hair was straight and shining and almost the color of strained honey. Her delicate-featured face was luminously pale. She was tall, and long-legged, and graceful. She wore a pale-green lamé dinner dress and a pair of ostrich-feather mules. She smiled up at him as he came in and said, "Hello. Have some coffee."

The man sprawled at the other end of the sofa was big and bony and ungainly. He had badly mussed red hair, surprisingly blue eyes, freckles, and a friendly grin. He looked up and said, "Boy, I bet you feel terrible."

The third person in the room didn't even stir. He was short and stocky, with thick shoulders. Someone had been playing tick-tack-toe on his shirt front, and his necktie was under one ear. His round face was reddish and perspiring, a lock of black hair fell over his forehead. He was beginning to need a shave. He was slumped in a big easy chair, snoring.

The blonde girl poured a cup of coffee, held it out, and said, "Sit down. I'm Helene Justus. This is my husband, Jake Justus. He runs a saloon in Chicago; he won it on a bet.* That's John J. Malone over there, the best criminal lawyer in forty-eight states. If you ever commit a murder, let him know."

The young man took the coffee, felt for a chair, and said, "I'm Dennis Morrison. Thanks for bringing me home with you. I——" He took a sip of the coffee, put the cup down suddenly on the table, jumped up, and said, "*My wife!*"

"She'll forgive you," Jake said easily. "They always do."

"You don't understand," Dennis Morrison said. "We were just married yesterday. At four o'clock. We had dinner. Then we came here, to the hotel." He realized that the little red-faced man, John J, Malone, was awake now, looking at him with wise, almost sardonic eyes. "Bertha had a little unpacking to do. I felt—well, not embarrassed, but—— Oh hell, you know what I mean."

The blonde, Helene, smiled at him sympathetically, and her husband, Jake Justus, said warmly, "I certainly do."

"Well," the young man said, "well, I thought I needed a drink. And I thought maybe she wanted to be alone. You know. So I went down to the bar to get a drink. I had a couple. Then I met some people. We had a couple more. And then," he paused, frowning, "I'm not very sure what did happen. I remember something about a floor show in some night club. It wasn't a very good floor show. And riding in a taxi, I remember that. But I

* The Casino. See *The Right Murder*.

don't remember meeting you, or coming here, or anything——" He paused, and said, "*Bertha!*"

"Young man," said John J. Malone, "what you need
is a drink *now*. There's some bourbon in the bathroom."

He poured an inch and a half of bourbon into a water
glass, handed it over, and said, "I've never been married
myself, but this stuff fixes anything."

Dennis Morrison said, "Thanks," and gulped. The raw
liquor went down like water and hit like liquid fire. But
his nerves began to settle down to something almost near
normal. He shuddered and said, "Guhhhh."

"See," the blonde girl said brightly. "You feel better
already."

He managed to smile at her. "I know this sounds silly,"
he said, "but where did we meet?"

"Downstairs in the lobby," she said. "You were trying
to steal the lilies from the flower display to take upstairs
as a present to the most beautiful girl in the world, and
the room clerk was being a little difficult about it. You
looked sort of helpless, so we adopted you."

"Oh," Dennis Morrison said. He looked down at the
rug. "I don't know what you think of me, doing a thing
like this, on my wedding night."

"Think nothing of it," Jake Justus said. "On our wedding night, Helene was in jail for reckless driving." *

"And assaulting an officer in the attempt to do his
duty," Helene said proudly. "The next night, Jake got
mixed up with some Southern moonshine and didn't get
home for eighteen hours."

"Stop reminiscing," John J. Malone said wearily. "This
young man has to get home to his bride. What is he going to tell her?"

* *The Wrong Murder.*

Dennis Morrison looked up at him, groaned, buried his head in his hands, and said, "I'm a louse."

"That is not the thing to tell a bride," Helene said sternly. "You were kidnaped."

"You had an attack of amnesia," John J. Malone said.

"You were shanghaied," Jake said.

There was a little silence. Then Helene rose, smiled, and said, "Oh hell, tell her the truth. She won't care. We'll all go with you and convince her it's the truth."

The young man looked up, a gleam of hope in his eyes. "Would you? Really?"

"Sure," Helene said. "But put your clothes on first. We won't take you home to your bride in Jake's pajamas."

"You're very good to me," he said. "I don't know why you should be so good to me."

Helene said, "Because you're so beautiful, and because we're so kind, and because you're so helpless. Now go put your pants on."

He pulled himself to his feet and stumbled into the bedroom.

Jake waited till he was out of sight and then said sternly to Helene, "Now look. We didn't come to New York to get mixed up in other people's troubles."

Helene looked at him for a long time before she said quietly, "No, we didn't. We have enough of our own."

Jake looked away and turned a trifle pale. Malone got up again, swayed toward the window, and looked dismally at Fifth Avenue, ten stories below.

"I don't like New York," he said unhappily. "I want to go home."

The door to the bedroom opened and Dennis Morrison came out. His face was white, but he was smiling. His dinner jacket didn't fit him very well, but, even so, it was becoming. "I'm really not worried about what Bertha will think," he said. His voice was unconvincing.

"But you'd like us all to go along and back up your story," Helene said. "O. K. We'll make it a parade."

Jake and Malone went with her to the door. The young man stopped them there, one hand on the knob.

"I don't want you to think," he said, and then paused. "I mean, I want you to understand," he began again, "you see, Bertha——"

There was a thunderous knock outside the door. Jake and Helene glanced at each other, and then Jake threw it open.

There were two policemen there, and a house detective. They looked from Jake to Malone to the young man, and one of the policemen said, "Which one of you's Dennis Morrison?"

The young man said, "I am. Why?"

The two policemen looked at each other and one of them said in a low voice, "O. K., so the elevator boy was right." He turned to Dennis Morrison. "You in suite 713?" Dennis Morrison nodded. "Got a wife?"

Dennis Morrison nodded again. "Bertha. What—— Is she all right?"

"I'm afraid not," the policeman said. His voice was rough, but kind. "I'm sorry, boy, but I'm afraid she's dead."

There was a silence, and then Dennis Morrison said, "Oh God, no!" His face was dead white and perfectly expressionless. He swayed a little.

Helene reached a hand out to grasp his arm, looked at the policeman, and said, "This isn't any time to make jokes."

Dennis Morrison shook himself loose. He stared at the policeman and said, "*No!*"

"Pull yourself together, boy," the policeman said. He sounded almost gentle now as he spoke. "Because I'm sorry, boy, but I'm afraid she's been murdered."

Chapter Two

"IF I HADN'T gone out," Dennis Morrison said in that flat, emotionless voice, "if I hadn't left her alone. I just went downstairs to get a drink. If I'd only come right back upstairs again. I could have fought him off. I could have protected her. But I wasn't here. It must have been a robber. It must have been a maniac. It couldn't have been anything else. Because everybody loved Bertha. Nobody would have wanted to kill her. Only a robber." He drew in a long breath and began again, "If I hadn't gone out. If I hadn't left her alone."

"That's enough," Helene said sharply. "You're a big boy now." Her face was pale; her eyes were big and dark and shadowed. She smiled at him.

"But we'd just been married," he said. "Only yesterday. And she had some unpacking to do, and I went downstairs to get a drink, and I met some people. If I hadn't left her, it wouldn't have happened. I could have fought him off." There wasn't any emotion in his voice.

"You'd better have a drink, fella," John J. Malone said. He reached down behind the sofa cushions and pulled out the gin bottle he'd carried from Jake and Helene's suite, concealed under his coat. There wasn't any glass in sight, so he held the bottle to the young man's lips.

"Thanks," Dennis Morrison said automatically. He shuddered. Then he began again, as though someone had dropped the needle back on a phonograph record. "Crazy accident. Why did it have to happen to us? We were only married yesterday. We hadn't even—you know what I mean. Bertha hadn't an enemy in the world. She was sweet. Everybody loved her. With all the rooms there are in this hotel, why did a fiend have to break into this one? Why *us*? We'd only been married yesterday. If I only hadn't left her alone——"

"If you don't shut up," Jake Justus said grimly, "I'm going to smack you square in the kisser."

Dennis Morrison looked up at him, and said, "I'm sorry." He glanced at the closed door to the bedroom and said, "Damn it, why don't they get through in there?" Then he drew a long, gasping breath, and said, "*Bertha!*"

The door opened and the young man from the Homicide Bureau came out. Arthur Peterson. He was slender and not very tall. His light hair was thinning on his dome-shaped head, his skin was an unhealthy yellow, and he wore thick-lensed glasses. But his eyes were friendly and for just a moment he seemed almost embarrassed at speaking to the man who'd been a widower before he'd been a bridegroom.

"Tell me," Dennis Morrison said. "Was she——?"

"No," Arthur Peterson said. "No, it wasn't that." He managed not to look at Dennis Morrison even for a moment. "Your wife was a very wealthy woman, wasn't she?"

"I guess she was well fixed," Dennis Morrison said. "I never asked."

Arthur Peterson looked at the ceiling and said, "I'm sorry to have to bother you with all these questions, at a time like this. But you understand, it's purely a matter of routine. You aren't exactly wealthy, are you?"

"My God," Dennis Morrison said, "are you suggesting I married her for her money?"

"Nothing of the sort," the pale man said hastily. "But you will inherit it, won't you?"

Dennis Morrison said, "I have no idea."

John J. Malone couldn't stand it any more. He stepped up and said, "If you're going to examine this young man, I insist on his lawyer being present."

Helene whispered, "Attaboy, Malone."

The man from the Homicide Bureau looked at him and said, "Indeed. And who is his lawyer?"

"Me," John J. Malone said, drawing a long breath.

"That's fine," Arthur Peterson said. "And you are present, so we can go right ahead." He raised his thin eyebrows. "Assuming you are a lawyer."

"I am the damnedest fine lawyer that ever came down the pike since Portia," John J. Malone said a trifle thickly. "And if you attempt to intimidate my client, you'd better stay away from the city zoo in the future. Because I'll make such a monkey out of you that they'll be chasing you with butterfly nets." He pulled the gin bottle out from behind the cushion and said, "Shall we drink to it?"

"No thanks," Arthur Peterson said, wincing. "Liquor is poison to my stomach."

"Routine questions," said John J. Malone. "That's all I'll let him answer."

The routine questions covered the details of where Dennis Morrison had been the night before, and why. The man from the Homicide looked a tiny bit sympathetic. Not very much, though. Then the door to the bedroom opened, and everyone looked at it.

Assistant Medical Examiner D. Royale St. Blaise came out, a tall, dark, tired-looking man. He ignored everyone in the room except Arthur Peterson and said with professional callousness, "Beautiful job of decapitation. A surgeon couldn't have done better. Of course, she was killed about two hours before. I need further tests to determine the exact cause of death. But it was a beautiful job. Cut off neat as a——" He realized the presence of the widower, and said hastily, "I—beg your pardon."

"*What happened to her?*" Dennis Morrison said.

"Someone called her on the telephone," Arthur Peterson said. "When there was no answer, this party—we haven't located him—said he was sure she was in and someone had better investigate. The house detective went up. He found the door unlocked and went in and found Mrs. Morrison in bed, the covers pulled up over her chin, almost up to her nose. She was dead. Her head had been cut off."

Nobody looked at anybody else. Jake instinctively reached for Helene's hand, then drew back again.

Then Dennis Morrison stood up. "But why *Bertha?*" he said. He reached inside his left-hand coat pocket for his cigarettes, tried the right-hand pocket, then the inside pocket. Suddenly he stiffened. "*This isn't my coat,*" he said suddenly.

"Come, come now," Arthur Peterson said. "Let's not play games."

"No," Dennis Morrison said. "No, look. My God, it doesn't even fit." He moved his shoulders. The dinner jacket definitely didn't fit. He reached in his pocket, pulled out a cigarette case engraved Q. P. Z., reached in another pocket and pulled out three blue match folders printed in red, Q. P. Z. Then he pawed in the inside pocket and brought out an expensive monogrammed wallet, black leather, and crammed with folding money. The monogram was Q. P. Z. But there weren't any identification cards, not any at all. Not even a driver's license.

"That's the coat you had on when we picked you up," Jake Justus said. "I know, because I took it off you."

Dennis Morrison didn't seem to hear him. He glanced down to his left, then reached suddenly for his breast pocket and pulled out his handkerchief. "It isn't my coat. But this is my handkerchief. Look." There were initials on the handkerchief. D. M., for Dennis Morrison. He stood looking at it for a long time, not saying a word.

Then, "Listen, buddy," Arthur Peterson said in his expressionless voice. "You've got to do this sooner or later, so you might as well do it now as have to come down to the morgue. You've got to identify her."

"All right," Dennis Morrison said. He stood up. "What do I do?" He seemed to be in a daze.

Arthur Peterson and the medical examiner looked at each other, and then the examiner said, "Just take a quick look, that's all. It's nothing but a legal formality and it won't take but a second. Just look at her face, that's all. She looks pretty good, don't worry. We'll be right with you. It's just the formal identification."

"All right," Dennis Morrison said. "Where is she?" He moved mechanically toward the bedroom door. Royale St. Blaise took his arm and began mumbling the trite condolences long memorized by a doctor in the medical examiner's office. The door closed behind them.

One of the two uniformed policemen mumbled to the other, "Bet you two dollars he gets sick." His buddy mumbled back, "I'll take you. He looks strong. Besides, the doc fixed her up so you can't even tell her head was cut off."

The bedroom door burst open suddenly. Dennis Morrison appeared there, his face not white now, but ghastly gray. His eyes were staring, dark with horror.

"But that isn't Bertha," he said. "That isn't her at all." His hand grasped the door jamb, tightened on it. "That's someone else." His voice rose, almost to a scream. "Where is Bertha? *Where is she?*"

Chapter Three

"THERE is a train for Chicago," Malone said, "at six-forty-five tonight." He stole a look out of the corner of his eye at Helene, and added firmly, "And I am going to be on it."

He waited hopefully for some answer from her. There was none. She didn't even seem to know he was there. She was gazing at a tiny speck on the polished surface of the bar as though it were the moon reflected on Lake Minnetonka, or Venus seen through the telescope at Yerkes Observatory. Malone reached out and brushed the speck away and said, "Tonight. Six-forty-five *tonight*." She sighed faintly and transferred her gaze to a minute puddle of beer which, from the look on her face, might have been Lake Michigan seen from the top of the Palm-olive Building. Malone turned to the bartender, waved, and called, "Two more." Still there wasn't a peep from Helene.

There was something about the look on her face that he didn't like. He'd seen her under many circumstances and in many moods. White-faced, blazing-eyed, and still cool and calm, on a day when a friend had been accused of and arrested for murder. That had been the first time he'd seen her; she'd had on pale-blue satin pajamas, a fur coat, and galoshes, she'd just met Jake Justus, ex-reporter and press agent, and there had been a Look on her face. There had been a delicate glow in her cheeks the day she'd announced that she and Jake were engaged.

He'd seen her looking scared, happy, and starry-eyed the day she and Jake were married. He'd seen her terrified but grimly brave when Jake was missing, probably kidnaped aand possibly murdered. He'd seen her with her lovely, patrician face smudged with dust and soot, with cobwebs entangled in her shining hair. He'd seen her happy, worried, thoughtful, sad, gay, drunk, sober, angry, indignant, sympathetic, and bored. But never like this, absent-minded and, somehow, faraway.

Malone paid for the beers, cleared his throat, and began again. "I came here," he said loudly, "under false pretenses. You long-distanced me yesterday afternoon and lured me into coming to New York. You said you had a problem and you needed my help immediately. You said I could spend a pleasant vacation in New York and have a wonderful time." He paused to drink his beer and relight his cigar. "I came to New York, breaking a date with a very charming young lady to do so. I caught the train. I got here. And what did I find?"

He waited for a moment. He might have been talking to someone in the next room for all the attention she paid him. He cleared his throat a second time, and went on. "I got off the train at quarter past seven this morning. You and Jake met me. I'll ignore, for the moment, the fact that both of you were in evening dress. We went to the hotel, where I expected to find a bed. Instead, I found some strange drunk who has a murder on his hands." He snorted loudly. "I haven't had any sleep, I haven't had any breakfast, the only cheap liquor on the train was terrible, and I lost twenty-four dollars in a poker game between Buffalo and Albany." He didn't add that he'd also lost his return fare to Chicago. That could be considered later. "And," he said, "I am going back to Chicago at six-forty-five tonight." He looked at Helene's exquisite profile, counted ten, and then said angrily, "Well, what do you have to say?"

Helene frowned. She said, "I wonder where Bertha Morrison *is*."

"I don't know," Malone said, "and I don't care. And who the hell is Bertha Morrison?"

She shoved the newspaper that had been lying by her elbow in front of him. Malone glanced at it, trying to pretend he wasn't interested. The headline was a little too much for him, and he went on reading.

HAVE YOU SEEN THIS WOMAN?

"Never in my life," Malone said gloomily. He looked at the three photographs, Bertha Morrison, née Bertha Lutts, at seven, a plump, dull-looking child. Bertha in her graduation dress, a heavy-set, dull-looking girl. Bertha's wedding picture, a round-faced, dull-looking woman.

WHERE IS BERTHA MORRISON? a caption read.

"I haven't the faintest idea," Malone told the caption. He didn't want to read any more, but he couldn't help it. He took one more look at the two-column full-face picture of her, and shook his head sadly. It was going to be damned hard to convince anybody that young Dennis Morrison hadn't married Bertha Lutts for her money. Malone went on reading.

Bertha Lutts hadn't attracted any attention during the

thirty-three years of her life. Then she'd made up for it fast, and all at once.

She hadn't been numbered among the richest girls in the world, and she'd never appeared in the *Social Register*. She hadn't made a debut, and her name had never been in Winchell's column. Her picture had never been in a newspaper until now.

But she owned a couple of Cadillacs, she had a chauffeur and a maid, she lived in an expensive apartment, she had charge accounts in all the best stores. She had a big block of A. T. & S. stock, a good-sized section of profitable real estate in Brooklyn, an unquenchable yen for life, and no friends.

There were a lot of girls like Bertha Lutts. Born to be plump and dull, and born to a father who made a lot of money and invested it wisely. They were well fed and well cared for, they had their teeth straightened and their eyes protected with expensive glasses, but they never went to fashionable boarding schools or joined exclusive sororities. They grew up to buy costly clothes, with good labels, that never fitted very well, but they never had any place to wear them. Usually they were left orphans at an early age. Papa died from the strain of making money; Mamma died from the strain of living with Papa.

A few of them went into business and made more money. Others hired companions and became perpetual tourists. Some met congenial nurses and became chronic invalids. Some went in for tweeds and heavy shoes and managed dog kennels. Some moved to southern California and became religious, giving their time and their incomes to little groups with no money, a small meeting hall, and an exalted name, like The Society of the Lavender Lily. They organized bridge clubs, they became unpaid social workers, they sometimes (unfortunately) became interested in politics. Occasionally they joined Lonely Hearts clubs. ("Attractive man, 42, world traveler and scholar, would like to meet lady interested in discussing poetry.") And once in a while, ōne of them got married.

Rich old maids—who began being old maids at the age of fourteen. Bertha Morrison, née Lutts, had been one of them.

"A perfect fortune-hunter setup," Helene commented. "Only usually it turns out that when a rich thirty-three-year-old orphan marries a poor but charming young man, she's found ten weeks later stuffed under a culvert somewhere in Nebraska. This happened another way, and it doesn't make sense."

"I am not interested," Malone said stiffly. "I am not even curious."

"And I," Helene said, just as stiffly, "am not talking to you. I'm talking to myself." She looked at the newspaper again and scowled. "They met and they loved. It could have been like that. Just because she had money doesn't mean he married her for it. Well, anyway. They get married. Then on his wedding night this guy gets a terrific attack of bashfulness and goes out and gets plastered and doesn't come home. He turns up wearing a dinner jacket that belongs to some perfect stranger with the initials Q. P. Z. but with his own handkerchief in the breast pocket." .

"Nicely folded, too," Malone said.

Helene was silent for a moment. "Maybe it happened like this. Someone slipped him a mickey with the idea of robbing him and walked off with his jacket. That could explain how he lost his own jacket."

"Then a fairy godfather in a well-fitted dinner coat comes along and slips our hero a new coat." Malone said gloomily. "Besides, he said he didn't have much money in his own wallet. While Q. P. Z.'s wallet was stuffed with ten-buck bills."

"All right," Helene said. "You find an explanation."

"It's none of my business," Malone said. He got tired of trying to attract the bartender's attention and drank Helene's beer.

Helene said, "He woke up in the morning full of remorse at having walked out on his bride. But his bride is missing. Malone, where the hell could she be?"

"Gone home to Mother," Malone said.

"But she's an orphan," Helene said.

The little lawyer sighed. "That remark is supposed to lead into a very bad vaudeville joke, but for the life of me I can't remember how it goes. Will you shut up and stop bothering me." He raised his voice and addressed the bartender. "Put down that *Racing Form* and pay attention to your customers."

"It isn't the *Racing Form*," the bartender said. "It's *The New Republic*. Was there something you wished, sir?"

"I do my wishing on four-leaf clovers," Malone said. "But since you're here, you can bring us two beers. And give me a double rye for a chaser."

"Yes, sir," the bartender said. He was a tall, thin, blond young man with melancholy eyes and a Boston accent. He began filling the glasses, then suddenly caught himself and looked questioningly at Malone.

"You heard me," Malone said hoarsely. "Where I come from we always drink rye as a chaser for beer. I'm a Chicago gangster and I shoot people when they don't serve me properly. Now gimme those drinks."

The bartender said, "Yes, *sir*," shoved the glasses across the bar with shaking hands, and fled back to *The New Republic*.

"This," Malone growled, "is a hell of a saloon."

"It isn't a saloon," Helene said. "It's a cocktail lounge. And you're a big bully, and you ought to be ashamed of yourself." She lit a cigarette. "Malone, what could have happened there last night? The bride vanishes. In her place is a beautiful woman, still unidentified, wearing a very elegant nightgown, and neatly decapitated." She glanced back at the newspaper and added "Decapitated after she was killed. She'd been strangled, and she'd put up a terrific struggle. Bruises and contusions all over."

"That just goes to show," Malone said in a morose voice, "never struggle while you're being strangled. You get bruised."

"All Bertha's jewels are missing," Helene went on relentlessly, "and so is Bertha. Where is she? What's it all about?"

"At eleven o'clock in the morning," the little lawyer moaned, "you bring up problems like that."

"Dennis Morrison is being held for questioning," she said. "Malone, they can't keep that poor young man in jail, can they?"

"Ask them," Malone said, drinking his rye. "Or ask his lawyer."

Helene said, "But you're his lawyer."

Malone put down his glass and turned to her. "This is New York, not Chicago."

"Perfect nonsense," Helene said. "Besides, you don't have to go into court, or even talk to the police. All you have to do is find Bertha, find out who strangled and decapitated that unidentified woman, and get Dennis Morrison out of jail."

"At six-forty-five tonight," Malone told her firmly, "I will be on the train for Chicago." He lit his cigar. "Funny damn thing, though, about that dinner jacket." He decided it was time to change the subject. "Where's Jake?"

"I don't know," Helene said. She tried unsuccessfully to make it sound like, "I don't care."

Malone looked at her, opened his mouth to speak, and closed it again. Something—he didn't know what—was wrong. He didn't like to admit how much it worried him. There were just two people in the world he loved very dearly. Jake and Helene.

Whatever was wrong was serious enough to make Helene send for him. But what the hell was it? She'd tell him about it when she got good and ready, he reminded himself, and in the meantime there was no use asking questions.

"Jake goes out," Helene said suddenly, "and stays away for hours at a time. He says it's business, and he'll tell me about it later. But what is it, and why doesn't he tell me now? And why does he insist on staying on in New York, when we'd only intended to be here a week or two?"

"It takes time to look over Radio City," Malone said.

Helene sniffed scornfully and said nothing.

Was it another woman? Impossible, Malone told himself, looking at Helene. He was sure there was no woman in the world—indeed, no woman had ever been born—who could compete with Helene. And Jake had worshiped her since the first day he set eyes on her, the day of the Inglehart murder, dressed in blue satin pajamas, a fur coat, galoshes, and with a quart of gin in the side pocket of her high-powered car. No, it couldn't be another woman.

"And he's worrying about something," Helene said. "I can tell."

Malone said, "It's all your imagination."

He'd realized that Jake was worried when he first stepped off the train. He too could tell. Financial troubles? Hardly. The Casino back in Chicago was out of debt and doing a rushing business. Anyway, if Jake was worried about money, he wouldn't be here in New York, he'd be tearing back to Chicago to do something about it.

What the devil kind of trouble could Jake be in that he wouldn't tell Helene? Maybe he was being black-mailed. No, that was absurd. There wasn't any sin or crime Jake could ever have committed that he wouldn't tell Helene about.

One thing was certain, it wouldn't do any good to go to Jake and say, "Look here, what the hell's the matter with you?" When Jake had anything to tell, he'd tell it in his own way and his own time. Meanwhile——

"There is a train for Chicago," he began again.

"At six-forty-five tonight," Helene said acidly. "I heard you the first time."

The little lawyer sighed. He did want to be on that train. There was, of course, the unfortunate fact that he'd lost his return fare in that poker game.

Financially speaking, it had been a particularly bad time for him to take the trip. When Helene's call had reached him, he'd been sitting in his office, looking admiringly at a very lovely little bracelet that had cost him exactly half of all the money he had in the world. And he'd been con-templating the date he had that evening with a charming young person from the Casino floor-show chorus.

Regretfully he'd broken the date and taken back the bracelet. Then he'd bought a shirt, a pint of cheap rye, and a ticket for New York. Of the remaining money, there was nine dollars left after the disastrous poker game.

Naturally Helene had asked to pay his fare, and natu-rally he'd refused, informing her that he had more money than he knew what to do with. He knew she didn't be-lieve him, but he hadn't expected her to.

Of course, he could wire Joe the Angel to wire him the price of a ticket home. Maybe he'd better do it right now.

His thoughts were interrupted by a voice saying, "Oh, here you are. The desk clerk told me he thought you were in the bar."

It was Dennis Morrison. He looked very tired. He still had on the mysterious dinner jacket, and his dark hair was mussed as though he'd been running his hands through it. His eyes were just faintly swollen and pink-rimmed.

"They let me go," he said hoarsely. "But I could see they didn't believe a word I said. Tell me, what am I going to do?"

"You're going to sit down," Malone said sternly, "and have a drink. You need one."

The bartender leaned over the bar and said, "Oh, aren't you the gentleman who——"

Malone fixed a cold eye on him and said in an ominous voice, "In Chicago, when we find curious bartenders——"

The bartender fled for the second time.

"Stop scaring him," Helene said. "It's mean."

"I don't like him," Malone said.

He moved over to the next stool so that Dennis could sit between them. A train for Chicago, he reminded himself. Six-forty-five. Wire Joe the Angel for money. No mixing up in this affair. He avoided Helene's reproachful eyes, and tried not to look at the expression on Dennis Morrison's very young and very handsome face.

"They haven't found Bertha yet," Dennis said. "They haven't identified that other woman. Nobody knows what's happened to Bertha. Where is she? And the police don't believe me. I can tell they don't believe me." He looked up helplessly. "I don't know why I should bother you two with this. I only met you this morning.

But I haven't any other friends in the world." He buried his face in his hands.

Malone crushed out his cigar, took a fresh one from his pocket, and began unwrapping it slowly and thoughtfully. There would be a train for Chicago at six-forty-five tomorrow night, too. After all, he hadn't seen anything of New York yet. Not that he was going to get involved in this——

But it wouldn't do any harm to give the young man a little good advice. Besides, if Helene got interested in the case, it might take her mind off her anxiety about Jake.

He carefully looked away from her, though, as he said, "My dear boy, you have nothing to worry about. You couldn't be in better hands. Now let's move over to a booth, where we can talk in private."

Chapter Four

JAKE JUSTUS watched from behind an enormous armchair in the lobby of the hotel until he saw Helene and Malone emerge from the elevator and head toward the bar. Even at that hour of the morning, tired and distracted, he realized for possibly the two-thousandth time how gorgeous she was. He saw heads turn to look at her as she walked across the lobby, and the sight created a pleasant little glow in his mind.

She was wearing something made of a dull, pale-blue stuff, she had a wide-brimmed, darker-blue hat pulled down over her shining hair, and her fur coat was thrown carelessly over her shoulders. He found himself imagining he was seeing her for the first time, with her delicate, perfect profile, her pale skin and fair hair, her lovely, long, slim legs. He realized that if he were seeing her for the first time, he'd follow her. It took a great effort of will to keep from following her now.

Instead, he waited until she and Malone were out of sight, and then walked hastily to the elevator, with a large, brown-paper-wrapped package under his arm. He'd been there in the lobby for nearly two hours now, holding the package he'd received from the desk clerk, waiting until Helene was out so that he could go upstairs and open it.

He'd never kept secrets from Helene before. He didn't want to now. But it was necessary, if he was to surprise her the way he'd planned.

Jake closed the door behind him and locked it. Then he sat down and stared at the package. There would be a letter inside it. He knew exactly how it would begin.

DEAR MR. JUSTUS:
Thank you for letting us see your novel, *The Mongoose Murders,* which has been read with a great deal of interest. We feel, however——

He knew how it would end, too;

. . . We shall be happy to consider any future work which you may submit to us.

He knew because he already had four letters tucked away in his wallet, all beginning and ending the same way. The only difference between them was in the letterheads, the signatures, and the words immediately following the "however."

Perhaps he ought to give the whole thing up and go home to Chicago. Jake closed his eyes and pictured the dingy, shabby old La Salle Street station as it would look in the early morning. Outdoors, it would probably be raining, cold and dismal, and it would be dark and noisy under the el as the taxi went through the Loop, bumping over the old paving on Van Buren Street. But over on Michigan Boulevard he would be able to see the faint mist rising from the lake, and the trees in Grant Park would be putting out their first, pale-green leaves.

Only, he couldn't go back to Chicago yet. If he did, he would never be able to explain to Helene why he'd insisted in staying on in New York all these weeks, and why so often he'd been unaccountably absent for hours at a time. He'd never be able to surprise her when there wasn't a package left at the desk, just a letter, beginning:

DEAR MR. JUSTUS:
We want to publish your book and——

Jake Justus sighed, took out his penknife, and began cutting the strings around the manuscript package. There was always a ghost of a chance that the enclosed letter wouldn't contain that word "however." It might, instead, say, "If you will make certain changes——" In that case, he'd make them so fast that the paper would scorch. He'd make every certain change required. In fact, he'd change every blessed word in the manuscript except the "By Jake Justus" on the title page and the two-word dedication.

Those two words, *To Helene*, had required a week of thought and soul-searching. He'd tried such variations as *To my wonderful and understanding wife*, and *To the*

most beautiful girl in the world, and even experimented
with a dedicatory poem beginning:

> *Whatever I write,*
> *Whatever I do,*
> *My inspiration is You.*

From there he'd moved to the purely literary, such as
To One Who Knows, and to the purely corny, such as
To You, My Guiding Star. Once during the week, in a
Loop bar, he'd composed a marvelous dedication of
which, later, he could only remember that it contained
one line, "You are the light of all my nine lives," which
didn't seem to make much sense the next day; and something about Helene's legs being the loveliest in ten million years of time, which, later, he considered to be true,
but irrelevant. He'd written it on a paper napkin which
he lost in the taxi on the way home. Following that experience he'd settled for just plain *To Helene.*

After all, what it really meant was, "I love you, I love
you, I love you." It didn't matter how it was phrased.

He finished cutting the string and pulled off the heavy
brown paper. Two pages from the manuscript slid off his
lap and fluttered to the floor. One of them was blank save
for *To Helene.* The other began with "Chapter One,"
and, *It was a dark, dismal, dreary day in the County Jail.*"
Jake picked them up and slipped them under the rubber
band around the manuscript.

For a moment or so he held the unfolded letter in his
hand. Then he went into the bathroom and poured himself a drink. Then he sat down in the big easy chair, lit a
cigarette, and took a long, slow drag. And then he unfolded the letter.

"With certain changes" would be as good as an acceptance. He'd already rewritten the book four times. Jake thought over the last months, and smiled wryly. *The Mongoose Murders* had started out as *Memoirs of a Reporter,* by Jake Justus. Publisher A had written, "We feel, however, that a volume of personal reminiscences would not, at this time——" and had suggested that the material could be incorporated in a novel sometime.

Jake had rented a typewriter and some office space, and written *In the Shadows of the Jail,* A Novel, by Jake Justus. Publisher B had written, "We feel, however, that while the characters are interesting, there is not sufficient plot to hold them together——" Jake had added a homicide, a jewel robbery, a fire, and a wreck on the North Side elevated. Publisher C had written, "We feel, however, that while there is an interesting story, the characters are not sufficiently convincing, and the lack of love interest——"

Jake had finally submitted *One Wonderful Hour,* A Romance, by Jake Justus, to Publisher D. Jake had great hopes for Publisher D, who finally wrote, "We feel, however, that while this is an unusual love story, and the characters are interesting, there is a lack of suspense——"

Then Jake had come to New York, and just about when Helene was beginning to get a little restless and to ask difficult questions about their long stay, *The Mongoose Murders,* a Mystery Novel, by Jake Justus, had gone to Publisher E. And now——

Jake crushed out the cigarette in the ash tray at his elbow and read the letter.

DEAR MR. JUSTUS:
Thank you for letting us see your mystery novel, *The Mongoose Murders,* which we have read with a

great deal of interest. We feel, however, that while the background material and your handling of it are unusual, the plot shows an unfortunate lack of knowledge of crime-detection methods. Therefore the book as a whole is not sufficiently convincing as a murder mystery. We shall be happy to consider any future work you may submit to us.

Sincerely,
LEE WRIGHT
Simon and Schuster

"What the hell!" Jake said out loud. Lack of knowledge! Why, as a reporter on the *Herald Examiner*, he'd helped to solve one of Chicago's most baffling murders, when, within a month, four apparently inoffensive postmen had been found slain at the same point in their routes. That was when he'd first met John J. Malone, who'd been the lawyer for the suspected slayer. And then there had been the time when a rich old woman had been found murdered in a house where every clock had stopped precisely at three. And the whole series of murders that had involved his best publicity client, the radio star Nelle Brown. Why, hell's bells, his ownership of the Casino had come about through his helping to find the murderer of three men who had all seemed to be named Gerald Tuesday. And then there had been the murder of ex-Senator Peveley, in a sleepy little Wisconsin town, and the murder of a nasty-tempered midget in Jake's own night club. Lack of knowledge indeed! He'd tell the writer of that letter—what was his name?—Oh yes, Lee Wright—he'd tell Lee Wright where to get off!

Only, he realized suddenly, Lee Wright, editor of the mystery department of Simon and Schuster, couldn't have been expected to know about Gerald Tuesday, or ex-Senator Peveley, or even about the strange little man named Joshua Gumbril, who'd been murdered at the corner of State and Madison Streets, on the busiest shopping day of the year. Because Jake had always kept his part in those affairs out of the newspapers.

The tall, red-haired ex-reporter and ex-press agent rose and began walking slowly up and down the room. Maybe, he reflected, he'd better become an ex-author.

As he paced back and forth, he glanced absent-mindedly at the newspaper that had been left on the coffee table. On his first glance he read, HAVE YOU SEEN BERTHA MORRISON, and muttered, "No, and I never want to." On the next trip he took in HEIRESS MISSING IN MYSTERY MURDER, and on the third trip he paused a moment to read, UNKNOWN BEAUTY FOUND SLAIN IN SWANK HOTEL. By the time he reached his fourth lap, he'd picked up the paper and was reading the story that began with, "One of the most baffling crimes that ever——"

He carried the paper with him for one more trip around the room, and then sank down in his chair, the paper on his knees, staring at the letter he'd left on the end table.

". . . an unfortunate lack of knowledge of crime detection . . ."

Lack of knowledge, hm! He'd show them!

He hadn't been a press agent for nothing!

By the time he'd found the missing Bertha Morrison, identified the Unknown Beauty, and handed over the murderer to the police, he'd be able to walk into that editor's office with his manuscript under one arm and a book of press clippings under the other, and say, "*What* lack of knowledge?"

Jake folded up the letter and tucked it away with the four he'd already received. He hid the rejected manuscript under his clean shirts in the bureau drawer. Then he settled down to study the newspaper account of the crime and to compare it with his personal knowledge of the case.

He was going to have to work fast. But he'd worked fast before, and he could do it again. Maybe that surprise for Helene was going to come off after all.

Chapter Five

CATHARINE McCLOSKEY, seventh-floor chambermaid of the St. Jacques Hotel, was a cheerful and agreeable soul. There was nothing, she liked to say, that she wouldn't do for a friend.

She considered that nice Mr. and Mrs. Justus in 721 to be special friends. It wasn't only because Mr. Justus was so lavish with tips, nor because Mrs. Justus had discarded a number of expensive and beautiful dresses which could be made over elegantly for Mrs. McCloskey's daughter, Mary Margaret. Nor was it even because neither of them appeared to notice the occasional inches that disappeared from the bottle of John Jameson's Dublin Whisky that stood on the bathroom shelf.

No, it was simply because Mr. and Mrs. Justus were friendly people. There was nothing she wouldn't have done for them.

So when the nice Mr. Justus asked her to use her passkey and let him into 713, where that awful murder had been committed last night, giving as his reason a curiosity which she found perfectly understandable, she was delighted to oblige. And she promised by a number of saints, her honor, and her dead mother that she'd never tell a soul.

"Now myself," she said, unlocking the door, "you couldn't drag me into there, not with a herd of wild horses, you couldn't. The housekeeper, she sez to me, 'Katie, don't you touch that room until the cops get back and get through with it.' And I sez, 'Don't you worry, I won't even touch it when the cops *do* get through with it.' That poor lady, lying there with her head sliced off just as neat as you please, all dressed up in a lace and satin nightie that must of cost fifty dollars if it cost a penny. No, I didn't see it myself, but one of the elevator boys told me. Yes, indeed, I will forget I let you in. Oh, thank *you*, Mr. Justus. For ten dollars, I'd forget my dead father's name, rest his soul."

Jake closed the door behind him and stood looking around the parlor of 713. What could there be to find here? He had no idea. The police had already been through the suite with a whole series of fine-tooth combs. The finger-print men, the police photographers, and all the rest of the specialists.

Yet he felt that in order to find a murderer and iden- tify his victim, the place to start was where the murder had occurred. Similarly, in order to locate a missing person, the search should begin at the place from which the person had disappeared.

He looked hopefully around the room, as though he expected a clue to be written on the walls, or Bertha Morrison to come popping out from behind a chair. The parlor of 713 was almost a twin to the parlor of the suite he shared with Helene, save that it was in reverse. The windows were on the left side instead of the right, and the imitation fireplace was on the right side instead of the left. The walls were a pale blue gray instead of a pale green gray, and there was a corresponding difference in the colorings of the draperies and the framed flower prints on the walls.

A charming room, furnished in the best and most unobtrusive of taste by a costly interior decorator. But what did it have to tell him? For that matter, what did searching the scene of a crime tell anybody?

Clues? If the murderer was smart and clearheaded and knew what he was doing, he didn't leave any vest buttons lying on the carpet, or fingerprints on the doorknob. If he was dumb, or reckless, or in a violent rage, he usually got caught without benefit of clues. Nevertheless, the first thing to be done in the event of murder was to search the scene of the crime.

Catharine McCloskey had made this search possible. But what in blazes was he going to look for? Fingerprints? Jake grinned wryly. He didn't know how to find a fingerprint, or what to do with one if he did find it. These scientific cops picked up bits of lint from the carpet and dust from the window curtains. Maybe he should have brought along a vacuum cleaner. But even if he collected a bushel of lint, he wouldn't know what to do with it except stuff a pillow.

He started moving around the room, not so much looking or listening as trying to *feel*. The hell with fingerprints, dust, lint, and vest buttons; a room itself could answer questions, once you knew what questions to ask.

Dennis Morrison and his bride had planned to leave this morning on a honeymoon tour. They'd checked into the St. Jacques yesterday afternoon. Then why were all the bride's clothes put carefully away, the dresses on hangers, the lacy lingerie folded neatly in the dresser drawers? There should be handsome and expensive luggage somewhere. If it wasn't here—and it wasn't—it would be in the hotel storeroom.

People didn't unpack like that to stay overnight in a New York hotel.

But only she had unpacked. Dennis Morrison's shaving things were in the bathroom, his brushes were on the dresser, one suit was hanging in the closet—a business suit—and a clean shirt and brand-new tie were on the top of the bureau. There was a locked and obviously unpacked pigskin suitcase in one of the two bedroom closets, and another pigskin suitcase left open—the shaving things, brushes, shirt, and tie had evidently been taken out of it.

Bertha Morrison had unpacked and settled herself as though she intended to stay a month. Dennis Morrison had been packed and ready to leave in the morning. Jake closed his eyes and stood thinking. They'd been married at four in the afternoon. They'd had dinner. Then they'd arrived at the St. Jacques, and Dennis had started out on his bender. She must have unpacked after he left.

The hotel manager had said that the suite had only been reserved for one night. Dennis Morrison had said they planned to leave for Banff, Sun Valley, Victoria, Yosemite, and the Grand Canyon in the morning. Then why the devil had Bertha Morrison done such a complete unpacking job?

The police, looking for fingerprints, lint, dust, and vest buttons, didn't notice things like that. Jake prowled around the bedroom, reflecting on how a room could tell what had happened in it. Bertha Morrison had taken a bubble bath. He knew from looking at the marks on the bathtub. She'd smoked two cigarettes while she was in the tub; the stubs were in a tray propped up on the soap dish. And she'd drunk a glass of—he sniffed—champagne. He looked under the bathtub and found an empty bottle. Not just a glass of champagne, a quart. She'd used body oil, bath powder, hand lotion, pancake make-up, and two kinds of perfume. She'd put curlers in her hair—they were still faintly damp when he found them in the drawer of the dressing table—and then sprayed her hair with Lakker-Myst. She'd put on mascara, eyebrow pencil, rouge, and lipstick. A hell of a thing, Jake reflected, going to all that trouble expecting your bridegroom to come in the door—and then having your bridegroom go out and get drunk as a goat, and a murderer coming in the door instead.

Only, Bertha Morrison hadn't been murdered. Some unidentified woman had been murdered in Bertha Morrison's bed, wearing a lace and satin nightgown. And Bertha Morrison, bathed, curled, made-up, and perfumed, and probably a little drunk, was missing.

All this is very fine, Jake told himself, but it doesn't tell you where Bertha Morrison is, who was murdered, and who murdered her.

The police had hardly touched the desk, save for dusting fingerprint powder over its polished top. Jake stood looking at it thoughtfully. Bertha Morrison had not only unpacked her clothes and her cosmetics, but also her portable typewriter and letter case as well. He scowled at the typewriter. It was pale-blue enamel; the keys were pink with dark-blue letters. And it was monogrammed, too. B. L. in gold, for Bertha Lutts. Jake thought the typewriter ought to tell him something about Bertha. As a matter of fact, it did. Jake began to dislike her.

There was a sheet of letter paper in the typewriter. The design in its left-hand corner was a badly drawn but beautifully printed queen bee. Jake shuddered. There

were a few words typed on the paper. The typewriter
ribbon was blue.

April 29th

Dear Uncle George:
  We are deliriously happy . . .

Jake stared at it. There was something wrong about
that letter, just as there was something wrong about the
whole setup of the room. Not just the words "we are
deliriously happy," written in a room from which the
writer of those words had disappeared, and in which an
unidentified woman had been brutally slain and muti-
lated. But something else. It was a moment or so before
he realized what it was.

The unfinished letter was dated April 29th. But this
was April 9th.

Oh, well, everybody made mistakes in typing.

But if Bertha had made such a mistake, she'd have cor-
rected it immediately or put in a fresh sheet of paper.
Everything he'd learned so far of Bertha, from looking at
her closet, her dressing table, and her bureau drawers,
indicated correctness, order, and methodical neatness.
Bertha would never have made a mistake like that.

Had the police already searched the Florentine-leather
letter case? Jake stared at it. There was a faint dusting of
finger-print powder over its top. But there was also a little
heap of cigar ash. It had fallen, he remembered, from
Malone's cigar, earlier in the day. Malone had been pacing
up and down the room and sounding off to the guy from
the Homicide Bureau, with that big Irish mouth of his.

He wished Malone was here with him now.

The letter case, then, was virgin territory. The cops
certainly hadn't explored it before the time Malone

dropped that cigar ash, and, obviously, save for the finger-printing, they hadn't explored it since.

Jake lifted the lid gingerly, as though he expected Bertha Morrison, or the murderer, or perhaps a brace of leopards to jump out, and looked down at a neatly typed page.

Write to:
Olive Eades
Josephine Diehl
Dorothy Finny
Eunice Olsen
Melva Engstrand
Martha Chalette
Dagmar Slagg
(See address book.)

He fished out the address book, bound in white leather, with B. L. tooled on the front. At the top of page one was *Abramson, B.*, and an address and phone number. Underneath was written *bootlegger* in faded blue ink, crossed out in brighter ink and supplanted with *merchant*. Below it was *Adams, J.*, address, phone number, and *doctor*. Then *Allenberg, J.*, with the notation *dentist*, very recently crossed out, by the look of the ink, and supplanted with *retired*.

Jake turned quickly to the C's. *Martha Chalette. Lex. 2-5762. 345 W. 34th St. Married to an artist. Bridge Club.* He turned another page.

Josephine Diehl. Biddeford, Me. Martha Washington Hotel when in town. Bridge Club.

The next page indicated that Olive Eades worked for an advertising agency as a typist, and that Melva Engstrand was getting a divorce. Jake decided not to spend time checking up on Dorothy Finny. He stuffed the typed page and the address book in his pocket and went on examining the contents of the letter box.

There was a little sheaf of bills, neatly clipped together, from Altman's, The Colony Lingerie Shop, Lord and Taylor, and Chez Rosette, all with *paid* and the date carefully written in a fine Spencerian script in blue ink. There was a paid-up bill from the World-Wide Mailing Service. There was a bill from Prendergast's, Inc., with a notation *Ask about 74¢ overcharge on brassière.*

There was a letter from a Bohemian orphanage in Indiana, giving thanks for a generous contribution, and there was a fat package of letters asking for money, all bound together with a rubber band, and with a notation clipped to them reading *Investigate.*

There was a letter signed *your Uncle George* and beginning *Dear Bertha: I hope you'll be very happy, but after all you hardly know the man.* Jake stuffed that in his pocket for future reading.

Nothing, so far, Jake told himself, that was worth slipping Catharine McCloskey ten bucks, save for the knowledge that Bertha Morrison would have made somebody a damned efficient secretary. Every letter had the date of its receipt and the date of its answer carefully marked at the top. Even one that read *My dearest, darling, angel Bertha—our evening at the opera was so wonderful. Say that we'll meet again, and soon. Your helpless slave, Dennis* had a notation in the corner in the fine Spencerian handwriting and the light-blue ink, *Rec'd February 23rd. Answ'd February 25th.*

Well, at least, Jake comforted himself, he was getting a good picture of neat, methodical, depressing Bertha Lutts Morrison.

There was a letter, typed on shadow-thin paper, with

italic type and brown ribbon, at the very bottom of the letter box.

Bertha—
Cruel are the pitiless hands . . . and cruel laughter stains the lips . . . and nearer every day the night . . . when stars look down and weep—to see how Death with stealthy tread creeps in to keep his rendezvous with love. How bright, how gay will be the April day when you are bruised and dead.

UU. UU.

What the hell!

Someone had written to Bertha Morrison, before last night, threatening to kill her. Someone who signed himself, or herself, UU. UU. Damned silly signature, unless it was written by Siamese twins. Damned silly letter, for that matter.

Besides, it hadn't been Bertha who'd been found murdered. Bertha had disappeared.

Just the same, this was the closest he'd come to a clue. If he could find the writer of that letter——

Perhaps, if he went through the desk drawers, he'd find something more. He dropped the letter on the blue enameled typewriter and pulled open the top right-hand drawer. It was empty, save for a sheet of notepaper reading:

> *hairdresser, 10* A.M.
> *reducing class. 3* P.M.
> *buy new girdle* (important)

The top left-hand drawer contained a copy of Dr. Stopes' *Married Love.*

The rest of the desk was empty. Jake was just closing the bottom left-hand drawer when he heard a key rattling in the front-door lock. He ducked into the bedroom, fast, and stood just inside the door, listening.

He heard footsteps, heavy footsteps. There seemed to be three people coming in. One of them was whistling *Just a Memory*. Another voice said, "Cut that out!" and the whistling stopped. Then an unhappy-sounding voice said, "I don't know what the inspector wants us to look for."

Cops!

If they found him here, then his chance of solving the case was lost and gone forever. Where could he hide? No draperies big enough to duck behind. The closets were likely to be searched as a matter of routine. The bed was so close to the floor that only an underfed worm could crawl under it.

"Well, we gotta look around," one of the voices said.

Jake managed to cover the distance between the bedroom door and the bathroom without making a sound. He stepped inside the shower bath and pulled the curtains around him.

This was just another one of those routine searches, he reassured himself. The cops would be through in a few minutes, and then he'd be able to make his escape.

Not until he heard one voice say, "Aw, there's nothing here," and another one answer, "Just the same, we better search. Peterson might check up," did he realize he'd left the letter signed UU. UU. in plain sight on the desk. And by then, it was too late.

Chapter Six

THERE WERE two advantages to hiding in the shower bath. Jake could hear everything said in the outer rooms, and by parting the curtains half an inch he could see most of what was going on.

There was, however, one disadvantage. The last person using the shower hadn't turned it off completely, with the result that a thin stream of cold water ran down inside Jake's shirt no matter how he shifted to avoid it. He didn't dare monkey with the faucet, because that would undoubtedly make a noise, and this was obviously a time for silence.

He could hear, and occasionally see, three men in the room beyond the bedroom. Two plain-clothes men and a uniformed cop. The cop was a big, bored-looking guy who moused around the room looking for cigars. One of the dicks was a little shrimp with a shrill, angry voice, and the other was a tall, thin, unhappy-faced dope who looked as if he had stomach trouble.

"This is just a routine search," the little guy said. "Peterson said we have to make a routine search. Personal possessions. That sort of dope. Don't know why *we* should be stuck with it but we are."

The tall one said, "Wonder if there's any bicarb in this place."

He came into the bathroom and opened the medicine cabinet, while Jake held his breath. He found a bottle of soda mints, took four, slipped the bottle into his pocket, and went out again.

Jake encouraged himself with the reminder that the cops, after all, weren't expecting a man to be in the apartment, and therefore they wouldn't search for one. In fact, they were in the same position in which he had been; they didn't know what they were looking for.

"For Chrissakes, Birnbaum," the little guy said, "why don't you take a layoff and get your stummick fixed up."

"Because I'd have to stay home with my wife, that's why," Birnbaum said gloomily. "I'd get worse than ever. It's her cooking that's the trouble, anyway."

"Hey, O'Brien." The uniformed cop called from the bedroom where he'd opened a bureau drawer. "Come lookit all these swell lace underpants. D'ya think one of 'em would be missed? I know a girl in Canarsie about this size."

"Lay off that stuff, Schultz," the little man, O'Brien, said. "We're here to look for evidence."

"Maybe you are," Schultz said, "but I'm still looking for a cigar."

They inspected the closet, the dressing table and the bureau, just as Jake had done, commenting favorably on their contents. "Imagine one babe owning all those nighties," O'Brien said. Birnbaum took another soda mint, belched, and said, "My wife wears flannel ones." O'Brien opened the perfume bottle, sniffed, and put a drop on his handkerchief. "Never could resist perfume," he explained apologetically.

It was Schultz who found the sheet of thin paper, typed on with brown ink. Jake heard him call out, "Hey, lookit, fellas. A t'reatenin' letter!"

The two plain-clothes men beat it into the parlor.

O'Brien read it out loud. When he came to the signature he said, "What the hell!" and then, "It was wrote by some nut."

"O. K.," Birnbaum said, "so it was a nut murdered her. It didn't make sense anyway, strangling a dame and then cutting her head off and then tucking her in bed. So we arrest this You-you You-you, and there's the case." He took another soda mint.

"You take too many of those pills," O'Brien said. "Maybe that's what's the matter with your stummick."

Birnbaum said crossly, "I know what's good for me and what isn't."

"Lookit, fellas," Schultz said. His voice was puzzled. "This here t'reatenin' letter says 'Bertha' at the top of it. Only it wasn't this Bertha babe who got murdered. It was some other babe."

O'Brien sighed and said, "Listen, Schultz, to a nut it don't make no difference whether the right person gets murdered or not, so long as somebody gets murdered."

"It don't make no sense to me," Schultz said stubbornly.

"So why does it have to make sense to you?" Birnbaum said. "Let Peterson worry about it. That's what they made him an inspector for."

"O. K., O. K.," Schultz muttered. "Just make out like I didn't say nothing." He turned over the wastebasket and began examining its contents.

The two plain-clothes men rummaged through the desk. They didn't have any more luck than Jake had had. O'Brien read out loud the letter from Dennis, and Birnbaum said, "Give me that. I bet you're making it up." He read aloud "your helpless slave" and O'Brien whistled, "Wew-wew-wew!"

Schultz said, "Quit clowning, you guys. I can't concentrate."

"Don't make so much noise, Birnbaum," O'Brien said mincingly. "Schultzy can't concentrate."

There was silence for a few minutes, broken only by the rattling of papers. Then suddenly Schultz said, "Hey, lookit, fellas, I found the envelope what the t'reatenin' letter come in. Same fancy paper, same typewriter."

O'Brien said, "Give it here." Then "I'll be damned, it's got a name and address on it."

Jake mentally swore at himself for not having gone through the wastebasket. He was praying that he wouldn't sneeze. The trickle from the shower was slowly soaking his left shoulder, and he didn't dare shift his position. Oh, well, if he got pneumonia, it was in a good cause.

"It sure as hell must be from a nut," Birnbaum said. "Imagine putting your name and address on a threatening letter before you go and murder the person you sent it to."

"But the person it was sent to wasn't murdered," Schultz said firmly, and Birnbaum said, "Nobody asked you. Shut up."

"Wildavine—Williams," O'Brien read slowly. "That's double-you double-you, all right. Must be a dame."

Jake made a mental note of the name.

"Then what was the idea of that you-you-you-you gag?" Schultz wanted to know.

"Because she's a nut," O'Brien said patiently, as though he were speaking to a slightly retarded child. He read, "Twenty-three Morton Street. That's down in Greenwich Village. There's a lot of nuts down there."

Jake hastily memorized the address. 23, 23, 23. Wildavine Williams, 23 Morton Street. Oh, if he could only get out of this damned shower and start for 23 Morton Street!

"All right," Birnbaum said. "So phone in and report and let's get out of here. I want to get to a drugstore and get some Pepto-Bismol."

"And let Peterson take all the credit?" O'Brien said. "Listen, my mother didn't raise any half-wit children. We'll go down there and pick her up ourselves. These nuts always break down and confess right off the bat. Then we'll take her in to headquarters with the confession."

Birnbaum said, "I don't feel so good."

"You'll feel swell," O'Brien said, "if we get a promotion outa this."

Schultz said, "Yeah, but lookit, fellas, this Wildavine dame wrote the t'reatenin' letter to Bertha, and it wasn't Bertha who got killed."

"Schultz, I don't like you," O'Brien said. "Come on, Birnbaum, let's get going."

Jake breathed a sigh of relief. Once those three cops got out of the apartment——

The sigh of relief turned into a faint groan when he heard O'Brien say, "And your orders, Schultzy, are to stay here and watch the apartment. Peterson says he don't want nothing moved out of here."

"O. K.," Schultz said, "only I wish there was some cigars."

"I'll send up some from the lobby," O'Brien said. "You just be sure nobody takes nothing out of here, that's all."

Schultz said, "O. K." again, and added, "get all Havana."

The door closed behind the two plain-clothes men. Jake peered through the crack in the shower. Schultz waited until he was alone, then took the copy of *Married*

Love out of the desk, unlaced his shoes, unfastened his collar, stretched out on the davenport, and began to read.

A quick dash might do it, Jake reflected. Through the bedroom, along the back of the other davenport, and then a rush to cover that last ten or twelve feet.

But Schultz's service revolver was within an instant's reach, and these big, lazy-looking cops could move disconcertingly fast.

Besides, he'd have to cover the distance, and then open the door. By that time Schultz would be chasing him, and the hotel corridor was no place in which to try to escape from a cop.

Dope! He'd forgotten about the bedroom door that led into the corridor. There was one, of course, so that the suite could be split up into individual rooms. It would be locked, but with the same spring lock as the other doors, opening from the inside.

He made sure that Schultz was still absorbed in his reading matter, and then slowly, cautiously, stepped out of the shower. He paused just long enough to mop his neck, and as far as he could reach under his collar with a bath towel. Then he began tiptoeing through the bedroom.

He'd just rounded the foot of the bed and passed the chaise longue when the cold water that had been dripping down his back took effect. He sneezed. Loud.

Schultz automatically said, "Gesundheit," without looking up from his book. A second later he leaped off the davenport and yelled, "Whozat?" as he started for the bedroom. Jake ducked, fast, back of the bedroom door.

He knew, of course, that Schultz would immediately look back of the door. Schultz did. In the split second while they faced each other, a lot of things went through Jake's mind.

He didn't like to do this. In the first place it was bad business to sock a cop. In the second place, he liked Schultz. He felt that Schultz was the brainiest one of the trio who'd searched the apartment. Brainy, and with a certain charm. Just the same, it had to be done. As Schultz reached for his revolver Jake swung, and connected.

Chapter Seven

NOT MUCH TIME had elapsed since the two plain-clothes men had left the suite, and elevator service in the St. Jacques was on the slowish side. O'Brien and Birnbaum were still in the corridor in front of an elevator door that was just opening when Jake stepped out of the suite.

Jake called, "Going down!" and ran down the corridor. He stepped in, catching his breath and looking as unconcerned as he could. Then he took a good close look at the two men.

O'Brien had sandy hair, a red face, and eyes that were as blue and bright as marbles. He might have been a bartender, or a bookie, or a flyweight fighter, or a retired jockey. And yet he still looked like a cop. So did Birnbaum. No one, Jake reflected, had ever figured out a way of making a plain-clothes man look like anything but a cop. Birnbaum had a long, sallow face, dark hair that was thinning over his forehead, unhappy eyes with faint shadows under them, and a scar on his upper lip.

"Maybe I'll get an Alka-Seltzer instead of Pepto-Bismol in the drugstore," he said, "while you're sending up Schultz's cigars."

"You just don't eat right," O'Brien said unfeelingly.

"I know I don't," Birnbaum said. "My wife is a lousy cook, that's why."

The elevator reached the lobby floor. Birnbaum headed for the drugstore, O'Brien for the cigar counter, and Jake for the sidewalk.

His first thought was a taxi. Then he changed his mind. Even with the start he had on O'Brien and Birnbaum, they were in a squad car. The only driver Jake knew who could beat a squad car, in any traffic, was Helene. And at that maybe in *this* traffic——

He reproached himself indignantly for holding such a disloyal thought, and headed for the subway station at Fiftieth Street and Sixth Avenue.

There was a subway train roaring down toward the stop as he cleared the last few steps. He shoved through the turnstile, raced across the platform, and caught the train. It was crowded with the Saturday noon-hour rush; he squeezed in with difficulty and stood there, held up by the crowd.

Schultz had the right idea, good old Schultzy. Wildavine Williams had written that letter to Bertha. But it wasn't Bertha who'd been murdered; it was some perfect stranger. Well, at least a stranger to the police and to him.

Maybe Wildavine Williams could explain it all, if he got to her before the police did, and kept her out of the way of the police until he could ask her all the questions that were in his mind. Of course that wouldn't be much good if O'Brien and Birnbaum had the correct theory, and she was insane. The letter, and especially its signature, did seem to bear out the theory.

Just as the train began to pick up speed beyond the Thirty-fourth Street station, an idea came to him, one that might possibly explain the presence of the unidentified beauty in Bertha's bridal chamber, and some of the wording in the letter. Jealousy would be the motive. Wildavine Williams had arrived on the scene, murdered the unidentified beauty, and spirited Bertha away. That would be a simple, easy explanation.

Only, in that case, why had the unidentified beauty been decapitated several hours after she'd been brutally slain and beaten in an insane rage?

And besides, Bertha had had a bridegroom, Dennis Morrison. The simple, easy explanation didn't fit at all with the fact that Bertha Lutts, in her thirties, and rich, who went to a reducing class and considered buying a new girdle important, had married Dennis Morrison, in his twenties, handsome and charming.

Just how the hell did this business of Dennis Morrison's dinner jacket fit in? Jake sighed, and wished that Malone and Helene were with him. He'd never tackled a problem like this entirely on his own before.

He got off the train at Fourteenth Street, hailed a taxi, and said, "Twenty-three Morton Street. Fast."

As the taxi turned into Morton Street, he looked around for a police car parked along the curb. There was none. He made a silent prayer that Officer Birnbaum had lingered awhile over his Alka-Seltzer, and that traffic conditions had been bad on the way.

Twenty-three Morton Street was a dingy, red-brick building set at an off-angle to the street, three stories high, and gable-roofed. There was a tiny triangle of decayed lawn in front of it, littered with wastepapers and soaked with April rains. Three steps led down to a mud puddle and the front door. A typewritten sign thumbtacked to the doorjamb read, "Sublet; charming atmospheric garden apartment. Furnished. Two rms. and bath. 100% colonial. Wood-burning fireplace. Antiques. $150 mo. Ask Janitor." The sign looked as though it had been there a long time.

In the vestibule was a row of doorbells, with name frames beside them. About half the frames were empty. Jake had located "Wildavine Williams" and pushed the button beside it before he noticed the sign reading, "Buttons don't bell. Pleaz to knock. Joe, Janitor." That sign, too, looked as though it had been there a long time. Joe, Janitor, was evidently in no hurry about fixing the bells.

Both the vestibule and the downstairs hall gave Jake a twinge of homesickness. They reminded him of that rooming house on upper Wabash where he'd lived while trying to land his first job on a big city newspaper. The same discolored, bilious-green calcimined walls, marred with dirty finger marks and pencil notations around the pay telephone. The same battered table where the postman left the mail, always littered with unforwarded letters, grocery-store circulars, and neighborhood giveaway newspapers. Even the same smell, a mixture of yellow soap (though nothing ever seemed to get washed with it), musty carpets, coal smoke, and the back-yard garbage container.

That rooming house on upper Wabash had called itself a studio building. This house advertised a "charming garden apartment." He could picture the charming garden apartment without any strain on his imagination. Lots of Atmosphere, magnificent high ceilings, and fifty-year-old plumbing.

Wildavine Williams lived in 3-C. That would be the

rear apartment on the top floor. Jake started to climb the stairs. Someone was practicing a Chopin Etude in the second-floor rear. Two people were having a loud, angry quarrel in the second-floor front. Jake started up the next flight, hoping Wildavine Williams would be home. He wondered, indeed, just what he would find. Not a homicidal maniac, in spite of O'Brien and Birnbaum's quick and simple solution. Maybe he'd find Bertha Morrison, Maybe he'd learn the identity of the murdered woman. Or maybe he wouldn't discover a damn thing. But, at least, he was here ahead of the police.

The door to 3-C was slightly ajar. Jake knocked on it. A thin, reedy voice called, "Come in," and, as Jake opened the door, added, "If you're the grocery boy, just set your box on the table."

"I'm not the grocery boy," Jake said. "I want to see Miss Wildavine Williams."

"All right, just a minute," the voice called. It came from behind a curtain hung across one corner of the room, hiding, Jake guessed, the kitchenette.

The room was half dark, but he could make out a few of its details. The walls appeared to be painted a chocolate brown, and the paintings hung on the wall must certainly have been given to Wildavine by artist friends. There was no other way to account for them. A Paisley shawl hung over the fireplace. There wasn't much furniture: a double-bed-size spring and mattress combination which tried to masquerade as a studio couch with the help of a slightly rumpled black sateen cover, a folding table and two chairs, enameled Chinese red, and a writing desk of the same color. There were cushions on the floor, in the corners, and heaped along the back of the couch.

A sweet-potato vine was growing in an empty peanut-butter jar on the one window sill. There was Mexican pottery all over the place. A pair of pink rayon panties were draped over the back of one chair, evidently the day's laundry. The only light came from two candles in Woolworth candlesticks on the mantel and another one in a pottery candlestick on the table.

"Hurry up," Jake called. He added, "What's the matter, is your electricity off?"

Wildavine Williams came out from behind the curtain and said, "I never use anything but candlelight. Electricity seems to stifle me."

She was a medium-height, thin, stringy woman somewhere in her thirties. Her hair, as near as he could tell, was brown—what Helene called just plain hair color—and it hung down to her shoulders, with a limp bang in front. She had on rimless glasses and no make-up. She was wearing a batik smock, a pair of bright-orange pajama pants, and rope sandals.

Jake said, "I haven't time to talk to you now. Get a coat on and come out of here quick with me. The police are on their way down here from Fifty-fifth Street, and I don't want them to find you."

He could see her eyes widen behind the rimless glasses. She said, "The police?" Her voice squeaked a little. Then she said, "Are you insane?"

"Not that I know of," Jake said, "but the police think you are. They think you murdered that woman in Bertha Morrison's bridal suite last night because they found the letter you wrote Bertha. So grab your coat and let's scram."

"Murdered," she said, "who was murdered?"

"Nobody knows yet," Jake said. "Listen, I told you there's no time to talk, understand? Believe me, I'm here to help you. So just do as I say and don't ask questions."

She stared at him. "Who are you? What do you do?"

"I'm Jake Justus," he said, "and I'm a writer."

"Oh," she said, "have you ever read any of my poems?"

"All of them," Jake said desperately, "and I'm crazy about them. Now, look, we've got to get out of here before the cops arrive."

"Did you like them?" she said. "What did you think of them?"

"The cops?" Jake said. "I liked them very much. I usually like cops and they usually like me, only now and then we don't understand each other . . ."

"That isn't what I mean," she said. "Did you like my 'Kaleidoscopic True-Views of the Heart at Eve' that was printed in *Fragmentaria*?"

Jake said, "I adored it." He wondered if he could knock her out, carry her down the stairs and into a taxi, and be out of reach by the time O'Brien and Birnbaum drew up at the curb. Then he decided it would not only be difficult and dangerous, but also untimely. It might raise unfortunate suspicions in Wildavine Williams' mind. Besides, she looked fairly heavy.

"And my 'Afterechoes of a Yestermath, at Ferryboat in the Offing,'" she said excitedly, "what did you think of it?"

"I thought it was magnificent," Jake said. "A great inspiration. And now listen to me. The police read something you wrote and they construed it as a threat, and they're on their way down here to arrest you."

"This all seems rather silly," Wildavine Williams said. "What possible interest could the police have in me?"

Jake bit his tongue just in time to avoid saying, "What possible interest could anybody have in you?" and said instead, "Because of you I stood under an ice-cold shower bath for two or three hours, I knocked out a cop who was eight feet high and four feet wide, and I rode down here on a crowded subway train, two jumps ahead of a squad car, just to rescue you. Now get your coat and let's get the hell out of here."

"Do you know what I think?" Wildavine Williams said. "I think you're suffering from a neurosis."

"And I think," Jake said, "you're going to be in jail in about thirty minutes if you don't do as I say."

"But for *what*?" Wildavine insisted.

Jake sighed loudly and said, *"Murder!"*

"Whose murder?" Wildavine demanded.

"I don't know," Jake said. He stopped himself. The conversation seemed to have got back to its starting point. "Miss Williams, there's no time to explain. You'll just have to trust me. Please believe me, that I'm only trying to help you out of trouble."

"But," Wildavine said, "I'm not in any trouble."

From down on the street came the unmistakable moan of a squad-car siren. It stopped in front of the door.

"Oh, aren't you?" Jake said grimly.

Wildavine stared at him. There were voices in the vestibule and heavy footsteps. One of the voices—Birnbaum's—said, "Maybe we should have brought Schultz in case she resists arrest."

"Why," she gasped, "you meant it!"

"For the love of Mike," Jake said, "did you think I was playing twenty questions? Where the hell can we hide around here, fast?"

She blinked twice and then said, "Next door. Here." She opened a door on the side of the room; it led into a room similar to hers, save that the walls were navy blue and the furniture orange and that a cheap India print covered the couch. She locked the door behind her.

"This is Zora's," she whispered. "A friend of mine. She leaves the door unlocked so I can come in and feed the cat." She pointed to a big, thin Siamese, the color of a mushroom, asleep on the bed.

There were footsteps on the stairs.

"Good," Jake whispered. "Now, get this. They don't have a description of you. Or me. They'll probably come here to ask where Wildavine Williams is. Tell them—she's gone to Jersey City, or someplace. Anything. Only don't let them know who you are."

She nodded. "Only why do they want me?"

"I told you," Jake murmured, "there's been a murder."

"Yes. But what murder?"

"Please," Jake whispered, "let's not get into that routine again. Keep quiet and listen."

There was a knock on a door of the apartment they'd just left, then the door was opened. There was a faint murmur of voices. After a few minutes the voices came nearer. O'Brien and Birnbaum were evidently standing out in the hall.

"Well, we'll try next door," O'Brien said.

Jake cleared his throat, and said loudly, "And, madam, if you'll take a three years' subscription to the magazine no home should be without, *The Household Friend*, we will give you absolutely free of charge this magnificent five-hundred-page book of——"

There was a thunderous knock at the door. Jake nodded to Wildavine, who rose and opened it. The two plain-clothes men came in.

"Good afternoon, lady," O'Brien said. "Do you live here?" When she nodded, he said, "We're looking for a Miss Wildavine Williams."

"She lives next door," Wildavine said.

"We know she lives next door," Birnbaum said. "We were just there, and she's not in. Where is she?"

Wildavine looked blank for a minute and then said in

a slightly quavering voice, "She said—she was going to Jersey City."

"Where in Jersey City?" O'Brien asked.

"I don't know."

"What'd she go there for?" Birnbaum asked.

"She didn't tell me."

"When's she coming back?" O'Brien asked.

"I guess—next week sometime," Wildavine said weakly.

O'Brien fixed a cold eye on her. "If she's gone to Jersey City and she ain't gonna be back till next week, how come she left her door unlocked?"

"I don't know," Wildavine said. "She's—very absent-minded."

Jake decided it was time to help. He stepped forward and said, "Would either of you gentlemen be interested in a three-year subscription to *The Household Friend*? As a special introductory offer——"

"Come on, O'Brien," Birnbaum said, "let's get out of here."

Jake began to breathe easier. Then he heard the sound of heavy steps hurrying—no, running—up the stairs. A voice called, "Hey! O'Brien! Birnbaum!" His blood froze.

A second later Schultz appeared in the doorway. He said, "Hey, listen, fellas——" Then he stopped and stared at Jake. "There he is," he exclaimed. "There's the son-of-a-bitch that socked me."

"He did, huh," O'Brien said, taking a step forward.

Well, anyway, Jake consoled himself, they hadn't caught up with Wildavine. If she had sense enough to stay under cover, everything would still be O. K. As soon as he'd talked his way out of this—and he had no doubt that he could—he'd get back to her and start asking questions.

Then there were more footsteps on the stairs, light

footsteps. They came to the landing, down the hall to the door, and stopped. A short, plump, freckled young woman with reddish hair stood in the doorway, a grocery bag in each arm. Her mouth was round with surprise.

"Why, Wildavine!" she exclaimed. "What's going on here?"

O'Brien and Birnbaum stared at her. Then they said, in perfect unison, "*Wildavine?*"

Chapter Eight

"DON'T BE SILLY," Helene said firmly. "I'm not in the least worried about him. He can stay away all day as far as I'm concerned. All I said was that he's never stayed away as long as this before."

"And all I said," Malone growled, "was that he'd probably be along any minute."

"If he isn't," Helene said, "I don't care." She lit a cigarette and sat breaking the match into tiny pieces.

They'd brought Dennis Morrison upstairs. The hotel manager was having the young man's clothes and personal possessions moved out of the suite he was to have shared with his bride, and into another room, and had brought one complete change of clothing into the Justus suite. Malone had given Dennis stern orders to take a bath, shave, and dress before he tried to talk or even to think.

"Malone," Helene said, "what time is it now?"

The little lawyer ignored the question and said, "He's probably been delayed in traffic."

Helene sniffed and said, "I hate you."

The bedroom door opened and Dennis Morrison came out. He'd put on a well-cut gray worsted suit, a white shirt, and a maroon tie. He was newly shaved, his dark hair was shining, and he was doing his best to smile. But his face was still very pale, and there were still shadows around his eyes.

"That's better," Malone said. "Sit down there on the sofa and relax. When did you eat last?"

"Dinner," Dennis Morrison said. "I had dinner last night. With Bertha."

Helene and the lawyer looked at each other. Helene said, "We'd better not wait lunch for Jake. It's nearly two o'clock now."

She telephoned downstairs for three double orders of scrambled eggs, three double orders of bacon and large quantities of toast, marmalade, and coffee.

"My clothes," Dennis Morrison said. "I left them in there." He nodded toward the bedroom, paused, and said, "The dinner jacket——"

"It stays right here," Malone said. "That dinner jacket is evidence."

"The police kept the cigarette case and the wallet," Dennis Morrison said. "They said that was evidence. But they let me keep the jacket."

"Haven't you even the faintest idea of where you got it?" Helene asked.

He shook his head. "I've been trying to think. All day. Trying to remember the names of people I met. But I can't. I can't even remember where I was."

"Well, stop trying until you've had some food," she

said. "All discussion is hereby postponed until the last crumb is off the tray."

Conversation during lunch was hardly sprightly, but somehow Helene and Malone, between them, managed to keep it off brides, disappearances, and murder. A little color had begun to come into Dennis Morrison's face by the time the tray was carried out.

"The police would inform me the minute they discovered anything, wouldn't they?" Dennis said anxiously. "So if I don't hear anything, it means they haven't found out anything yet, isn't that right?"

Malone nodded and said, "Don't worry, you'll get a call from them as soon as they have any news."

"If I could only do something," Dennis said. "If I could only go out and find her. If there was only some way I could help the police." He paused. "The thing is, you see, I did marry Bertha for her money."

Malone stole a quick glance at the tortured young face and then blew a cloud of cigar smoke toward the ceiling before he said, "That's nothing so remarkable. I always planned to marry for money myself. Only I never could find a woman with enough money who agreed it was a good idea." He was rewarded by a faint smile on Dennis Morrison's face.

"She knew about it, though," Dennis said. "So it was really all right. Besides, it was her idea, anyway. And I meant to make her happy. Just as if it had been really love. Maybe we would have fallen in love. Eight years' difference in age isn't so much."

"Try beginning at the beginning," Helene said. "It might make more sense that way. Where did you meet her and how did it all happen?"

"I was working for an escort bureau." He paused,

looking at the floor, and said, "I know, it sounds like a silly way to make a living. But I didn't seem able to do much else. I thought making a fortune in New York would be a cinch, but—oh, well, you don't want to hear my whole life story."

"Indeed we do," Helene said warmly.

"I can think of nothing more interesting," Malone said, sternly repressing his conscience and a yawn. It had been a long time since he'd had any sleep.

"I guess it's just Small-Town Boy Tries to Make Good, and Flops," Dennis said. "Small town. My folks didn't have any money, but we got along. Summers I spent on Grampa's farm. He did have money, some, anyway. He bought me a bicycle, and when I was in high he bought me swell clothes and gave me spending money, and a flivver when I was in my last year. I was pretty popular. And then Grampa died and left some dough for me to be sent to college. A good college. I guess he figured that there wasn't anything more important than going to a good college."

Malone squeezed down another yawn and reflected that he wouldn't know anything about that. He'd worked his way through night law school driving a taxi.

"I bet you were pretty popular in college, too," Helene said.

"Well," Dennis said, "well, yes. I was friends with all the right guys, if you know what I mean. I didn't go in much for athletics, but I was president of my class one year. And when I finished I thought I was sitting on top of the world, coming to New York, with a job waiting. I thought selling insurance was going to be a cinch. I guess I just wasn't a good salesman. I had a couple of other jobs, and then finally, a few years— about three years—ago, I ended up with this escort bureau." He paused to sip his drink and said, "I'm afraid I'm boring you."

Malone murmured, "Think nothing of it. Go on."

"Well, I had to earn a living somehow," Dennis said defensively. "My folks were all dead and I couldn't write home for money. I made enough to pay for my room and get clothes and meals. And sometimes I had fun. Then I met Bertha."

"A client?" Helene asked.

Dennis nodded. "She was—well, sort of different. Most clients were a terrible pain. She was just—oh, I don't know, pathetic. She'd never had any dates or boy friends or gone out dancing, or stuff like that. Only, she didn't hire me from the escort bureau because she wanted to go out dancing."

Malone opened his eyes and said, "Howzat?"

"It was because of her girl friends," Dennis said. "She had a bunch of them that she'd gone to school with. Most of them were married or getting married, or having careers, or something. She wanted to show them she could at least have a guy to take her out on dates. So she had a regular schedule for me at the escort bureau, three nights a week. Then one night I called for her and she looked like she'd been crying. She'd been to a shower for one of her girl friends who was going to get married. So I said, joking, 'Why don't you get married yourself, just to show those girls?' And she looked at me a minute and said, 'That's an idea. Will you?' "

"It's as simple as that, eh?" Malone said. He rose, walked to the bathroom, and poured himself a short slug of gin. He hoped it would wake him up, because he wanted to hear what Dennis Morrison was saying. It was hard to concentrate. Life stories were hardly the prescription for a man who'd spent twenty hours on the train, had no sleep at all and a great deal of hangover.

"Are you sure this interests you?" Dennis Morrison said.

"My dear young man," Malone assured him, "if it interested me any more, I'd be in a state of nervous collapse." He lighted a fresh cigar.

"So you married her," Helene prompted Dennis.

"Well," Dennis said, "you see, she wanted to get married. Most of her girl friends were married, or getting married, or divorced, and they sort of looked down on her. The ones that weren't married were in business or something, and they looked down on her, too. Except for one or two, they were really just nice to her because they all went to the same school. So she thought that if she suddenly had a big romance, and got married—see?"

Helene said, "Well, it's a rather drastic kind of glamour build-up. But go on."

"There was another thing," Dennis said. "She used to say she didn't want to be a rich old maid with a companion. She'd much rather be a rich old divorcee with a past."

"A perfectly reasonable ambition," Malone said. He got up and moved a little closer to the window.

"I tell you, it was pathetic," Dennis said. "All she wanted of me was to marry her, and be wonderfully attentive when other people were present, and stick around for a couple of years, and then she'd pretend to run away with another man and I'd divorce her. That was all I had to do, and she was willing to make me comfortably fixed for life. Only—well, look, I figured that we already liked each other and—well, we might be able to make it stick. It would have been better." He smiled wryly. "She'd have been happier with a husband to show off to her girl friends in the bridge club than a divorce decree. A husband, and a nice home, and all that." He paused. "Of course, if she'd wanted to stick to the original bargain, I'd have agreed."

"Tell me," Helene said, "was this to be a marriage in name only?"

Dennis Morrison looked embarrassed. "Well," he said at last, "well, in a way."

"Young man," Helene said sternly, "to that question you can only answer yes or no."

Malone said, "*Helene!*"

"Well," Dennis Morrison said, "I mean—well, it was like this. It was—well, it was implied. I mean, yes. That is, 'yes' was implied. If you know what I mean."

"Vaguely," Helene said.

Dennis said, "I just assumed—you know. I'd never kissed her, or anything. And it was all arranged in such a business-like way. It—just never was discussed. I don't know what she thought."

Malone opened one eye and said, "What did *you* think?"

"I didn't think," Dennis said. "Not until we were married and we had a wonderful dinner at the Rainbow Room, and we came back to the hotel. And then I began to think about it. You know. I could have slept on the sofa in the parlor overnight. But then there was that long trip on the train, in the same drawing room. And resort hotels, and all that. I didn't know if I ought to say something, or just what."

"So you excused yourself and went out to get drunk," Malone said sleepily.

"Oh, no," Dennis said. "It wasn't like that."

"He didn't go out *to* get drunk; he went out *and* got drunk," Helene said. "There's a distinction."

"Stop quibbling," Malone said crossly, "and give me the facts. Never mind her, Dennis, just go on."

Dennis said, "She told me she wanted to unpack a few things and take a bath. So I said that was fine, I wanted to drop down at the bar for a nightcap. I sort of figured that—well, that was up to her, after all, only I wanted to find out what she expected, without asking. And I figured if I waited long enough, if you know what I mean, I could—well, you know, figure it out from the way things were when I got back."

"A very gentlemanly idea," Malone murmured, his eyes closed. "Only you fell among drunkards."

"You know how it is," Dennis said. He looked very young and very embarrassed. "You get to talking with people at a bar. And I hadn't eaten such a lot of dinner. And I was kind of upset and jittery, anyway. And this guy I was talking to—I don't remember much about him—suggested we go up the street and catch the show at some club—I don't remember which one it was. And I looked at my watch and thought, well, that would just about fill in the right amount of time. I remember that. So we had a couple more drinks and we left, this guy and I."

"Was it a good floor show?" Malone asked. "And where was it?"

"I guess it was good," Dennis said. "I'm pretty vague about it. And I can't remember where it was. I do remember there was a comedian and a girl who sang and a chorus. I know I got separated from this guy I'd met, but I got mixed up with some other people there. I don't remember anything about them, just sitting down at their table. Only there's just a dim recollection—well, more of a feeling than really a recollection—about going to a bunch of other night clubs and bars. And that's all."

"When did you start on this tour?" Malone asked.

"It was about eight o'clock. Maybe half-past. Not later than that, I'm sure."

Helene said thoughtfully, "And it was after four when we found you down in the lobby, trying to pick lilies. You must have covered a lot of territory."

"But how did I get back here?" Dennis said.

"There's a kind of instinct drunks have," Malone told him. "Drunks, and homing pigeons." He scowled. "That's a lot of time, too."

Malone and Helene looked at each other in silence.

"What is it?" Dennis demanded.

"Your night's adventures make an interesting story," Malone said slowly, "but if the police get any unpleasant notions about the murder that happened to be committed in your rooms, they won't consider it much of an alibi."

Dennis groaned. "I know it," he said, "but what can I do? Because that's exactly what did happen."

"It may not be much of an alibi," Helene said to the lawyer, "but it's all the alibi he's got."

Malone chewed savagely on his cigar for a moment. "Personally," he said at last, "I distrust alibis. People who turn up able to account for every minute of their time, with proof and witnesses, when a murder happens to be committed, rouse my suspicions. Because alibis like that always seem to me to indicate a certain amount of preparedness. Under ordinary circumstances people can't account for their time that way. But," he said gloomily, "sometimes the police take a very conventional view of things."

"If he could only remember the places he went to last night," Helene said thoughtfully. "Or even if he could find out which ones they were. Because he mightn't re-

member being there, but people would remember him."
Her eyes narrowed. "That's it. See, there's a solution to
every difficulty!"

"Now," Malone said. "Remember. At six-forty-five
tonight——"

"There's a train for Chicago," Helene said. "And you
won't be on it. Because this nice young man needs an
alibi. And we're going to find it for him."

Chapter Nine

"FOR THE one hundredth time," Malone said firmly,
"I am not going to accompany you on an insane tour
of all the night clubs, saloons, dives, and heaven knows
what in New York City, asking waiters and bartenders,
'Did you see a young man with dark hair in here last
night?'"

"You're very unco-operative," Helene said. "Besides,
we'd take his picture along. He's got one. I saw it."

Malone snorted. "Do you think that when some stranger pokes a photograph in a bartender's face and says,
'Did you see him last night?' the bartender is going to give
any information?"

"He would to me," Helene said with serene self-
confidence.

Malone reflected that she was right. He had yet to see
the man Helene couldn't talk out of anything she wanted.
He tried another approach.

"It's none of our business," he began. "Just because you

and Jake happened to pick up a strange drunk in the hotel lobby last night——"

"We're the only friends he has in the world," Helene said. "He told us so himself."

Malone lit a fresh cigar and said, "Jake won't like it. Murders aren't a hobby to him, they're a damned nuisance."

He was immediately sorry he'd said it. The expression changed on Helene's face, and she said, "Malone, what time is it now?"

"Five o'clock," Malone said. He added hastily, "He's been delayed."

"Since ten o'clock this morning?" Helene said.

He couldn't tell if the tone in her voice indicated fury or alarm. He said, "All right, he's probably stumbled into an honest job for once, and he's ashamed to tell you about it."

"*Jake?*" Helene said witheringly.

"The truth is," Malone said, "he's probably out with another girl. So stop worrying about him."

Helene sniffed. She was silent for a moment. Then, "But, Malone, he's never been away as long as this." And after another moment, "If he isn't here by six o'clock, I'll——"

"You'll do what?" Malone said.

"I'll——" She stared at him, drew a long breath, and said, "I'll get all dressed up and we'll go out to dinner, and after that we'll find Dennis' alibi, and the hell with Jake."

"Oh, no," Malone said, "not me. Let Dennis find his own alibis."

They'd tucked the exhausted Dennis Morrison into bed half an hour before, and left strict orders at the desk that he was not to be disturbed. Since then Malone had been carrying on a losing argument with Helene over the evening's plans. Losing, he reminded himself, but not lost.

"Damn it, Malone," she said, "aren't you even curious?"

"Not in the least," the little lawyer said with his last ounce of determination. "I don't care where Bertha Morrison is, or why she disappeared from her bridal chamber after going to so much trouble and expense to get a bridegroom. I don't care who the unknown beauty was. I don't care how she got into the aforementioned bridal suite, or why. I don't care who murdered her, or why her head was cut off. I don't care one damned thing about it, and I'm getting rapidly less interested every minute." He glared at Helene, attempted to land an inch of cigar ash in the ash tray, and landed it on his vest instead. He brushed at it ineffectually for a minute and then said, "It is a hell of a funny thing, though, about that dinner jacket." He looked at Helene and added, "Stop giggling."

"I'm not giggling," Helene said. "That was just a staccato sneer. If you're so curious about that dinner jacket, why don't you find out where it came from and how it got on Dennis Morrison's back? A smart man like you!"

"Shut up," Malone said almost dreamily. "Let me think." He paused. "It was an expensive, custom-made jacket. There must be a tailor's mark on it. Good tailors keep records of the clothes they make."

Helene said, "You're still a smart man," jumped up, raced into the bedroom, and returned with the dinner jacket. "I was hoping you'd think of that before I did." She tossed it on his lap. "Too bad the owner didn't leave an identification card in his wallet. That would simplify everything."

"He was probably out on a bender," Malone said, "and

wanted to be able to pass himself off as John W. Smith of Keokuk, Iowa, in case of necessity." He examined it carefully. "Mawson and Mawson," he reported, "New York."

Helene ran for the phone book. There was no Mawson and Mawson in the phone book. Malone tried information. There was an eighteen-months-ago number, which turned out to have been disconnected. Helene started calling all the Mawsons in the phone book; on the third try she got the widow of the senior member of Mawson and Mawson.

Mr. J. L. Mawson, Sr., had died eleven months ago. The firm had gone out of business right after his death. Mr. J. L. Mawson, Jr., was touring Mexico. The widow of J. L. Mawson, Sr., had no idea what had happened to the records of the firm, or where any of its old employees could be reached.

Neither did J. L. Mawson, Sr.'s married daughter who lived on Long Island, nor a niece in Bridgeport, Connecticut. But an older brother (quite deaf) on Staten Island remembered that the head cutter of the firm had been a Mr. A. Garabedian, who lived somewhere on East Thirty-fourth Street.

It turned out that Mr. A. Garabedian was now on the West Coast, employed by the Hollywood Costume Company.

"Well," Helene said, after forty-eight minutes of telephoning, "it was an idea, anyway."

"Just a temporary setback," Malone said grimly. "I'll find who that jacket belongs to and how Dennis Morrison got it if it takes till Christmas."

"But, Malone," Helene said innocently, "I thought you weren't interested."

Before Malone could find a suitable and reasonably unprofane answer, Helene said reproachfully, "Such language! Now I'm going to get dressed for dinner. I'll meet you in the bar in forty-five minutes."

That would be six-forty-five, Malone reflected as he went out the door, just the time that train was going to leave for Chicago, without him.

He went to the room Jake and Helene had reserved for him, let himself in, turned on the light, and sank down on the edge of the bed. It was a pleasant room, with maroon and apple-green printed draperies, hunting prints on the cream-colored walls, a comfortable bed, a big easy chair, a handsome bureau and writing desk, and thick, spongy carpets. But he didn't appreciate it. He was too worried about how he was going to pay for it.

There was, he felt, an overwhelming load of assorted worries on his mind. The fare back to Chicago. The trouble between Jake and Helene, whatever it was. Jake's mysterious absence. The tough spot Dennis Morrison was in, though that was none of his business. The dinner jacket. Making up the sleep he'd lost on the train. Paying for the hotel room. And now, one more. Paying for Helene's dinner and the other incidental expenses of the evening.

He hadn't had a chance, what with one thing and another, to wire Joe the Angel for immediate funds. Besides, all he could count on from Joe the Angel was return fare to Chicago. And the nine dollars in his pocket was all he had in the world.

Malone rose wearily, stripped off his coat, took off his shirt and tie, and prepared to shave. Helene would, as usual, want to pick up the check. As usual, he wouldn't allow her. She was one of the two best friends he had in all the world, but he'd never let her pick up the check.

Nor Jake either, for that matter. To be perfectly accurate, he practically never let even a perfect stranger pick up the check. That was one of his great troubles.

He looked crossly at his half-lathered face in the mirror. With all the money he'd made, he told himself, here he was with just nine dollars. And where had it gone? Thrown away. Women, liquor, poker games, and friends. Still, he reflected, rinsing out his shaving brush, what the hell could you do with money except spend it on women and liquor, lose it in poker games, and lend it to friends.

The hotel would probably cash a fair-sized check, considering that Jake had made the reservation for him. Not so good though, when the check bounced three days later.

He finished shaving, and stood under the shower for a full ten minutes, letting the soothing water stream down over his broad, brown hairy chest, his small paunch, and his short, stocky legs. It refreshed his body, if not his mind. He toweled and dressed himself, rubbed talcum on his round, reddish face, and brushed his dark, unruly, and slightly thinning hair.

Maybe he'd better just tell Jake and Helene that he was broke.

No!

There must be a drink left in that pint of rye he'd bought in Chicago just before he left. He burrowed through his suitcase and found the bottle tucked into a bedroom slipper. There were three drinks left in the bottle. He took two of them, fast.

The phone rang, and he picked it up. Maybe Jake was back. Or maybe Dennis Morrison had heard from the police.

It was the switchboard girl. "A Mr. Proudfoot to see you, Mr. Malone."

"Send him right up," Malone said. He wondered who the hell Mr. Proudfoot was. Probably more trouble. Another worry.

Where was he going to get some dough, fast?

Where the hell was Jake?

Who did that dinner jacket belong to?

When was he going to get back to Chicago?

There was a knock. He opened the door and saw a tall, angular man with iron-gray hair and a grim gray face. A well-dressed man, though everything he wore, save his white shirt, was dead black, from his highly polished shoes to his well-brushed derby.

"Mr. Malone?" the man said, almost without moving his mouth. "I'm Mr. Proudfoot."

Malone murmured that he was delighted to meet Mr. Proudfoot. He invited Mr. Proudfoot to come in, apologized for the mussed-up condition of the room, and regretted that he didn't have a drink to offer.

The visitor seemed to have no time for these social amenities. He came straight to the point, sitting down on a straight chair and parking a black calfskin brief case on his knees.

"Mr. Malone," he said, "I read of you in this afternoon's paper. I took the liberty of telephoning a number of people in Chicago and checking up on you."

Malone felt a cold wave starting through his blood stream. Like a drowning man doing a split-second autobiography, he thought over every sin he'd committed in his life, and ended up wondering if he were being arrested or sued.

"I reached the conclusion," Mr. Proudfoot said, "that you are a very remarkable man."

"That all depends," Malone said cautiously.

"And I am given to understand," Mr. Proudfoot went

on, "that you have done some very remarkable things."

"Well, that's one way of describing it," Malone said·
airily. "Have a cigar."

Mr. Proudfoot appeared to be a man who talked but
didn't listen. "Therefore, I have come to the decision," he
said, "that you are exactly the man I am looking for. I,"
he said, "am the trustee and lawyer for Bertha Lutts—I
suppose I should say, Bertha Morrison. I have become
convinced that this is what her late father would wish me
to do."

"I'm sure of it," Malone said, in a daze. He began to
wonder if he should have taken that last drink. Or maybe
it was because he'd lost a night's sleep.

"Mr. Malone," Mr. Proudfoot said, leaning forward a
little, "I would like to engage your services. Not in any
legal capacity, but in connection with the disappearance
of Bertha Lutts—or, rather, Morrison. In short, I desire
you to find her."

Malone started to say that he was not a walking lost-
and-found column, took another look at Mr. Proudfoot's
black broadcloth suit, estimated its cost, and said instead,
"Well, that might be a difficult task. It might take time,
and time is money——"

Mr. Proudfoot cleared his throat. "As Miss Lutts'—I
mean, Mrs. Morrison's—trustee, I am taking it upon myself to offer you five thousand dollars as a fee. Plus any
expenses which might be incurred."

"There would be immediate expenses," Malone said.

"And of course," Mr. Proudfoot went on, as though he
hadn't heard, "a five-hundred-dollar retainer. In fact, I
have the check right here in my wallet." He reached into
his wallet and drew out a long, narrow, pale-yellow slip
of printed paper. "I trust that you'll accept the case, Mr.
Malone. It is simply a matter of finding Bertha Lutts—

Morrison—and producing proof that she did not murder that woman who was found in her bed—proof that would convince a jury."

Malone folded his hand over the check. If he took it to the hotel desk, he could draw all the money he needed, including the price of a ticket to Chicago. The hell with Joe the Angel. "My dear Mr. Proudfoot," he said, "I assure you, your case couldn't be in better hands."

Then he wound up the slowest double take in his life. "What was that," he said hoarsely, "you wanted me to do?"

Chapter Ten

"BUT LOOK HERE," Malone said. "What makes you think Bertha killed that woman?"

Mr. Proudfoot looked at him fixedly. "Can you suggest any alternatives?"

"As a matter of fact, yes," Malone said. He began unwrapping a cigar. "Is that what I'm hired for? To find an alternative and make it stick? Because that last part may take a little doing. It isn't so easy these days to pin a murder rap on somebody, especially if it's somebody who didn't do it."

"No one is suggesting that you do anything even remotely illegal," Mr. Proudfoot said. His eyes and voice were like ice.

"O. K.," the little lawyer said mildly. "I was just asking. Let's get back to where we were. What makes you think Bertha killed the woman?"

"My dear Mr. Malone," Abner Proudfoot said, "since her childhood, Bertha has been strong-minded and stubborn, and a creature of whims."

Malone coughed. "Murder and decapitation," he said, "are hardly whims."

"I suspect," Mr. Proudfoot said, trying not very successfully to look as though he were smiling, "that you choose to be humorous. No thank you, Mr. Malone, I have never smoked. However, if you will permit me——"

Malone had been betting with himself that Abner Proudfoot took snuff. He won.

"By a whim," Abner Proudfoot said, "I refer, naturally, to her rash and thoughtless marriage to this indubitably charming but nevertheless completely unknown young man. Until yesterday," he added in a wounded tone, "*I* had never heard of him."

"She must have been very impetuous," Malone murmured.

"Impetuous," Abner Proudfoot said, "in a determined way. But does that have anything to do with the situation?"

"Well," Malone said, "no." He was beginning to wish that his visitor would go away. He could feel a pleasant warmth emanating from his inside coat pocket, where he'd stowed the check. He would, he resolved, have the cashier give him five one-hundred-dollar bills. That would settle Helene's hash once and for all. She'd looked entirely too skeptical when he'd refused her offer to pay his train fare. Well, tonight he'd take out a hundred-dollar bill to pay the dinner check and say apologetically, "I'm sorry, waiter, I haven't anything smaller——"

"I beg your pardon," he said, "I didn't hear what you were saying——"

"I said, I would have been glad to have given her advice," Abner Proudfoot repeated, "if she'd come and asked for it. If she had, it would have saved all this trouble."

"You'd have advised her against marrying Dennis Morrison, I assume," Malone said.

"Naturally. I feel that we may safely assume," Proudfoot went on, "that this man is an adventurer. What was he when they first met? A professional escort. The word for it, I believe, is gigolo."

Malone knew several other words for it, but he kept them to himself.

Abner Proudfoot took another pinch of snuff. "Under those circumstances," he said, "I feel that we may also assume that if he preyed on one wealthy woman, he preyed on others." He sneezed and blew his nose on an enormous, snow-white handkerchief. "The murdered woman was obviously wealthy."

"Did you know her?" Malone asked. "Or are you psychic?" He wondered if Jake was back yet. Probably not. Helene would have phoned.

"I did not know her," Proudfoot said, "and I am not psychic, although I had a great aunt——" He paused. "I examined the unfortunate woman's remains, at the morgue. Her hair was dyed, a shade which is known, I believe, as moon dust. A costly process, and one that can only be done at two or three beauty salons in New York. She wore false eyelashes, of a type which can only be applied one at a time, each lash fitting over the natural hair —a slow and difficult process, requiring the services of a highly skilled operator. And her manicure——" He paused again.

"There was something odd about her manicure," he admitted. "It had obviously been done at one of the best salons. And yet, her hands had not received the same fine care in the past. For some reason, that struck me as rather strange."

"I'm not surprised," Malone said. "Say, maybe you could tell me a good place to buy a nightgown for a present I want to give a girl."

"I would recommend Karole's," Abner Proudfoot said promptly. He named an address on Forty-fifth Street.

Malone pretended to write it down. Then he said, "How do you know all these things?"

Abner Proudfoot winked at him. It was a little as though a minor earthquake had cracked the Great Stone Face.

Malone said, "Oh," and wished he hadn't asked. His imagination started to work on a picture of Abner Proudfoot in a playful mood, and gave up fast. "So this dame was well-fixed, huh?" he said. "Well, I'll take your word for it temporarily. But how does that make Bertha a murderess?"

"Jealousy," Proudfoot said. "This other woman felt that she had a prior claim on Dennis Morrison's attentions. It is quite conceivable that she may even have been providing him with the necessities of life. In which case, hearing of the marriage, it is not unnatural that she should come here to confront the bride. There was, as you know, a struggle. There were bruises and contusions on the body, in addition to the fact that death was caused by strangulation, a fact which is in itself an implication of emotional violence. I am quite sure that if the circumstances of the case were to be carefully examined, it would be readily proven that the murder was committed in self-defense—a circumstance which I trust will not arise, if you succeed in what you have been engaged to do."

"Brother," Malone said, "for five grand I could prove

to any jury in the world that old man Macbeth murdered in self-defense. Only I gathered that what I'm engaged for is to find the dame, prove she didn't done it, and find some guy we can prove did done it. That should be worth more money than you're paying, but I'll do it for you because you're a pal. But a couple of little things bother me. After Bertha had strangled this visiting babe in self-defense, why did she bother to undress her, rig her out in a fancy lace and satin nightgown, and tuck her in bed?"

"When you have located Bertha," Abner Proudfoot said coldly, "we will ask her."

"Oh, sure," Malone said. "And another thing. When Bertha scrammed, she took all her jewelry along. Nothing else. There was a coat hanging there in the closet that looked as if it had been carved out of a whole herd of chinchillas, but she didn't take that. She just took the rocks. How come? For dough? Didn't she carry enough mad money in her purse to take care of her in case she impetuously committed a murder?"

"I take it you are being facetious," Abner Proudfoot said. His lips curved in what might have been a smile on almost any other face. "When you locate Bertha——"

"We'll ask her," Malone said. "O. K. Just one more little problem bothers me, do you mind? After she'd strangled this babe with the expensive hair-do in self-defense, why did she stick around for three or four hours, and then cut her head off?"

"Bertha——" Proudfoot began. He stopped, and his lips shut like a bear trap.

"I know," Malone said. "She's a creature of whims." He put out his cigar. "All right, I'll find her. You might toss in a couple of hints, though, about where to look. Where might she have gone? Any family? Any friends?"

"Her entire family consists of an uncle, George Lutts, and a cousin, Howard, or Howie, Lutts," Abner Proudfoot said. "They live in Brooklyn. It had once been planned that she would marry Howard when she attained her maturity, but for some reason the match never came off. Howard can be a rather difficult individual. I have, naturally, investigated the Luttses since Bertha's disappearance. She has a number of friends, mostly female, and it goes without saying that I have similarly investigated them. I very much regret, Mr. Malone, that I am afraid I will be unable to give you any suggestions."

Malone said, "Oh, well, she'll probably turn up holed out at the YWCA. "That's the least of my worries. I've always been wonderful at finding women. Now when that little chore is attended to, who do you want me to put the finger on?"

"I beg your pardon?" Abner Proudfoot said stiffly.

"Talk English, pal," the little lawyer said, "and don't try to kid John Joseph Malone, because, just between ourselves, he isn't kiddable. You want me to find some guy or some babe we can pin this murder rap on and make it stick. Only I want to know, do you have any suggestions?"

"Naturally," Proudfoot said, "I should be delighted if you were able to discover, and to hand over to the proper authorities, the perpetrator of this heinous crime."

Malone said, "Wow!" and then, "You don't fool me, brother. You've got yourself a soft snap as this Bertha babe's trustee, and don't try to tell me you're doing it because you knew her old man by his first name. There's a fat per cent connected with it, and of course if any money should stick to your fingers now and then, you can always lick it off. If Bertha should bow out via the electric chair, you'd be right down in the pickle jar, because you'd have to look for another job, and at your age that mightn't be such a cinch. So, you hire me to find her, find a dope to pin the murder on, save her neck and your income."

Abner Proudfoot rose and stood, holding his black derby in one hand and his black brief case in the other. He said, "I find your attitude most reprehensible, Mr. Malone. I am afraid that we must consider our arrangement terminated."

Malone didn't get up. He relit his cigar and said, "Oh, no, bub, you hired me, but you can't fire me. Because I've got your check in my pocket, and if you stop payment on it, I'll sue you, and think how embarrassing that would be. Besides, it isn't your money, anyway. And if I don't do this little job for you, you're going to be in a hell of a fix."

For a minute Abner Proudfoot stared at him. Then he said, "There is something in what you say, Mr. Malone. I feel that I must retract my statement of a moment ago."

"Now you're talking," Malone said. He rose, went to the writing desk, and started pawing through it. "Just for the fun of it, bub, let's put it in writing." He pulled out a sheet of letter paper, took his fountain pen out of his pocket, unscrewed the cap, and handed it over. "Just put it this way. I, Abner Proudfoot, as trustee for Bertha Morrison, née Lutts, do promise to pay to John Joseph Malone the sum of four thousand five hundred dollars, in the event of the said Bertha Morrison, née Lutts, being found and proved innocent of the murder committed in suite 713 of the St. Jacques Hotel on the night of April eighth. And sign it."

Abner Proudfoot frowned, took the pen, and wrote, Malone prompting him now and then. He signed the paper with a flourish, recapped the pen, and returned it.

"I doubt very much, however," he said, "if, in view of

its informal terminology, that paper could be construed as a legal document, should it ever be brought into court."

"Buddy," Malone said, "you let me worry about that. And if this little document ever gets into court, I'll drop dead from surprise and it won't matter anyway." He folded the paper carefully and tucked it in his pocket, next to the check. "You know I think we're going to get along swell."

There was a knock at the door, and Malone jumped up to answer it. It was Helene.

A pale-gray woolen evening cape, embroidered with silver thread and reaching to the floor, hung from her shoulders. A paler-gray chiffon dinner dress clung to her like a cloud of cigarette smoke, a dress that was powdered with minute rhinestones. Her hair was sleek and shining, the color of honey, and her delicate-featured, patrician face was white under its make-up. There was a big silver bangle just below her slender throat.

"Ah, yes," Malone said. He turned to Mr. Proudfoot. "This is Cleopatra Carmichael, one of my concubines." He smiled at Helene and said, "Carmelite, my dear, this is Mr. Abyssinia McSnitch, my great-great-grandfather."

Abner Proudfoot mumbled something, and Helene just stared. Malone said, "Don't mind her not speaking to you, poor child, she was born deaf and dumb. Well, it's been nice seeing you again, uncle Ed, and be sure to open the door before you go out."

Abner Proudfoot picked up his brief case for the second time. Again his face threatened to crack into a smile. "I am convinced that I was not misinformed as to your abilities, Mr. Malone," he said. "I feel sure that our relationship will be a happy and profitable one. Good night." He bowed elaborately to Helene and went out.

Helene waited until she heard the elevator door close

down the hall before she said, "For the love of Mike——"

"A client of mine," Malone said, "a harmless madman, but a lovable one."

"Malone, Jake isn't back yet. It's seven o'clock."

"Oh, hell," Malone said, "he probably got drunk and he's sleeping under a bar somewhere."

"Jake couldn't get that drunk in nine hours."

"All right, he's out with another girl."

He was relieved to see that this time she definitely looked more angry than alarmed.

"Listen," he said, picking up his topcoat, "tell me something. If you were headstrong, and a creature of whims, and you'd just beaten, strangled, and decapitated another babe just for the hell of it, where would you head for?"

"The elevator," Helene said promptly, "and then the lobby, and then the bar."

"Then that's where we're headed," Malone said. "The elevator, the lobby, and the bar. Because we're a couple of bloodhounds. And if we don't reach that last-mentioned place soon, I'm going to begin to bark."

Chapter Eleven

THE EVENING was not an unqualified success in the matter of taking Helene's mind off Jake's unexplained absence. She pointed out at intervals that she was not worried, but Malone observed that she ate only approximately ten per cent of her dinner.

Tracing Dennis Morrison's progress of the night before was considerably more successful. The night bartender in the small bar of the St. Jacques (Malone didn't like him any better than the day bartender) remembered him well. He'd come in about eight o'clock, drunk three whisky sours and two straight bourbons, got into conversation with someone at the bar, and drifted out—nine or thereabouts, the bartender thought. No, he hadn't recognized the man Dennis had conversed with. He couldn't say what kind of mood Dennis had been in. "I am not hired as no psychologist," he added with wounded dignity. "I am hired to serve drinks."

Helene decided that they would have dinner right there at the St. Jacques. Not that it really mattered, she explained casually, but it would make it easier for Jake to join them if he arrived in time. They lingered over coffee and brandy for an extra half-hour, on the same theory. Jake did not arrive. They left.

The night club down the street that had been Dennis Morrison's first stop was of the intimate, underlighted and unventilated variety. It was also crowded, but they managed to be squeezed in at a table the size of a piano stool.

Malone ordered two ryes, lit a cigar, looked around the room, and reflected that the murals would make him terribly nervous after about six drinks. Helene located the waiter who had served Dennis Morrison the night before and started to work on him, a process which was interrupted by the floor show. It was exactly like every other floor show Malone had seen in his life. He did manage to find out the name of the cute little redhead in the chorus, but he wasn't sure how to get acquainted with her. New York techniques might be different from those employed in Chicago.

Helene telephoned the hotel to see if Jake had come in yet. He hadn't. Fortunately the floor show was over and the waiter came back before she had much chance to brood about it.

Dennis Morrison had come in a little after nine, in the company of a tallish man in a brown suit. "He seemed a little high," the waiter said, "but more nervous than high, if you know what I mean. He didn't pay much attention to the floor show and kept looking at his watch. He acted as if he was waiting to keep a date."

"He was," Malone said.

"Well, he had a few drinks and he felt better," the waiter said. "He was drinking brandy and champagne. I guess his friend went home, I didn't notice him go. Your friend paid the check when he left. After he'd been here awhile he got acquainted with the party at the next table and joined them."

Malone reflected that that was not surprising. It was practically impossible not to get acquainted with the party at any next table, in this place. Right now, a thinnish girl at his left had her elbow poked into his ribs, and a plump man on his right was leaning on his shoulder.

"He left with them," the waiter went on. "I heard one of them suggest going to El Morocco, but of course I don't know if they did or not. There were six of them. One of the women was blonde and she had on a green dress. They were all feeling pretty happy."

"Were the men in dinner jackets?" Helene asked.

The waiter thought a minute, then shook his head. "Nope."

Malone sighed. He paid the check, wondering as he did so if he'd been drinking rye or distilled platinum.

They traced Dennis Morrison to El Morocco, to Monte Carlo, where Helene called up the hotel again, to the 1-2-3 Club, where Malone switched from rye to gin, to the Stork Club, to Copacabana, where it appeared that Dennis had deserted his new friends and wandered off by himself.

The first thing to do, Helene declared, was to try all the places within easy stumbling distance. Malone suggested that a better idea was to go home and sleep, but he was promptly squelched.

Dennis Morrison had not been seen at the Savoy Plaza or the Persian Room, but he was well remembered at Café Society Uptown, where he'd been thrown out. The trail seemed lost, but it was picked up again in a bar about fifteen blocks away, on West Forty-ninth Street, and followed to another bar on Broadway below Forty-sixth Street. Malone began to feel a little more at home; indeed, in the second bar he felt that he could switch to a cheaper gin. It wasn't that he was economizing; he just liked the taste better. The bartender not only remembered Dennis Morrison, but suggested that his next stop had probably been Marty's Bar and Grill, on Eighth Avenue.

At Marty's Bar and Grill Helene called the hotel again and learned that Jake had not come in. Malone organized a quartet to sing *The Harp That Once Through Tara's Halls,* and Marty remembered that Dennis Morrison had come in about quarter to two, bought drinks for the house and several for himself to celebrate his marriage, and left half an hour later, headed in a more or less northerly direction. He suggested inquiring at the Idle Hour, half a block up the street.

The bartender at the Idle Hour was very helpful. Dennis Morrison had been in, sometime after two, celebrating his marriage. "I never thought he'd marry her," the bartender commented, "but he fooled us all. Nice, pretty girl, too. I put him in a taxi about half-past two or quarter to three. Wait a minute, I think I can find the taxi for you. The driver's a friend of mine."

While they waited, Malone experimented with pouring

his gin into a glass of beer and drinking the results, and got into a fight with one of the customers over the relative honesty of New York and Chicago cops, gaining a cut on his lip and losing his necktie in the process. The bartender threw out the customer and said to Helene, "Louie shouldn't of said that to your friend. And any friend of yours, lady, is a friend of mine. The next one is on the house."

The taxi driver said, "Yeah, I picked him up here. Yeah, thanks, I will. Just a short one though. I quit work in another hour and my old lady's allergic to the smell of alcohol."

He'd picked up Dennis Morrison at quarter to three and driven him around for nearly an hour. They'd stopped at an all-night drugstore, where Dennis had bought a pint of bourbon, and then they'd driven through Central Park, while Dennis discoursed on love and marriage, and sipped at his bourbon, ending up by flinging the bottle through the cab window at the General Sherman statue. "We damned near got pinched," the driver said. He'd left his passenger at the St. Jacques at quarter to four.

"And that's where you're going to take us and leave us," Malone said, "at"—he consulted his watch—"quarter after four."

"Jake will surely be there," Helene said, "by the time we are."

Jake was not.

Malone went into the bathroom and held a cold washcloth against his swollen lip for a few minutes. Then he poured himself a pickup drink from one of the bottles on the shelf, rearranged his collar, and smoothed down his hair.

By the time he came back Helene had finished calling the hospitals. He said, "Stop worrying," again, and she said, "Who the hell's worrying?" Then she picked up the phone again and said, "Get me the morgue."

Jake wasn't there.

"He's been kidnaped," she said in a thin little voice.

"For the love of Mike," Malone said. "He's probably socked a policeman and been thrown in jail."

He watched her thoughtfully as she picked up the telephone again. She looked very tired and young and pale. And helpless. She was, he knew, about as helpless as a company of marines, but the sight of her still tied a knot somewhere between his stomach and his heart.

She called police headquarters. They had no record of any Jake Justus. She hung up the phone and said slowly, "Malone, do you think we ought to report him missing?"

"*No!*" Malone said. He added, a little more mildly, "There's no telling where Jake may be or what he may be up to. But there's always a better than even chance he might not appreciate having the cops out looking for him. At least wait till morning, and get some sleep first."

"I'm not—sleepy," Helene said, her eyelids drooping. She lit a cigarette, dropped it in the ash tray, and left it there.

Malone looked at his watch. It was four-forty. "After all," he said, "you were awake all last night, too."

"Do you think I could settle down and go to sleep with Jake missing?" Helene said drowsily. "I'm going to sit right here by the phone in case he calls, and wait for him."

"Fine," Malone said. "In that case, I'm going to wait with you."

He watched her going to sleep, slowly, little by little, and fighting it all the way, like a small child on Christmas Eve. Her eyes closed and then opened again fast, and she said, "I'm going to wait for Jake." She smothered a yawn, lit another cigarette, and abandoned it in the ash tray. And then at last her delicate eyelids fell shut and didn't open again.

Malone waited for a full ten minutes. She didn't stir so much as an eyelash. Finally he picked her up from her chair by the telephone table and carried her to the sofa. He went into the bedroom and brought back a pillow and a big satin-covered comforter.

He slipped the pillow under her head, took off her shoes, and tucked the comforter around her. She half opened her eyes for a moment and whispered, "Jake." Malone stood still, holding his breath, until he was sure she was not going to wake again.

Then he emptied the ash tray, opened the window, and tiptoed out, pausing at the door for one last look at Helene.

If Jake was just out on a bender, he reflected, closing the door softly, then a certain red-haired ex-press agent was going to get one hell of a punch in the nose from a certain lawyer named Malone, when he did show up. And if he wasn't just out on a bender——

Jake was all right. Nothing could have happened to Jake. Nothing ever had. He'd been missing before and turned up alive and well. He would this time. He had to.

Malone realized that he felt wide-awake and restless, the usual result of being overtired. The little hotel room, for all its skillful interior decoration, didn't appeal to him.

Maybe he could go out and look for Jake.

A fine idea, but this was New York, not Chicago. Where in blazes would he look?

Maybe he could find an all-night bar.

That was no good, all by himself in a strange city. Besides, he'd been in enough bars already.

Maybe he ought to call up that cute redhead from the chorus.

Very good, only he didn't have her telephone number, just her name.

Maybe he just ought to go to bed and catch up on his sleep.

The elevator opened, and Malone stepped in. The elevator boy winked at him and carried him past his floor. After the one other passenger in the car got off, the boy grinned at Malone and said, "Are you the gentleman who was looking for a poker game?"

Malone wrestled with temptation for just thirty seconds, during which he told himself that his having been taken for someone else was obviously a lucky sign, that it was, after all, only five o'clock, and that he still had $437 in his wallet.

"Boy," he said happily, after thirty seconds. "You not only read my mind, you write it."

Chapter Twelve

"THIS IS not complete failure," Jake kept telling himself during the ride in the squad car. "It's only a temporary setback."

It wasn't a comfortable ride. He was wedged in between O'Brien and Birnbaum, manacled to the latter. In front of him, Schultz sat beside a silent, alarmed, and bewildered Wildavine Williams. His prospects weren't comfortable, either. He was going to have a lot of explaining to do.

"Watch him, Birnbaum," O'Brien said. "He's one of those moor-ons."

Wildavine said, "This is all some ridiculous mistake. I shall see to it that a full report reaches the newspapers."

"The mistake," Birnbaum told her, "was when you put your name and address on the envelope of that threatening letter."

"I assure you," she said stiffly, "my uncle George will hear all the particulars of this outrage, and he is the best lawyer in Platteville, Wisconsin."

"Do write him," O'Brien said. "You probably owe him a letter, anyway. Only," he added, "you'd better not threaten him in it, because the police in Platteville may not be as friendly and easy to get along with as we are."

She sniffed and was silent.

"Yeah, but listen," Schultz said in a worried voice, "the dame she wrote the t'reatenin' letter to wasn't the dame who got murdered."

"Shut up, Schultz," Birnbaum said. "You talk too much."

"Yeah, but wait a minute, fellas," Schultz said. "How'd this guy get into the apartment while we was searching it, and then how'd he get down here ahead of us? That's what I want to know."

"I manifested myself," Jake said in a sepulchral tone. "I'm really not a magazine salesman, I'm the spirit of the murdered woman, and I can appear and disappear whenever I choose."

O'Brien crossed himself and then said hastily, "Shut up, you."

Jake said, "*Boo!*"

"See what I mean?" O'Brien said to Birnbaum. "The guy's a moor-on."

Birnbaum said, "I wish we could stop by a drugstore. I'd like to get an Alka-Seltzer."

"You eat wrong, that's all," O'Brien said.

There were, Jake reflected, two things he could do. He could tell the whole truth, what he had been doing, and why. It wouldn't be difficult to prove it. Only, if he did so, the cops would probably keep an eye on him till the case was finished. He wouldn't have a China-man's ghost of a chance of finding Bertha Morrison and the murderer of the unknown beauty. He'd never be able to prove to that editor that he knew all there was to know about crime detection.

Besides, Helene would find out. Not that she wouldn't understand and sympathize. In fact, if she knew what he was doing she would enthusiastically insist on helping. He'd welcome her help, but this time he wanted to surprise her.

The other thing he could do was to go on playing dumb, and pray that the cops would rapidly find out that he had nothing to do with the crime. The trouble with that was, it might take anywhere from an hour to a week, and in the meantime, Helene would worry her-self frantic.

Suddenly a third possibility occurred to him and, think-ing it over, he began to feel better. That inspector from the Homicide Bureau, Arthur Peterson, had looked like an understanding and reasonable guy. He'd tell Peterson the whole story, the book, Helene, everything. A good guy like Arthur Peterson would appreciate the situation, turn him loose, and keep the secret. Hell, Peterson would probably be glad to have the help of a well-grounded, though strictly amateur, criminologist.

Everything was going to be swell, if only Wildavine

could be released, too. Because he still had a lot of questions to ask Wildavine. The chances were good, he told himself. The police really didn't have anything on Wildavine.

At headquarters he assumed an air of great dignity and importance, and announced, "I have valuable information to give, but it can only be given to Inspector Arthur Peterson. Take me to him at once."

The sergeant wasn't impressed. He ignored Jake's statement and barked, "What's your name?"

Jake stared at him silently, trying to look as though he weren't thinking hard to find a usable name.

"He says he's the spirit of the murdered woman," Birnbaum said.

"Yeah," Schultz added, "and he says he can manifest himself anytime he wants to and disappear any time he wants to. Personally, I don't believe it."

"I said, what's your name?" the sergeant said to Jake, grim determination in his voice.

"Edward J. Kelly," Jake said promptly. It was the first name that had come into his mind. "Listen, I want to talk to Arthur Peterson."

"Shut up," the sergeant said. "Where do you live?"

Jake said, "Chicago."

The sergeant looked at him for a moment, then picked up an interoffice phone and dialed an exchange. "Say," he said, "I've got a nut down here who's mixed up in that St. Jacques hotel killing. He thinks he's the mayor of Chicago."

That hadn't occurred to Jake before, but he said coyly, "Maybe I am. Then wouldn't you be surprised."

"Shut up," the sergeant said again to Jake, and then into the telephone, "O. K., I'll send him along to you."

"What I want to know is," O'Brien said, "do we get the credit for this guy, or does Peterson?"

The sergeant said, "Depends on what he done. Take him on upstairs."

"He socked me," Schultz said. His voice sounded hurt.

"He was in the place where the babe was murdered," O'Brien said, "and then we found him hiding out with this dame."

"Who'd written the threatening letter," Birnbaum added.

Schultz said, "Yeah, but lookit, fellas, the dame she wrote the t'reatenin' letter to didn't get murdered."

"For two bits, Schultz," O'Brien said, "I'd sock you myself."

"Wait a minute yet," the sergeant said, "is he booked for resisting an officer, or is he a material witness, or what?"

"Put him down as held for questioning," Birnbaum said. Then they took Jake upstairs.

A soft-voiced young man in a gray double-breasted suit smiled pleasantly at Jake, offered him a cigarette, and said, "I'm sure this is just a simple little misunderstanding which can be cleared up very quickly if you'll answer a few questions." He unscrewed the cap of his fountain pen and shook a drop of ink over the wastebasket. "Your name, again?"

"I'll tell that to Mr. Peterson," Jake said. He wondered what was happening to Wildavine.

"He says he's the mayor of Chicago," O'Brien said.

The young man in the gray suit frowned and wrote something down. Then he smiled at Jake again. "I know this is all a great nuisance, but it really is quite important. Now tell me, just how did you happen to be in that suite at the St. Jacques?"

"I'll tell that to Mr. Peterson, too," Jake said. "Along with a number of other things."

"In another minute he'll start hollering for a lawyer," Birnbaum said gloomily. "They always do."

"Please," the young man said, "I want you to consider me your friend. I'm only trying to help you out of what is really a very serious situation. You do believe I want to help you, don't you?"

"Sure," Jake said. "So get me Arthur Peterson so I can talk to him quick and get the hell out of this lousy jail."

"You are not being very co-operative," the young man said reprovingly. "Just why do you insist on seeing Arthur Peterson?"

"Because I want to tell him something," Jake said.

"Ah," the young man said. "Won't you tell me what you want to tell him?" His voice was so friendly it almost cooed.

"Sure," Jake said. He nodded his head and grinned broadly.

"See, he's a moor-on, all right," O'Brien said.

The young man in the gray suit scowled at him. Then he chirruped at Jake, "Ah, that's fine! Just tell me what you want to tell Arthur Peterson.

Jake tiptoed over to the desk, looked all around him cautiously, laid a finger on his lips, leaned over the young man, and finally whispered, "A secret!"

The young man leaned back, sighed, and said, "All right, boys, turn him over to Doc Grosher."

Eventually, Jake reflected, they'd get tired of him and deliver him to Arthur Peterson.

Doc Grosher turned out to be a big, impressive man with a scrubbed-looking pink skin, eyeglasses, a mane of iron-gray hair, and a well-cultivated reassuring manner. He had a couple of assistants in white coats.

Birnbaum, O'Brien, and Schultz vanished. Jake hoped Birnbaum got his Alka-Seltzer.

"Fine, fine, fine," Doc Grosher said, beaming and giving his hands a dry wash. "Lovely day, isn't it? Now, young man, just take off your coat, tie, and shirt."

"I'm not sick," Jake said, "and I'm not going to take off my shirt. I just want to talk to Arthur Peterson."

"Of course you do," Doc Grosher said soothingly. "Yes, of course you do. But let's get through with this little routine first. Now just take off your coat, tie, and shirt." He signaled to his assistants with his eyes.

Jake took off his coat, tie, and shirt. He was silent and patient while his chest, his blood, his blood pressure, and his reflexes were tested. He was even amiably quiet while the measurements of his skull were taken and the doctor murmured, "Hm. Yes, yes, yes." But by the time he was allowed to dress again, and was seated cozily at a corner of the doctor's desk, he was getting pretty damn tired of it all.

The doctor stared at him dreamily and then said, "Tell me quickly. What is the first thing you remember?"

"Trying to find Arthur Peterson," Jake said. He said it quickly, too.

"No, no, no," Doc Grosher said. "I mean the very first thing you can remember."

Jake gave the same answer. They went through that routine several times before the doctor gave up.

"When did you first become aware," Doc Grosher went on, "that you were the mayor of Chicago?"

"When I started looking for Arthur Peterson," Jake said.

There were a number of other questions concerning his birthplace, his childhood memories, his home life, his education, his occupation, and a few more questions which Jake considered insultingly personal. He gave the same answer to all of them. He'd tell Arthur Peterson.

"Now tell me this," the doctor said, in the same dreamy manner, "have you ever felt an impulse to kill, a momentary impulse?"

"I'm going to feel a momentary impulse to give somebody a bust in the nose," Jake said, "if you don't quit playing games with me and take me to Arthur Peterson."

"Definitely an interesting type, isn't he, doctor?" one of the assistants said. He was a thin young man with glasses and curly dark hair. "Threatening, and yet not violent."

The doctor said, "Sssh!" to him, and then snapped at Jake, "Quick! Are you asleep or awake?"

"Neither," Jake said. "I'm dreaming. Dreaming of getting to see Arthur Peterson."

"What day is this?"

"The day on which I'm trying to see Arthur Peterson."

"Who are you?"

"The guy who wants to see Arthur Peterson."

"Where are you?"

"In the office of some damn-fool doctor who's trying to keep me from seeing Arthur Peterson." Jake was beginning to get impatient.

"Rather a definite feeling of persecution there, don't you think, doctor?" the other assistant said, an anemic-looking young man with sandy hair.

"I think the hell with it," Doctor Grosher said, dropping his reassuring manner. "I think the guy's nuts."

The sandy-haired assistant said, "You don't want me to write that down, do you, doctor?" and the dark-haired assistant said, "Shall I give him Test A, doctor?"

The doctor said a rude word and lit a cigarette.

"Tests A and B are routine," the assistant said earnestly. "They have to go on the charts."

Dr. Grosher snorted. The curly-haired assistant sat Jake at a desk, handed him an eight-page leaflet and a pen, and said, "Try to answer all the questions in eleven minutes."

Jake drew faces all over the chart, labeled them all "Arthur Peterson," and handed it in in six minutes.

The sandy-haired assistant led him into a small adjoining room and seated him before an immense wooden board covered with variously shaped holes. Beside the board was a pile of variously shaped wooden blocks. The idea, he informed Jake, was to fit the blocks into the proper holes. Then he went away and shut the door.

Jake built a magnificent house out of the wooden blocks. Over the door he lettered, "Arthur Peterson lives here."

"He seems to have a definite fixation about Arthur Peterson, doctor," the sandy-haired assistant said.

Dr. Grosher said another very rude word. Then he said, "All right, let him talk to Arthur Peterson."

Jake's heart leaped. A few minutes—half an hour, at most—of man-to-man discussion, and he'd be out of here. A taxi would take him back to the hotel in another half-hour, and he'd straighten things out with Helene somehow. Maybe he'd tell her he'd been having a tooth filled. Anyway, he'd be there in time to take her to dinner.

"You don't think we ought to give him Test C?" the curly haired assistant said.

"The hell with Test C," Doc Grosher said. "The hell with him. Just get him out of here."

As Jake was being turned over to a uniformed cop, he

heard the sandy-haired assistant say to the curly-haired assistant, "Doc Grosher must be getting old. He seems to be losing his grip."

Jake had expected to land in Peterson's office. Instead, he landed in a cell. He protested indignantly and loudly. After all, time was fleeting.

The cop said soothingly, "Sure you're going to see Arthur Peterson. Only just settle down and make yourself at home, and you'll get a nice little dinner, and a nice little sedative the doc ordered. On account of Arthur Peterson is some place up in Connecticut and he ain't coming back until ten tomorrow morning, and so you can't see him till then."

He locked the cell door, and said, "So long, buddy. Sleep well."

Chapter Thirteen

"THIS IS not Chicago," Arthur Peterson said sternly. "We do things differently here. Scientifically and efficiently. And we don't need help from amateurs."

Jake nodded his head apologetically and said, "Yes, of course. I realize that." He looked hopefully for a sympathetic gleam in the police official's eye, and saw none.

"Particularly," Peterson added, "amateurs who disturb the morale of the entire department."

"I'm really very sorry," Jake said humbly. "It was just"—he remembered Doc Grosher's words—"a momentary impulse."

Arthur Peterson looked at him, a cold gleam behind his thick-lensed glasses. "Momentary impulses," he said, "impair efficiency."

"I'm sure of it," Jake said.

He felt tired, miserable, and worried. His night in jail had not been a restful one, punctuated as it had been by busy young men from the Behavior Clinic who kept popping in to test his reflexes and ask him questions. Besides, he'd been too disturbed about Helene to sleep. He could just see her, sitting by the telephone, waiting, when she could have been out showing Malone the town. A couple of times he'd considered giving the whole thing up and telling the next busy young man who came in, "I'll tell you everything, if you'll only let me phone my wife."

But every time, when the young man appeared, he'd thought better of it. After all, he was doing this for Helene, wasn't he? When it was all over, and he'd succeeded in what he was trying to do, they'd laugh over it.

Now, however, it was beginning to look as though it had been for nothing. He'd told Arthur Peterson the truth, and all he'd got had been the kind of scolding a schoolboy might expect for throwing a rock through a window. He'd been apologetic and sorry and humble, but so far it hadn't done any good, and his patience was beginning to wear thin. In about sixty more seconds he was going to pop Arthur Peterson right on the end of his long, thin nose.

"Of course," Peterson said suddenly, "I do appreciate the circumstances. I have a wife myself. And I've always had a kind of feeling that I could write a book."

Jake felt hope leap up in his chest for the first time in hours.

"In fact," Peterson went on, "sometime I'd like to tell you about the book I have in mind. I really have a lot of material. Maybe I could give you some good ideas, too."

"That would be wonderful!" Jake said ardently.

"I even have a few things jotted down. Just roughly, you know. Maybe you'd like to look at them."

Jake said, "I'd be delighted! They must be extremely interesting."

Arthur Peterson's thin lips almost smiled. There was a moment's silence. Then he said, "Letting you go is going to be hard to explain to Doc Grosher. But I guess I can do it."

He spent several minutes trying to get Doc Grosher on the phone. Then he said, "Funny, the doc's home with a hangover. I never knew him to go on a bender before."

Jake said nothing. He mentally apologized to Doc Grosher.

"I shouldn't let you go," Peterson said, "but of course, as a fellow writer——" He paused, coughed mildly, and went on, sternly, "Remember, though, we don't allow this sort of thing here. Detection is not a pastime for amateurs. Stick to your writing and don't bother us."

Jake said, "Oh, don't worry," and hoped the officer would take it to mean, "Yes, I will."

There was another brief silence, and then Arthur Peterson looked up from behind his shiny and orderly desk. "Just between ourselves, though," he said, "as a matter of idle curiosity, did you happen to stumble on anything important yesterday?"

Jake's heart jumped for joy a couple of times. The only difference between New York and Chicago cops was in the words they used! "Well," he said slowly, "not exactly. There were a few things that struck me as interesting." He went on to tell about the fact that Bertha Morrison had unpacked as though she expected to stay at the St. Jacques forever, instead of just overnight, even to having her luggage taken to the storeroom, but that Dennis Morrison hadn't unpacked, save for a few overnight necessities.

"You have a very keen eye," Arthur Peterson said reluctantly, making a few notes. "Anything else?"

Jake decided to keep Bertha's notes and her address book to himself. "Just the letter—if it was a letter—from Wildavine Williams. It should have occurred to me to look in the wastebasket for the envelope, but your cops beat me to it."

"Our department is very efficient," Arthur Peterson said, a little purr of pleasure in his voice. "It wasn't a letter, of course. Miss Williams, it develops, is a poetess. She had, quite innocently, sent Bertha Morrison a copy of her latest poem. One of the last things Bertha Morrison did before her disappearance was to write her a letter thanking her for it."

He pulled out a cardboard file and took out a letter. Jake immediately recognized the handsome stationery with the engraved queen bee in one corner.

"Dearest Wildavine," Arthur Peterson read aloud, "I think your last poem is very beautiful. Thank you for sending it to me. I am sure that someday you will be a famous and successful poet like Shakespeare and Robert Burns and Ella Wheeler Wilcox. Do not let hardships discourage you, someday you will be grateful for the good effect they have had on your character. I am sorry I cannot make you the loan to take the course of study you are interested in, but I am sure the trustees would not allow it. Thank you again for your poem and for the good wishes you expressed over the telephone. I am very happy, and looking forward to our Manhattan honeymoon. Affectionately, Bertha."

He put the letter back in the file. "The whole business," he said, "was quite discouraging to O'Brien and Birnbaum, but Schultz claimed to have suspected it all the time."

Jake repeated slowly " 'Our Manhattan honeymoon.' That might explain her unpacking job. Maybe there was a change of plans at the last minute. It could have happened that way."

"It could," Arthur Peterson said, nodding.

"Only," Jake went on, thinking out loud, "Dennis hadn't unpacked. And he said that they planned to leave in the morning on their honeymoon tour." He frowned. "Maybe she decided on a Manhattan honeymoon and was going to break the news to him when he came back. Women do things like that sometimes."

"Yes, they do," Arthur Peterson agreed. "When Clara and I were married——" He paused, and coughed.

In the silence that followed, the telephone rang. Arthur Peterson answered it, and as he listened, a light came into his pallid yellowish face. His eyes gleamed. The thin, straw-colored hair on his high-domed head seemed about ready to stand up straight.

He hung up the phone and said, "Well, the murdered woman has been identified."

Jake said, "Oh," and tried not to sound disappointed. Learning the identity of the murdered woman was one of the things he'd counted on doing himself. Still, if he found Bertha Morrison, and discovered the murderer——

"I've got to go right over there," Peterson said, getting up. He looked at Jake speculatively and said, "Maybe you'd like to come along. Strictly unofficially, of course. But you might be able to pick up some literary material."

"Oh, sure," Jake said. He might be able to pick up some information he could use, too. He considered saying, "Do you mind if I call up my wife first," and then thought better of it. His explanation, if he could think of one, had better be delivered in person.

Schultz accompanied them in the police car on the way to the morgue. He didn't have anything to say, but he kept looking thoughtfully at Jake.

A white-faced, middle-aged man was waiting for them in an office adjoining the police morgue. He was an ordinary little man, with receding gray hair, rimless glasses, and a shiny dark-blue suit. He looked friendly and intelligent and, at the moment, tired, worried, and stunned. He was introduced as Dr. William Puckett, of Puckett's Mills, Ohio.

"It's Hazel, all right," Dr. Puckett said. "I mean, Gloria. She didn't like us to call her Hazel in front of out-of-town folks. Gloria Garden. Legally I guess, though, she's still Hazel Puckett." He took out a pipe, tapped it absent-mindedly against the desk, and then put it back in his pocket, still empty. "She was a model. Maybe you've seen her picture on some magazine covers. She was on quite a few. I'm her pa." He took the pipe out again and began absent-mindedly fiddling with it. "Do you know yet who did it? This is going to be a terrible blow to Mrs. Puckett."

Arthur Peterson said with surprising gentleness, "No, we don't know yet. Yes, naturally it would be a great blow. To you, too. My deepest sympathy." He waited a moment and then said, "How did you happen to come in and identify her?"

"Saw her picture in the paper," Dr. Puckett said. He blew his nose noisily. "That drawing that was made of her face. I'd been trying to find her anyway, so when I saw that drawing I knew it must be her, and it was."

Jake said, "Trying to find her? Had she been missing?"

Arthur Peterson gave him a look that said, "I'll ask the questions," but Dr. Puckett didn't seem to notice.

"Missing since yesterday," he said. "I came into town to attend some medical lectures. We country doctors have to keep up, you know. First thing, I went to see Hazel— I mean, Gloria—and she wasn't there. Didn't have her telephone number, so I went back two or three times. Last time was about midnight. This morning I tried again, and she still hadn't shown up. Then I saw that picture in the papers, and came right over here."

"Did you know Bertha Morrison?" Arthur Peterson asked.

Dr. Puckett shook his head. "Never heard of her. Never heard of her husband, either. 'Course, Hazel knew a lot of people I never heard about." He sucked noisily on the empty pipe. "Read the whole story, beginning to end, in all the newspapers. None of it told me anything."

Further questions elicited the information that Hazel Puckett—Gloria Garden—had been a pretty baby, that she'd starred in high-school dramatics, that the summer after her graduation she'd clerked in Wirtz's Variety Store, saved up her salary, and run away to New York to become a great actress. That had been seven years ago.

"Guess she wasn't much of an actress," Dr. Puckett said, "but she sure was a mighty fine model. Never knew much of anything about her friends here. Whenever I come into town, we'd go out to dinner and a real good show, and she'd take me all around and show me the sights. She always came home for Christmas, and once in a while for a few days in the summer. But she never could get along with Irma—that's my son Ed's wife, they live with us. Irma never did like her."

He put the pipe away in his pocket. "She made a lot of money. Always was sending little presents to Ma, fancy nightgowns and silk underwear and stuff like that. Ma never did wear 'em, but she was pleased as punch." He paused. "How soon can I take her home?"

"A day or two," Arthur Peterson said gently.

"As long as that? All right. Well, I guess that's all I can tell you. If you need me in the meantime, you can get in touch with me at my sister-in-law Mabel's house. I always stay there when I'm in New York." He named an address on Staten Island, which Arthur Peterson wrote down and Jake memorized. "That's all, I guess. G'by."

"Wait a minute," Arthur Peterson said. "I'll have you driven home."

"Oh, no thanks," Dr. Puckett said. "I always kinda enjoy the subway and the ferry. It's a change from riding around in the old car back home."

Jake and Arthur Peterson watched him as he went down the corridor, a stoop-shouldered little figure, walking slowly.

"Damn shame," Jake said at last.

"Always is," Arthur Peterson said. "Every time some man or woman is murdered, somebody loses a relative or a sweetheart or a friend. It doesn't help to get sentimental about it, though."

"I know," Jake said. "It impairs efficiency.'"

Arthur Peterson said, "Exactly. Well, we'll start checking up on this Gloria Garden. I'll get in touch with you soon, Mr. Justus, and we'll get together. I'd like to talk with you about this book of mine."

"Delighted," Jake said again. They were out on the sidewalk before he realized that he was being sent home. "Look, don't you want me to come along?"

"Remember what I said about amateurs?" Arthur Peterson said.

Jake said, "Yes, but—I was just thinking of getting literary material——"

"I'll tell you all about it," Arthur Peterson said, "when it's all over. So long, and stay out of trouble. Schultz here offered to drive you to your hotel."

Birnbaum and O'Brien were waiting in a car at the curb. Jake watched while Arthur Peterson climbed in and the car drove away. There wasn't, he knew, a chance in the world of his examining Gloria Garden's apartment and prying into her private life ahead of the police. He'd just have to take the chance of finding something they overlooked. Or getting some hunch they missed out on.

Suddenly he became aware of Schultz standing in front of him, and of the look in Schultz's eye. "Sock me, will you," Schultz said.

Jake tried to duck, but not in time. A sledge-hammer blow landed on his jaw, and the world dissolved in a shower of pretty colored lights.

When he opened his eyes again, Schultz was bending over him solicitously.

"Hope I didn't loosen up none of your teeth," Schultz said. "I didn't mean to sock you quite so hard."

Jake wiggled his jaw experimentally and said, "Nope, no harm done."

"O. K.," Schultz said. "No hard feelings, I hope." He gave Jake a hand getting up. "C'mon, let's get going. Before I take you home, I'll buy you a beer."

Chapter Fourteen

THE TELEPHONE by his bed went on ringing for quite a while before Malone answered it. At first it didn't wake him to more than a vague realization that there was an objectionable noise somewhere near his ear. Then when he recognized it for what it was, he relaxed and just let it ring.

Whatever the telephone had to inform him, he didn't want to hear it. Probably bad news, anyway. For a moment his better self insisted that he answer, but Malone immediately told his better self just where to get off.

After a few minutes the phone stopped ringing. See, Malone told his better self, I told you that if we just ignored it, it would get tired and go away.

He felt distinctly uncomfortable and depressed. During the night some evil practical joker had come in and pumped his head full of some lighter-than-air gas. He suspected that if he moved too suddenly, he might explode. A pair of squirrels had evidently been nesting in his mouth, while he slept. And in addition, he was filled with a vague sense of past calamity and a more acute premonition of future ones.

Malone wondered what the past calamity could have been. Whatever it had been, it had been terrible. Maybe he'd been murdered in his sleep. That would account for the way he felt right now.

The phone began to ring again, insistently. Malone said, "Oh, all right," reached for it, missed it on the first two tries, finally got it to his ear, and mumbled, "Go away. I'm a very sick man."

"Malone," Helene's voice said. "Wake up. Get up right away. I need you."

"Good night," Malone said. "Sleep well. I'll see you in the morning." He hung up.

The phone immediately rang again. Malone counted slowly to a hundred, hoping it would stop. It didn't. He sighed, propped himself up on one elbow, and answered it again.

Helene said, "It's the middle of the afternoon. Do you want me to come down there and drag you out of bed with my own little hands?"

Malone instinctively pulled the sheet up over his bare chest and said, "*No!*"

"Well, then," Helene said, "don't hang up on me again. Malone, Jake's back."

"That's nice," Malone said. "All your worries are over. Now go away and let me sleep."

"*Wait*," she said. "He hasn't explained a thing. He just came in, kissed me, and said good morning. Now he's taking a bath and shaving. And he has a bruise on his chin."

"The cop probably socked back," Malone said, with the voice of a prophet. "What do you want me to do, come down and wash his back?"

"And, Malone, they've identified her."

"Who?" Malone said, blinking. He wondered if he'd missed a sentence.

"The police. They've identified that girl. The one who was murdered. It's all in the papers."

"That's nice, too," Malone said. "Now everybody can stop worrying. Good-by—wait a minute." It suddenly flashed through his mind that he'd accepted a five-hundred-dollar retainer to find Bertha Morrison and prove that she hadn't murdered the unidentified girl. And he began to have a horrible idea of what the calamity had been. "Stay where you are," he said. "Keep calm, don't do a thing. Wait for me. Don't lose your head. I'll be right there."

He heard Helene sniff scornfully into the phone as he hung up the receiver.

Malone sat up, swung his short, plump legs over the edge of the bed, wrapped a sheet around his shoulders, and sat wiggling his toes. It was always a bad sign when he went to bed with his socks on. Just what had happened, anyway? He didn't look forward to finding out.

At last he rose and began looking around the room. He located his pants under the bed, his vest on a hanger in the closet, his coat hung over a towel rack in the bathroom, his shirt neatly folded and tucked under his pillow, and his tie knotted carefully around a floor lamp. One shoe was in the bathtub (luckily dry) and the other on top of the dresser.

He went through all his pockets, through all his luggage, in all the bureau drawers and under the rug. Then he tore the bed apart sheet by sheet. All he could locate was some two dollars in silver in his pants pocket, and a twenty-dollar bill in his vest.

Malone staggered into the bathroom and looked at himself in the mirror. He saw several inches of broad, brown hairy chest, a thick neck, and a round, reddish, haggard, unshaven face. His black hair looked as though someone had been knitting with it during the night, and his blue eyes were faintly pink-rimmed. He told the face exactly what he thought of it, and began, slowly and uncertainly, to shave.

By the time he'd shaved, stood under the shower for

ten minutes, and dressed, he felt vastly improved in body. The inch of rye that had somehow been overlooked in the bottle completed the job of putting him back to normal physically. Mentally, though, he'd been going down like a Radio City elevator.

He wasn't bothered by the fact that the $437 he'd started out with had melted down to $20 and a handful of change. That had happened more than once in his life, though usually under circumstances he enjoyed remembering. It was the fact of losing at poker. Because Malone didn't lose at poker. When he needed money, which was often, he could always run a small stake up into a comfortable sum, by finding a friendly poker game. He knew all the tricks of professional cardplayers, having successfully defended a number of them in court, but he never used them. He simply relied on the Malone luck, which had never failed him before now. The events of the night before were a grim warning that his luck was running out.

Not that he was superstitious, *but*——

The poker game on the train from Chicago didn't count. Because then he had, as he realized too late, been playing with sharpies. Whereas last night——

He paused in the middle of knotting his tie, and swore at the mirror. Then he finished with the tie, put on his coat, picked up his hat, and went out, slamming the door. He wasn't depressed now, but he was beginning to get mad.

Helene was going to have to wait a few minutes. He had other things to attend to first.

By asking a few questions he was able to locate the elevator boy who'd steered him to the poker game the night before. He was off duty, and Malone found him in the locker room, shooting craps.

Malone had broken the twenty-dollar bill at the cigar counter, and he handed the boy five. It was, he considered, a good investment.

"Gee, thanks, Mr. Malone," the boy said.

"Oh, you know me," Malone said. "That's nice. I just wanted to ask you, confidentially, who tipped you off last night that I was looking for a poker game?"

"Why," the boy said, surprsied, "the gentleman who came to see you last night. Tall, skinny gentleman, all in black except for his shirt. Some friends of his were having a little game here last night and he said you'd probably want to join in later."

"Thanks," Malone said. "I thought so."

"Nothing wrong, I hope," the boy said anxiously.

"No-o-o, not a thing," Malone told him. "If these poker players hang out here regularly, you might let them know I'm expecting some real money by wire today, and I might like to plunge a little heavier tonight, that's all."

He went up to the lobby and sent off a wire to Joe the Angel. "Wire me hundred dollars. Urgent."

Helene was coming out of the elevator just as he left the telegraph desk. She wore a navy-blue dress trimmed with big gold buttons, and a wide, navy-blue hat that framed her pale, exquisite face. A big fluffy fur was draped over one arm.

"I thought you were coming right down," she said accusingly.

"Important business," Malone told her. "Just looking after some investments of mine. Where's Jake?"

"He came down just ahead of me. Maybe he's still here in the lobby." She paused. "Malone, there he is. In the phone booth. What call could he be making that he couldn't make from upstairs?"

They looked at each other for a moment, then Malone said in a firm voice, "In a situation like this, eavesdropping is perfectly ethical." He took her arm and led her around behind the phone booth. They got there just in time to hear Jake say, "Is that you Wildavine? Did you get home all right?"

Helene gasped. Her fingernails dented Malone's arm through his coat. Malone whispered fiercely, "*Shut up!*"

"I must see you," Jake was saying. A pause, then, "Tonight? Can't you make it sooner? This afternoon? I don't want to wait till tonight." Another pause, and, "Oh, all right, if you insist. I think it would be safer if I didn't come to the house. Where? The Blue Cat Club? Eight-thirty? Fine." The receiver clicked.

Malone glanced at Helene out of the corner of his eye. What he saw was the Great Stone Face, done in marble, and beautifully carved. He'd seen more expression on fast-frozen oysters. He wanted to say something— he wasn't sure what, just something—but his mind and his speaking apparatus appeared to have become disconnected.

He tightened his grip on her elbow and led her around the phone booth, back of the flower stand, and past the cigar counter in time to meet Jake face to face in the center of the lobby.

The tall red-haired man looked tired and pale. An unsuccessful attempt had been made to powder over a bruise on his chin. His hair was mussed, and his eyes were heavy with lack of sleep.

"Hello," Malone said. He couldn't think of anything else to say.

Jake looked up from lighting a cigarette and said, "Oh. Hello." It appeared he couldn't think of anything else either.

"Just going out?" Helene said brightly. "I thought we'd show Malone the town. You know. Radio City. Grant's Tomb. Central Park. The Statue of Liberty."

"Chinatown," Malone added helpfully. "The Bowery. Wall Street."

"Wonderful idea," Jake said. "Don't miss Trinity Churchyard and the Bronx Zoo." He finished lighting his cigarette; Malone noticed that his hand shook a little. "Wish I could come with you, but I've got an important business appointment." He looked at his watch. "Let's meet at six o'clock sharp. Have an early dinner. Is that all right with you?"

"Perfectly," Helene said. "It'll give us more time to do the town afterward."

"What happened to your chin?" Malone asked.

"This?" Jake said, touching it. "Oh, nothing. A door ran into me."

"As I remember," Malone said, "the last door that ran into you got his nose broken. How did this one come out?"

Jake laughed hollowly and said, "That's very funny. Well, I'll see you at six."

Helene looked at the revolving door for a long moment after Jake had disappeared through it, and then said, "Malone, what was the name of that place? The Blue Cat Club?"

"I don't think so," Malone lied. "I don't remember just what it was."

"The Blue Cat Club. Eight-thirty," Helene quoted. "We'll just happen to drop in accidentally at quarter to nine. I just want to see what she looks like, Malone."

Malone lit a cigar and said, "I make no promises. I have important business to attend to."

"What business?"

He considered telling her. There were good arguments both ways. If he did, she would insist on coming along and helping, which might lead to well-nigh disastrous results. On the other hand, it would take her mind off Jake. Still, he would have to tell her about Abner Proudfoot and the five hundred dollars and the poker game. She might, of course, be a great deal of help. However, after all he'd had to say about keeping out of the affair, to confess that he'd accepted the job of finding Bertha Morrison——

"It's a secret," he said stiffly. "I can't tell."

Helene sniffed. "I'm not even curious," she said. "It just happens I have important things to attend to myself. And neither you nor Jake are going along."

"Wait a minute," Malone said. He'd seen that light in her eyes before. Usually it spelled t-r-o-u-b-l-e. "What kind of important things?"

"It's a secret," she said coldly. "I can't tell." She glared at him, her eyes a nice mixture of frost and flame. Then she said, "An early dinner. We'll meet here."

"Wait," Malone said. "Where are you going? Wait, I'll go with you——"

But by that time, she was gone.

Chapter Fifteen

MALONE went into the coffee shop and consumed a double portion of country-fried ham and eggs, with fried potatoes and a side order of pancakes. That, he decided, would hold him till dinner, which was only a couple of hours away.

Then he bought the latest editions of all the newspapers in the lobby, went into the bar, slid onto a barstool, and said automatically, "Bring me a double rye."

Life seemed very complicated and much too difficult to get along with. Jake and Helene keeping secrets from each other. Jake making a date with some girl, and Helene insisting on turning up, quite by accident, at their meeting place. A murder of an especially unpleasant nature, a pathetically bereft bridegroom with a bad hangover, and an inexplicably missing bride. A gloomy guy who hired him, Malone, to find the missing bride and prove her innocent of the murder, one way or another, and paid him a handsome retainer. Then a crooked poker game, rigged by the gloomy guy (Malone mentally called him by a more explicit name) to win back the retainer. And now—what?

The double rye was slid in front of him. Malone looked up and recognized the thin, melancholy bartender with the Boston accent. The bartender recognized him in the same moment and looked just faintly alarmed.

"What's this doing here," Malone snarled. "I distinctly remember ordering a double-gin-and-beer highball."

"Oh, yes, sir," the bartender said. "I'm very sorry." He started to take away the double rye.

"Leave that there," Malone snapped. "For a chaser."

The bartender seemed to have a little trouble making the gin-and-beer highball, but he finally arrived with it, shuddering. Malone growled at him wordlessly, waited until he was again buried in a secondhand back number of *New Directions*, and then poured the gruesome mixture into the nearest cuspidor. He set the empty glass back on the counter, began sipping his rye, unfolded the newspapers, and looked at the headlines.

REPORT MURDERED
WOMAN IDENTIFIED
     (*The New York Times*)

SLAIN BEAUTY WAS ARTIST'S MODEL
    (*New York Herald Tribune*)

WHO KILLED LOVELY GLORIA GARDEN?
     (*Journal-American*)

MODEL SLAYING
NOT SEX CRIME
POLICE SAY

     (*Daily News*)

MURDERED MODEL WAS
MODEL UNION MEMBER

     (*PM*)

Malone sighed, finished his rye, and began reading.

Gloria Garden had been a gorgeous girl, judging from the slightly undressed photo on the front page of the *News*, the portrait in the *Herald Tribune*, and the reproduced cigarette ads in *PM*. Otherwise, the newspaper stories didn't tell him a great deal. It was just the same old stuff. Some small-town girl grew up beautiful, and came to the big city to make hay out of it.

The newspaper stories didn't tell him anything about Bertha Morrison, except that she was missing, and he knew that already. "Dennis Morrison, husband of the missing woman, was reported in a state of near collapse." Malone grinned wryly. *Near* collapse! That reporter should have seen Dennis Morrison when he was tucked in bed, sometime yesterday. "Police are searching for Bertha Lutts Morrison——" Malone knew that too, and he crossed his fingers that the police wouldn't find her before he did.

The melancholy young bartender tiptoed up and whispered, "Was your drink quite satisfactory, sir?"

"It was terrible," Malone said. "Bring me another, and don't forget, a double rye for a chaser." He glanced once more at the newspapers and wadded them into a ball which he sent rolling down the bar, overturning the luckily empty beer glass of a customer who was absorbed in reading the day's *Racing Form.* "You'd better give me two of them at once. I feel an attack of melancholia coming on."

"Yes, *sir*," the bartender said. He forgot the chasers, slopped over the glasses in his haste to shove them across the counter, and hurried back to his stool where he hid behind *The Southern Review.* Malone disposed of the gin-and-beer highballs in the cuspidor, waited thirty seconds, and then roared, *"Service!"*

The young bartender raced back the length of the bar, realized his oversight, poured out two double ryes fast, noticed what had happened to Malone's newspapers, said, "Would you care for something to read, sir?" plucked a magazine at random from in back of the cash register, shoved it at Malone, and fled.

Malone glanced at the magazine. It was covered in expensive violet paper, and it's title was *Whither? The Poetry of Tomorrow.*

The little lawyer sighed, turned to the title page, sat bolt upright, and bawled at the bartender, "Hey! You!"

By the time the bartender had skidded to a stop in front of him, Malone had remembered the axiom that indirect questions brought forth direct answers. He scowled and said, "Bring me a double brandy and a double vodka." He scowled a shade deeper and added, "Chasers for the rye."

While the bartender was unsteadily pouring them, he said, "Where did you get this magazine?"

"That? Oh," the bartender said. "A lady left it here."

"When?"

"Night before last." He spilled a half ounce of vodka on the bar, and Malone mentally warned himself not to light a cigar within three feet of it.

"Make out my check," Malone said.

He disposed of the vodka, the brandy, and one of the double ryes, in the cuspidor, while the bartender was bent over the adding machine. By the time the harassed young man turned back, he was sitting nonchalantly behind an array of empty glasses.

"Now," Malone said grimly, taking the check, "I won't stand for any nonsense. In Chicago, when I ask questions and a bartender don't answer them, do you know what I do?" He paused, wondering just what he would do. "Tell me about this lady who left the magazine here night before last."

"She didn't really come in to get a drink," the bartender said. "She came in to use the telephone. She bought a thirty-cent highball and sat drinking it for an hour and a half. Every few minutes she got up and tried a number on the house phone. She seemed a little upset. Finally she got up and went out, and she left her magazine on the bar. I stuck it behind the cash register with a bunch of other junk."

"You have a fine memory, and a fine critical sense," Malone said. "I'll remember you in my will." He signed the check with a flourish, and glanced again at the inside page of the magazine where was written in pencil, *Wildavine Williams.*"

"You can have the magazine," the bartender said.

"A lovely thought, but I insist on paying for it," Malone told him. He laid a half dollar on the bar and immediately regretted the impulse.

"Oh, thank you," the bartender said. He leaned forward and lowered his voice. "Mr. Malone, tell me. Just as a matter of sociological research. Do you really carry a gun?"

"Four of them," Malone said, patting himself. He leered across the bar and added, "Usually, I carry a knife in my teeth, too."

For the rest of his stay in New York, he reflected, he'd find another bar. A sudden pang of homesickness for Joe the Angel's City Hall Bar seized him, a pang that was intensified when the girl at the telegraph desk informed him that the hundred dollars had arrived.

Malone changed the check into twenty-dollar bills and stood in the lobby, fingering them in his pocket. Six forty-five. A train. He could pay his hotel bill, his bar check, buy a ticket, and still arrive in Chicago with enough to stake him in a friendly little game at one of Max Hook's joints. He'd be home again.

But there was the problem of Jake and Helene. It had to be straightened out, somehow.

And he'd taken on a job. Finding Bertha Morrison and proving her innocent of murder.

Then there was that small matter of Abner Proudfoot and the poker game.

Finally, before he left New York, he had a little score to settle, on Helene's account, with a dame named Wildavine Williams.

Chapter Sixteen

"PRETEND we just happened in here to buy a drink," Helene said, "and everything will be all right."

Malone hoped so, but he wouldn't have made a bet on it. He didn't like the situation, he didn't like the exterior of the Blue Cat Club, and he had a premonition he wouldn't like the interior of it any better.

Jake had been pleasant, polite, absent-minded, and hurried during dinner. Helene had started out by being a shade too bright and gay, and had ended up doing a creditable imitation of the sphinx. Malone had managed to preserve an air of normality—and missed most of his dinner—by keeping up a spirited conversation, almost entirely with himself. No one mentioned the murder, Gloria Garden, the missing Bertha Morrison, or Dennis.

Jake had excused himself at eight-thirty. A business appointment. He'd be back early. Helene had waited fifteen minutes, then called a taxi. Malone had made a feeble protest which was not only overruled, but scarcely heard. Now, they were at the threshold of the Blue Cat Club.

"I just want to get a look at her, that's all," Helene said. She added firmly, "Don't be jittery, Malone."

"I'm not jittery," Malone said in an indignant tone, putting a match in his mouth and trying to light it with his cigar. His stomach felt as though it were harboring a nervous octopus.

He tried to imagine a girl that Jake would make a date with, when he could have been with Helene, and failed. He mentally pictured Salome, Cleopatra, Madame du Barry, and the brunette adagio dancer at Chez Paree, and then he gave up. His imagination was fairly vivid along such lines, but it refused to go as far as conjuring up a girl who could come between Helene and Jake or, for that matter, Helene and anybody.

He was prepared for anything by the time he entered the Blue Cat Club, including a lady hypnotist. He wasn't prepared though, for Wildavine. Neither, from the look he saw on her face, was Helene.

She picked a table in the brightest-lighted and most conspicuous part of the room, and said, "Let them notice us first." She sat down and slid her white wool cape off her shoulders. The white-and-gold jersey dinner dress she had on under it made her look like a particularly well-dressed angel. "And look as if you were having fun, damn you, Malone."

Malone glanced again at Wildavine and said gloomily, "If you ask me, we might as well go home."

Helene said, "Sssh!" She smiled at the waiter, ordered two champagne cocktails, leaned her elbows on the table, and managed to look gay, entertained, and animated. "Malone, if she were really homely, I could understand it. There's something fascinating about terribly homely women. But she isn't. She's just ordinary plain. And dowdy."

"Stop being catty," Malone said. "I think she's beautiful and fascinating." He glanced again at Wildavine.

She was wearing a yellowish-brown tweed skirt, and a blouse printed with monkeys, palm trees, and bananas. Her stringy brown hair seemed to have collapsed on her shoulders from sheer exhaustion, and her thin damp bangs looked as though they were tired of being pushed out of her eyes. A coat that matched her skirt had been thrown over the back of her chair, it had a worn tan caracal collar. Her face was bald of make-up, and her rimless glasses were slightly askew on her nose. "Fascinating," Malone repeated, "and wonderfully well dressed. Now if you could only get hold of clothes like that——"

"Shut *up*," Helene said. "Those are probably all the clothes she can afford, and nobody's ever told her about hair-dos, powder, and lipstick."

Malone looked sharply at Helene, at the white-and-gold dress, the flawlessly brushed and shining hair, the lovely and exquisitely made-up face. Suddenly he realized where Helene had been going when she'd left him in the morning, and how she'd spent the day. That white-and-gold dress was new, and it had probably taken a lot of shopping to find. And the hair and complexion job must have used up four hours in one of the best beauty parlors.

He realized something else. Helene had spent that time, trouble, and money to make herself more beautiful than the girl Jake was meeting. Now, seeing Wildavine Williams, she was sorry that she'd done so. Not because of Jake, either.

"Come on, Malone," Helene said. "Let's get the hell out of here."

Malone half rose and then sat down again. "You got me down here, and now you're going to stick it out. I never thought you'd turn out to be such a sissy, afraid to meet a girl because she's more interesting than you are."

Helene said between tight lips, "You don't know what I mean."

"Oh, yes I do," Malone said. "And the chances are she won't even notice what you have on, or how you look. She probably likes that suit and thinks her hair beats anything Charles of the Ritz ever turned out. Besides," he added, "don't look now, but we're being observed, and I think they're going to join our party.

He'd seen Jake's face turn pale, then red, then white. He'd observed Jake leaning across the table and whispering something that could only have been, "Psst! My wife is here." He noticed Wildavine looked startled, then puzzled, and finally worried.

Just as Jake pushed his chair back, Malone leaned across the table and said, "So what do you really think of the Cubs' chances in the World Series?"

Helene smiled at him brightly and said, "I wouldn't be at all surprised."

Jake said loudly, too loudly, "Well, imagine running into you here! Helene, this is Miss Williams, a business acquaintance. Miss Williams, this is Mrs. Justus, my wife. And Mr. Malone."

Helene beamed and said, "What a delightful coincidence! Do join us."

Wildavine Williams blushed, said, "Well—" and sat down.

"Miss Williams is a poetess," Jake said, pulling up a chair.

"What a fascinating hobby!" Helene said.

Wildavine looked at her as though she'd said, "What fun it must be to poison babies!"

Helene added hastily, "I meant, avocation."

"Poetry is not an avocation," Wildavine said. "It is a directive."

"Exactly what I've always maintained," Malone said. "I can see that we see eye to eye, cutie. And what are you drinking?"

She didn't seem to know, and nobody else seemed to care. He ordered more champagne cocktails.

"I wrote a poem once," Helene said, a reminiscent gleam in her eye. "It began, 'I wish I were an angleworm, a little wiggling angling worm——" She broke off suddenly, as though Jake had kicked her under the table.

"That's very interesting," Wildavine said. "It displays a remarkable exposition of the subconscious desire to return underground, and a nice feeling for movement."

"Exactly what I thought at the time," Helene said happily. "Would you like to hear the next verse, about how the angling worm meets his mate, under a cabbage root?"

Jake said quickly, "Miss Williams' poems are different, Helene."

"And how magnificently different," Malone said gallantly and enthusiastically. He lifted his glass. "Let's drink to the magnificent difference of Miss Williams' poems." He drained off the champagne cocktail, sneezed, and said, "Do you mind if I call you Wildavine? I feel as if I'd known you always."

"Please do," she said. Her thin cheeks reddened a trifle.

"I feel that we have a great deal in common," Malone said. "Tell me, do you know a magazine called *Whither*?"

"Oh, of course," she gasped. "Who doesn't?" There was an awed pause in which no one even whispered, "Not me."

"I buy it every week," Helene said brightly, after the pause had gone on long enough.

"You must be mistaken," Wildavine said. "It only comes out four times a year." She turned to Malone, obviously a kindred spirit. "If *Whither* would only print one of my poems, I'd know I was a Success. I've been trying for four years, and I always get back such lovely letters, but nothing ever comes of it." She turned back to Jake, a prospective kindred spirit. "You know, of course, about *Whither*. The Zabel Publishing Company."

"Naturally," Jake said. He did know the Zabel Publishing Company. It was second from the top of the list he still meant to send his book to.

"Well, *Whither* is old Mr. Zabel's love child," Wildavine said. She tittered, and said, "You understand, I mean a spiritual love child."

"We understand, a spiritual love child," Malone said, wondering how a magazine of verse could be anything else.

"He edits it himself," Wildavine said, "and reads every word that's submitted. Though the Zabel Publishing Company prints hundreds of books, *Whither* has a very limited, but devoted circulation. But he's refused everything I've offered him, even my last poem, a lovely, simple little thing that I call 'Caravan over a Brooklyn Unlimited Lamppost Good night.'" She sighed deeply and looked persecuted.

"It sounds wonderful," Helene gasped. "I can't imagine how he turned it down. I'd love to read it!"

Wildavine brightened and said, "I'll recite it to you. It just happens that I memorized it." She leaned back, closed her eyes, and looked as much as possible like a chromo of Saint Cecilia at the organ.

> *Eeeny*
> *catch a toe*
> *meeny miny*
> *nigger*
> *mo.*

She paused and said, "I'm attempting to be subtle, you see, in a poetization of the racial problem."

"Oh, of course," Jake murmured.

She closed her eyes again and went on:

> *Christopher*
> *Chronology,*
> *chrysanthemum*
> *O herald the herald the*
> *tomorrow*
> *tomorrow*
> *chronic.*

She paused again. "You grasp the social significance of that, of course?"

Helene said, "We couldn't miss it."

Wildavine beamed and said, "An interesting verse pattern, too, I thought. Well, I'll go on." She drew a long breath. "This last verse, of course, deals purely with spiritual values. And I'm told there's just a touch of the occult."

> *Yesterday.*
> *Hello.*
> *Tomorrow.*
> *Good-by.*
> *The worm turns*

regards,
regards,
regards.
Western Union.

In the awed pause that followed she said, "Do you know, it took me four months to write that?"

"I can easily believe it," Malone said. He signaled the waiter and said, "Four more champagne cocktails. And put a slug of gin in mine."

Across the table, he could see Jake and Helene looking at each other. Jake's eyes were saying, "I can explain everything," and hers were answering, "I won't ask any questions."

That was all very fine, but he was damned if he was going to take Wildavine home. His next drink rubbed a little of the fur off his brain. Night before last Wildavine Williams had been in the St. Jacques bar. She'd been upset. She'd made a number of calls on the house phone. She had, indeed, been sufficiently upset to walk out and leave a copy of *Whither* lying on the bar.

Malone leaned confidentially across the table and said, "When did you meet Jake Justus?"

Her eyes widened behind the rimless glasses. "Yesterday. Why?"

"Idle curiosity," Malone said. It hadn't been Jake that Wildavine Williams had called every few minutes on the house phone from the St. Jacques bar on the night Gloria Garden was murdered and Bertha Morrison disappeared.

He wanted to talk with Wildavine Williams, but not when Jake and Helene were around. That meant finding out where she lived, and he wasn't going to ask Jake.

From the look on Jake's and Helene's faces, they had a great deal to say to each other, without an audience. Something had to be done about Wildavine.

Malone looked around. The bartender had all the appearances of a good guy. He excused himself, headed toward the men's room, and ended up at the far corner of the bar.

The bartender was a good guy, and co-operative. For ten bucks. A worth-while investment, Malone reflected, all things considered.

The next round of drinks arrived two minutes after Malone returned to the table. Malone rose, lifted his glass, bowed to Wildavine, and said, "To your future!"

She giggled, returned his bow, and drank her drink. It worked fast. Five minutes later she mumbled, "Mus' tell you about m'chil'ood sometime." One more minute and she added, to the world in general, "S'beautiful world, beautiful." Another minute, and she was fast asleep.

They took her home and put her to bed. Malone surreptitiously wrote down the address. He pretended not to notice that Helene put Wildavine's clothes carefully on hangers, and tucked the sheets under her chin. He likewise pretended not to notice that Jake looked embarrassed and uncomfortable. Finally, he pretended to be ignoring Jake and Helene and be looking out the window during the taxi ride back to the St. Jacques.

He looked at his watch as he entered the lobby. It was still early. He could still make it to that poker game.

Everything was swell. Everything was going to be fine and dandy. Jake and Helene were holding hands under the cover of her white wool cape. They'd explain the whole affair to each other. As for him, all he had to do was win back his dough from Abner Proudfoot, find

Bertha Morrison, prove she hadn't murdered lovely Gloria Garden, collect the rest of his dough, and catch the next train back to Chicago.

He said he had to buy a newspaper, and let Jake and Helene go on into the elevator unattended. Their reconciliation was their own business. He waited till the elevator doors closed, and then began feeling in his pockets for the slip of paper that had the poker-game room number written on it.

A voice behind him said, "There he is. That's the guy."

Malone wheeled around, in time to see the desk clerk pointing him out to three men who were eying him closely. One of them was short and stringy, another was tall and sad, and the third was a beefy uniformed cop.

"Where is he?" the short guy demanded. "Where have you hidden him?"

"You claim to be Dennis Morrison's lawyer," the tall guy added. "What have you done with him?"

Malone said, "Who the hell are you?"

The big beefy cop said, "None of your damn business."

The little stringy guy said, "Shuddup, you," and to Malone, "I'm O'Brien, this is Birnbaum, and he's Schultz. Where is Dennis Morrison?"

"Last I saw," Malone said, feeling for a cigar, "he'd just settled down for a long winter's nap. Why don't you try looking in his bed? Or even under it."

"Oh, a wise bird, huh?" O'Brien said.

"Now be reasonable, Mr. Malone," Birnbaum said placatingly. "We're only asking you to co-operate. In return, we'll co-operate with you."

"Yeah," Schultz said, nastily.

"I'm in a very unco-operative mood," Malone said.

"I'm a busy man. If you don't go away, I'll call up the mayor." Suddenly he realized he was in New York now. Just as suddenly the significance of what they were telling him began to percolate through his mind. He was hired to find Bertha Morrison, and now—— "Sure, I'll be glad to co-operate with you boys," he said genially. "Just ask me anything you want to know. If I can't answer it, I'll buy you a drink, and if I can answer it, I'll still buy you a drink."

"Just one question," O'Brien said. "Where is Dennis Morrison? Because he's disappeared. And if you've hidden him somewhere, you'd better turn him up damn fast. And if you haven't"—he grinned unpleasantly—"then you can come along and help us look for him."

Chapter Seventeen

"You overestimate me, gentlemen," Malone said, biting the end off a cigar. "I only operate as a one-man bureau of missing persons on alternate Thursdays. Call me up some Thursday and I'll find Dennis Morrison for you. Judge Crater, if you prefer. Or, with a little coaxing, I'll find you Charlie Ross."

"Oh, a wisenheimer, huh?" Schultz said, moving up.

"You're damned right," Malone said joyously. "And what's it to you, you dumb Dutch son-of-a-bitch?"

Schultz squealed with rage and made a remark which not only reflected on Malone's immediate ancestry, but on the whole Irish race. Malone, in one quick move, stuck the cigar back in his pocket and kicked Schultz in the stomach. Schultz kicked back just as Malone ducked. The girl at the cigar counter screamed.

"Lay off that stuff, Schultz," O'Brien said. "You'll have the cops in here in another minute."

"Cops, hell," Schultz roared. "We're the cops." He butted Malone in the chest. Malone landed, in a sitting position, on the floor, with a surprised grunt.

"He said 'lay off,'" Birnbaum said.

Schultz growled a little and subsided.

"We came here for a nice gentlemanly conference," O'Brien told Schultz reprovingly, "with this nice gentleman." He assisted Malone to his feet.

"And Peterson said we should be quiet about it," Birnbaum added.

Malone brushed himself off, looked around at the awed spectators in the lobby and the white-faced cigar-counter girl, and decided to be co-operative. He'd settle the more personal aspects of the matter later with Schultz, somewhere up an alley.

"Don't be alarmed," he told the spectators, "this is just the way I prefer to take my daily exercises. You know, keeping fit, and all that sort of thing." He offered Birnbaum a cigar, grinned at O'Brien, and said, "Shall we retire to the bar, gentlemen?" adding under his voice, "And get the hell out of this crowd?"

O'Brien and Birnbaum looked at each other and O'Brien said, "It's in line of duty, isn't it?"

Malone led the way to the bar and into a secluded booth. He waved for a waiter and said, "I understand, of course, you can't drink a drop, on duty." The waiter arrived then, and Malone said, "Bring each of these gentlemen a glass of water and bring me four double whiskies, all at one time."

He waited till the waiter was out of earshot, then looked across the table at Schultz. "We'll discuss this further at some more propitious time," he said. "But I want to get this on the record right now. I don't like you. Not because your mother wasn't married to your father and wouldn't have recognized him if she'd seen him again. Not just because your mother was obviously an ape and your father a kangaroo. No, not even because you have halitosis and B.O. and a repulsive personality. I don't dislike you just because you're illiterate, illegitimate, and unwashed, and because you stink. It's just because——"

"Hold him, Birnbaum," O'Brien said.

Birnbaum said, "Calm down, Schultz. You've been in trouble before, getting into fights on duty."

Schultz relaxed and mentioned something unpleasant about Malone's personal habits.

"Take it easy now, Malone," Birnbaum said.

Malone leaned back and muttered a comment on the unusual manner in which Schultz had been conceived.

The waiter arrived with the drinks just in time.

"This is very nice of you, Malone," O'Brien said, lifting his glass. "Malone-Malone-Malone-Malone. It's a very familiar name."

"My uncle, Patrick Joseph Malone, was a police lieutenant in Detroit," Malone said helpfully.

O'Brien thought for a minute, then shook his head. "I never was in Detroit. But I had an aunt who married a Malone and lived in Cincinnati. Where did your people come from?"

"My father," Malone said, downing his drink, "Francis Ignatius Malone, was born in County Limerick. My mother, Esther Levinsky, was born in Bialystok."

Birnbaum brightened and said, "One of my cousins married a Levinsky from Bialystok. Louis Levinsky. In the wholesale shoe business."

"Say," Schultz said, "one of my mother's nephews married a Malone."

"He must have had to buy a hell of a lot of perfume to do it," Malone said.

"Lay off him, Malone," O'Brien said. "He's not such a bad guy when you get to know him. You order the next round of drinks and I'll pay for it."

"Oh course he's not a bad guy," Malone said. "I love him like a brother. Well, a cousin. Oh, all right, a second cousin, with the smallpox."

The drinks arrived. Birnbaum downed his, groaned, and sighed, "Oh, what this is doing to my stomach."

"The trouble with your stomach," O'Brien said unfeelingly, "is that you don't put enough alcohol in it. It kills germs."

"Sure," Malone said. "Every stomach needs fumigating now and then." He downed his own drink. "Now, what's all this about Dennis Morrison?"

"He's gone," O'Brien said. "Vamoosed. Scrammed. Out of sight."

"*Farschwinden*," Birnbaum said.

"He ain't here," Schultz said. "In other words, he's gone. And where the hell is he, you——"

"Calm down, Schultz," O'Brien said. "This guy is one of my cousins."

"Well, he's Dennis Morrison's lawyer, ain't he?" Schultz said. "And Dennis Morrison is missing. Which means this guy must have hidden him out someplace."

"I am Dennis Morrison's lawyer," Malone said delicately, "in a purely metaphorical sense." He twirled his glass between his fingers. "I allowed myself to be carried away by my sympathy for him yesterday morning, and made certain utterances which I later felt had been unfortunate and uncalled for. Therefore, I am not responsible for his disappearance. And besides, how do you know he's disappeared?"

"Because he's gone," Schultz said. "Because he ain't here, that's why."

Malone shrugged his shoulders. "He may have just stepped out to buy a newspaper, or go to a movie."

"This guy is entirely too smart," Schultz said to his companions. "I say, we oughta arrest him."

"I don't like your friend," Malone said to O'Brien. "You ought to do something about his personality."

"Never mind him," O'Brien said. "Schultzy's O. K. We know Dennis Morrison disappeared because he was supposed to come down to headquarters and never showed up. This dame who was killed up in his place got identified, and Peterson sent for him to come down and answer a few questions. He said he'd get a taxi and be down there in half an hour, and that was the last we heard of him. So Peterson sent us up here to look for him, and he's gone. Left right after that telephone call."

"Maybe he got lost," Malone said helpfully.

"It's been six hours," Birnbaum said. "He couldn't get that lost."

"I don't know," Malone said. "I knew a fellow once——"

"He's trying to change the subject," Schultz muttered. "That's a sure sign he's got something to hide."

"Shut up, Schultz," O'Brien said.

"The chances are," Malone went on, "the murderer has been watching the scene of the crime. When he discovered that Dennis Morrison was going down to police headquarters, he became alarmed, fearing that Morrison had discovered his identity. Therefore, he murdered Dennis Morrison and disposed of his body."

"Say," O'Brien said. "That's a very interesting theory. I never thought of that."

Malone smiled and looked modest.

"Yeah," Schultz said scornfully, "only how did this here murderer find out Dennis Morrison was going down to police headquarters?"

Malone looked around, and whispered, "Telepathy!"

A split second later O'Brien said, "*Sit down, Schultz!*"

"Just the same," Birnbaum said, "it is a very interesting theory. Maybe we ought to call up Peterson and tell it to him."

"And let Peterson take all the credit?" O'Brien said. "Don't be a dope. We'll find the body and the murderer ourselves, and get a promotion out of it."

"So we find him ourselves," Birnbaum said gloomily. "So where are we going to look?"

"Ask this guy," Schultz said, "he's smart. He knows all the answers, and if he don't, he makes 'em up."

This time O'Brien said, "*Sit Down, Malone.*"

"You know, I think that's right," Birnbaum said, "about alcohol being good for my stomach. Let me buy a drink this time."

While it was being brought, Malone decided to change the subject before he was asked any embarrassing questions. He said, "Well, at least you've got the dame identified, anyway. That's something."

"Yeah," O'Brien said, "but does that do us any good? Do we get the credit?"

Birnbaum sighed and said, "Here we are, knocking our

heads against the wall trying to figure out who she is, so now this no-good *momser* walks in—just like that—and he tells *us* who she is. How do you like that?"

"I see what you mean," Malone said.

"And the Kansas City police wired us they had Bertha Morrison, only it turned out it was somebody else," O'Brien said.

Birnbaum added, "When people are missing, the Kansas City police always report them first, and always it's the wrong one."

The drinks arrived. O'Brien lifted his glass. "Well, here's to finding Morrison's body, and his murderer. You know, Malone, you're a swell guy, and besides you're a relative of mine. Maybe you ought to come along with us. I bet you'd be a lot of help."

Before Malone had started thinking up plausible excuses, Schultz leaned forward and said earnestly, "You know, there's one thing I still can't figure out. It was Bertha Morrison got that t'reatenin' letter. But it wasn't her that got killed."

"For cripes sake," O'Brien said, "are you off on that again? Listen, that letter didn't mean a thing."

"Peterson said it didn't have anything to do with the case," Birnbaum said.

"Who's Peterson?" Schultz demanded belligerently.

Malone said quickly, "Rich women are always getting threatening letters, usually from cranks." He'd just remembered that he was hired to find Bertha Morrison. "Who sent it?"

"Oh, some crazy dame," O'Brien began.

He was interrupted by a bellboy paging him, and hurried away. Birnbaum groaned and said, "So they've found Dennis Morrison's body. We're too late again. I wonder if they have any soda mints here."

"Maybe Peterson's coming down here," Schultz said. "Maybe we'd better get the hell out of this bar."

They went into the lobby just as O'Brien turned away from the telephone.

"Hell," O'Brien said. "They found him. Morrison."

"Alive?" asked three voices.

"Yeah," O'Brien said. "He caught amnesia or something and instead of going to headquarters like he said he would, he's been riding back and forth on the ferry boats. Peterson turned him over to Doc Grosher, and Grosher stuck him in the hospital overnight."

"Well," Malone said, lighting a cigar, "it was a nice theory, anyway. Glad to have been of help to you."

"And we gotta beat it back to headquarters," O'Brien said. "All those reports we made yesterday turned out to of been made wrong, and we gotta straighten 'em out."

"I don't feel so good," Birbaum said.

"It's all the fault of that moor-on we picked up yesterday," O'Brien said. "He rattled me." He turned to Malone and said, "Say, there was a screwy guy. I'll tell you about him sometime."

"Do," Malone said cordially.

They made a solemn promise to get together soon, and the three policemen left, Birnbaum murmuring, "Y'know, maybe I should try taking vitamins——"

Malone stood in the lobby, looking after them. The picture of young Dennis Morrison breaking down and spending hours riding back and forth on ferry boats gave him an unpleasant pang. The picture of Dennis Morrison in the hands of the police was even more unpleasant. Malone didn't like to see anyone in the hands of the police, even his worst enemies.

Yet, there was nothing he could do about it now. By

this time, Dennis had undoubtedly been given a sedative and put to bed. In the morning——

Meanwhile he did have the job of finding Bertha Morrison, and the first part of it was winning back the money old man Proudfoot had paid him. He located the helpful elevator boy and headed for the poker game with most of Joe the Angel's hundred dollars in his pockets, hope in his heart, and larceny in his mind.

Chapter Eighteen

MALONE WOKE up with a mild hangover, a clear conscience, a slightly blackened eye, and a bit over seven hundred dollars hidden behind one of the pictures in his room.

The clear conscience was due to the fact that four hundred and thirty-seven of the dollars belonged to him by right, and a hundred to Joe the Angel. His possession of the remaining two hundred-odd dollars seemed to him a simple matter of poetic justice, though he doubted if Abner Proudfoot would see it that way when he learned about it. The black eye had been gained during a discussion of whether or not he should be allowed to take his winnings away with him, and because of Malone's quite natural objection to being called a crooked poker player. The hangover was entirely his own idea, and made him a trifle proud. Malone's feeling about a hangover depended entirely on the circumstances which had accounted for it.

He was even humming a little when he met Helene in the lobby.

"You've been fighting again," she said reprovingly.

Malone shook his head. "A mosquito bit me on the eyelid, and I slapped him harder than I'd intended."

Helene sniffed. "That was a wonderful mosquito, to fly into a New York hotel room during April."

"This mosquito rode in on a rocket ship," Malone said.

They went into the coffee shop, where the little lawyer ordered a double pot of black coffee, and implored the waitress to bring it fast.

"I suppose the mosquito bought you a drink, too," Helene said.

"I bought the drink," Malone said. "After all, he was my guest, wasn't he? Where's Jake?"

"Out," Helene said. She was silent for a minute, frowning. "He went out early this morning. He said he had important business to attend to, and he didn't know when he'd be back."

"He's probably gone to see Wildavine," Malone said, starting on his second cup of coffee. His head was beginning to clear now.

"Malone, what does he see in her?"

"It's her poetry," Malone said. He'd been wondering the same thing. "It would fascinate anybody."

"And Wildavine telephoned me this morning and invited all three of us to dinner tomorrow night."

"Tell her I've broken my leg," Malone said. "Tell her I'm coming down with the measles." Still, he did want to find out what Wildavine had been doing in the St. Jacques bar the night of the murder. "On second thought, tell her I'll be delighted. Her poetry fascinated me, too." He signaled the waitress and ordered ham and eggs, fried potatoes, pancakes, and a piece of pie. "Maybe you ought to write a poem, too. That would fix everything up."

"Maybe I will," Helene said ominously. "And I'm worried about Dennis Morrison. I wanted to invite him to breakfast with us, and the desk clerk said he went out yesterday afternoon and hasn't come back. What could have happened to him?"

"He's in jail," Malone said, before he thought.

Her eyes widened. "In jail! Why? What for?"

"For riding ferry boats," Malone said.

"Malone, they can't put people in jail for that."

The little lawyer sighed. "The answer to that line was thrown out of vaudeville a year before you were born," he said wearily. He decided it would be better to tell her all the circumstances of how Dennis Morrison got in jail. She'd read them in the papers later, anyway.

She listened attentively, sipping her coffee. When he'd finished she said in a determined voice, "I'm going with you."

"That will be wonderful," Malone said. He blinked, and added hastily, "You're going with me where?"

"To see Dennis Morrison, of course," she said, "and get him out of this mess."

"Purely a delusion," Malone said. "I'm not going anywhere, and I'm certainly not going to take you with me."

Helene looked at him reproachfully and said, "That poor young man!"

Malone muttered something unintelligible into his coffee.

"And what am I going to do all day?" she went on, in an accusing tone. "You busy with Dennis Morrison, Jake out somewhere. I've already been on six sight-seeing tours of New York, and I've lost one of my knitting needles."

Malone said in a faltering voice, "There is a train for

Chicago at six-forty-five tonight, and I've got to spend
the day packing——" His voice trailed away. He knew
when he was licked. Besides, Helene did need to have
her mind taken off her personal worries. "But for the
love of Mike, behave yourself. This is New York, and
you won't be dealing with Chicago cops."

"Cops are cops," Helene said, with self-confidence.

There was a moment when Malone shared her self-
confidence. That was when O'Brien, loitering in the anteroom outside Arthur Peterson's office, looked at Helene,
at her serene face and shining hair, at her wide-brimmed,
violet felt hat, at her pale violet suit and the honey-
colored fur collapsed over her arms, at her slender, lovely
legs, decorated with stockings the exact shade of corn
silk. O'Brien just said, "Gosh!" He said it almost reverently.

As though by some interdepartmental telepathy, Birnbaum and Schultz appeared magically in the anteroom.
The three of them converged on Malone with smiles of
greeting, looking admiringly at Helene.

During the introductions Helene smiled dazzlingly and
impartially at them all. Then she said, wide-eyed, to
O'Brien and Birnbaum, "Are you really detectives? I've
always wanted to meet one!"

They assured her happily that they were, offered to
show her through headquarters, and to tell her some really
exciting stories about detection.

"Him, though," Malone said, gesturing at Schultz, "he's
just an ordinary uniformed cop."

Schultz held back a comment about Malone, bridled,
and tried to look like a composite rotogravure picture of
New York's Finest.

Helene flickered her long eyelashes at him and said,
"It's wonderful how much handsomer a uniform makes

any man look! I imagine policemen must live terribly dangerous lives, don't they!"

Schultz purred, and agreed that they did.

By the time the brisk young secretary came to usher Malone and Helene into Arthur Peterson's office, O'Brien, Birnbaum, and Schultz were Helene's adoring slaves, and Malone's self-confidence had soared to a new high.

It fell to a momentary all-time low, however, when Arthur Peterson looked up from behind his desk, turned first red, then white, and finally said, "What the hell are you doing here?"

If the little lawyer had known the reason behind Arthur Peterson's confusion, he might have felt better. After all, Arthur Peterson prided himself on being an upright and conscientious man, to whom keeping secrets between a husband and wife was definitely reprehensible—in spite of the fact that he liked the husband, and that the secret was designed to bring a pleasant surprise to the wife sometime in the near future. The business of finding it necessary to keep the same secret from the newspapers and from his immediate superior was even more bothersome. It was not only unethical, it was the sort of thing that created departmental inefficiency. And then, after a sleepless night of worrying about the rights and wrongs of the situation, to have the wife in question drop in, accompanied by that drunken, probably ignorant, and undoubtedly crooked Chicago lawyer! It was too much!

He added, coldly, "Well?"

Malone was saved from answering, "Well, yourself, you damned squarehead," by Helene's bringing one of her high heels down on his toe.

"How nice to see you again!" she said brightly. "I'm sure you don't remember me, but we met that awful morning at the St. Jacques, after that perfectly frightful murder. I know, I thought at the time, how fortunate it was that someone was in charge of the case who was really understanding and humane. And," she added, after a quick glance at Arthur Peterson's marvelously arranged desk top, "someone so efficient!"

Arthur Peterson said very lightly and casually, "Oh, we try to do our best." He wondered if Jake Justus really appreciated not only the rare beauty but the fine intelligence of his wife.

Malone had been holding his breath, now he relaxed. He'd seen Helene giving that double-barreled smile to policemen before, all the way from Captain von Flanagan of the Chicago Homicide squad to the Sheriff of Jackson County, Wisconsin. It had never failed yet, but there always had to be a first time, and Arthur Peterson had looked like a peculiar customer.

Malone beamed, and said, "We're here about Dennis Morrison, of course." He took out a cigar and began unwrapping it.

"Oh, yes, naturally," Peterson said, still admiring Helene. "You're his lawyer, aren't you?"

"Well," Malone said, lighting the cigar, "in a sense, yes."

"More than that," Helene said, with just the right touch of mild indignation in her voice, "we're his friends." She looked anxiously at the police officer. "I hope you aren't going to keep him in jail very long."

"We aren't going to keep him in jail at all," Peterson said, half sharply. A note of bitterness crept into his voice. "He hasn't broken any law."

The little lawyer said, "Glad you see it that way. I didn't think there was any law against having some perfect stranger murdered in your bridal suite, while you were out on a big bender, or having your bride run away from home. So unless he was drunk and disorderly, or gone insane——"

"He wasn't," Peterson said quickly. "Neither one. He was disturbed and confused, and showed all the evidences of having been under a terrific strain."

"And no wonder," Malone said, chewing savagely on his cigar. "How would you have felt if your bride had disappeared on your wedding night?"

Arthur Peterson blushed a little and said sternly, "In this job, we find it necessary to avoid personal comparisons."

"I don't suppose you've found any trace of her yet," Malone added casually.

"That's in another department," Peterson told him. "Missing Persons."

"Maybe she's been murdered, too," Helene said, round-eyed, and in an awed voice.

"In that case, it would come into this department," Peterson said. "Homicide."

Helene looked fascinated, beautiful, and said, "Oh!"

Arthur Peterson reflected on what a fortunate and probably undeserving individual Helene's husband was. He said, "Dennis Morrison is on his way here. There are a few little formalities we must go through before his release. Meanwhile, perhaps, as his lawyer, you'll want to have some private conversation with him."

"Of course," Malone said. He imagined that the police officer had figured on some private conversation with Helene. He was right.

"And maybe you'd like to look around a little," Arthur Peterson said, beaming fatuously. "Our crime-detection laboratories are really interesting."

"I'd adore it!" Helene said, in a thrilled voice. As they went out the door, she was saying, "Is it really true that you can tell, just from looking at a person's finger-prints—" and Arthur Peterson was saying happily, "I'll be glad to explain about that to you."

Malone sighed, shook his head, and relit his cigar. Helene, as usual, had been right. Cops were cops.

O'Brien brought in a pale, tired-looking Dennis Morrison, who smiled wanly and said, "Good of you to come all the way down here."

"Think nothing of it," Malone said. He was wondering if Dennis Morrison had any money. Probably not. He was always getting stuck with clients who had to pay off with cigarette coupons. Then he remembered suddenly that he was already engaged by Abner Proudfoot to find the missing Bertha Morrison, and that Dennis, unknowingly, might be a help. "I was glad to come."

"You can trust him," O'Brien said to Dennis Morrison. "He's a good guy. Cousin of mine." He grinned at Malone and went out.

"Now tell me," Malone said, "what the hell were you doing on that ferry boat?"

"Just—well, just riding," Dennis Morrison said. "It's a little hard to explain. You see, they called me up. I guess you know that. I'd been lying down, trying to think things out, trying to decide what I ought to do to find Bertha. And then this police detective telephoned. They'd identified that girl. I felt a lot better, at first. You know. It seemed so awful to think of her lying there in the morgue, without anyone knowing who she was. Mr. Peterson said her father had identified her, and he was at police headquarters now. They just wanted to ask me a few questions and I said I'd be right down." He paused.

Malone threw away the stub of his cigar and began unwrapping a fresh one. "It's taking you a long time to get on that ferry boat," he said amiably.

"I told you this was hard to explain," Dennis Morrison said. He frowned. "I got a newspaper in the subway station." He paused again. "Habit, I guess. I took the subway instead of a taxi. And I read the paper on the subway train. It told all about Gloria Garden, and about her dad, an old small-town doctor, identifying her. I didn't mean to stay on the train, but I did. I just didn't notice when I got to my station. And then I was at South Ferry, and I got off there and realized where I was, and suddenly I decided I'd ride back and forth on the ferry just once, to clear my head a little. No, I hadn't been drinking, it was just that I couldn't face meeting that old small-town doctor, after I'd murdered his daughter."

"Quite naturally," Malone said, very calmly. He bit off the end of his cigar and lighted it very leisurely. *"After you'd done what?"*

"Murdered his daughter," Dennis Morrison repeated. He sounded almost irritable. "Because I did, of course. By my absence." He laughed harshly. "That's it, you see. I murdered her by my absence. I don't know who she was, or anything about her, I don't know how she got into our suite or why she was wearing Bertha's blue satin nightgown, or why and how she was killed. But if I'd been there, instead of being out on a bender, she wouldn't have been killed. See what I mean? So I'm her murderer, really. And I rode back and forth on the boat, thinking about her old dad, and how he'd come all the way here from someplace in Iowa or Ohio or wherever it was, only to find her in the morgue, and that it was my fault. I kept thinking about jumping off the ferry boat, but I couldn't, I had to stay alive and find out what had become of Bertha, and then when the boat docked again there were the police, and they brought me here." He drew a long, sighing breath. "They've been very nice to me, really. I told them exactly how it was, and why I felt the way I did, and they were very nice. Some doctor, a Dr. Grosher, I think his name was, gave me an examination and asked me a lot of questions, and then he gave me something to make me sleep, and I just woke up about an hour ago."

"I see," Malone said, puffing furiously on his cigar. He distrusted kindliness on the part of the police, and especially he distrusted police doctors.

"Now," Dennis Morrison said, "before they let me go, they're going to make me look at that girl—Gloria Garden—again. Why should they do that? I've already told them I didn't know who she was. So why, now that they've identified her——"

"Purely a formality," Malone said automatically. He flicked a nonexistent ash off his cigar and said, "No, it isn't a formality. They think that you do know her, and that they can shock you into showing it. An old trick. Just keep your nerve, that's all. Don't worry, I'll be right——"

The door opened and Helene's voice trilled, "—but that's *dangerous*, Captain Peterson! Aren't you ever *scared?*"

"Pure routine," Arthur Peterson said, shutting the door. His voice had a definite purr in it now.

Later, Malone was never sure just how Helene talked herself into going along when Dennis Morrison was taken to view Gloria Garden—or Hazel Puckett—for the second time. He rather doubted if Arthur Peterson knew, either. Yes, definitely, New York or Chicago, cops were cops.

And morgues were morgues. The same dreary anteroom, the same green steel filing cases. The same unpleasant, hygienic smell. The same bored attendants reading movie magazines.

He realized suddenly that this was his own first look at the corpse, and his nerves tightened. He was not more than half aware of Dennis Morrison's white, sick face, or of Helene's murmur to Arthur Peterson that indeed she did want to go along all the way, and that she wouldn't be the least bit frightened with him right at her side.

"Don't get disturbed," the attendant said, "she's fixed up real nice." He slid out the drawer and said, "Pretty, wasn't she?"

Malone wasn't conscious of Helene's little gasp, or of Dennis Morrison's moan. Gloria Garden, née Hazel Puckett, hadn't been pretty, she'd been beautiful. The newspaper photographs, even the magazine covers, hadn't begun to do justice to her, to the soft, moon-colored hair, the exquisite skin, the lovely face. He wondered what color her eyes had been.

"No," Dennis Morrison said, half sobbing. "No, I've never seen that face before. Never in my life."

Malone tautened. He caught his breath before he said, "Maybe you haven't seen the face before, but how about the body?"

"This isn't any time or place for humor, Mr. Malone," Arthur Peterson said harshly.

"I'm not being humorous," Malone said. "I'm just pointing out something that you cops have been too dumb to catch onto before now." He wished he were anywhere else in the world than here in the morgue, because never before in his life had he wanted the feel of a cigar between his fingers as badly as now. He'd spent the longest split second of a lifetime decided whether to follow up his hunch himself or to let the police follow it up for him.

He'd decided on the latter. "I was just asking if our young friend here could identify the body, without the face."

Helene said, in a thin little voice, "Malone, you're out of your mind."

"I'm not out of my mind," the lawyer said indignantly. "I'm just using my mind, which is more than these police dopes have done. Because, when women are beaten and strangled, in a room that shows all the signs of a terrific struggle, their faces get bruised and marked, too."

There was a half-strangled gasp from Dennis Morrison.

"That body is bruised and marked," Malone went on ruthlessly. "You can see where hands tore at the arms and shoulders, and where the blows landed. But look at the face. There isn't a tiny scratch on it, or even the faintest discoloration."

Arthur Peterson said, "Good God! Of course!"

"Therefore," Malone said, ignoring him, "obviously, you have two murdered women here. The two pieces fit together very neatly, like two pieces of a jigsaw puzzle that match in everything except the design. Only, it's the head of one, and the body of another."

Chapter Nineteen

"DON'T be so downcast about it," Malone said sympathetically to the young assistant medical examiner. "People seldom find things they're not looking for. You had what seemed to be the body of a murdered and decapitated woman. Certainly you weren't looking for it to be parts of two murdered and decapitated women. You were looking for the cause of death and anything that might lead to identification, and you did the best you could."

The young doctor smiled wanly. "That's very kind of you, Mr. Malone. But how did *you* know?"

"Me?" Malone said modestly. "I guessed."

Schultz snorted rudely, O'Brien beamed admiringly and muttered something about Malone being a cousin. Arthur Peterson looked cold and said, "I hope you're telling the truth about it being guesswork. Because withholding information from the police is a serious business."

"I wouldn't dream of doing such a thing," Malone said, in his smoothest voice. He looked around, and decided it was perfect etiquette to light a cigar here in the medical examiner's office. "I noticed the fact that the head and the body didn't seem to belong together, because I wasn't looking for it."

Schultz growled that Malone was obviously a lying scoundrel who should be promptly arrested. He was immediately shushed by O'Brien and Birnbaum.

"I thought I just made it plain," Malone said. He bit off the end of the cigar with loving care. "If you're looking for something specific, like the cause of death, or the motive for a murder, you're not inclined to notice what may seem like irrelevant and unimportant facts." He paused to light the cigar. "But if you're only a mildly interested bystander, like myself, just looking, you may accidentally see something important. That's all." He expelled a cloud of smoke. "I just thought I'd help you out."

"We appreciate your co-operation," Arthur Peterson said stiffly.

"And you were right, of course," the young medical

examiner said, almost wildly. "Those tests should have been made before, but there didn't seem to be any need for them. But there are two different blood groups, the skin texture is dissimilar, and the hair type——" He paused. "Only, the head and the body fitted together so perfectly"—he paused again—"the thing is, though—where is the other head and the other body?"

"The head has been identified," Arthur Peterson said. "Hazel Puckett's father is on his way here now to view the body. If we can identify the body now——"

"*Bertha!*" young Dennis Morrison said hoarsely. He buried his face in his hands, gasping.

Helene said sharply, "Stop that, Dennis! You don't know that it is."

Birnbaum pulled out a cigarette, lit it, and stuck it into Dennis Morrison's hands. O'Brien said, "C'mon, fella," and Schultz said, "Cut it out. It prob'ly ain't her, even if she did get a t'reatenin' letter——" at which Peterson said, "*Shut up,* Schultz."

"The thing is," the young medical examiner said, "the cause of death was the same in—both cases. Asphyxia. Undoubtedly as the result of manual strangulation. Decapitation followed, in both cases, within a matter of hours. Examination of the head, after scalp reflection——"

"Now *you* shut up," Helene said. She slipped her hand over Dennis Morrison's arm.

"Yes, but the thing is," the medical examiner said again, "where is the other body, and where is the other head?"

"That isn't in your department," Arthur Peterson told him.

"All right, but the thing is this," the young medical examiner said, his face very pink, "the head's identified, but the body isn't. Whose body is it?"

Arthur Peterson said, "That isn't strictly in your department either," but nobody heard him. Everybody was looking, instinctively, at Dennis Morrison.

"I don't know," Dennis Morrison said. "How could I know? We'd just been married. That afternoon. We had dinner. We went to the hotel. She wanted to do a little unpacking, so I went downstairs to get a drink——"

"We've heard all that before," Arthur Peterson said.

"He's just trying to tell you," Malone said, "that he married her sight unseen."

"And therefore," Helene finished, "he can't identify the body."

O'Brien looked sympathetic, and Schultz blushed. There was a brief silence.

"She was about five-foot-eight," the medical examiner said helpfully, "and weighed about one hundred forty pounds. Her general skin tone was blondish."

Dennis groaned, rubbed his hand over his forehead, and whispered, "It must have been. But I couldn't swear to it. I couldn't identify her. Not possibly."

"Don't worry," Arthur Peterson said gently. "We've sent for her family doctor, and we've sent for the father of——" He started to say "the father of the head," stopped himself, and said, "Dr. Puckett. I'm sure we can manage an identification without troubling you further."

Within the next half-hour Bertha's family doctor and her gymnasium teacher from boarding school arrived to view the body. Neither one was able to offer a positive identification. The doctor, an embarrassed and nervous middle-aged man, highly excited at his first brush with police procedure, explained that he'd removed Bertha's tonsils at the age of seven, treated her for a severe cold which threatened to develop into pleurisy when she was ten, and explained the facts of life to her, at her father's request, when she was twelve. Since then, he'd prescribed a tonic for her during her adolescence, treated her for a sprained ankle at twenty-two, and worked out a reducing diet for her two years ago.

Body number 147 might be Bertha's, or might be the body of any healthy, slightly overweight young woman. He couldn't say for sure.

"In my profession," he said apologetically, "you see so many——"

The gymnasium teacher, a Miss Hazlett, was no more help, and turned out to be a lot of trouble. After she was through being ill, and had downed a dose of spirits of ammonia, she took center stage, patted her stringy reddish hair, blushed unbecomingly, and started to deliver a little lecture on the importance of daily gymnastic exercises.

As far as Bertha Lutts was concerned, and the Thing she'd been asked to look at—she refused to refer to it as a body—she couldn't say yes, and she couldn't say no.

"I was her gym teacher, yes," she said. "For three years. But naturally, I never"—she looked coyly at the floor— "saw her in the flesh, so to speak."

"It's her, though," Schultz repeated, after they had come and gone. "Because she was the one that got the t'reatenin' letter."

"That letter business was settled yesterday," Arthur Peterson said.

Schultz said, "Well, anyway, it's gotta be her. Because if it ain't her, then how did the body get into that hotel suite? You can't just go carrying headless bodies up and down in hotel elevators. So that means it's her, and therefore——"

Dennis Morrison turned white. Helene said, "That's enough. Stop it."

"Yes, but, lady," Schultz said, "when you've got a headless body—if you were a man, and it might be your wife, wouldn't you want to know——"

Dennis Morrison uttered a half-strangled sound.

"You shut your mouth," Helene said to Schultz, "or I'll shut it, and good, you tactless ape."

"Don't you call me no ape," Schultz said.

"I'll call you worse than that," Helene said, and did.

Dr. Puckett arrived at that moment, a providential diversion. The room was instantly hushed, and Malone put down his half-smoked cigar. Dennis Morrison was the anguished husband of a missing and possibly murdered bride, but here was the father of an identified and authentically murdered girl.

Malone looked curiously at the small, gray-haired man, trying to imagine him as the father of the girl who had been born Hazel Puckett and died Gloria Garden. It wasn't easy to imagine.

Dr. Puckett took out his pipe, tapped it against the palm of his hand, and managed to put everybody at ease. "Kind of surprising, isn't it?" he said mildly. "It turning out that this isn't Hazel's—I mean, Gloria's—body at all, only her head. I'm mighty sorry, I'd figured on taking Hazel home to her ma, right after the inquest, and now it looks like I can't." He fiddled with the pipe for a minute, then stuffed it back into his right-hand coat pocket. "Hope you can find out who this other girl is, without calling in her folks. Hard on a girl's folks, to be called into something like this." He took the pipe out again.

"Have a cigar," Malone said, his throat dry.

"Thanks," old Dr. Puckett said, "I will." He reached for it, carefully snipped off the end with a knife that hung from his watch chain, and lit it. "My name's Puckett. What's yours?"

"Malone," the little lawyer said, hoping his voice wouldn't break.

Arthur Peterson gave Malone a grateful glance and said, "Dr. Puckett, if you don't mind——"

"Oh, sure, I'll view the body," Dr. Puckett said. "That's what I'm here for, isn't it? Hope I can help you out, that's all." He walked toward the inner door, handed his cigar to Birnbaum, and said, "Hold this, will you?" and went on in, just as though the head of number 147 wasn't that of his only daughter.

He came back a few minutes later, plucking the cigar from Birnbaum's nerveless fingers as he came in through the door, and shaking his head.

"Sorry," he said apologetically, "I can't help you out. Never saw her before. It isn't Hazel, that's about all I can tell you, and I guess you know that already. Hazel had a scar on her——" He bowed toward Helene and said, "Pardon me, ma'am, left backside. Where a neighbor's dog bit her when she was seven. It wasn't a vicious dog, just nervous."

He puffed at the cigar. No one moved or made a sound.

"Well," he said at last, "sorry I can't tell you who she is. Was, I mean." He managed a wan smile in the direction of Arthur Peterson. "I guess now you'll be looking for Hazel's—I should say, Gloria's—body. I guess you'll call me up if you find it. I hope you do. I'd like to take her home." The cigar had gone out. He relit it. "Maybe some of you've seen Hazel's picture in the magazines. She was a beautiful girl."

There was another silence after he had gone.

Then Arthur Peterson jumped up and said briskly, "Well, that's all." At the downstairs doorway of the gloomy building he added to Dennis Morrison, "Don't go out of town. We'll telephone you if we need you again."

O'Brien and Birnbaum grinned at Malone and climbed into the police car. Schultz followed them, muttering, "I still say, you can't take no headless body up in no elevator——" The slamming of the car door shut off any further thoughts on his part.

They stood on the curb for a moment, looking after the police car.

Malone said, "Let's go home. It's not much of a home, but it has a bar. Home is where the bar is." He waved at one of a pair of taxis parked down the street.

Both taxis approached, one a Yellow, and one a Checker. The Checker got there first. Malone gallantly opened the door for Helene and ushered her in. Then he looked around for Dennis Morrison. Dennis Morrison wasn't there. The other taxi, the Yellow, was speeding down the street.

Malone jumped in and slammed the door. Helene leaned forward and said dramatically, "Follow that cab!"

"Which cab?" the driver said gloomily.

The Yellow cab was already out of sight around a corner.

"On these streets," the driver added, even more gloomily, "a bloodhound couldn't follow a snail. Where d'ya want to go?"

With a little prodding, the driver went around the corner the Yellow had turned. They caught a brief glimpse of it far down the street, then it disappeared again. Finally they found it, beside a subway kiosk, empty save for a disinterested driver reading the *Racing Form*. He had no idea where his passenger had gone.

Dennis Morrison had disappeared again.

Chapter Twenty

GETTING into Gloria Garden's apartment hadn't been as difficult or expensive a task as Jake had anticipated. It was just a matter of getting acquainted with the janitor.

The janitor, one Carl Burns, was sufficiently impressed by Jake's Chicago *Herald Examiner* press card not to notice that it was eight years old, or to remember that the *Herald Examiner* was no longer in existence.

He was even more impressed by the fact that a copy of *The Nation* protruded from Jake's coat pocket. After all, he had no way of knowing that Jake had hung around the corner bar long enough to get a line on one Carl Burns, janitor, and on Carl Burns' political preferences.

When Jake whispered to him about the social significance of the Gloria Garden slaying, and the articles that could be written about it, he nodded wisely, and uncapped one of the bottles of beer Jake had brought along. Only, he said, shoving a glass of beer across the oilcloth table in the basement kitchen-apartment, it should be a book, not a series of articles. Now he, Carl Burns, had always planned to write a book——

When Jake confided that he, too, planned to write a book, Carl Burns came through with the key to Gloria Garden's apartment. When Jake unobtrusively left a ten-dollar bill under one of the beer bottles on the table,

Carl Burns ignored it and offered to keep an eye out for intruders.

Jake took the key and went up the carpeted stairs. It was a small, three-story building, in the East Sixties, with an antique shop on the ground floor. Someone announced as "Detweiler, Dress Designs, Closed until May 15th" had the second floor; Gloria Garden had lived on the third. Carl Burns inhabited the rear basement.

Jake listened for a moment outside the door before he thrust in the key and opened it. Not a sound. He went in, closing and bolting the door behind him.

Gloria Garden, née Hazel Puckett, had been a person of bad and expensive taste. The beige carpet was thick and spongy as June grass; over it were tossed, with an unsuccessful air of carelessness, bright little scatter rugs that pretended to have been made by hand in colonial looms. The heavy lace curtains would have done credit to an expensive boarding house, and an immense oil painting of a tired-looking man in a red coat and plumed hat hung over the fireplace. There was maple furniture everywhere, so much that Jake found himself wondering if he should have brought along a bucket to collect sirup.

There were glass ash trays and tiny china figures everywhere, and a magnificent pipe stand designed to look like a startled owl. End tables were placed strategically beside every chair, and glass-topped coffee tables turned up everywhere. In one corner, looking lost and incongruous, was a big, well-worn, red-leather armchair, with a footstool before it.

The effect was of much money spent, frantically, in an attempt to buy comfort and luxury. Jake looked around the room and reflected that the attempt had been successful, too, regardless of what interior decorators might think of it. It was a comfortable, costly, ugly, pleasant room, a room to be lived in.

Jake prowled around it aimlessly. He wasn't searching, he was trying to get impressions. There couldn't be anything to find in this apartment. But it could tell him something about Gloria Garden.

The living room told him a great deal. A girl with money she'd made herself, who wanted nice things and didn't care how much she paid for them, and picked them all wrong. A girl who put on the dog. That portrait over the fireplace—an ancestral portrait, no doubt, whenever friends dropped in. Had she ever told anybody about old Doc Puckett, the general practitioner in a small town? The maple furniture was damn near antique. Gloria had probably given it a family history, and comfortably forgotten the mission-style fumed oak back home.

But the pipes in the owl pipe stand had been smoked, and the big red-leather chair was worn and dented. A permanent boy friend? A husband?

Jake went into the tiny hall that led to the kitchen, and wished that Helene were with him. She could interpret a lot of things that didn't make any sense to him. Still, he could figure out a few things for himself. Whoever had used this kitchen had worked at cooking. There were gadgets everywhere, electric mixers, juicers, beaters. He pulled open the cupboard shelves and saw Bisquick, Aunt Jemima Pancake Flour, vanilla, raisins, and a long shelf of spices and flavoring. Molasses, and sage and garlic, and onion and celery salts. Cooking sherry, and dinner wines, and five quarts of cheap bourbon, one opened.

The table in the tiny dining room was set for two; it looked as though it were permanently set for two. Tall white candles, burned down an inch or so, lace mats, roses,

that should have beeen thrown away two days ago, dropping their brown-edged petals from a crystal bowl.

Jake opened the door to the bedroom and paused there.
So far the apartment had baffled him. It fitted a girl who
had married well, and been allowed to pick her own furnishings, but who had made a concession in the matter of
the red-leather chair. A girl whose husband or boy friend
loved good food, a girl who loved to cook for him. A girl
with bad taste and a warm heart, raised on Grand Rapids
Furniture and a country-school cooking course. But it
didn't fit Gloria Garden, the lovely model, with her
moon-colored hair.

The bedroom walls were pale gray. The bed was enormous, its padded headboard was an obscene pink, and it
was covered with a heavy lace spread. The windows were
curtained with thickly gathered chiffon of the same unpleasant pink. There were mirrors everywhere.

At one wall was an immense dressing table placed art-
fully against a mirror that stretched from floor to ceiling,
bordered on both sides by curtains that matched those at
the windows, mirror-topped, and covered with immense
jars, perfume bottles and atomizers.

There were half a dozen large paintings on the walls,
brilliant in color, slightly Oriental in tone, and all dealing
with the facts of life.

The room was heavy with perfume. On the floor
around the immense bed ran what seemed to be a strip of
silver; it turned out to be a plate-glass mirror, set in the
carpet.

Jake felt like murmuring an apology as he closed the
door.

He wondered what O'Brien, Birnbaum, and Schultz
had made of the furnishings and decorations of the bed-

room, and what Arthur Peterson had thought of the pictures on its walls. Jake grinned.

He opened the door to the bathroom; it smelled of cologne, bath salts, perfumed soap, and shaving cream. There was a design of tropical fish along the edge of the dark-green tiling. The towels were thick and enormous, monogrammed with an immense G.

Jake stood in the hall, frowning. So far the apartment had told him a great deal about Gloria Garden, née Hazel Puckett. It had told him, among other things, that she had a husband or a boy friend, and that she was hell-bent on keeping him by one means or another.

But it hadn't told him why Gloria Garden had been found murdered in a suite in the St. Jacques Hotel, dressed in a pale-blue satin nightgown, and neatly decapitated.

Suddenly his nerves tightened; he paused in the act of lighting a cigarette. The clothes hanging in the closet at the St. Jacques certainly hadn't belonged to Gloria Garden, no, none of them. Then what had happened to her clothes? She must have gone to the St. Jacques alive. But she hadn't gone dressed in a blue satin nightgown. Besides, the nightgown had belonged to Bertha Morrison.

Jake finished lighting his cigarette and called himself several kinds of a fool for not remembering that before. The clothes Gloria Garden must have worn to the St. Jacques that night were not in the suite where she'd been murdered. Had the murderer carried them away? Or worn them away?

He prowled around restlessly, his face knitted into a scowl. There was something wrong about this place, too, something he couldn't quite put his finger on.

He went, almost aimlessly, from room to room. In the

bathroom he opened the big mirrored medicine cabinet. Toothpaste, iodine, hangover remedies, odds and ends of medicine. But no razor, and no shaving cream. That was it. The bathroom smelled of shaving cream, but there wasn't any in the medicine cabinet, and no razor.

Jake went back into the bedroom and flung open the closet door. Dresses, furs, a ski suit, riding clothes, negligees. He looked through the bureau drawers. Lacy and embroidered lingerie, blouses, filmy stockings. But nowhere any shirts or ties or pajamas.

That was all wrong. This apartment had been lived in by two people, one a man. Even if the man had maintained his official home somewhere else, which was likely, there should at least have been a dressing gown. And a razor.

Had there been a quarrel before Gloria Garden's murder; had the man packed his belongings and left? There were empty hangers in the closet that might have been used for a man's clothes, and there was a blank space on the shelf reserved for shoes and slippers.

He finally reached Gloria Garden's little mahogany desk, went through it, and stood looking at it reflectively. There was a half-empty bottle of violet ink, a pen, and a well used blotter. There was a package of pale-gray writing paper with the name Gloria Grden. But save for a few receipted bills, there were no letters, not anywhere.

That too was a wrong note. A girl like Gloria Garden wrote letters and received them and, what was more, kept them. There should at least have been letters from her family.

The letters might have been carried away, or Gloria Garden might have hidden them. Jake thought it over. Either one was possible, if the letters contained anything of value. The missing letters might tell him a great deal that he needed to know, answer a great many questions.

Jake looked at his watch and sighed. Helene would be waiting. Still, it couldn't be helped. He lit another cigarette and settled down to search in earnest.

Chapter Twenty-One

"THERE's no point in our telling the police that Dennis Morrison's beat it again," Malone said crossly. "They'll find it out soon enough. And there's no point in our trying to find him ourselves, because New York is a big city, and I'm tired. Maybe he just got another irresistible yen for those ferry boats."

Helene sighed, and tossed her furs over the back of a chair. "I wish I knew where Jake is?"

There had been a message waiting at the desk of the St. Jacques. Jake had been unavoidably delayed, by important business, but he'd be back by four. It was now a little past five, and there had been no further message.

"I wish I was back in Chicago," Malone said, in a gloomy voice. "I wish I'd never left Chicago."

He didn't want to admit to Helene that he was worried about Dennis Morrison. Indeed, he didn't want to admit it to himself. He had enough on his mind without it.

"I've sent downstairs for a fresh bottle of bourbon and the afternoon papers," Helene said. "They ought to have a wonderful time writing about your discovery. Malone, where do you imagine the other body is?"

"I have no further interest in the case," Malone lied stiffly. "I went there today because of a feeling of responsibility for Dennis Morrison. Since he ran out on us this afternoon, that feeling of responsibility has ceased to exist. The bourbon is a timely thought, but I am not concerned about what the newspapers have to say."

He managed to pretend, when they arrived, that he was reading them only to humor Helene.

The newspapers made a great to-do over the discovery, which they attributed to detective work on the part of that brilliant young police inspector, Arthur Peterson. Malone grinned, again reflecting that cops were cops, wherever you found them. The newspapers were particularly excited over the fact that the body, which they unanimously assumed to belong to Bertha Morrison, could not be identified. They speculated on the whereabouts of the head and on whether it would ever be found. There were more pictures of Bertha Morrison and Gloria Garden, and a slightly smudged picture of old Dr. Puckett leaving police headquarters.

Helene pushed aside the last newspaper and shook her head sadly. "I had it all figured out so nicely," she complained. "Gloria Garden was an ex-girl friend of Dennis'. She went to see Bertha that night, they had a quarrel, and Bertha killed her and then ran away. This shoots it all to hell."

"It wasn't a very good theory, anyway," Malone told her consolingly. He didn't add that he'd had the same one himself. "It left too many things unexplained."

"I was leaving those for you to figure out," Helene said. "Malone, where do you suppose Bertha's head is?"

"It'll probably turn up in a trunk in the baggage room of the railway station in Keokuk, Iowa."

He was wondering if, once the body was identified as Bertha Morrison's, he could collect half the fee from Abner Proudfoot. Probably not. Abner Proudfoot would probably hold out for all of Bertha or nothing.

"Malone, who could have murdered both those women and switched them around like that?"

"It isn't *who* that interests me," Malone said, "but *why*. That is, if I were interested at all, which I'm not, that would be the most interesting," He added hastily, "Stop bothering me with stupid questions."

Helene giggled. "It is funny, though, about that dinner jacket," she said slyly.

"Damned funny," the little lawyer murmured, without thinking. "I can't help wondering if——" He caught Helene's eye, glared at her furiously, and snapped, "I said leave me alone."

He poured himself a drink, crushed out his cigar, and began unwrapping a fresh one.

"Just the same," Helene said, "I bet I can find out who it belongs to."

"Bet you can't," Malone said automatically.

"Watch me," Helene said. "I bet I can find the owner of that jacket, and how Dennis Morrison got it, before you find the murderer."

"I'm not looking for the murderer," Malone said. He frowned. "Dennis Morrison——" He paused. Their eyes met.

"If he murdered Bertha," Helene said slowly, "he did it for her money. But the murderer disposed of her head so that she couldn't be identified. Whether that was his reason or not, I don't know. Dennis wouldn't have done it. Because with Bertha unidentified, he couldn't inherit her money." She frowned. "Still, he could have known both Bertha Morrison and Gloria Garden."

Malone shook his head. He aimed his cigar ashes at the

tray; most of them landed on his vest. "That look on his face when he came out of the murder room that morning was genuine. He couldn't have been acting."

"And," Helene added thoughtfully, "his hangover was genuine. I'd swear to that. The problem is to find someone who wanted to murder Bertha and didn't want her body to be identified."

"The problem," Malone said gloomily, "is to get back to Chicago."

"But, on the other hand, if it isn't Bertha's body, and it might not be, whose is it?"

"Little Red Hooding Ride's," Malone said.

"Malone, what happened to Bertha's jewels? There was about two thousand dollars' worth of jewelry missing from the bridal suite."

"The murderer found he'd left his fingerprints all over it," Malone said, "so he dropped it down the toilet. If you don't change the subject pretty damn quick, I'm going out to the movies."

She sighed. "You're a very mean man, Malone. I can't help wondering, though, why Dennis left us so suddenly and unceremoniously, and where he went."

"I wonder if there's a good Western picture showing anywhere," Malone said.

Helene muttered something about unsympathetic Irishmen. "How do you suppose the murderer got Gloria Garden's head up here? A recently severed human head is an awkward thing to carry through a hotel lobby, even at night."

"He dressed up like an all-American fullback and carried it under his arm," Malone said. He paused and scowled. "Maybe Gloria Garden was murdered right here in the hotel."

"In that case, where is her body, and where is Bertha Morrison's head?"

"This is where I came in," Malone said, "and this is where I go out." He looked at his watch. "If Jake doesn't get here pretty soon, I suppose I'm stuck with taking you out to dinner again."

She looked at him icily. "I could always call up an escort service." Suddenly she was silent, staring at him. "Malone!"

"Oh, no you can't," the little lawyer said, getting to his feet.

"Oh, yes I can," Helene said. "Can, and will." She began thumbing through a pile of notes on her desk. "I have the name of the one Dennis Morrison worked for written down here somewhere."

They argued about it while she looked for and located the telephone number, though Malone knew it was a losing argument. Finally she gave the number to the operator, and said to Malone, "Get out of here while I dress. And don't you dare tell Jake where I've gone."

"I won't," Malone said. "And I don't care if you never come back, either." He slammed the door as he went out.

As he walked down the hall, he reflected on the futility of arguing with a woman, especially Helene. Not, he admitted, that she'd had such a bad idea.

Well, anyway, he could unobtrusively follow her and make sure that she was safe.

The telephone was ringing when he reached the door of his room. Malone flung open the door, switched on the light, and glared at the telephone for a moment. Still, it might be Jake. He grabbed up the receiver.

It was a thin, nasal, masculine voice. The voice said, "Mr. Malone? This is Mr. Proudfoot's secretary. Mr.

Proudfoot wishes you to come to his home." The voice named an address in the East Sixties. "And, at once."

Malone said, "Listen, you tell Mr. Proudfoot to——"

But the voice had hung up.

Chapter Twenty-Two

MALONE spent a futile fifteen minutes trying to get Abner Proudfoot's secretary back on the phone. Mr. Proudfoot's residence, it appeared, had an unlisted phone, and the offices of Proudfoot, Schwartz, Van Alstine, and Proudfoot failed to answer. Malone talked to a succession of telephone operators, supervisors, and superintendents about the importance of talking to Abner Proudfoot at his home. Finally, after threatening to call in a medium and talk to Alexander Graham Bell in person, he gave up and slammed down the receiver.

He spent an equally futile, but somewhat more satisfactory fifteen minutes talking profanely and colorfully about Mr. Abner Proudfoot's private life, personal habits, and probable future.

It would take a while for Helene to dress. Malone peeled off his coat, tie, and shirt, and began a comfortable, leisurely shave.

He was torn between temptation and his sense of responsibility. The summons from Abner Proudfoot constituted the temptation. It wasn't just that he was curious as to what Abner Proudfoot had to tell him so urgently. But there were a few things he was looking forward to telling Abner Proudfoot.

On the other hand, he knew Helene's proclivity for getting into trouble, and this wasn't Chicago, this was New York. At various times in Chicago she'd managed to get herself kidnaped, arrested, and nearly murdered. Heaven only knew what might happen here.

He was just rubbing after-shave lotion into his cheeks when the phone rang again. He dried his hands on his shirt, mistaking it in his haste for a towel, and ran to answer it.

The nasal voice said, "This is Mr. Proudfoot's secretary calling back. Mr. Proudfoot wants to know what's detaining you."

"Tell Mr. Proudfoot my secretary hasn't finished washing my neck and ears," Malone snarled, "and that I only make appointments a week in advance." This time he managed to hang up the phone first.

He selected a clean shirt and changed leisurely into his navy-blue suit. The phone rang twice during the process; he ignored it. He moved his possessions from the pockets of his brown suit to those of his blue suit, fussed with his tie, and brushed his hair. He stuck the slip of paper with Abner Proudfoot's address on it into his vest pocket. Maybe tomorrow morning he'd call on Abner Proudfoot, if he felt in the mood.

He picked up the phone and called Jake and Helene's suite. Helene answered, and he said, "Well, how about dinner?"

"Not tonight," Helene said. "I have a date."

"Is Jake there?"

"Not yet." Her voice was almost gay. "I'm leaving a message for him. See you tomorrow, Malone." The receiver clicked sharply in his ear.

All right, then he'd follow her. He stuffed a heavy glass ash tray in the toe of an old sock, knotted the sock, and placed it conveniently in his right-hand pants pocket. Not that he anticipated any trouble, but it was always well to be prepared. He put on his topcoat, fished his hat from under a chair, and went out.

Damn New York. Damn Abner Proudfoot. Damn everybody. Damn Helene.

She was ahead of him, in the lobby, cashing a check at the desk. Her long, full-skirted chiffon dress was the pale-green color of a field of new wheat; over it she wore a gleaming evening coat the color of gold. The net scarf over her shining hair was dotted with golden flecks.

Yet—had she dressed hastily, or in anger? There was too much make-up on her exquisite face, carelessly applied. She wore earrings and four bracelets of diamonds, and a diamond chain from which was suspended a glowing emerald. Helene, wearing all that jewelry? He couldn't understand it. Particularly, with the golden evening coat, and gold-flecked scarf.

She moved toward the door; he followed, keeping her in sight. Near the door she paused to greet a big, handsome, blond bruiser in evening clothes. The blond bruiser showed her a card, she beamed, rested her hand on his arm, and sailed out the door beside him.

Malone reached the sidewalk just as they stepped into a waiting cab. The cab moved away, Malone raced across the sidewalk and dived toward the next cab, just drawing up. The doorman said, "Sorry, sir," and elbowed him aside. A party of four got in the cab and drove off. Malone gritted his teeth and started for the next cab and was nearly knocked to the sidewalk as the doorman opened the cab door for a white-bearded gentleman in an opera hat. A hurried young man with a brief case under his arm got the third cab.

"Sorry, sir," the doorman said, "you'll have to wait your turn."

Malone, speechless and growling, pointed in the direction Helene's cab had taken.

"There's three ahead of you," the doorman said. "I'm sorry sir, but——"

Helene's cab was now out of sight.

Malone considered giving the doorman a punch in the nose, and then decided against it. It might make him feel better, but it wouldn't accomplish anything. Besides, he suspected (rightly) that Helene had bribed the doorman.

After all, he told himself, Helene was over twenty-one, and she hadn't been raised in the backwoods.

He went up to the desk. Had Mr. Justus come in yet, or had there been any message?

Mr. Justus had not come in, and there had not been any message. But there had been several calls for Mr. Malone from a Mr. Proudfoot. Mr. Malone stopped at the cigar stand, replenished his supply, and made a mental note to get acquainted with the cigar-stand girl as soon as he had the time. He went out to the street again and called for a cab. This time he got it right away.

He didn't like the looks of Abner Proudfoot's house any better than he'd liked Abner Proudfoot. He stood for a moment on the sidewalk, after the cab had driven away, regarding it. It was four stories high, one of them an English basement, with a narrow front. There were ornamental iron grilles over the windows, and the shades were all tightly drawn.

There was another iron grille set in the heavy wooden door. Malone found the bell with a little difficulty, and rang it. There was a long wait, during which the little lawyer's patience wore down to its last thread before a middle-aged butler opened the door and announced that Mr. Proudfoot was not at home.

"I'll wait," Malone said, elbowing his way into the hall. "This is a business call."

"Yes, sir," the butler said nervously, "I'll tell Mr. Proudfoot's secretary, sir. What is the nature of the business, sir?" He was a thin, horse-faced man, slightly shabby, with graying hair and a worried look. Malone felt an inexplicable rush of sympathy for him.

"Mr. Proudfoot seduced my daughter, and I'm here to make him acknowledge that he's the father of her unborn child," Malone said.

The butler took his hat and said, "Yes, sir. I'll call Mr. Proudfoot's secretary. If you'll just wait right here."

Malone waited, looking around the hall. It looked very high-class and expensive, like a first-rate undertaking parlor. Only, on closer inspection, it was shabby. The carpet had been picked out a long time ago by someone with a lot of money, but it was slightly frayed along the edges and the seams. Perfectly dusted, though. The long plate-glass mirror was beautifully polished, but its frame was faintly tarnished. One of the bulbs was out in the chandelier.

A thin, sickly-looking young man with ginger-colored hair and thick glasses came into the hall, looked at Malone, and said in a high-pitched, nasal voice, "You'll have to have an appointment to see Mr. Proudfoot."

"I'm making an appointment," Malone said nastily, "right now." He poked a thumb through the pocket of his coat.

The secretary squeaked, on an even higher pitch, and backed through the lighted doorway. Malone followed him into a library that looked like the place where the corpse was found in any "B" picture made before 1930.

"You have a quaint sense of humor, Mr. Malone," Abner Proudfoot said coldly. He didn't rise from his chair.

"Thanks, pal," Malone said. "I think so, too." He noticed that the gilding on the coat of arms over the fireplace was chipped. "Did you want to see me about anything important, or did you just want me to drop in for a friendly little drink, pal?"

"Bring Mr. Malone a drink," Proudfoot said to the ginger-haired secretary. He folded his hands over his knees and sat silently looking at nothing. The firelight made his black suit and black tie look even blacker.

Malone was glad when the drink arrived. Any minute now, he expected a bat to fly across the room, or Boris Karloff to crawl out of the fireplace.

"I asked you to come here," Proudfoot said, "to inform you that I consider it necessary that our arrangement be terminated, and at once."

Malone half choked on his drink, gulped down the rest of it, and said, "How's that again?"

"I have come to the conclusion," Abner Proudfoot said, "that Bertha will get in touch with me, of her own free will, whenever she deems it advisable to do so. Therefore, no further necessity exists for you to search for her. I appreciate the efforts you have already put forward in behalf of this case and naturally I shall not expect you to return the advance fee I have already paid to you, on my own responsibility."

Malone drained the last half inch of bourbon from his glass before he answered. The upholstery on the big chair might be almost threadbare, and one bulb might be missing from the immense crystal chandelier, but it was damned good bourbon.

"You want me to stop looking for Bertha Morrison,"

Malone said. "I wonder why. Is it because she's already been found, or because you're afraid I'll find her?"

"My reasons for arriving at this decision are none of your concern," Proudfoot said stiffly. "I consider that you have been adequately compensated for the efforts you have put forth on my behalf, and I will appreciate your returning to me the paper which you induced me to sign."

"It's in my safety-deposit box," Malone lied. He knew that Proudfoot didn't believe him. He rose, and said, "I'm a hard man to fire, buddy. Once I'm hired to find a dame, I find her, come hell or high water. And if I do find this one, I'm just as like as not to insist on being paid for finding her. That's the mean kind of a cuss I am."

"You may consider this interview at an end," Abner Proudfoot said coldly. He raised his voice and called, "Dudley!"

"You don't need to yell for the bouncer," Malone said. "I don't like this joint." He grinned at the pallid young secretary who'd come in the door and stood hesitantly, just inside the doorway. "Don't worry, toots, I'm leaving, anyway." He turned another grin on Abner Proudfoot, who'd risen and was standing before the fireplace, his hands clasped behind his back. "Naturally, you want me to stop looking for Bertha Morrison. Because you know I'm a damn smart guy, and now that a body's turned up in the morgue that might be hers, you're afraid I'll find her head. And that's the last thing you want to have happen, isn't it, pal?"

Abner Proudfoot said, "I do not consider my interests to be any further concern of yours, Mr. Malone."

Malone puffed at his cigar. "You must have thought she was alive, when you hired me to find her and to keep her out of the chair. Because as long as she's alive, you can go on milking her old man's estate. But if she's identified as dead, her husband will inherit all that dough, and the management of it, and you'll be out of luck. So as soon as you read in the papers that that might be her body in the morgue, you called me up quick, to tell me to lay off." He knocked a fleck of ash on the carpet.

"Only I'm a guy with a lot of natural curiosity, and when I start out to find a person, I find her. On my own time, if I have to."

The gray-haired butler appeared in the door and said, "Can I be of assistance, Mr. Proudfoot?" Mr. Proudfoot didn't seem to hear him.

"Or, if I should stumble on the missing head," Malone said, "which is necessary to identify her, then maybe we can make a deal."

Abner Proudfoot looked at him quickly and said, "Do you know where it is?"

"I was beginning to think you'd brought it here and stuffed a pillow with it," Malone said, "but I guess I was wrong. No, I don't know where it is, but I'll look around. You'll hear from me, pal. And don't think you've fired me, because you haven't."

He took a backward step toward the door, looking into the room. Abner Proudfoot, tall, dressed in black, standing before the carved fireplace. The paneled walls, the gloomy oil paintings of unpleasant-looking men. The drawn blinds. The gray-haired butler standing near one door, and the spectacled secretary near another. It made, Malone thought, a swell scene.

It was marred, though, suddenly. Another door was flung open, and a chubby, yellow-haired young woman, dressed in a bright-violet negligee, a pair of ostrich-plume slippers, a string of pearls, and nothing else, ran into the room and up to Abner Proudfoot.

She said petulantly, "Honey, I can't stick around here waiting for you all evening——" Then she saw Malone, pulled the negligee together, and said, "Oh, I'm sorry, I didn't know you were entertaining a friend."

"He's not entertaining," Malone said quickly, "and we're not friends. But you and I could be."

She giggled, caught a nasty look from Proudfoot, and was hastily silent.

Malone backed slowly to the door, carefully keeping all of them in sight. He paused at the door.

"Good night," he said, "and thanks for the drink. You'll hear from me."

"Sylvester," Abner Proudfoot said, "show Mr. Malone to the door."

Malone let the gray-haired man precede him and waited with his back against the wall while the door was opened.

"Good night, Mr. Malone," the butler said.

"Good night, Sylvester," Malone said, in the same grave tone.

He heard the heavy door bang shut behind him, and restrained a sudden impulse to run like hell down the sidewalk. So, Abner Proudfoot was trying to tell him, John J. Malone, what to do, was he! Well, he'd find Bertha Morrison now, dead or alive, if it was the last thing he ever did.

The street was dark and shadowy, there wasn't a cab in sight. A thin, cool April rain was beginning to fall. Which way was west? He wasn't sure. Far down the street, though, he could see lights, as of a main thoroughfare. If there wasn't a cab there, he could at least find a phone with which to call one. He headed toward the lights.

He wished with all his heart that he wasn't doing this alone. Always, in similar circumstances in the past, Jake and Helene had been right along with him. But this time,

Jake was off on some mysterious business of his own, and Helene was out night-clubbing. He needed them. He needed Jake's determined single-mindedness and Helene's flashes of intuition.

Besides, on the off chance that Abner Proudfoot was really out to get that signed agreement back—Jake was always a good man in a fight.

By the time Malone had gone half a block he was definitely uneasy. Something about the street itself depressed and worried him. The darkness, the rain, the lack of cross streets. The great, gloomy apartment buildings, the tightly shuttered houses. The emptiness of the sidewalk. If a guy needed to holler for help here, he'd be lucky if he even got an echo.

He walked faster and faster. Were there footsteps behind him? Utter nonsense. Just his Irish imagination again. He was damned if he'd look back.

An even darker section of the sidewalk stretched ahead of him in the next block, beside a great, shadowed, cavernous excavation. Malone speeded up a little more. It wasn't so far to that lighted street, now.

He passed a street lamp; it threw his shadow on the walk before him, huge and distorted. It produced another shadow, too, right behind him, moving up closer, with an upraised arm.

Malone wheeled around, just as the arm moved. He was thrown against the frail railing of the excavation, and a hard object grazed the side of his head.

The little lawyer had learned his art of self-defense on Chicago's West Side, and he hadn't forgotten it. He brought up one knee sharply and, at the same moment, drove one fist toward a stomach and the other toward a jaw. His unseen opponent yelped and fell back just long enough for Malone to get away from the railing and pull the improvised blackjack from his pocket. He swung his weapon. The other man, with a startled cry, slid through the railing and into the excavation.

But there had been two of them. Malone spun around just in time. A blow aimed at the back of his neck shunted harmlessly across his shoulder. He drove his fist into what he hoped was a face, but another blow caught him on the side of the head, and he fell to the walk.

He lay still, pretending unconsciousness. His second assailant knelt beside him, picked up the abandoned black-jack, and put it into his own pocket. Then he began to search Malone. He was reaching for the inside coat pocket when Malone managed another, even more savage kick. The man, cursing, fell backward, and Malone tried to get up, with a desperate hope of getting away.

A car came slowly down the street, a police car. It slowed down still more as it reached the excavation, and a split second later Malone's attacker was out of sight, leaving the lawyer alone on the sidewalk. The car stopped, with a little moan from its siren, and a searchlight was turned on Malone. He tried to get up, stumbled, and half fell. There was a sharp pain in his head, tiny lights danced in front of his eyes.

Two men came running out of the car, one of them slipped a hand under Malone's arm. A voice said, "Are you O. K., Malone?" and then "Good thing Peterson told us to tail him."

In the last instant before everything went black, Malone felt a twinge of surprise. He'd never thought the time would come when he'd be so glad to see Schultz.

Chapter Twenty-Three

JAKE's first thought had been to sit down and read the letters right there in Gloria Garden's apartment, they were that tempting. Then he'd looked at his watch, realized how late it was—already nearly seven—and that Helene was waiting. He's stuffed the packet inside his coat and started back to the hotel.

He'd wasted an hour looking for the letters in all the places where he—or any other man—would have hidden them. For a while, he'd been about to give up. Someone else must have been here ahead of him. He was sure of it.

Then he'd thought about the little desk. Yes, he remembered, and positively, one of the empty drawers had been open a crooked inch, as though it had been hastily closed, and there was the fact that the desk drawers had been so completely empty. Gloria Garden might have taken out any important letters and hidden them away. But whoever had been here ahead of him must have simply scooped out letters, bills, clippings, ads from the Book-of-the-Month Club, everything, to be read and sorted out later.

Still, there was a chance that Gloria Garden might have hidden her important letters somewhere else in the apartment. He certainly wasn't going to give up now, after spending all this time.

He thought about Helene, about where she always hid his birthday and Christmas presents, and the letters from her Aunt Agatha whom he didn't like and who was always writing for money. Then he went into Gloria Gar-

den's bedroom, lifted up the top section of the double
mattress, and there were the letters, tied with grocer's
string into a neat little bundle.

Jake felt a sudden joyous elation. He'd found something, anyway. He didn't know yet where he was getting,
but he was getting somewhere.

He wanted to rush straight to Helene, not to tell her
what he'd accomplished, not to tell her what he hoped to
do, but just to look at her. He'd glance over the letters in
the privacy of the bathroom, or maybe he'd save them to
read and study later. He'd take Helene out for a celebra-
tion, even though she wouldn't know what they were
celebrating. Malone too, of course.

The cab got stuck in four different crosstown traffic
jams, and seemed to take at least a week to reach the hotel.
The talkative driver apologized all the way for the series
of delays, and Jake politely pretended that he was in no
hurry and didn't mind.

He had to wait another month or two for the elevator,
and then it moved like an exhausted snail, and stopped
for days at a time at every floor.

The corridor to his door looked a mile long, and he
raced the full length of it. At the door he paused, to make
sure that the packet of letters didn't create a bulge under
his coat. Then he found his key, unlocked the door,
opened it, went into the suite, and discovered that Helene
wasn't there.

It was past seven, but possibly she and Malone hadn't
come back from sight-seeing. No, they'd been back, there
were cigar butts in one ash tray, cigarette stubs in another, and a litter of newspapers on the floor. He inspected Helene's wardrobe. The pale-green chiffon
wasn't there. She'd gone out, dressed for the evening.

He called Malone's room. There was no answer.

Jake pulled the packet of letters from under his coat, threw it across the room, plopped down on the davenport, and sat there swearing.

It was true he was three hours late.

But obviously Helene hadn't worried about him. She'd dressed up in the new pale-green chiffon and gone out to have a good time.

Maybe he should have confided in her, long before this, about what he was doing,

But he wanted to surprise her.

And Malone, the bastard, his best friend, Malone hadn't worried because he came home three hours late. He might have been lying murdered in a gutter somewhere. But Malone had gone out to do the town.

Jake grabbed the telephone, called the desk, and asked if Mrs. Justus had left a message for him when she went out. There was a brief pause for investigation. It turned out Mrs. Justus had. The desk read it over the telephone in a businesslike, emotionless voice. "Have a date for dinner and the evening. Be home early."

Jake said, "Thank you. And do you have any idea where I could reach Mr. Malone?"

There was a very long pause while the desk checked. Mr. Malone hadn't left any message. But he'd been in the bar about an hour ago. Just a minute, please, Mr. Justus. A still longer pause. Mr. Malone left in a taxi. He didn't say where he was going.

Jake thanked the desk very politely, hung up, and restrained an impulse to throw the telephone across the room.

Where the hell was Helene?

Where the double-hell was Malone?

Why had they gone off and left him?

He'd been surprised and bewildered at his first discovery that they were gone. Now, he began to get mad.

Of all the inconsiderate people! Going off to have a good time, without him, just because he happened to be a few minutes late!

He slammed the bedroom door, hard, and kicked a wastebasket across the room. That made him feel a little better, but not much.

Treat him like that, would they! He'd show them! He'd call up a girl and take her out to do the town. Maybe he'd run into Helene somewhere.

He ripped off his tie and began unbuttoning his shirt, preparatory to bathing and changing into evening clothes. At the third button, he paused. He didn't know any girl to call up, in all of New York, except Wildavine. And Wildavine was at home, reading his manuscript. Jake definitely didn't want to interrupt her. She'd promised to give him her opinion of it tomorrow.

All right, he'd stay home and sulk. He refastened his shirt and put on his tie again. He'd do a job of sulking that would go down in history.

For that matter, though, whom did Helene know here in New York to go out with? She hadn't gone with Malone. She didn't know anyone in New York worth putting on the new green chiffon evening dress. Or did she? Come to think of it, she'd been behaving rather oddly these past few days.

Jake put on his coat and went downstairs to the lobby. Someone must have seen Helene leaving. He inquired at the desk, at the cigar stand, and of the doorman, and got exactly nowhere. "I'm sorry, sir, I didn't notice Mrs. Justus leaving." No one, it seemed, had noticed Helene.

That, Jake reflected, was a rank impossibility. People always noticed Helene. And, in that pale-green dress——

He had the feeling of being surrounded by a wall of silence, a conspiracy. Then he realized that of course it was a conspiracy. The desk clerk, the cigar girl, and the doorman didn't remember noticing Helene because they thought they were talking to a jealous husband. They were right.

Jake went back to the suite, baffled, frustrated, and miserable. He was all over being mad, now. He just wanted Helene.

Maybe she'd misinterpreted his behavior. Now that he thought it over, he'd been keeping a lot of secrets from her. He'd been away for long periods of time without explanation. And tonight he'd been unusually, inexcusably, and unforgivably late.

The idea of treating Helene like that! He ought to be ashamed of himself. He was. No wonder she'd gone out with someone else. He didn't blame her.

The only thing he could do to redeem himself was to solve Gloria Garden's murder and find Bertha Morrison. Then he'd be a public hero, some publisher would buy his mystery novel, and Helene would be pleased and proud.

Therefore, he might as well start on those letters, right now. Maybe he ought to have dinner first. Hell no, there wasn't time. He could get along without dinner. Besides, there was a bottle of bourbon on the end table.

Jake pictured Helene, in the new pale-green chiffon dress, eating *filet mignon* and broiled mushrooms. He sighed, poured himself three fingers of bourbon, and untied the string around the packet of letters.

It was, he discovered, a complete set of correspondence. The first letter in the collection was written on white ten-cent store paper, with blue-black ink, in a masculine hand. The second was on pale-gray paper, violet ink, and in a lacy, feminine hand, with little circles serving for dots and periods.

There were no envelopes, nor addresses written on the letters, but the letters were dated. Whoever had put them together in this packet had had an orderly mind, and had arranged them according to dates. Jake noticed, flipping a finger through them, that her letters had become longer than his, toward the end of the correspondence, and that she had written two or three to his one.

He opened the first one. It was dated almost two years ago.

Lovely Gloria:

Our week end in Atlantic City was so wonderful. I wish these could be pearls I send you, instead of flowers. Tell me we'll meet again, and soon, soon, soon.

Adoringly,
Ducky

Dear Ducky:

Thank you for the lovely flowers. I'm free for dinner and the evening a week from Tuesday. Let's meet in the Astor lobby at 6.30.

Sincerely,
Gloria

Gloria, my beautiful:

Every hour I spend away from you seems a century . . .

Dear Ducky:

Thank you for the book of poems. Perhaps someday next week . . .

Adored Gloria:

Night after night I dream of beautiful you, and the wonderful hours we've spent together . . .

Darling Ducky:
The flowers were so lovely. I've always loved violets.
Why don't we have dinner here at my apartment to-
morrow, instead of going out . . .

Jake glanced through a dozen more. Ducky remained
flowery and fervent, Gloria seemed to be slowly warming up. After about five months of the correspondence,
she'd begun a letter with *Dear, dear Ducky, my Dream
Man.* Jake stopped right there to pour himself another
drink.

The letters of the next few months were ardent and
anatomical. They would have sounded swell, read in the
dry, singsong voice of a clerk of the court. Jake reflected
that no one had ever told Ducky about beginning his letters, *My dearest sweetheart, and gentlemen of the jury.*

By the end of the first year, Ducky's letters had cooled
down a little. They began, simply and chastely, *Dear
Gloria.* Gloria, now, was the one who was going all-out.

Ducky-wucky-darling:
Please don't worry about the little loan. I'm so glad
I was able to help. You mustn't let it trouble you. After
all, aren't we . . .

Dear Gloria:
I don't know why you should be so good to me. Believe me, someday soon . . .

Ducksie-dearest:
Will the enclosed be enough? Please don't be so discouraged, I'm sure you'll find another job . . .

Now, Jake reflected, we're beginning to get somewhere! He began to read with more interest.

Dear Gloria:
Believe me, sweetheart, I'm going to pay you back
every penny, the minute I am earning money again. And

some sweet day, when I'm able to offer you the home you deserve . . .

My Wonderful Ducky man—
Oh, it's going to be so wonderful, just you and me, in a little house of our own . . .

Then there was a long gap, nearly three months.

Dear Gloria:
How can you be so unjust? I've been working, trying to save up enough to repay you. Meanwhile I've had back rent, dentist bills, and other things. I thought you'd understand . . .

Oh my own, wonderful Ducky:
I'm so happy that you've forgiven me!

One nice thing about the letters, Jake reflected. Reading them, it was possible to fill in the missing conversations that had taken place in between.

Object matrimony really reared its head about a month later.

Ducky-lovey:
I don't see why we should have to wait until you have a job again. After all, I'm earning more than enough for both of us. And why should we lose all these precious days and nights together . . .

Dear Gloria:
You are so understanding and fine . . .

However, there had evidently been problems:

Dear Ducky: [*Hm, a shade of coolness there.*]
I'm sorry I was so angry last night, but I've always dreamed of being married in the little old church back home . . .

Dear Gloria:
We mean so much to each other. How can our marriage concern anyone but ourselves . . .

Dearest Ducky:
I can see what you mean about any public announcement of our marriage interfering with my work as a model, but . . .

Dear Gloria:
It's your career I'm thinking of . . .

Evidently, Ducky had got his way. The letters ended there. But there was a penciled note:

Gloria—be sure to leave ten dollars on the table for me when you go out, and make some fresh coffee so it will be hot when I get up.

None of the newspaper accounts of Gloria Garden's life had mentioned a husband. Ducky must have succeeded in selling her on that idea of a secret marriage.

Finally, at the end of the packet, there was a letter on thin, ruled paper, spidery handwriting, and black ink.

Dear Daughter:
I'm sorry your marriage turned out so unhappily. Just remember he couldn't have been much good or he wouldn't have taken up with another woman. Don't try to get him back. Willy Bark's wife (remember him, he works in the post office) ran away with another man. Willy got her back and she's made his life miserable for the last twenty years.

Maybe you ought to come home for a little visit. Your ma is ailing a little, nothing serious. But she would sure like to see you, and so would your old pa. Looks like we're going to have an early thaw this year. The snow is going fast and Joe Beebie says he saw a robin in his yard last week. Henry Parsons has gotten married to a girl from Janesville, Wisconsin, and Harlow Larsen has twin boys. I've had all my teeth out and it's taking me a little time to get used to my plates. The river is high, Pearlie Rodell's basement was flooded a couple of days ago and her cat was drowned. They're repainting the city hall. Write soon. I hope you can come for a visit.

Your loving Pa

Jake folded it up, put the letters back together, and tied the string around them again. He wished Gloria had been able to get home for that visit.

She'd met Ducky somewhere, he'd courted her, she'd fallen for him. He'd needed money, and she'd lent it to him. They'd been secretly married. He'd left her for another woman. That was all.

The case was all sewed up. Dennis was Ducky, and Bertha Morrison was the other woman. There had been a divorce, Gloria Garden, or better, Hazel Puckett had taken her pa's advice. Then she'd learned of Ducky's marriage to the wealthy woman, and gone to confront her. Maybe to tell her that Ducky insisted on having his coffee ready when he woke. There had been a quarrel, a fight. Bertha, the stronger of the two, had strangled Gloria, decapitated her in a jealous rage, dressed her in the pale-blue satin nightgown and tucked her in the bridal bed. Then Bertha had donned Gloria's clothes and fled the city.

It was as simple as that. Jake stretched, yawned, got up, and hid the packet of letters in his shaving kit. Now, all he had to do was find Bertha Morrison, and force a confession from her.

He wished Helene were here.

Maybe he ought to get some dinner.

No, a drink would do just as well. Alcohol was a food too.

He poured himself a drink, picked up one of the newspapers from the floor, and began aimlessly glancing through it. More pictures of Gloria Garden and of Bertha Morrison. Hm. Must be a story about the murder.

Well, he'd give them a better story, in a couple of days. He read on, lazily.

Astute work on the part of Arthur Peterson. Gloria Garden's head. Verification from the medical examiner's office. Unidentified body. A speculation on the part of the newspaper as to the identity of the body.

Jake sat up, said, "What?" and downed his drink, fast.

He read through the rest of the papers hastily. Beautiful model. Brilliant detective work. Arthur Peterson. Missing bride. No marks of identification on body. "Body had no identifying scars, doctor says." "Has Bertha Morrison Been Found?" " 'We try to be efficient,' Inspector Arthur Peterson of the Homicide Bureau said modestly tonight, in an exclusive interview . . ." Search for a Missing Head. Search for a Missing Body. Search for a Missing Murderer.

Jake read through to the last paragraph in the last paper, crumpled them all up into a football-shaped wad, and hurled that across the room.

All his time and efforts and deductions had been wasted. Because Gloria Garden's head had been found on Bertha Morrison's body. And Gloria Garden's body was missing, and so was Bertha Morrison's head, and so was Ducky. Who the hell was Ducky, anyway, and why the hell had he scrammed? Maybe he was the murderer. Sure, that was it. Now all he had to do was to find Ducky.

Jake yawned. He picked up the roll of crumpled newspapers and carried it out to the waste chute. Then he emptied the ash trays, wiped them out, and put them back where they belonged. He took the empty glasses into the bathroom and rinsed them under the cold-water faucet.

No use letting the room look like a shambles when Helene came back.

What would he say to her? "Where the hell have you been?" Or, "Sorry I got home so late." Or maybe just ignoring the whole thing, with "Hello, darling, how nice you look."

Jake untied his shoes, loosened them, and stretched out on the davenport. His watch said five to ten; she'd be home any minute now. He decided he'd pretend he hadn't noticed how long she'd been gone, and that he hadn't come home three hours late. Yes, that was the thing to do. He wouldn't even need to say, "How nice you look," because every time he looked at her, his eyes said, "How beautiful, how beautiful you are."

He closed his eyes, just for a second, opened them, lit a cigarette, and lay staring at the ceiling through the smoke. Helene's eyes could be like smoke, blue gray. Who had Ducky been? Had he murdered Gloria Garden and Bertha Morrison, and why? How was he, Jake, going to find out? What would Wildavine think of his book? Where was Helene, and how soon would she come home to him?

He yawned again. It had been a long day. Traipsing around, trying to locate some of the people in Bertha Lutts Morrison's address book. Most of them moved away, none of the others home. Then the searching of Gloria Garden's apartment. The gloomy skies. The cold dripping of April rain. He was tired.

He poured himself one more drink, downed it, and put out his cigarette. Gloria Garden had been beautiful, she could have had her pick of all the men in New York, and she'd fallen for a louse. Old Doc Puckett sounded like a swell guy. Who could have taken Helene out to dinner? Oh, well, she'd tell him when she came home, which would be pretty soon now. He wished they were back in Chicago. What had he ever wanted to write a book for, anyway?

Jake closed his eyes. The room was warm, the davenport was big and comfortable, even for his long legs. He let himself relax, and thoughts began to run around aimlessly in his mind. Bertha Morrison's head. Ducky. How could he find Ducky, and who was Ducky? A son-of-a-bitch, whoever he was. Pretty soon that door would open and Helene would come in, cool and lovely. Willy Bark should never have taken his wife back. What would Wildavine Williams think of his book? He hoped Dennis Morrison was all right. Helene was the most beautiful woman in all the world. A little sleep wouldn't do him any harm. Where the hell had Malone gone? Zz-z-z-z. Bertha Morrison's head. Ducky. Gloria Garden. Murder. Zzz-z-z-z-z. Helene—Helene—Helene—Helene——

Zzzzz-z-z-z-z-z-z

There was a sharp pounding on the door, Jake leaped to his feet and stumbled across the room, rubbing his eyes. He glanced at his watch and paused, oblivious of the pounding on the door.

Three-fifteen! Good God! Could he have been sleeping that long? Helene, where was Helene? Jake rubbed his eyes again, blinking the sleep out of them. She must have found Malone and gone somewhere with him. That was it. That had to be it. He brushed the hair back from his forehead and threw open the door.

There was Malone. His face was gray, a bandage was plastered over one eye, his jaw was swollen, and one cheek showed an ugly cut. His tie was missing, his collar was torn, his coat was ripped down one side. His left hand was bandaged, too, and when he walked into the room, he showed a slight limp.

"Malone!" Jake gasped. "What happened to you? Where have you been all this time?"

"Oh, I just ran into a few friends," the little lawyer said airily. He didn't see any point in explaining that after he'd been revived and bandaged, he'd spent the next four hours buying what had started out to be a couple of beers for Schultz, to celebrate the capture and incarceration of the thugs who'd held him up.

"Good thing they were friends," Jake said, "or they might have really done you some damage. Where's Helene?"

"Isn't she home yet?" Malone asked.

"Wasn't she with you?" Jake asked.

Malone sagged against the doorpost. Jake sank down on the couch. "It's quarter past three," he said.

"I tried to follow her," Malone said.

Jake said, "Maybe we'd better call the police," and Malone said quietly, "Yes, maybe we had."

The phone rang.

Jake looked at it and said, "Maybe you'd better answer it." Malone looked at Jake and said, "Yes. Maybe I'd better."

Chapter Twenty-Four

THE BLOND young man from the escort bureau said that his name was Harris Lawrence.

Helene giggled and said, "I'm Helene Johnson. My name's really Harriet, but you don't think it's silly of me to call myself Helene, do you?"

He said, "It sounds to me like a beautiful name, to fit a beautiful personality." He said it as though he were reciting a set speech. "I'm delighted to meet you, Mrs. Johnson. Where would you like to go?" He helped her into a cab. "You understand of course——"

"Oh, yes, I know," Helene said gaily. "It was all explained to me over the phone. I give you, in advance, enough money to cover the evening's expenses, and you give me back any change that's left over when you bring me home." She opened her rhinestone bag, took out a hundred-dollar bill, and gave it to him. "Do you suppose that will be enough?"

"Amply," Harris Lawrence said, closing his fingers over the bill.

"Because if it isn't," Helene said innocently, "I have more. Now, you pick the places we'll go. I've never been in New York before, we just got in a couple of days ago, and my husband says we've got to go home tomorrow. He's been busy every minute of the time we've been here, and I haven't gone anywhere, except shopping of course. Tell me, you don't think I'm silly to call up an escort bureau, do you?"

"Not at all," Harris Lawrence said, folding the bill into

his vest pocket. "May I suggest that we have dinner in the Rainbow Room?"

"Oh," Helene said, with a wide-eyed gasp, "I'd love to have dinner in the Rainbow Room! I've heard about it, in the papers back home, but I never thought I'd really go there myself!"

She exclaimed excitedly about the Rainbow Room, and ordered champagne cocktails and lobster salad.

The blond young man did his best with conversation. He tried politics, baseball, and literature, and finally seemed relieved to find that Helene Johnson was mostly interested in the movies and in seeing celebrities.

She finished her *bombe glacée*, and then said, "I've always read that a dinner like this should be followed with a glass of brandy. Do you think I'd be terribly silly to order a glass of brandy?"

"Not at all," Harris Lawrence said. He refused a brandy for himself, explaining that he didn't drink.

"I don't, either," Helene said. "Not at home. But I don't come to New York every day, do I?"

She dawdled over her second brandy, adroitly slopping most of it onto the tablecloth, until it was too late to go to the theater. Then she said, "Oh, well, what I'm really interested in is seeing Night Life. You'll show me every-thing—I mean, *everything*—won't you?"

"Everything you say," Harris Lawrence said gallantly, slipping her gold wrap over her shoulders.

He took her to a fifth-rate night club that was an imitation of El Morocco. Helene was pleased and excited, ordered three drinks, two of which were surreptitiously poured under the table, and said, "Oh! Isn't that Walter Winchell at the table over there?" At the cheap night club that was an imitation of Twenty-one, she gasped and said, "Oh, look! In the corner! Cary Grant! Anyway, it certainly *looks* like him." And, in the even cheaper imitation of the Stork Club, she giggled and said, "Tell me, you don't think I'm silly to wear all my diamonds at one time? Because at home they just sit in the deposit box."

They're very becoming to you," Harris Lawrence said.

"Joe—he's my husband—doesn't know I brought them with me," Helene confided. "He's pretty conservative. I have copies of all of them, of course, and that's what he likes me to wear. But I always say, why not put the copies in the safety-deposit box and wear the real thing? I wouldn't say that to Joe, of course. He wouldn't understand. But you do understand, don't you, Harris? You don't mind if I call you Harris, do you?"

Harris Lawrence said, "No, not at all. I'd like you to."

"Harris!" Helene said, beaming. "You know what I think? I think you're cute." She giggled again. "Please, tell me you don't think I'm silly."

"I think you're wonderful," Harris said. "I only wish you were going to stay in New York for a long, long time."

"Oh," Helene said, rapturously, "I just wish I was going to stay here *forever*! But since I've got to go home tomorrow, please, take me everywhere, will you? Just —*everywhere*?"

He took her to a Harlem night club, announcing apologetically at the door that more money was needed. It turned out that she had another hundred-dollar bill, but that was all. That had to last through the evening.

"And your fee, or whatever you call it, has to come out of that," she told him. "That's all the money I could save out of what Joe gave me to spend on clothes. And he'd kill me—I mean, really kill me—if he knew I was doing anything like this."

In the night club she pretended prettily to be shocked and delighted by the floor show. She ordered five more drinks, and drank one of them. Harris Lawrence was a smooth-looking customer, but he evidently wasn't wise to the trick of emptying the little glass into the sugar bowl.

Helene toyed with a sixth drink, and said, "Y'know why I called the office tha' sent you out? B'cause a friend of mine gave me the number, tha's what. Friend, name of Josephine. Know her? A'right, you don' know her. She went out with somebody from your office and she thought he was pretty cute, I think you're pretty cute, too. But y'know what? I mean, y'want me to be perfectly frank? When I called up your office, y'know what I thought? I thought I'd get him."

She looked again at Harris Lawrence. He had thick yellow hair that looked as though it might have had a henna rinse, a broad face, glassy blue eyes, and moist lips. He didn't look suspicious, though.

"Y'know Josephine's friend?" she asked. "Name was Dennis—Dennis something." She accidentally knocked over her drink and said, "Ooops! There I go, being clumsy. Tell me, y'don't mind my being clumsy. Oh, I remember my friend's friend's name. Dennis. Dennis Morrison. Works for your escort bureau. J'ever know a man named Morrison?"

"He isn't there any more," Harris Lawrence said. "He left about a year ago." He looked searchingly at Helene, smiled, and said, "Do we have to talk about him?"

"Uh-uh," Helene said, shaking her head. "Let's talk about us now."

"How about another drink?"

She shook her head again, vigorously. "Le's get out of

this dull place. I gotta leave N'York tomorrow, I haven't got much time to spend. I wanna see something really exciting, I mean *really* exciting."

"Well," Harris Lawrence said slowly, and speculatively, "maybe I can suggest a place——"

"Le's go," Helene said, rising and staggering gracefully. "But, 'member now, I wanna see something, well, *really*——" She gave him a long wink.

"I know exactly what you mean," the blond young man said.

In the taxi, suddenly, Helene felt that maybe she'd taken on something too big for her to handle. It was the first time she'd ever attempted anything like this, entirely on her own. She'd been in a few tight spots before, but always with the knowledge that Jake and Malone were somewhere within screaming distance or, at least, knew what she was doing, and would arrive when she needed them. But this time—Jake was involved in some strange business he wouldn't tell her about, Malone was absorbed in some weird affair of his own, and—here *she* was. The three of them, all going three different ways. It had never been like this before. She tried to choke back a little, involuntary moan, and didn't succeed.

"There, there," Harris Lawrence said, in a voice like ice.

A sudden spasm of fear froze the flesh to her bones. She wished with her whole heart that Jake—Malone— *anybody* was there. Not that she was frightened because the blond young man was making passes at her in the taxi, but because he wasn't. If he had, she'd have stopped being frightened. Helene had learned how to cope with that during her freshman year in boarding school. But this was something else.

She stole a look at Harris Lawrence out of the corner of her eye. He looked disinterested, polite, and calm, entirely too polite and calm. She was frightened.

But, she told herself, this wasn't any time to start swimming back to shore. Besides, the events of the evening had borne out her ideas about the escort service which had once employed Dennis Morrison.

The desk clerk at the hotel had given her a list of recommended escort services, and warned her against any which were not on the list and were, therefore, unregulated and unsupervised. There were, the desk clerk explained, plenty of legitimate escort services with which you could even trust your dear old white-haired grandmother. But some of the others——

The service Dennis Morrison had worked for had not been on the recommended list.

Of course, she could always scream. This was a well-populated street, and there would probably be a cop at the next corner. But she'd started this, and she wasn't going to give up now.

She fell heavily against Harris Lawrence's shoulder and lisped, "My frien' Josephine—everybody calls her jus' Jodie, Jodie-wodie, she told me that the young man who took her out was pretty wunnerful. Tha's why she gave me th' name an' number of your office. Tell me, d'ja ever know him? Was he a frien' of yours?"

"Who?" Harris Lawrence asked.

"My frien's frien'. Jodie's frien'. Name of—Dennis. D'ja know him?"

"Not very well," the blond young man said.

"S'too bad," Helene said. "He mussa been a wunnerful man. I think you're wunnerful, too, honey. Min' if I call you honey?"

"Not at all."

She yawned, long and loudly, and said, "Very s'eepy. Maybe I oughta go back to the hotel an' go to s'eep. Min' if I go back to the hotel 'n' go s'eep."

"Oh, you don't want to do that," Harris Lawrence said. "Why, you haven't spent all your money yet."

Tha's all righ'," she told him. "Y'can keep the rest of it."

He reached over and took her hand. His hand was cold and damp. "Have you forgotten," he said, in a bad imitation of tender confidence, "I promised to show you something *really*——" He pressed her hand.

"Oh yeah," she said, "Oh sure. Y'bet I wanna go there." She managed another giggle. "Joe would murder me!"

"But you've got to keep quiet about it," he said. "If the escort bureau knew I was taking anybody there, I'd lose my job."

She wondered where he was taking her. She pretended to muffle a coloratura hiccup and said, "I think you're cute."

"I think you're cute too," he said grudgingly.

"Where're we going, honey?" she said. "Sure you don' min' if I call you honey?"

He said, "Well, it's a kind of night club."

It turned out to be a cross between a fifth-rate speak left over from 1929 and an Elks' Smoker. There was a great show of secrecy, and a great to-do about being admitted. Inside, there were a stuffy, smoke-filled room, a dozen untidy tables, a few drunken customers, and a bored-looking waiter who consented to bring Helene a glass of alleged Scotch, tasting faintly like sweet varnish. Three tired colored boys were creating a terrific din with a piano, a guitar, and a bass fiddle. On the tiny platform that pretended to be a stage, a rather chubby girl, dressed in one adroitly placed oak leaf and a carelessly applied coat of body paint, was inexpertly dancing something that might have been a hula.

"Oh," Helene gasped. "If Joe's mother could see *this*! She's terribly strict, you know. And Joe would just die. I mean, absolutely die." She remembered to hiccup again, and prattled on, "Joe thinks I'm spending the evening with a girl frien', but I don' have any girl frien's in N'York, y'know what I mean?" She pretended to avert her eyes from the platform, and said, "I'm kinda scared, honey. Maybe I'd better g'wan home. I d'want to get in any trouble."

"You don't want to go home now," Harris Lawrence said, with an unsuccessful attempt at warmth. "Why, the show's just starting."

She combined the giggle and the hiccup this time, and said, "Well, if you say so, honey."

He patted her hand all the way up to the elbow, with disinterested fingers, and said, "Pardon me just a minute, beautiful."

He didn't go toward the men's room, he walked over to the bored waiter and spoke a few, quick, low-toned sentences. Helene poured the glass of imitation Scotch under the table. How could she get out of this place, if she had to? Again she felt a moment of almost pure panic. If only Jake were here! If only she were anywhere else in the world, and with Jake! Maybe she could get out of here, if she pretended to be going to the ladies' room.

Harris Lawrence came back and sat down beside her. She looked at him anxiously and said, "Oughta go home. Oughta go home ri' now."

"Oh, you want to see the rest of the show," he said. "You won't see anything like this anywhere else."

There were exactly fourteen other customers in the

place. Helene wondered how many of them were legitimate. There were four giggling, intoxicated, middle-aged, expensively dressed women at one table. There were three glassy-eyed men at another table. There was a party of four in one corner, two men and two girls, none of them paying any attention to the chubby dancer. There was a hard-faced man sitting alone at a table near by, and two more hard-faced men at a table near the door.

The waiter unobtrusively whispered to the party of four. A moment later they left, just as unobtrusively.

"I hope you're enjoying the show," Harris Lawrence said.

"S'wunnerful," Helene assured him. "Jus' wunnerful. Only, oughta go home."

The music came to a long drum roll, the chubby girl whirled around, vanished between the dingy green curtains, and returned without the oak leaf. Two of the glassy-eyed men applauded, not very loudly.

Helene wondered how the trick was going to be worked. A fake holdup, or a fake raid? Or maybe the old gag of a furious wife bursting in with a six-shooter.

The colored piano player took a drag on his cigarette and put it out. The music suddenly hit a new high, as far as sound volume was concerned. From behind the dingy curtains, a thin, brown-haired man darted, dressed in a minute scrap of imitation leopard skin. The middle-aged women put down their drinks and began to watch the show. The chubby girl fell to the floor, posing like an ungraceful Eve. One of the hard-faced men nodded to the waiter, who stepped out into the anteroom. The thin, brown-haired man dodged behind the dingy curtains, came back without the leopard skin, and struck a pose. One of the middle-aged women gave a little scream. Then there was a shrill whistle from the front, and the lights went out.

Harris Lawrence grasped Helene's arm, right. "Come with me," he whispered. "This is a raid."

She let him lead her through the dark room. It was more than a fake raid, she reflected. There had been a sudden white flare that could only have come from a flash bulb just as the lights went out; the camera, she guessed, must have been aimed to take in the party of middle-aged and expensively dressed women, and the Adam-and-Eve scene on the stage.

"Don't worry, I'll hide you," he said. "Just stay there and keep quiet." He thrust her into a dark closet and shut the door.

She stood there, listening for sounds outside. There were none. The freezing fear began to come back. She wished that Jake were here. It seemed like a very long time before the door opened again. There was the blond young man, and, beside him, one of the hard-faced men.

"This is a friend of mine," Harris Lawrence said. "He can get you out of this."

Helene whimpered (softly, though) and said, "Wanna go home."

"Shut up and mind me," the man said, "and you'll get home." His voice changed suddenly. He said very smoothly and persuasively, "You don't want your husband to know there's been any trouble."

"Oh, no, no, no," Helene said.

"I can fix it with the cops," he said. "Have you any money?"

She shook here head and burst into tears.

Harris said, "She's such a nice lady, I don't want

to see her picked up in a raid. Only I haven't any money with me."

Helene sobbed, and said, "Maybe they'd take my jewelry."

"She has copies," Harris Lawrence said quickly.

"That's right," Helene said. "I have copies. Joe wouldn't ever find out."

"Well," the man said, "maybe——"

"Oh, please," Helene gasped. "You look so kind. Please, help me!" She stripped the bracelets off her wrists, pulled off her necklace. "Joe would kill me, if he found out!" She snatched off her earrings, and dumped the whole lot in the hard-faced man's hands. "Jus' get me outa here. I wanna go home, I wanna go home!"

"Jeez, where do you find them!" the hard-faced man murmured to Harris Lawrence.

She whimpered, "Wanna g'home." She managed another hiccup, not coloratura this time, but almost baritone. "I don't feel so good." Then she burped, as loudly as she could.

"You'd better get her out of here," the hard-faced man said.

Harris Lawrence nodded and said, "Oke. Shall I call Louie?"

"Hell no," the hard-faced man said. "Go out and hail a legitimate cab. They may be looking for her when she gets back."

"I think you're cute too," Helene burbled to the hard-faced man. "Min' if I call you honey?" She burped again, louder this time and said, "Feel sick."

"For Chrissake," the hard-faced man called, "hurry up with that cab."

"O. K., O. K.," Harris Lawrence called back, from half-way down the stairs.

If they thought she might remember where she'd been, they would send someone with her in that cab. She didn't want that to happen.

She fell over a shadow on the carpet, and sprawled against the hard-faced man, who pulled her to her feet.

"Wanna take my clothes off," she giggled thickly. "Wanna take all my clothes off, righ' now." She moved a vague hand toward her shoulder strap.

"You want to go home," he said. "Remember? Home?"

"Whose home?" she said. She reached for the other shoulder strap.

He caught her hand and slapped it. She threw her arms around his neck and began crying noisily. She broke off in the middle of a sob and said, "Feel bad. Ri' here," and put a hand on her stomach.

He supported her with one arm and yelled down the stairs, "Hurry up with that cab!"

"O. K., it's here," Harris Lawrence's voice called back.

"Do wanna go home," Helene hiccuped.

He picked her up, carried her down the stairs, and dumped her into Harris Lawrence's arms.

"Are you sure it's safe?" Harris Lawrence said.

"Hell yes," the hard-faced man said. "Right now, she wouldn't remember the Johnstown Flood."

"Do wanna go home," Helene said in a childlike voice. "Pu' me down, ri' away." She struggled a little. "Pu' me down, I tallya. Wanna 'frow up, ri' away."

"*Put her in that cab*," the hard-faced man said, "*quick. Get her out of here!*"

Harris Lawrence didn't put her in the cab; he threw her in. He slammed the door and said, "Take her to the St. Jacques. The doorman will pay you."

The cab shot down the street. Helene sat up and took a long breath of fresh, clean air. She lit a cigarette.

"Never mind that St. Jacques business," she told the driver. "Just take me around the block."

The driver slammed on his brakes in surprise, nearly throwing her to the floor. "Howzat?"

"I said, take me around the block," Helene told him, "and slowly."

The cab moved about a hundred feet, then the driver said, "But, lady, you looked——" His voice broke off.

"Do I look that way now?" Helene said serenely.

"Well——" He looked back over his shoulder. "Well, no."

Suddenly she realized how much afraid she'd been. The blond young man who'd called himself Harris Lawrence, the hard-faced man, the dingy room, the feeling of being entirely on her own. She was still afraid. Even the shadows cast by the street lamps were dark and menacing.

"Turn the corner," she said. Then, sharply, "No, to the right."

A broad red face looked back at her from the driver's compartment. "Are you gonna tell me how to drive? Nobody can make nothing but a right turn at that corner." His face matched the picture in the driver's card. Stanley Sczinsky. "You're sure you feel O. K., ma'am?"

"I feel fine," Helene said, slowly releasing her fingernails from the palms of her hands. She threw away her cigarette and lit a new one, to prove to herself that she wasn't really trembling. "Just drive around the block, and don't go too fast. How are you at following people, Mr. Sczinsky?"

"Just call me Stan," the driver said. "And I could follow a herring down Forty-fourth Street." He slowed down, looked over his shoulder again, and said, "Lady, you aren't one of those G-men, are you?"

Helene straightened the gold-spangled scarf and said,

"Not me." It was an almost unendurable temptation to say, "Take me to the St. Jacques." She'd be safe, and warm, and comfortable. But no, she'd started this, she had to see it through. "Take it easy around this next corner, Stan, turn off your lights, and slide up to the curb."

"Whatever you say, lady," Stan said.

People like Harris Lawrence and the hard-faced man didn't let a lapful of diamond jewelry just lie around loose. The hard-faced man had said, "I'll take care of the stuff," and Harris Lawrence had said, "Not unless I'm with you." They'd had to do some nice, fast work, taking in a discontented young wife who was leaving town tomorrow. Now they'd do some equally fast work, cashing in on her jewelry.

The street was dark and quiet. They parked against the curb, turned off the lights, and watched. Stanley Sczinsky turned around and said, "Lady, you know you have to pay for waiting time."

"Don't worry, I will," Helene said. "If I have to wait all night."

But it was only a few minutes before two men came out of the dingy, unlighted building. Even from across the street and halfway down the block, she could recognize them. The hard-faced man. The hennaed hair of Harris Lawrence.

"Hold everything, Stan," Helene whispered. "Here we go."

The two men got into a waiting black sedan and drove south. The cab followed discreetly, a block behind.

"I dunno what you're up to, lady," Stan said as they crossed Forty-second Street, "but I'm glad to help."

Was there another car following? She couldn't be sure. The street was dark and deserted, but there was a pair of headlights that seemed to keep about a block behind. Well, that was a risk she had to take.

The car ahead stopped in front of an underlighted pawnshop. Helene said, "Pssst!" The cab passed the pawnshop, Stan switched off the lights and slid silently up to the curb half a block beyond. The car behind slowed down and turned the next corner.

Helene, said, "Wait for me," and stepped out. Stan said, "Don't you want I should come with you, lady?" and she shook her head. No use involving anyone else in this.

She wanted a look through the windows of that pawnshop. She wanted to memorize its location, and the face of the man behind the counter.

Were there steps behind her, on the sidewalk? She wasn't sure. She paused a moment, listening. Yes, there had been steps. They'd paused when she paused. Maybe she ought to turn back and run, maybe she ought to yell for Stan. No good. To turn back would be to confront whoever was following and Stan was out of earshot by now. There was no way to go but ahead.

Her limbs were stiff with terror as she walked on. Only one light showed in the entire block, the window of the pawnshop where Harris Lawrence and the hard-faced man had gone. By now, they must have discovered that her diamonds had come from the Forty-second Street Woolworth's. She couldn't go on, someone was coming down the walk toward her, someone who'd got out of the black sedan. She couldn't turn back; the footsteps were right behind her now. She couldn't scream for help, because her throat was frozen shut with fear.

A car crept up the street and slowed to a stop beside her. She turned quickly and went into the pawnshop.

New horrors might be waiting for her there, but at least it was lighted.

A gray-haired hunchback was behind the counter, facing Harrison Lawrence and the hard-faced man. There was a tray in front of him, glittering red and green and white. He moved the tray and lights flashed from it, and he said, "I got gypped on this stuff from the Morrison dame, and now I'm damned if I'll even look——"

The door creaked. Harris Lawrence and the hard-faced man spun around; their faces grew long with surprise. The hard-faced man said, "It's a trap——"

Helene thrust her hands deeper in the pocket of her evening coat and said, "If anybody moves, I'll shoot." She hoped her voice didn't sound as trembling as it felt. There was an answer to that line, she remembered it from a long-ago vaudeville act. "And if anybody shoots, I'll move." She didn't say it out loud.

The footsteps had stopped just outside the door, then they'd begun again, coming in. The three men in the pawnshop moved a step toward her, then stopped.

She hoped Jake wouldn't be too sorry. She hoped he'd marry again, and have a happy life.

The blond young man turned white, and gave a little cry.

A voice behind her said, "Duck, Mrs. Justus."

A shot whistled past her cheek. A hand struck her on the back of the neck, throwing her to the floor. There was another shot, and she saw the hard-faced man collapse. The gray-haired hunchback ran toward a rear door, a shadowy figure hurtled past her, dived at him, and brought him down. Harris Lawrence stood in the farthest corner, screaming.

Someone came running in the door. It was Stan. He was saying, "I heard shots. Is the lady all right?"

"She's all right," someone said.

Helene looked up. Her face hurt, where she'd hit the floor. The green chiffon dress had been badly torn. Oh, well, she hadn't liked it very much, anyway. She looked up into the anxious face of O'Brien.

"Are you O. K., Mrs. Justus?" he asked anxiously.

Helene nodded and struggled to her feet. Something had happened to her knees. They seemed to have liquefied.

"Peterson said we should keep an eye on you," O'Brien said. There was a note of apology in his voice. "I hope you *are* O. K. Because he'll raise hell if you aren't."

"I feel wonderful," Helene gasped. She pointed a shaking hand toward the tray and said, "Jewels. Bertha Morrison's. He said so."

The gray-haired hunchback shrieked, "I didn't know they were hers. I didn't know anything. I'm an honest businessman trying to make a living. I didn't know anything. I'm an honest businessman——"

No one paid any attention to him. A man who'd come in with O'Brien said, "By God, they are Bertha Morrison's. I saw a picture of that clasp."

Stan supported Helene with one arm, pulled a half-pint flask from his pocket, and poured cheap whisky between her chattering teeth. The cold began to recede from her bones. "You'll be all right, lady," he assured her.

The man who'd come in with O'Brien picked up Helene's necklace and bracelets and said, "Are these yours?"

Helene nodded. "But they can keep them. They came from the Woolworth's on Forty-second Street."

Harris Lawrence stopped screaming and began to laugh hysterically. O'Brien took his hand off Helene's arm and said, "Come out of that corner, you. Before I drag you out."

The other cop prodded the blond young man into the middle of the room and under the lights. Then he beamed unpleasantly and said, "Well, as I live and breathe! Howie Lutts!"

Chapter Twenty-Five

"STOP WORRYING," Malone said to Jake. "She's all right. nothing's happened to her." He gave up trying to light a cigar.

"Of course she's all right," Jake said. He managed to make his teeth stop playing the Habañera from *Carmen.* "Just because they called from police headquarters——"

Malone made another try with the cigar, almost setting the taxi on fire. He tried to think of something helpful to say to Jake and finally fell back on, "Stop worrying."

"Me worry?" Jake said. His teeth finally settled down to a slow samba. "Helene's all right. Nothing could happen to Helene. She could look after herself anywhere." He drew in a quick breath and said, "You stop worrying."

"Who's worrying?" Malone said. He threw the cigar out the window and put the burnt match back in his pocket. Then he leaned forward and said to the cab driver, "For the love of Mike, step on it!"

The cab driver said, "Don't worry."

Conversation lagged.

Helene had been murdered. Helene had been kidnaped. Helene had been arrested for something.

The cab drove up in front of police headquarters. Jake was out before it stopped and flung a bill at the cab driver. The elevator inside the building moved slowly, and Malone said, "Hurry *up*, damn you."

There hadn't been any information in the telephone call. Simply, "Are you the husband of Mrs. Helene Justus? Will you please come down to police headquarters, right away?"

Helene had been in a traffic accident. Helene had been robbed. Helene had been raped.

It was a hell of a long way from the elevator to Arthur Peterson's office.

Helene had been run over by a subway train. Helene had fallen out of a window. Helene had been trapped in a burning building. Helene had——

Helene was sitting in the most comfortable chair in Arthur Peterson's office, looking beautiful and serene. She was saying, "It really was just an accident. I didn't have any idea that Bertha Morrison's jewels—I mean, it just happened that Mr. Justus had to be out on business this evening, and I didn't want to stay home alone, so I called up this escort bureau. And then——" She turned her head, her eyes grew wide and bright, and she said, "Oh, *Jake*!"

He saw then that there was a bruise on her cheek, that her dress was soiled and torn. He walked over to her fast and put his arms around her. She was trembling a little, and she buried her face against his chest. He held her very close, pressing his cheek against her soft hair. It didn't matter, right now, that the room was full of plain-clothes men. It didn't matter that a sleepy-eyed

Arthur Peterson was watching from behind his desk. Only one thing mattered. Helene was here, and safe, and in his arms.

Arthur Peterson cleared his throat, loudly. Jake looked up. What was this about Bertha Morrison's jewels? What had Helene been up to this time? Had Arthur Peterson given away any secrets? Arthur Peterson's eyes told Jake that he hadn't, and that he wouldn't. Jake relaxed. He stood up, glared at Helene, and said, "I ought to give you a good punch in the nose."

"Mrs. Justus has been a very great help," Arthur Peterson said coldly. "She's a brave little woman."

A big blond bruiser, handcuffed to O'Brien, snorted and said a very rude word. O'Brien slapped him across the mouth with his free hand.

A little gray-haired hunchback, who'd been weeping silently into a big handkerchief, looked up and said, "I'm an honest businessman just trying to make a living. I didn't know it was stolen jewelry."

A hard-faced man, wrapped in a gray police blanket, and with one arm bandaged, said, "Honest businessman——"

"You shut up, too," O'Brien said.

Malone managed to get his cigar lighted, and said, "Would somebody mind telling me what goes on here? I missed the first few reels."

A red-faced man in a cab driver's uniform said, "I dunno who you are, Mac, but believe me, if you know this lady you oughta be proud."

"Single-handed," O'Brien said, almost reverently. "Single-handed, she trapped this whole bunch of crooks."

The gray-haired hunchback wailed, "I'm no crook. I got a family. I got to make a living."

Arthur Peterson repeated, this time to Malone, "Mrs. Justus has been a very great help."

"I didn't mean to be a help," Helene said. "Honest." She looked at him appealingly. "I told you. Mr. Justus had to be out on business. Mr. Malone was busy. I didn't want to stay home alone all evening, so I thought it might be fun to call up an escort bureau. I remembered Dennis Morrison had mentioned he once worked for one, and I called it up, that's all." She reflected that the police already knew Dennis Morrison's life history, she wasn't giving anything away. "Honestly, that was all. Then I began to get a sort of funny feeling. Like, well, something was wrong. I can't explain it, really. It was a sort of hunch."

"Intuition," Arthur Peterson said admiringly.

"So I thought it might be fun to play along and see what the racket was. And I did. And they got me to this place and pretended there was a raid. I knew it wasn't a real raid because of the flashlight going off."

Arthur Peterson looked up and said quickly, "Did you pick up those four women?"

"We sent 'em home," a plain-clothes man said, "and we got the picture and destroyed it." He added, "One of 'em's the sister-in-law of a councilman."

"Oh," Peterson said. "Well, there's no use dragging innocent victims into this." He smiled at Helene and said, "Go on, Mrs. Justus."

"That's about all," Helene said limpidly. "I was curious to know what they were going to do with my jewelry, so Mr. Sczinsky and I followed them."

"Just call me Stan," the cab driver said modestly.

"And you know the rest," Helene finished. She beamed up at O'Brien and said, "It's so lucky you were there."

Jake looked at Helene, at O'Brien, and at Peterson. He said, "What the hell was the idea of having my wife followed?"

"And having me followed?" Malone added. He looked almost agreeably at Schultz, who'd come in just behind him, and said, "Not that it didn't turn out to be a good idea."

"Well, to be frank," Arthur Peterson said, "I felt a little uneasy about all three of you. You know Dennis Morrison, you'd been with him the night of the murder. I thought it might be a good idea to keep all of you in sight." He scowled and said, "I don't know what's happened to Birnbaum." He changed the subject quickly. "This is a pure and simple extortion case. It really shouldn't come into this department. This overlapping of cases from one department to another impairs efficiency. But in view of the fact that those were Bertha Morrison's jewels, and that this young man is Bertha Morrison's cousin——"

Malone wheeled around to look at Howie Lutts. He was the one Abner Proudfoot had described. *It had once been planned that she would marry Howard when she attained her maturity, but for some reason the match never came off. Howard can be a rather difficult individual.* He didn't look like a very difficult individual right now. He looked like a rabbit.

"Listen," Howie Lutts said hoarsely. "Listen to me. I haven't seen Bertha for years. I used to know her when we were kids, but she was always a pain in the neck to me. And you know I was working the night she was bumped off. You know that."

"We've checked his alibi," a plain-clothes man said. "It's O. K. He took a Mrs. Carl Browne, from Kansas City, to dinner at the Rainbow Room, and to a series of night clubs. They ended up in a hotel on Amsterdam Avenue, where a babe, pretending to be his wife, broke in, raised a rumpus, and Mrs. Browne paid her off. We've got the babe locked up, Mr. Browne has heard the whole story and he's being very nice about it, and Mrs. Browne is filing a complaint against this guy."

"O. K.," Howie said. "You hear that? Maybe you got me for extortion, but you ain't got me for murder. And I'll get a good lawyer, I'll get a light sentence. I'm young yet." There was a half sob in his voice. "It ain't my fault. I never knew what it was all about. He got me into it." He jerked his head toward the hard-faced man. "He's the guy you ought to send up, not me."

The hard-faced man spat on the floor, and said, "You're a lying son-of-a-bitch. I was trying to run a nice quiet little night club——"

The gray-haired man howled out something about being an honest businessman.

Arthur Peterson cut short the uproar by pounding on his desk. Then he said, "*Keep quiet!* All this is in another department." He looked coldly at Howie Lutts and said, "Did you introduce your cousin Bertha to Dennis Morrison?"

Howie shook his head and whimpered, "I never knew he even knew her. I never knew him, neither. Not well, I mean. He was just another guy who worked for Al."

Al, the hard-faced man, looked up and said, quickly and smoothly, "Dennis Morrison did work for me. Sure, I run an escort bureau. It was a little side line of mine. I'm in the entertainment business, and I like to see people have a good time. There's a lot of lonely people in the world, and the escort bureau paired them up. It wasn't licensed or supervised because my competitors bribed the authorities, they were trying to run me out of business. Naturally, I couldn't control the activities of the people who worked for me. But the bureau was perfectly legitimate. It's resulted in some very happy marriages. But in every business like mine a few crooks get in, who take advantage of their opportunities. Like this young man. But I'm not responsible. I can prove I'm in the clear. I've got a good lawyer." He drew in his breath. "As far as Dennis Morrison is concerned, he was with me for a little while, and then left, about a year ago. I haven't seen or heard from him since."

Malone hoped he did have a good lawyer. He was sure as hell going to need a lot of coaching before he got on a witness stand.

"By the way," Jake said quietly. "Where *is* Dennis Morrison? I should think he'd be rather helpful right now."

Arthur Peterson said, "We're looking for him." The tone of his voice said, "And don't ask any more questions."

Jake pretended he hadn't noticed the tone of voice, and said, "How about Bertha Morrison's jewelry?"

O'Brien said, "Yeah, how about that, Mr. Prince?"

The gray-haired man looked up from his handkerchief. "Understand," he said. "I'm an honest businessman. I try to make a living for my family. My wife, she has to have operations, my daughters, they're in school yet, my son, he's out of college, he can't find a job, my wife's mother, she lives with us. I try to make them a living. Rent I have to pay, taxes I have to pay, the pawnbroker license I have to pay. Donations to the police benefits I still have to pay. Understand? But I'm an honest businessman, I pay the rent, I pay the taxes, I pay the license, I give to the police. So if somebody brings in a piece of jewelry he should pawn, am I asking questions?"

O'Brien scowled and said, "When these crooks thought they had a bunch of hot ice to dispose of, they brought it straight to you. How do you explain that?"

The gray-haired man smiled and said, "All right. So I'm open evenings."

Malone said, thinking out loud, "The guys in this fake escort racket disposed of their stuff through this fence. Dennis Morrison had worked for the outfit. If he had any jewels to dispose of——"

"Don't be silly, Malone," Helene said.

She was ignored. Arthur Peterson shoved a picture of Dennis Morrison toward the gray-haired man and said, "Who's this?"

Mr. Prince studied the picture, shrugged his shoulders, and looked apologetic. "I see so many people——"

"How did you get hold of Bertha Morrison's jewelry?" O'Brien demanded.

"Why, I bought it," Mr. Prince said. "Understand? I told you, I don't ask questions. Am I to know where the jewelry came from? Am I to know a young lady has been murdered? The jewelry is offered to me for sale and I buy it for a good price, maybe even I cheat myself a little. Then when I see the picture in the papers, should I go running to the police? Will that bring the poor girl back to life again?"

"*Girl?*" Arthur Peterson said.

Malone said, "What girl?"

"Why," Mr. Prince said, "she sold me the jewelry. Poor girl, she was so young. You know who I mean. Gloria Garden." He looked up, smiled, and said, "Understand?"

There was a little silence. Then Arthur Peterson said, "Gloria Garden sold you that jewelry?"

Mr. Prince smiled again, and said, "Who else?"

"Why didn't you tell me this in the first place?" Arthur Peterson demanded. His voice was a trifle hoarse.

Mr. Prince shrugged his shoulders. "Did anyone ask me?"

A barrage of questions brought out the rest of the facts. Gloria Garden had appeared in Mr. Prince's establishment about eleven o'clock on the night of the murder. She'd had on a black dress, studded with gold nailheads, and a tan polo coat. Jake remembered the dress and the polo coat; they'd been hanging in Gloria Garden's closet. There hadn't been any bloodstains on them.

She'd explained to Mr. Prince that her mother in Terre Haute, Indiana, was very ill. She had to fly there, immediately. She'd have to hire a very expensive specialist. So he, Mr. Prince, had bought the jewelry. Should he ask questions? Poor girl, and so young and pretty. Was he to know she was going to be murdered? Maybe it was for the money he'd given her, nine hundred dollars, and he'd cheated himself. Nine hundred dollars was a lot of money. People had been murdered for a lot less.

He might have seen Dennis Morrison sometime, he might not. Maybe yes, and then again, maybe no. He saw so many people, he couldn't swear to it, and he was an honest man, he wouldn't want to perjure himself. The girl, though, yes. He remembered her very well. So pretty. So young. Too young and too pretty to be murdered.

Nothing could shake his story. Probably, Malone thought, because it was the truth. He could tell that Arthur Peterson believed it, too.

Al? Mr. Prince wasn't sure. He might have seen him before, he might not. The same was true of Howie Lutts. Maybe he'd come in the store, maybe he hadn't. He, Mr. Prince, couldn't swear to one or the other.

Could he investigate everybody who came in the shop to pawn a dollar watch? If a young man came in to sell a necklace left him by his grandmother, could he, Mr. Prince, take time out to read the grandmother's will? He tried to be an honest businessman, but he had to make a living, didn't he? If a customer said his name was Smith, should he, Mr. Prince, ask for a birth certificate?

Yes, he did have the receipt for the money, signed by the young lady. He located it among a fat bunch of papers in his wallet and handed it to Arthur Peterson.

Jake edged over to Peterson's desk, looking over his shoulder. It was a standard form, dated April 8, 1943. *Received of Mr. Harry Prince, the sum of $900 for merchandise——*

It was written with an indelible pencil, it was signed in violet ink, Mary Brown. There might be a lot of girls who used violet ink, Jake reflected, but that delicate, angular handwriting had belonged to Gloria Garden. He was no handwriting expert, but he'd been reading her letters all evening, and he knew.

"Frankly," Malone said to Arthur Peterson, "I don't think you can pin a thing on this guy."

Mr. Prince looked happily at the little lawyer and said, "Believe me, I'm an honest businessman——"

Arthur Peterson called in someone from another department. It turned out that Malone was right. There were no charges against little Mr. Prince. He'd bought jewelry that had belonged to a murdered woman. He'd bought them from a woman who'd been murdered shortly after the transaction. But he'd bought them, paid for them, and made out a receipt to sign, all in good faith. He was in the clear.

The hard-faced man, Al, said he didn't know Mr. Prince from a hole in the ground, and how soon could he call up his lawyer?

Howie Lutts, looking white and scared, said that maybe he'd hocked his watch once at Mr. Prince's establishment, but he couldn't be sure.

"None of this is in my department," Arthur Peterson said. "I'm only concerned with evidence bearing on the murder. However"—he beamed at Helene—"if you wish to prefer charges against this man——"

It turned out that Helene couldn't, even if she'd wished to. She'd seen Al offering her dime-store diamonds for sale to Mr. Prince, but she hadn't seen Mr. Prince offering to buy them.

The honest businessman wanted to go home. He reiterated his evidence regarding Bertha Morrison's jewelry to a police stenographer, and signed it. There was a little difficulty over the matter of the jewelry itself. Mr. Prince wanted either the jewelry—impounded as evidence in a homicide case—or his money, which had last been seen stuffed into Gloria Garden's purse. He finally settled for a receipt made out and signed by Arthur Peterson, and left in the company of a plain-clothes man, threatening suit.

The hard-faced man and Howie Lutts answered more questions, willingly, but not very satisfactorily. Howie Lutts hadn't seen Bertha, his cousin, for years. He hadn't even known she was married. Al, the hard-faced man, had never seen her in his life. Never knew there was such a dame till he read about her in the papers. Neither of them remembered anything helpful about Dennis Morrison. Al repeated that Dennis had worked for the escort bureau at one time but had left about a year ago. Howie Lutts repeated that he'd met Dennis Morrison a few times, but hadn't known him very well.

Malone, chewing savagely on his cigar, reflected that Howie Lutts and Al were probably telling the truth. Particularly Howie, with his scared eyes, and his police record. Howie would have talked, if he'd known anything to talk about.

Arthur Peterson muttered something about efficiency and the need for departmental reorganization, and sent Howie Lutts and Al away, in charge of a policeman from another department.

Jake yawned, and muttered something about going home.

Arthur Peterson yawned, and said it was a good idea.

Birnbaum turned up, looking pale and worried. Seemed he'd dropped into the drugstore for a bottle of soda mints, and missed Jake's exit from the hotel. Arthur Peterson gave him a sleepy lecture and sent him home. O'Brien and Schultz had already gone off duty, with starry-eyed farewells to Helene.

Malone looked at his watch and observed that it was late.

Helene rubbed her eyes and said that she was tired, very tired.

Stan Sczinsky said happily that his cab was parked right outside.

The meeting adjourned.

In the elevator, Jake put his arm around Helene. She drooped her head against his shoulder, like a sleepy child. He tightened his arm, and brushed his lips lightly against the tip of her ear. In just a little while now, they'd be home. Maybe then, he'd tell her——

They had to wait, downstairs, until Stan Szcinsky brought his cab up to the door. A young man came racing down the hall, calling, "Hey wait, Mr. Peterson!" Jake told himself not to listen. Home. Helene. He listened, anyway.

The young man had a teletype message in his hand. He was out of breath. He said, "Gee, glad I caught you, Mr. Peterson. They identified that guy in the hospital. The attempted murder case."

Arthur Peterson frowned. "I don't know anything about any attempted murder case." He took the teletype message and said, "That's in another department, anyway."

"Not now it ain't," the young man said. "Because they finally got the victim identified." He paused, caught his breath, and said, "He's still alive, Mr. Peterson, so you'd better hurry over there." He paused again, panting. "I hadn't ought to run up these stairs so fast. He sure as hell is in your department, Mr. Peterson. Because he's the husband of that babe." He finally got his breath and said, "You know. Dennis Morrison."

Chapter Twenty-Six

"Luckily, it was only a superficial wound," the tired-eyed doctor said, "and very little water entered the lungs. The patient could have gone home several hours ago, except that he is suffering from shock."

Malone remarked that every time someone tried to murder him, he suffered from shock, too.

The doctor managed a laugh, a feeble one, but still pretty good for that hour in the morning. "He'll be able to go home tomorrow, unless you want us to hold him, Mr. Peterson."

Arthur Peterson said coldly, "I don't know what we could hold him for."

"Except being a damned fool," the doctor said.

"How is he, doc?" Malone said. "I'm his lawyer."

"He's sleeping," the doctor said, "peacefully."

"You ought to have let us know before," Arthur Peterson said to the doctor.

"We didn't know who he was," the doctor told him. "He was brought in about half-past six or seven. There wasn't any identification on him. We made a routine report, unidentified man. Assault with attempt to kill. You should have gotten the report."

"Attempt to kill isn't in my department," Arthur Peterson said. "Neither is identification."

"Well, anyway," the doctor said, "when I came back on duty about an hour ago, there was a new assistant here. He'd seen Morrison's picture in the papers and he recognized him. We checked, and it was him, all right. He came to finally and told us who he was."

"But what had *happened* to him?" Helene demanded.

"Why, some guy tried to kill him," the doctor said mildly. "He was standing on the edge of the platform at South Ferry, waiting to take the boat. It was rush hour, and there was a crowd. Somebody standing behind him stuck a knife in his back. Lucky, right that minute the ferry bumped hard against the slip. It was just enough to jar the knife to one side. Gave him a nasty cut under the arm, but nothing serious. Then this guy gave him a shove and he fell into the water. Good thing the ferry had gotten stalled against the slip or he'd have been smashed when it came in. Somebody dived in and pulled him out. That's all." He lit his pipe. "There wasn't any arrest. The guy got away in the crowd and the excitement."

Malone started to ask a question and stopped himself. After all, Dennis Morrison was, in a sense, a client of his. No use making the case any harder for himself.

It turned out though that the same question had occurred to Arthur Peterson. He said, "Doctor, could he have arranged this thing himself?"

"Huh-uh," the doctor said. "Oh, sure he might have got some guy to pretend to stick a knife in him. But not to shove him into the ferry slip. Because the guy wouldn't have had any way of knowing the ferry was going to jam for a minute against the palings. And if he had been shoved into the ferry slip, and the ferry hadn't jammed there, he'd have been squashed like a——" He remembered Helene's presence, coughed, and said, "No, this was a legitimate murder attempt, all right. It couldn't have been framed." He looked sympathetically at Arthur Peterson. "I know what you mean. A guy who's suspected of murder arranges it so it looks like somebody tried to murder him. Only that wasn't it this time. Somebody sure as hell did try to murder this Morrison boy. Why, Peterson, did you have him under suspicion?"

Arthur Peterson said, "No." Just plain no.

Malone sighed. He knew exactly how Arthur Peterson felt.

Arthur Peterson thanked the doctor for his co-operation, stated that he wanted a word with Dennis Morrison before he was sent home tomorrow, and remarked again that it was late.

Stan Sczinsky was waiting outside with his taxi. It was, he explained, past time for him to turn in his hack and go home, but he'd waited to take his friends home first. He hoped he'd have the pleasure of driving them again sometime.

It was almost daylight. The sky was a dirty gray. Stan turned west on Thirty-fourth Street and drove toward Fifth. Malone glanced once out the window and decided he didn't like Thirty-fourth Street. It was dreary. Helene had curled up in Jake's arm, she looked half asleep, childlike, and happy. The cab turned into Fifth Avenue. Malone glanced out the window again. This was the street heroes and heroines rode down on the tops of busses in all the magazine stories he'd read in dentists' anterooms. He didn't like it, either. The April rain had begun to fall again, thin and drizzly and cold-looking. Malone closed his eyes and pictured Michigan Avenue, or even State Street, at this hour, rain or no rain.

He pretended he was there. The cab was going south on Michigan, crossing the bridge, stopping for a red light at Randolph Street. There was Grant Park beyond Randolph Street, and a glimpse of the lake, cold and gray now, but threatening to turn pink when the sun rose. The cab would turn west on Madison Street and stop for another light under the shadowy el. And then——

Someone shook him. Malone opened one eye and said, "Changed my mind. Just take me to Joe the Angel's City Hall Bar, up on Clark and——"

"You're in New York now," Jake said, shaking him again.

Malone blinked, stumbled out of the cab, and said, "Yeah, that's the trouble."

Jake carried Helene across the lobby, shocking the desk clerk and surprising the elevator boy. The green chiffon dress hung in ribbons, her face was dirty, and she was fast asleep.

He saw to it that Malone got off at the right floor and headed toward his room, then he took Helene home.

He bathed her face with warm water and she woke up. She said, half awake, "Dennis Morrison would have known about that pawnshop. But he couldn't have taken Bertha Morrison's jewels there. How did Gloria Garden get them? Gloria Garden couldn't have murdered her, she was murdered herself, the same way. Now, someone's tried to murder Dennis." She was half swaying with weariness.

Jake said, "Listen. Keep out of that mess, understand? It's none of your business. Stay away from Dennis Morrison, and don't go monkeying around in other people's affairs."

She stared at him, wide awake now. He looked angry; his face was pale. She said, "Don't be silly. We're involved in it already, because we picked Dennis up that night. Don't worry about me, I can take care of myself."

"You do as I say," Jake said. He looked at her. She was pale, he'd washed the make-up from her face along with the dirt, her lovely hair was disheveled, and her dress was a wreck. She was the most beautiful thing in the world. He made his voice as stern as he could. "I mean it. Stay out of that business, completely out."

She wasn't too sleepy to be angry. "It's my affair whether I stay out of it or not."

Jake said, "Damn it, Helene——"

Her eyes misted over, she gazed at him through a fog of unshed tears. Here they were quarreling, the last thing in the world she wanted to have happen, the thing she'd been trying most to avoid. Especially, right now.

Jake's throat contracted. He stopped speaking; for a moment, he almost stopped breathing. He'd only quarreled once with Helene since they'd met, he'd promised himself it would never happen again. And especially, now——

"*Jake!*" she whispered.

He picked her up and carried her into the bedroom, like a sleepy child.

Daylight slowly invaded the room. It was pleasant, sometimes, Jake thought, to go to sleep like this, by day, Helene beside him.

He felt guilty and apologetic. He should have told Helene the truth long before this. He was a louse, keeping secrets from Helene. And there were a lot of things that needed to be straightened. out. A lot of questions he wanted to ask. Helene's going out tonight. He hadn't believed for one minute that story about her being lonely and calling up the escort bureau. Any more than he'd believed Malone's story about beating up a pair of holdup men. Maybe the whole thing ought to be talked over right now. He'd tell her about his book, about everything. And then he'd ask *his* questions.

"Helene," he whispered. Helene, listen. I want to tell you——"

There was no response. He raised up on one elbow and looked at her. She was asleep.

Well, he'd tell her when she woke. He'd explain everything. He yawned. Maybe they could even pack and catch a train back to Chicago tomorrow. He yawned again. Or maybe they'd stay, and see his project through to the end. It didn't really matter, as long as Helene knew. He slept. He slept like the dead.

When he woke, she was gone. Her beige wool suit with the lynx fur was gone too, and the wide-brimmed brown felt hat. There was coffee in a thermos jug by his bed. There was a note propped up on the dresser.

Will meet you and Malone at Miss Williams' for dinner.
Have important business to attend to meanwhile.

> Love,
> Helene

Chapter Twenty-Seven

A THIN, acidulous female voice said over the telephone, "Mr. Malone?"

Malone doubled the pillow under his head, rested the phone on his bare chest, and said, "Yes."

"Mr. Proudfoot calling," the voice said. "One moment please."

Malone hung up the phone and pretended he was going back to sleep.

A minute later the phone rang again.

"Mr. Malone, this is Mr. Proudfoot's office calling," the voice said. "We were disconnected."

"We weren't disconnected," Malone growled. "I hung up, and I'll hang up every time you call. Unless you bother me too much, in which case I'll come down to your office and stick the telephone——" He caught himself just in time and said, "Down Mr. Proudfoot's throat."

He slammed down the receiver and reached for the cigar he'd providentially left on the bed table the night before. Calling a man up at this hour of the morning! He lighted the cigar and lay staring up at the ceiling, wiggling his toes under the covers. Who did Abner Proudfoot think he was, anyway? He let the phone ring for a good thirty seconds before he answered it again.

He picked up the receiver and heard a male voice saying, "Let me talk to him," and the thin female voice saying, "Yes, sir." He waited fifteen more seconds and then said, sleepily and lecherously, "H'lo, sweetheart. Z'at you? 'Member, you said you'd call me soon's you wake up——"

There was the sound of a throat being cleared noisily at the other end of the wire. Then Mr. Proudfoot said coldly, "I fear that you are mistaken, Mr. Malone. This is Abner Proudfoot calling." There was a forced pleasantness in his voice. "I trust you're feeling well this fine morning."

"I've got one foot in the grave and the other on a piano stool," Malone said. "How do you feel?" He added coyly, "I thought we weren't friends any more."

"After considering the situation," Mr. Proudfoot said, "I have reached the conclusion that I was unnecessarily hasty in my statements of last night. In short, I have re-considered my decision. To put it briefly, I sincerely

hope that you will consent to ignore the little contretemps and continue our thoroughly pleasant and satisfactory relationship as previously agreed upon."

Malone didn't answer for a minute. He wanted to tell
Mr. Proudfoot to go jump in a tree. Or did he mean,
go climb a lake? On the other hand—there was a poten-
tial $4500 he still might collect, with any reasonable luck.
and besides——

Something must have happened between last night
and this morning to change Mr. Proudfoot's mind. Malone was curious.

The silence seemed to worry Mr. Proudfoot. He said,
"I greatly regret any little unpleasantness which may have
occurred during our conversation, and I trust that you
will accept my apologies. May I have the pleasure of
conferring with you at my office this morning? There
will be a young lady present who may be able to give
you information of great interest and considerable value."

"O. K., pal, I'll be there," Malone said. "Name the
time and place."

He looked regretfully at the clock as he hung up the
phone. Oh, well, he'd had four hours' sleep. That was better than nothing. He picked up the phone again, called
room service, and said, "Bring me a Spanish omelet, a
double order of French fried potatoes, a piece of lemon-
meringue pie, a pot of coffee, and a pint of bourbon."

By the time he got into his taxi, he was shaved,
bathed, fed, and felt like a new man.

He wondered who the young lady could be, and about
the interesting and valuable information. He wished it
could be the chubby blonde he'd seen at Abner Proudfoot's, and that the information might be her telephone
number. Only he knew, of course, that it wouldn't be.
He'd have to find his own girls.

The little lawyer sighed and lit his after-breakfast cigar. He reminded himself that this was his first—and last—trip to New York, and that he ought to look around a little. This taxi ride might also serve as a sight-seeing tour. He leaned forward as the cab turned into Fifth Avenue and said, "Do we go by any historic spots on the way?" He added, "I'm a stranger in town."

"We go by Rockefeller Center in a minute," the driver said. "And if you're here for a visit, you sure oughta take time out and go to the Bronx Zoo. Them lions is really sumpin'! Only take my tip and don't go there on a sunny day, because on a sunny day all them lions do is lie around and purr."

"I've seen Rockefeller Center," Malone said, "and I'm allergic to lions." He leaned back and looked out the window.

Fifth Avenue didn't impress him any more than it had just before dawn. There was the Public Library. Well, personally, he liked the Art Institute of Chicago better. What he could see of the Empire State Building left him cold. It couldn't hold a candle to the Wrigley Building, especially at night when it was all lit up like an octogenarian's birthday cake.

"That's the tallest building in the world," the cab driver volunteered.

"It don't look tall from here," Malone said coldly. "Looks like an old two-story false front." All right, the Empire State Building was tall. So what? Just proved New York builders didn't know when to stop at a good story. The phrase pleased him, he repeated it to himself and flicked his cigar ashes out the cab window.

Madison Square looked like any other dingy and cluttered little city park. What's more, he would have bet heavily that there were more bums per square foot back in Bughouse Square in Chicago.

He looked critically at the Flatiron Building. It did look substantial, but not as substantial as the Monadnock Block, and besides, it needed a good scrubbing. The only thing to recommend it was its shape, and that was not any tribute; rather it was a reflection on the inefficient layout of New York's streets. And even so, didn't Chicago have the narrowest building for its height anywhere in the world?

The cab turned into Broadway, passed Union Square, and crossed Fourteenth Street. The cab driver pointed out the City Hall. Malone observed that it wasn't as big as the Chicago City Hall. He looked at his watch and found he was early for his appointment, when he got out of the cab. He didn't want to be early. In fact, he'd decided to keep Abner Proudfoot waiting a few minutes. Well, he could always stroll around a little. After all, he might never be here again.

Wall Street didn't impress him, nor did the Subtreasury Building, nor the House of Morgan. The streets were too narrow. The city of New York had been laid out very carelessly and very badly, amateurishly, in fact. Now the Chicago Loop, on the other hand——

He walked down to Bowling Green and back, still unimpressed. This was historic ground on which he trod. All right, Chicago had history, too. Maybe it hadn't gone on for so long a time, but there'd been more of it. Hadn't anybody here ever heard of Father Dearborn, and the Haymarket Riot, and Abraham Lincoln, and the Iroquois Fire, and the Century of Progress Exposition, and Al Capone?

Malone had worked up a righteous wrath by the

time he got back to Trinity Churchyard. History! History——!

And who was Abner Proudfoot, to push him around?

He was fifteen minutes late by the time he got in the elevator, and he was glad of it. Abner Proudfoot would probably tell him that Procrastination was the Thief of Time. He had a few things to tell Abner Proudfoot, too.

The offices of Proudfoot, Schwartz, Van Alstine, and Proudfoot were impressive, at first glance. Nice paneling, fine old prints, leather upholstery. But the leather upholstery was slightly frazzled at the corners, and the pimply-faced girl at the switchboard didn't look like an experienced PBX operator, rather like a business school student working out an unpaid tuition fee.

He expected to be kept waiting, with the leather-upholstered chair and a 1938 copy of *Life* magazine. But the girl said, "Y'can go right in. Second door to yer left, down the hall." She went back to the letter she was writing, by hand.

The door marked Abner Proudfoot was gilt-lettered wood, the others in the hall were ground glass, a couple of them ajar. Malone glanced into one of the offices; it was empty, the desk bare. He opened the door into Mr. Proudfoot's anteroom.

The paneled walls here were done in walnut that needed refinishing. A thin, gray-haired woman sat at the receptionist's desk, reading a copy of the *Woman's Home Companion*.

Malone said, "Hello, cutie, I'm Mr. Malone."

"Yes, Mr. Malone," she said. She finished the sentence she was reading and laid the magazine aside. "I'll tell Mr. Proudfoot you're here." She reached for a plug on the switchboard and said, "You won't mind waiting a few minutes?"

"Oh, I would mind," Malone said. "Very much. Time and Tide wait for no man. I'm Mr. Tide, and time is fleeting. You won't mind if I go right in." He heard a faint squeak of protest from her as he opened the door to Abner Proudfoot's office.

It was an impressive room, magnificently furnished, well dusted, and slightly shabby. The curtains had been mended, and a corner had been chipped from the frame of one of the pictures of old New York. Abner Proudfoot sat behind his desk, his black-clad shoulders hunched, his gray head bowed. He looked up as Malone came in.

"Oh, Mr. Malone," he said. Evidently he decided to ignore Malone's informal entrance. "You're rather late. Fifteen minutes, in fact." He frowned. "Procrastination is——"

"Punctuality," Malone said quickly and smoothly, "is the virtue of a man who owns an expensive watch. What the hell do you want to see me about, anyway? I thought you fired me."

"I thought you refused to be fired," Mr. Proudfoot said, just as smoothly.

Malone sighed and began unwrapping a cigar. "All right," he said. "We seem to be working the same side of the street again. What happened between the time you threw me out of your house and had a couple of thugs beat me up, with the idea of finding that paper you signed and throwing my voiceless body in the river, and now? Did you have a change of heart?"

"Your attitude is very unconventional," Mr. Proudfoot said. He took a pinch of snuff. "Am I correct in understanding your statement, that you had some unfortunate accident after you left my house last night?"

"Think nothing of it," Malone said, lighting the cigar. "And it wasn't an accident." He threw the match away.

"Only if I keep on getting kicked around, my price is liable to go up, and I have a feeling you want something from me."

"I have great faith in your ability," Mr. Proudfoot said coldly.

The little lawyer said, "That's fine. Faith can move mountains. Which mountain do you want to have moved, pal, and which way?"

"I suspect you are being facetious," Mr. Proudfoot said, in a tone of voice that indicated he was accusing Malone of some unmentionable crime. "I engaged you to find Bertha Morrison. I wish you to carry out that assignment." Before Malone could say anything he added quickly, "She is, obviously, alive and well. If there are any traveling expenses involved, you may be assured——" The buzzer on his desk rang. He picked up the phone, listened a moment, and said, "Ask her to come right in."

It was only ten or fifteen seconds before the door opened. The gray-haired spinster said, "Mrs. Eunice Olsen, Mr. Proudfoot," gave Malone a disapproving look, and shut the door softly.

Before Malone had time to look at Mrs. Eunice Olsen, a small pigtailed bombshell ran across the room, threw over the wastebasket, pounded on Mr. Proudfoot's knee with tense little fists, and demanded, "What'ya got to gimme?" A voice just inside the door said, *"Bubsie! Please!"* and then, "I'm sorry, Mr. Proudfoot, I had to bring her with me, The Expressionality School is closed—some kind of financial trouble, I think—and I don't have a maid—*Bubsie, stop that*—really, I wouldn't have come here at all, only I remembered you were poor dear Bertha's trustee and that's why I called you up about the letter and you thought it was important so I brought it right down here, and—*Oh!*" There was a sound of breaking glass. "I hope it wasn't anything valuable! Bubsie, how could you do that!"

"I done it like this," Bubsie said. There was another sound of breaking glass.

"Just a trifle," Mr. Proudfoot said grimly. "I trust you brought the letter with you." He seemed to be breathing with difficulty. "Mrs. Olsen, this is Mr. Malone, one of my associates. You may speak freely in front of him, I assure you."

Malone gave Bubsie a hard shove toward Mr. Proudfoot and got a good look at her mother. She was a thin, anxious-looking little woman, with hair dyed an unpleasant orange shade. Her purplish alpaca suit was badly fitted and slightly dusty, her brown hat was a trifle askew. Bubsie, though, was an age-four fashion plate. Eunice Olsen's hair hung down in tiny wisps; the make-up was slightly smeared on her left cheek. Bubsie's hair, though, was sleek and shining; it stuck out in two stiff pigtails on either side of her cross, pink little face.

"I was afraid dear Bertha was dead," Mrs. Olsen said, "when I read the papers last night. And then this morning, I got this lovely letter from her, mailed yesterday. So I remembered you were Bertha's trustee, and I called you up, and you said for me to come right down. I wouldn't have brought Bubsie, only the school—*don't*, dear. *Put down those matches!*"

Bubsie put down the matches, marched over to Malone, and announced that she'd learned a new word yesterday. Malone, being polite, said, "Hm?" It wasn't a nice word.

"Oh," Mrs. Olsen said. "*Bubsie!* Well, anyway, here's the letter, Mr. Proudfoot." She fumbled for it in her bag and laid it on his desk. "I tell you, I was so surprised when it came, after I'd read that—— Bubsie, stop that! Oh, Mr. Proudfoot, I'm so sorry!"

"Quite all right," Mr. Proudfoot said, his face like ice. "The picture needed reframing, anyway." He read through the letter and pushed it toward Malone.

Bubsie struck a pose in the middle of the carpet and announced to all and sundry that she wished to go to the bathroom and immediately.

Abner Proudfoot pounded the buzzer on his desk and yelled for Agatha. The gray-haired spinster appeared in the doorway. A moment later she, Mrs. Olsen, and Bubsie vanished.

"You'll pardon me while you read that," Abner Proudfoot said, wiping his brow. He looked pale and shaken. "I'll rejoin you in a moment."

Malone wiped his own brow, relit his cigar, and examined the letter. The postmark on the envelope was Buffalo, the date was yesterday. He unfolded the letter, typed with a bright-blue ribbon on paper monogrammed with a queen bee.

My dear Eunice:
Thank you for your good wishes, and for the lovely gift. We are deliriously happy, and Niagara Falls is beautiful beyond description. Tomorrow we are moving on toward the Far West. Soon we shall be at home, and then I hope we will see you and your beautiful little girl. Until then, all my love.

Bertha

Malone stared at the letter. It was a conventional note, sent by a happy young bride. Only the bridegroom was here in New York, he'd lost his bride the night of his marriage, right now he was in the hospital, or on the way home from it, the victim of a murderous assault. And Bertha——

He didn't want to think about it. Not here, and not

now. He shoved the letter back on Abner Proudfoot's desk.

Of course the whole thing could be a fake. But, with a check of Bertha Morrison's past typewriting and handwriting, it would be easy to tell. Or, a hallucination. Only he'd never seen a hallucination neatly typed on monogrammed paper before. And Abner Proudfoot and Eunice Olsen had seen the same thing. He couldn't answer for Abner Proudfoot, but Eunice Olsen seemed a sensible, levelheaded young woman, in spite of Bubsie.

Maybe he was dreaming the whole thing. He wished that he were, but he had an uncomfortable certainty that he was awake.

The telephone rang. No one seemed to be in the anteroom, so Malone answered it. Mr. Proudfoot? He was out right now. But this was Mr. Proudfoot's confidential assistant.

What did Mr. Proudfoot want to put on what, in the seventh?

"Sorry," Malone said, "I'm not that confidential. I don't place Mr. Proudfoot's horse money for him." He hung up.

Funny a guy like Proudfoot, in an office as impressive as this one, in a fancy building like this, wouldn't have a brace of stenographers, secretaries, assistants, and office boys, instead of one gray-haired babe in the anteroom.

The telephone rang again, and again Malone explained he was Mr. Proudfoot's confidential assistant.

It was a female voice, a businesslike but rather pleasant one. "I'm Olive Eades. I went to school with Bertha Morrison, and I remembered Mr. Proudfoot was her trustee. Well, I had a letter from Bertha this morning, and in view of all that's been in the papers, I thought I'd better phone you."

"Thanks," Malone said. "I'm handling Bertha's affairs for Mr. Proudfoot. Would you be kind enough to read it to me over the phone?"

The businesslike voice read:

My dear Olive:
Thank you for your good wishes and your lovely gift. We are deliriously happy. Niagara Falls is even more beautiful than its description. We are leaving tomorrow for the West. As soon as we are home, I do hope you will come and call on us. Until then, all my love.

Bertha

Malone said, "That's very interesting. I'd like to talk to you about it."

"I feel a little confused," the voice said. "From her letter, she seems to be on her honeymoon, her husband is with her, and they're very happy. But from the newspaper stories I'd gotten the impression that Bertha was dead, and that her bridegroom was here in New York, in a hospital, and that someone had tried to murder *him*." The voice sighed over the wire. "It's really terribly confusing, Mr.—what did you say your name was?"

"Malone," the little lawyer said, "and don't believe everything you read in the newspapers. You have a very lovely voice. What color are your eyes?"

A soft and hastily repressed giggle came through the receiver. "My friends say they're hazel, but my enemies say they're green." Her voice grew sober again. "Really, there must be something terribly wrong. Bertha writing that she's happy and on her honeymoon, but the newspapers saying that her husband is here——"

"Pure propaganda," Malone said. "Did anyone ever tell you that you ought to be on the radio?"

"Honestly?" There was a little gasp. Then, "So many

friends of mine have said—but I haven't any experience, you know."

"I bet you could make up for that, fast," Malone said. He wondered how she looked. "It just happens I have a few connections in the radio business—tell me, where can I reach you?"

"At the office," she said. "Blackett, Barton, Sample, and Ayers. It's in the phone book. Just ask for Miss Eades. Extension 291. And if I happen to be out, just leave a message with Miss Joyce. She's a lovely girl."

"I'm sure she is," Malone said warmly, "if she's a friend of yours."

The anteroom door popped open, and the gray-haired spinster stuck her head in. She looked a trifle harassed. She said, "Will you watch this dear child a moment, Mr. Malone? I'm getting her mother an aspirin." She shoved the dear child into the room and shut the door, fast.

Malone said pleasantly and automatically, "Be a good little girl, and your mother will be here soon."

She stated emphatically that she didn't mean to be a good little girl.

Malone said, still pleasantly, "Shut your trap, or I'll shut it for you."

She bit him just below the knee, picked up an ash tray and poured out its contents, grinding them into the rug. Then she announced that she hadn't really gone to the bathroom and she was going to, right here and now.

"You're a liar," Malone said. It turned out he was right.

She stuck out her tongue at him; he retaliated in kind. She called him a name; he called her a noisier one. She pulled a book off the desk and threw it at him; he caught it adroitly and threw it back at her. Then she really got mad.

Five minutes later Mrs. Eunice Olsen returned. Bubsie,

looking peaceful and angelic, was serenely settled on Malone's lap, listening to a story about leprechauns.

Eunice Olsen said, "Oh! Mr. Malone!" Her china-blue eyes said, "How did you do it?"

Malone caught the look, and said, "Well, she kicked me. So I kicked her back." He turned a pleasant-natured and flexible Bubsie over his knee and showed the small, pinkish bruise. Then he turned her back again, finished the story in a few hurried sentences, said, "Now be a good girl and mind your mother," and delivered her back to Mrs. Olsen. "She's a fine, smart child," he said, "but you'd better take her out of that school and buy a hairbrush."

Bubsie sat down by her mother, a subdued and agreeable little girl. "Mist' Malone said," she announced, "that if I'm not good, you're goin' t' beat the b'jeez out of me."

Eunice Olsen looked at Malone, then at Bubsie. A little color began to come back into her sallow cheeks. She said, "He's damned right."

Abner Proudfoot came back. He thanked Mrs. Olsen for her help, and patted Bubsie on the head. They left, Bubsie swearing undying affection for Malone, and Proudfoot sat down behind his desk.

"I trust you understand," he said, "the circumstances which led me to reconsider my hastily arrived at decision. Bertha must be alive, but she must be mad. In which case, after you have succeeded in locating her, it will be necessary for the courts to declare her incompetent and appoint a guardian."

"Meaning you," Malone said.

"There was another letter," Mr. Proudfoot said, received by a Miss Dorothy Finny. She telephoned me this morning and read it to me over the telephone. Frankly, I was quite inclined to doubt the authenticity of the letter. Miss Finny appeared to be in a hysterical state. She is, I might add, assistant to a well-known medium. She appeared to believe that both Bertha and her husband were dead, and that this letter was a manifestation of some sort. I induced her to send it to me by special messenger, collect. I must admit to you, Mr. Malone, that I was baffled. And then when Mrs. Olsen——"

"Let's see the letter," Malone said.

It contained just what he'd expected.

My Dear Dorothy:
Thank you for your lovely gift, and for your good wishes. Niagara Falls is so beautiful, I wished that you could be here. Tomorrow we are going on West. Soon we will be home again, and then we will look forward to a visit from you. We are deliriously happy. All my love.

Bertha

"Bertha didn't have much originality, did she?" Malone said, handing back the letter. Mr. Proudfoot lifted his eyebrows, and Malone said hastily, "You're right. She must be nuts."

"Exactly what I maintain," Mr. Proudfoot said. "It is my thoroughly established belief that some shock must have unbalanced her mind, poor girl. Evidently she believes that she is happily married and on her honeymoon."

"Or," Malone said, "she *is* happily married and on her honeymoon, and she doesn't read the newspapers."

Proudfoot said, "I am principally concerned with finding her, and reassuring myself that she is safe and well. I am certain that is what her father would have wished me to do, were he alive today."

"Right," Malone said. "And if I do find her, and she is nuts, and the court does appoint you guardian, I think you ought to double my fee, pal."

Mr. Proudfoot stated immediately that that was impossible, and that Malone had an unfortunate attitude toward the whole situation. He had promised Malone too large a fee already. In fact, it might be wiser for him to end the arrangement and call in some more responsible party.

Malone stated that if Mr. Proudfoot did any such thing he would sue him, and that Mr. Proudfoot was obviously the offspring of an unwed half-wit and a shameless camel.

Mr. Proudfoot said that he regretted, deeply, the fact that Malone failed to appreciate the delicacy of the situation. His sense of responsibility to Bertha's father——

Malone said he was going back to Chicago on the six-forty-five train and the hell with the whole thing.

Mr. Proudfoot ventured a remark that he might offer a small bonus in the event that the courts did find Bertha incompetent and appoint him a permanent guardian.

Malone said, "I'll find her. And if she isn't crazy when I find her, I'll promise you——"

"I wouldn't even suggest," Mr. Proudfoot said, coldly, "that you do anything even remotely illegal."

Malone walked to the door and opened it. He was anxious to get out of the office, to smell clean, fresh air again. He smiled amiably at Mr. Proudfoot.

"And meantime, chum," he said, "if you find yourself with time hanging heavy on your hands, drop up some night for a game of poker."

"I never indulge in card games," Abner Proudfoot said, without turning a hair.

"That's all right," Malone said. "Just bring along a couple of your pals. Or a couple of your thugs, I'm not choosy. Only next time, bring along tougher ones."

Abner Proudfoot didn't answer and didn't move. But the flicker in his eyes told Malone that his guess was right. Last night Abner Proudfoot had believed Bertha Morrison dead, he hadn't wanted her to be found and identified. He had tried to protect himself by getting the signed agreement back from Malone, and by having Malone found, senseless or dead, at the bottom of an excavation. Now, Bertha seemed to be alive, and he'd changed his mind, fast. He sincerely hoped Malone would consent to ignore the little contretemps.

"I'll find her," Malone repeated. He closed the door and looked at the gray-haired, frozen-faced spinster at the reception desk. "Your boss," he said, "is the ringtailed, cross-eyed son of an unmarried mother."

To his happy surprise, she smiled at him.

Chapter Twenty-Eight

JAKE FELT a sense of exhaustion and futility. There had been no further word from Helene. Malone had gone out somewhere and not returned. After an hour's fruitless waiting, he'd decided to go ahead where he left off yesterday.

He'd gone over to Brooklyn to see Bertha Morrison's uncle, George Lutts, who turned out to be a gentle, slightly deaf, overweight, real-estate broker, not as successful as Bertha's father had been, but mildly prosperous. He didn't manage Bertha's property, he explained to Jake, a Mr. Proudfoot did that. Abner Proudfoot. He was in the phone book. Jake made a note of the name.

He didn't remember ever having heard of Dennis Morrison, Gloria Garden, Puckett, Wildavine Williams, or anyone else connected with the case. "I haven't seen so much of Bertha since she grew up," he explained apologetically. "Anyway, since her father passed away. He was a fine man, but I've always thought he should have made me Bertha's trustee. Not that she wasn't capable of managing her own affairs. Anything else I can do for you?"

A look of pain came into his mild blue eyes when Howie's name was mentioned. Jake wished he hadn't had to mention it. Howie was in trouble again. Of course Mr. Justus must know that, if he'd seen the papers. Jake nodded, and thanked heaven that Helene's name had been kept out of the story, and his own.

Howie had always been a bad boy. Not that everything possible hadn't been done for him. Old George Lutts' face looked tired and drawn. Howie had been arrested at eleven for stealing hub caps off parked cars and put on probation. "He never was a vicious boy," George Lutts said. "He had a real nice nature. Only he just never could seem to resist temptation." Howie had been arrested at fourteen for stealing cigarettes and candy from a cigar store. "Not that he hadn't been in trouble before that," George Lutts said, "only not with the police." At seventeen he'd been picked up on a morals charge.

"Not a girl, you understand," George Lutts said, looking embarrassed and unhappy. "Howie, he never would have anything to do with girls. Once we thought maybe he'd fall in love with Bertha when he grew up, only it didn't work out that way. A person never can tell about those things."

Howie had been committed to the House of Refuge. At eighteen he'd been paroled and given a job in a filling station. He'd worked as an usher, an office boy, and a soda jerk. "Howie never could keep a job very long," Mr. Lutts said.

At twenty-two Howie, in the company of three friends, had held up a junk dealer. The three friends had been arrested, convicted, and sent to Elmira, but Howie had got away.

"I hid him out, I didn't tell," George Lutts said. "Heaven forgive me. Only his mother was so sick. She died in a coupla months, and she never knew about Howie."

He'd been picked up looting the till of a filling station, and served four years. After he'd come out he'd returned home, borrowed a hundred dollars, and disappeared. George Lutts had only seen him once or twice since then, when he'd come back to borrow more.

"Now he's in jail again," George Lutts said, sighing. "Too bad. Howie had such a nice personality, too."

Jake got away as soon as he could. He hoped that Howie Lutts would draw a long term, at hard labor.

He hadn't learned anything of value from George Lutts, nor did he learn anything at Abner Proudfoot's office, where a pimply-faced young woman informed him that Mr. Proudfoot was out of the city and not expected back for six months.

This, by golly, was going to be his last visit today. He knocked lightly on Melva Engstrand's door in the Beaux Arts Apartments, resolving that if he didn't learn anything here, he'd give up and go back to Chicago.

He said, as the door opened, "I'm a reporter, and I wanted to ask you just a few questions——"

"*Oh*," Melva Engstrand said. "How *thrilling!* Come right in!"

She was a big, buxom woman with bright-red hair and a well-made-up face. She had on a jade-green housecoat that rustled as she walked, and tinkling little silver earrings. The apartment was expensive-looking, and tastefully decorated. Melva Engstrand mixed him a drink, offered him a cigarette, and curled up on the couch across the room from him, looking coy.

"You reporters *do* get around! How did you hear about my divorce suit so soon?"

"Oh," Jake said. He sipped the drink. "Oh—well, we get around. Tell me all about it."

She did, and it took an hour and a half. Her first husband had been a dear, but *far* too old for her. She'd been just a child out of school, and she'd wanted to go out and have fun. They'd finally parted friends, and he'd settled a *very* nice sum of money on her. Her second husband had been a simply *terrible* person, he'd obviously married her for her money, and as soon as he saw he couldn't get his hands on it, he'd left her. Her third had been a brute, an *absolute* brute. They'd quarreled *all* the time, every minute of it. Would you believe it, she'd *actually* had to go to a sanitarium for a nervous breakdown. And *mean!* The way she'd had to *fight* to get any alimony! And now? Well, Arthur Engstrand had a *lovely* disposition and he was *so* generous, and he had a fine business, but he was *unbearably* conventional. He'd actually objected to her going to the race tracks, and *that* had been the last straw.

Besides, she was engaged. She giggled and said, "Please, you mustn't tell anybody, because I haven't gotten my decree yet. But he's *such* a dear! Wait, I'll show you his picture!" She produced it, a thin-faced young man with sideburns. "He's a poet. Tell me, since you're on the case, what do you think my chances are of getting a cash settlement out of Arthur?"

"Excellent," Jake said, "and all this has been very interesting. And while I'm here, there's something else I wanted to ask you about. Didn't you know Bertha Morrison—Bertha Lutts?"

"*Know* her," she said, "why I'm her *very* best friend! I nearly went out of my *mind* last night when I thought she'd been murdered, *honestly* I did. We were *so* close. Why, she used to tell me everything about herself, *everything*."

Jake lit a cigarette to conceal his sudden excitement and said, "She did? Do go on."

"We had lunch together *just* last week," Melva said. "She told me all about her young man. How he was just *fabulously* rich, and came of such a *wonderful* old Southern family, and he'd been pursuing her—really *pursuing* her—for months! He was *madly* in love with her. Can you imagine? *Bertha*? Not, of course, that she didn't have a lovely nature and all that, but—well, I guess you never *can* tell."

For just a minute, Jake thought he had something. Further questions, though, brought out that Melva hadn't seen a great deal of Bertha since boarding school, except for class reunions and the bridge club that had been organized last year. In fact, as she talked, the friendship seemed to dwindle down to a faint and not too amiable acquaintanceship. She, Melva, hadn't liked Bertha very well in school, she'd been too much of a dud. And *terribly* stingy. She'd spend plenty of money on herself, but *never* on her friends. She, Melva, had borrowed a little money from her a year ago, and Bertha had positively *hounded* her until she paid it back.

Jake remembered the clothes, the perfumes, and the beauty aids in Bertha Morrison's apartment, and the letter she'd written to Wildavine, refusing a loan.

"*Not*," Melva said, "that I'm not *devoted* to her, because I am. She may not be pretty but she has *such* a sweet disposition, even if she *is* opinionated and stubborn. And I was *so* relieved to hear from her this morning and know that she's all right."

"You must have been," Jake said absent-mindedly, reaching for a match. His hand froze in mid-air, and he said, *"What?"*

"When I got her letter," Melva said, "I was *so* relieved. After all that had been in the papers. It just shows how they exaggerate, doesn't it?"

"Oh." Jake said. "Oh, yes. Her letter. Of course. Could I see it?"

Melva giggled and said, "Well—I don't see why not. It doesn't have any *secrets* in it."

She found it under a box of chocolates on her writing desk and gave it to him. He recognized the paper, the blue typewriter ribbon. The envelope was postmarked April 11. It had been mailed from Niagara Falls.

My dear Melva:
Thank you for your good wishes and your lovely gift. Niagara Falls is beautiful beyond description. To-morrow we are leaving for the West. We are deliriously happy. As soon as we are home, do come and call on us. Until then, all my love.
Bertha

Jake read it through three or four times, and then handed it back, saying, "Thank you." His throat felt numb. Had Bertha Morrison gone insane, or had he?

"Isn't that the silliest thing you ever *heard* of?" Melva Engstrand cooed. "I read in the papers that the police seemed to think that body in the morgue was Bertha's. As though *Bertha* would ever have such a thing happen to her! And that the nice young man Bertha married was in the hospital, a victim of an attempted murder! While *she* writes me from Niagara Falls that they're *deliriously* happy! It just goes to show, you can't believe a *thing* you read in the papers. Honestly, sometimes I believe these newspaper reporters cook up these stories just from *sheer* sensationalism." She glanced at Jake, remembered why he was there, and added hastily, "I don't mean *you*, of course."

"I'm sure of it," Jake croaked. He rose and reached for his hat.

"Oh, *must* you go? When we were just beginning to get so *nicely* acquainted! Really, I *never* thought a reporter could be *so* charming, and I've known *so* many of them! *Won't* you come back and visit me again—I mean, *informally*—one of these days?"

"I'll call you up sometime," Jake said. "We'll have lunch." He fled.

Bertha was murdered. But she'd mailed a letter, yesterday, from Niagara Falls. Bertha was alive and well. But she'd written that she was deliriously happy, and yet, her bridegroom was still here in New York.

What the hell?

He stopped at the nearest United Cigar store. Maybe he ought to call up a psychiatrist. Or maybe he ought to call up the police. He finally called the hotel and asked first for Helene, then for Malone. Neither was in.

Well, there was still one thing left on his schedule for the day. He'd go over to Staten Island and have a talk with old Dr. Puckett. Jake looked at his watch. Yes, there was plenty of time left to go there, get back, dress, and be at Wildavine's at the appointed dinner hour.

He walked to Grand Central Station, took the subway, and rode to South Ferry. A boat was waiting, he got on, found a seat in the cabin, picked up an abandoned newspaper from the seat beside him, and began working the crossword puzzle.

The movement of water past the boat made a lovely sound. He closed his ears to it. If he looked out the window, he could see boats in the harbor and the Statue of Liberty. He didn't look. If he went out on deck, he could look back and see the New York skyline. He stayed where he was. Someday he'd take this same ferry ride, and Helene would be with him. He'd wait until then to do his looking. What was a six-letter word beginning with *l*, meaning Egyptian skink?

He got off the boat, went to the information booth in the ferry building, looked again at the address of Dr. Puckett's sister-in-law. Mrs. Mabel Puckett. The information clerk told him what car to take and what station to get off at.

Jake had never been on Staten Island before, but he resolutely kept his eyes and his mind on the crossword puzzle, abandoning it only when his station was called. By then he'd got hopelessly stuck with a seven-letter word beginning with *poc*, defined as a genus of oceanic ducks.

He'd started his trip in the center of a great city; now, forty minutes later, he stepped off the car in a very small and very neglected town. He walked past a tiny, weather-beaten station and plowed his way through knee-high weeds to a wooden sidewalk.

The address he was seeking proved to be up a slight hill, a block and a half down an unpaved road, and across a vacant lot to where four small brick houses stood desolately along a paved street, a memorial to what had once been planned as a Development. The last house of the four was Mrs. Mabel Puckett's.

There was a vacant lot beside it, newly spaded and raked, and carefully laid out with plant markers and cord. Dr. Puckett was there, in old corduroy overalls, planting radishes. Jake picked his way carefully across the damp ground.

"Early for planting, isn't it?" Jake asked cordially.

Dr. Puckett stood up, grinning, and wiped his brow. "Well, might be. I don't think there'll be another frost, though. Just thought I'd get in Mabel's garden for her while she's away, and while I'm here."

Jake said, "Don't let me stop you. In fact, let me help. Where do you want to put in these carrots?"

"Right over there," Dr. Puckett said. "Next to the beets. Don't pat 'em down too hard. You gotta be careful with carrots, this time of year." He straightened up for a minute, rubbed his back, and said, "I gotta put my own garden in, soon's as I get home. Ma isn't real well, and Irma—that's my son Ed's wife—don't care much for gardening. And Ed's busy all day in his garage." He carefully raked the moist ground over the radish seeds. "But since Mabel's down in Florida, and since she was kind enough to let me stay in her house while I was here—not that she didn't always ask me to stay here, which I always did—and since she's my dead brother Henry's wife, well, I thought the least I could do was put in her garden for her. Look out you don't step on that hose line."

Jake put in a long row of carrots, being careful not to pat them down too hard. The feel of the moist earth was good on his fingers, and when he straightened up, he took pride in the evenness of the row. After all, he'd been brought up in a little town, and there had always been a garden in the back yard. He wondered how Helene would like living on a farm someday.

"Looks pretty good," Dr. Puckett said contentedly. "Fine sandy loam here. Well," he sighed, "seed and weed, that's the way it goes. You plant, but you never know what's going to come up. Same way with people." He stooped, picked up a stone, and tossed it out of the garden. "I remember, I delivered five babies in a family, good, honest, God-fearing people. All nice, healthy, handsome kids. Three boys and two girls. One girl's a school principal now, a fine respected woman. Her sister's married and has a nice little family, she's president of the PTA in Grove Falls. One boy runs a grocery store, the other's a real good farmer. The third boy ran away from home twice, got sent to the reform school once, stole a car, held up a bank, shot the cashier, and got hanged. It just goes to show." He rubbed the dirt from his fingers on the seat of his pants and said, "Let's go in the house and have a bite to eat, I'm hungry. Got a cigarette with you?"

Jake was hungry. He'd missed lunch. Come to think of it, he hadn't had any breakfast, either.

Dr. Puckett led him into a neat little kitchen, washed his hands and handed Jake the soap, brought out a half-gallon bottle of beer, a loaf of bread, a carton of eggs, a bowl of butter, a frying pan, and an onion. He put the frying pan on the stove to heat, poured out two glasses of beer, and said, "Drink up," put a hunk of butter in the pan and waited for it to brown.

"Hope you like an egg sandwich," he said. "That's one thing a country doctor knows how to make." He chuckled, breaking the eggs into the pan. "You go out to a farm to deliver a baby. Five o'clock in the morning you're ready to go home, but you're hungry. Somebody's thought to put a pot of coffee on the stove for you, but nobody's thought you might like something to eat. So you look in the icebox, and there's never anything but eggs. You make an egg sandwich, and go home." He shaved onion into the frying pan and said, "Why did you come out here, anyway?"

"Frankly," Jake said, "I'm damned if I know. I guess I just wanted to talk to you."

"All right," Dr. Puckett said. "Go ahead, talk." He sprinkled salt, pepper, and celery salt in the frying pan. "Only maybe you'd better eat first." He flipped over the eggs, sauced the browned butter over them with a big spoon, and slid them expertly on the thick slices of bread he'd been warming in the oven.

Jake took one bite and said, "Boy!" He took another bite and said, "I never knew anybody in my life could make egg sandwiches like this, except my grandpop." He took two more bites and said, "Funny, this is one of the things no woman can cook right."

"Ma never learned how to make a good egg sandwich," Dr. Puckett admitted. "But you should just taste her devil's-food cake once."

"I'd love to!" Jake said. He licked the last bit of egg off his fingers. "You'd never believe it to look at her, but my wife makes the most wonderful corned-beef hash."

"You should taste Ma's watermelon preserves sometime," Dr. Puckett said. He refilled Jake's beer glass and his own. "Hazel was a fine cook, too. Won a blue ribbon at the county fair for her grape jelly one year." He reached for his pipe. "Now, what was it you wanted to talk to me about, son?"

Jake lit a cigarette and stared for a long time at its smoke. "I want to find the man who murdered your daughter." He held the cigarette so tight that it went out. "I started out to, for the most selfish reasons in the world. Now, well"—he dropped the dead cigarette in his saucer —"I guess it's just——" He looked up. "I'd like to see the son-of-a-bitch in the electric chair. I came out here to pump you for any information that might lead me to him, that's all."

Dr. Puckett said, "You don't need to be so vehement about it, son. Murder's a terrible crime, but I don't know as it does any good to revenge yourself on the murderer. Murder brings its own punishment, one way or another. Now you take Lew Hays, back home. I knew he'd poisoned his wife the night he called me in to treat her. She died just a little while after I got there. In a way it seemed like an act of justice, because Minnie Hays had been an awful mean woman. Frankly, I always thought she starved her father while she was taking care of him on his deathbed, though when she inherited his farm she found out it was mortgaged. And I knew for sure she was behind driving a little schoolteacher out of town just because she'd made sheep's-eyes at Lew. The schoolteacher hanged herself out of the back window of a house of ill-fame in St. Paul six months after she'd been driven out of town. Still, you hate to see a person die like that, even an awful mean person like Minnie Hays. From poison that acts that way, I mean. Not just so much because it was painful, but because it must have been embarrassing. She was conscious all the time, and Minnie had always been a terrible prim woman. Still, maybe she had it coming to her. Well, anyway, next month Lew married a blonde girl who'd been working in Wirke's Variety Store, and she's made his life a hell. She's twenty years younger than Lew, and I guess she found out there wasn't as much money as she'd expected, and she has a lot of boy friends. Maybe it's just as well I made out the certificate 'Death from Natural Causes,' instead of calling up the sheriff. Seems to me like most people get punished for what they do, one way or another. Now that blonde girl who married Lew, she got herself a mother-in-law who's an old——" He paused, knocked his pipe against the side of the table, and said, "What were we talking about, anyway?"

Jake gulped down the rest of his beer and said, "The man or woman who murdered your daughter."

"Oh, him?" Dr. Puckett said. "Don't worry. He'll get his comeuppance, someday." He rose. "I'd better go out and wet down those seeds I put in. Hazel was a pretty girl, and her ma's going to feel awful bad about this, but she wasn't perfect either."

Chapter Twenty-Nine

MALONE STARTED his renewed search for Bertha Morrison by looking up a friend and client from the old days in Chicago, one Charlie Firman, whom he'd successfully defended against a variety of charges, beginning with running a horse parlor and slowly working up to selling stock in a nonexistent platinum mine. Charlie had become a smart operator in the stock market, made a million dollars, lost it and his shirt, after which he'd borrowed a hundred dollars from Malone and gone to New York, where, from what Malone heard, he had a series of very high ups and very low downs.

He seemed to be in the midst of one of the very low downs right now. Malone found him occupying desk space in a shabby building ("Desk space, incoming phone calls, mailing address, $2.50 weekly") from which he was mailing out extravagantly printed brochures urging his sucker list to "Own a share in a radium mine!"

Charlie greeted Malone joyously, showed him the brochure, and said, "They'll love it! Radium has glamour! Everybody's heard about radium."

Malone nodded critical approval of the brochure.

"I paid a thousand bucks to have a specialist write that page about the source of radium," Charlie bragged, licking a stamp.

"You're a damn liar," Malone said amiably, dropping the brochure back on the desk. "You lifted it word for word out of the encyclopedia. Listen, pal. Want to do me a favor?"

"For you," Charlie Firman said, "anything."

Malone told him what he wanted. One thing about Charlie Firman, he had an uncanny ability for weaseling out information about people's most private financial affairs. More than once in the past he'd obliged Malone by finding out if a client was really too hard up to pay a big fee, or if he had a secret bank account tucked away somewhere. He'd always come up with the facts, too.

"Brother, I'm your man," Charlie Firman said. He stuffed the last brochure in an envelope, sealed and stamped it, and said, "I'll get you the dope on this Proudfoot guy, right down to the last penny."

Malone went away, satisfied. Meanwhile, he told himself, there was no point to working on the Bertha Morrison matter. Not until he heard from Charlie Firman.

The report on Abner Proudfoot reached him late that afternoon at the hotel, sent (collect) by special messenger. Charlie hadn't missed a thing. Malone read it through slowly and with satisfaction. It answered his most important question, that Abner Proudfoot would be able to pay the rest of the fee for finding Bertha. It answered a number of other questions, too, that Malone hadn't thought to ask.

He yawned, and reached for the phone. Jake had come in, and gone out again. Helene had come in later, and was dressing. She'd be ready to leave for Wildavine Williams' in a few minutes. Dennis Morrison had returned from the hospital and was in bed; he was going to have dinner in his room.

The little lawyer shaved and dressed leisurely. He wasn't looking forward to dinner at Wildavine Williams', but he might find out a few things he needed to know. He had the curious feeling that he had all the facts in the case except one, and that when he stumbled on that one, everything would fall automatically into place. He didn't know what that one missing fact could be, or whom it concerned, but he was serenely confident that he was going to find it.

He joined Helene in the lobby. She had on her simplest dress and an unfurred coat, no jewelry, and very little make-up. Malone looked at her approvingly. She'd meant to give Wildavine a break. Not that it would do any good. Helene, Malone reflected, just couldn't help being beautiful.

Helene said, "We've a few minutes. Let's go up and see how Dennis Morrison feels."

Malone had had the same idea. He wasn't so much concerned with how Dennis Morrison felt, as with whether or not Dennis had ever known Howie Lutts.

The young man looked tired and pale, propped up against the pillows. A wisp of bandage showed at the collar of his pajama coat.

He was sorry he'd run off and left Malone and Helene like that. It had been an impulse, a sudden impulse. He'd wanted to catch up with old Dr. Puckett and tell him how sorry he was about Gloria Garden's murder, and—well, everything. "About my not being there. If I had, you know, there wouldn't have been any murder."

"You can't be sure," Malone said. "There might have been a murder, with you on the receiving end."

Dennis stared and said, "I never thought of that! Someone *did* try to murder me. Why? Why would anyone want to murder me?"

"If you don't know," Malone said, biting the end off his cigar, "I can't guess."

"The whole thing seems so *senseless*," Dennis said. "And now, even more so. Do you know about the letters?"

Malone said, "Yes," and Helene said, "What letters?"

"From Bertha," Dennis said. "It's mad. It's insane." He gasped, and said, "But it means she's alive." A Mrs. Martha Chalette had received a letter that morning from Bertha, and turned it over to the police. It had been mailed from Niagara Falls. Arthur Peterson had shown it to Dennis. Bertha had written it all right. It had been just a little note, thanking Martha for her lovely gift, saying that Niagara Falls was beautiful, and that Bertha was deliriously happy.

"But that's impossible," Helene said. She turned to Malone. "Tell me. What does it mean?"

"I haven't the faintest idea," Malone said, lighting the cigar. "Unless she's married to someone else she thinks is Dennis." He had an alternative theory he didn't want to voice. But Dennis said it for him.

"Or she's gone crazy," Dennis said wildly. "All this has driven her crazy. But, at least, she's alive." He sat upright and said, his eyes desperate, "I ought to be out looking for her. I shouldn't be here, in bed. I feel perfectly all right."

"You stay where you are," Malone said. "Don't forget,

there's some guy with a knife out looking for you, and the police are having enough trouble as it is without you getting murdered, too."

Dennis sank back against the pillows. He managed a very faint smile. "You're right, of course. But I feel so—useless."

Malone brought the conversation back to where it had started from. The results were unsatisfactory. Dennis didn't remember anything helpful about the murder attempt. He hadn't been able to catch up with Dr. Puckett, who'd taken the ferry by the time he arrived. He'd just missed that boat. He'd been standing there, in the crowd, waiting to catch the next one, when he'd felt a sharp pain. Then someone had shoved him. He remembered the cold feeling of the water, and that was all.

Yes, he had known Howie Lutts. Not well, though. And not as Howie Lutts, but as Harris Lawrence. Not until now had he known that Harris Lawrence was Bertha's cousin.

"She might have learned of the escort bureau through him," Dennis said. "I wouldn't know. I just know I was sent to take her out one night, and that was—the beginning. He wouldn't have been interested in her as a client, even if she was his cousin. He was strictly working a racket"—he smiled wryly—"as of course you know."

Did Dennis know about the pawnshop where Bertha's jewels had turned up?

He knew, vaguely, that there was such a place, but he hadn't known where it was.

Could Dennis have inadvertently stumbled on any information, while working for the escort service, that would have called for an attempt to murder him?

He didn't think so.

Did Dennis ever know a man named Abner Proudfoot?

Dennis knew the name. He was Bertha's trustee. He'd never met him.

It was getting late. Helene rose and slid into her coat. Malone picked up his hat.

Would Dennis be a good boy and stay put, and not run around and get murdered?

Dennis would.

Was there anything they could do, or get for him before they left?

Not a thing, thanks.

Malone observed contentedly that Schultz was sitting in the lobby, trying unsuccessfully to look inconspicuous.

Not a word was said until they were in the taxi. Then Malone glanced at Helene and, ignoring all the other puzzling facts in the case, said, "Funny damn thing, though, about that dinner jacket."

"Isn't it," Helene said serenely.

There was something about her manner that he didn't quite like. She was entirely too calm, and she looked a little too pleased with herself. Something was brewing. He couldn't guess what it would be, but he suspected he wouldn't enjoy it.

He likewise suspected he wouldn't enjoy the next few hours. Fortunate, he told himself, that he'd fortified himself during the afternoon with the pint of grape brandy and the six bottles of Coca-Cola. It had made an agreeable mixture to sip while he waited for Charlie Firman to call. Now it had left him with a pleasant feeling of warmth and a slight buzzing in the ears.

They climbed the stairs to Wildavine's apartment. The door was ajar. There was a smell of garlic and tomato paste that had reached all the way down to the first floor.

Wildavine was saying, "Magnificent! Such verve! Such significance! And three hundred pages long! Just a matter now of getting it into the right hands."

She was sitting on one of the painted chairs talking to Jake, who was sitting on the edge of the couch. She had on enormous loops of earrings, a green ribbon bound her hair, and she was wearing bright-orange house pajamas. There was make-up on her face, too. Too much of it, and not very carefully applied, but at least it was there. Evidently she'd decided to offer a little competition herself.

She greeted them effusively, invited them to sit down on the teetery couch. Malone looked around the room. Cooking was obviously going on behind the curtain. The pictures on the wall held him spellbound, particularly one, titled *Unfinished Symphony*. It looked like a bright-green angleworm between two pale-blue fried eggs. The little lawyer stared at it for a long time. He wished he was back in Chicago.

A very tall, very thin, very gloomy young man came in, carrying a jug. Wildavine bounced up to greet him. A small woman with a lot of fuzzy white hair came in just behind him. She was dressed in a bright-red sweater, a tight black skirt, red anklet socks, and tennis shoes.

"This is *Madame*." Wildavine said reverently. "She *paints*."

Madame said, "How do you do," in a deep sepulchral voice, and sat down in a corner, with an air of having said her last words for the evening.

"And Peter Kipp," Wildavine said. "A *very* great poet."

The young man put the jug down on the table, looked at Malone, and said, "Do you write, or do you read?"

"Neither one," Malone said, startled. "I'm illegitimate."

"*I* recite," the young man said. He poured red wine

into the Kraft-cheese glasses Wildavine had produced. "I compose orally."

A plump, red-haired girl with freckles emerged from behind the curtain to announce that the spaghetti was ready to serve.

"And this is Zora," Wildavine said. "She lives next door."

Malone, in a slight daze, wondered if Zora wrote, read, painted, or composed. It turned out that she was a night cashier in a neighborhood movie house, and that this was her evening off.

A plate of spaghetti was put on his knees. Malone looked at it dubiously. There seemed to be a lot more spaghetti than there was sauce. One very lonesome-looking little meatball reposed in the center of it. He gulped the glass of red wine to encourage himself, poked an experimental fork in one end of a piece of spaghetti, and pulled it upward. It was approximately thirty-six inches long.

"Like this," Wildavine said brightly, performing an expert but horrifying trick with a fork and a tablespoon. "See how easy?"

Malone tried it, became hopelessly entangled, and ending by nearly strangling himself. Maybe, he thought, he should have drunk only half the bottle of brandy before starting out. He ended up by employing a technique similar to that employed by a bird with an angleworm and finally slid his plate onto the table under the cover of a furious argument about art.

He wondered how soon he could get out and find a steak.

Peter refilled all the wineglasses and was prevailed upon to compose, orally. Then Wildavine refilled them and consented to recite a poem which, it just happened, she had memorized. Madame sat in her corner working on her fourth plate of spaghetti. Zora carried out the dishes and refilled the wineglasses for the fourth time.

When there was a faint lull in the conversation, Helene said brightly, "You know, I sold a poem today. To *Whither*."

There was an amazed silence. Then Wildavine gave a hollow titter and said, "Your wife has such a wonderful sense of humor, Mr. Justus."

Jake said stiffly, "I don't think that was very funny."

"But I wasn't being funny," Helene said, in a voice like a hurt child. "I got a check for it, too." She reached for her purse, opened it, and pulled out a long, narrow slip of green paper. "Zabel Publications" was printed on the top. The voucher stated that the twenty dollars had been paid to Helene Justus for a poem, "Toella." It was signed Quarles Zabel.

"But when?" Jake began helplessly.

"I wrote it this morning," Helene said. "And I remembered Miss Williams had spoken of *Whither*. So I took it to Mr. Zabel and he liked it and he bought it. He's a very charming man."

"You—met—Mr. Zabel?" Wildavine said. Her voice sounded as though Helene had remarked casually that she'd just had a conference with the Archangel Michael. Even Peter Kipp looked impressed.

"Why, yes," Helene said. "I looked him up in the directory and phoned him, and made an appointment."

Wildavine slumped down on a chair. She looked stricken. For just a divided second, Malone didn't quite like Helene.

Jake said suspiciously, "What is this poem?"

Helene said, "Would you like to hear it? It just happens

I memorized it." She clasped her hands in her lap and recited, like a small girl saying "The Night Before Christmas" at a school benefit.

> *Toella*
>
> *alone*
> *weep*
> *you and you*
> *laugh*
>
> *comma*
>
> *period*
>
> *with weep*
> *the world*
>
> *comma*
>
> *and laughs.*

She stopped, smiled, and looked around for praise.

Wildavine gasped and said, "Magnificent! What tragic emphasis! What movement! What a feeling for emotional form!"

"Oh, thank you!" Helene said. She beamed. "I told him all about you, too. He wants to meet you. He wants to see all your poems."

"*Me!*" Wildavine said. "*Mr. Zabel?*"

"In fact," Helene said, "I took the liberty of making a sort of tentative appointment for you, for tomorrow morning at ten. If you can make it, that is. I told him about that simply wonderful poem you recited for us, and I even quoted a little of it to him. I hope you don't mind. He was very impressed, and he wants to buy it." She beamed. "Ten o'clock, at his office."

Wildavine just said, "Oh!"

Malone took the liberty of pouring himself another glass of the sour red wine. He retracted everything he'd been thinking about Helene.

He had just a faint suspicion, though, about that poem——

He'd never heard of Helene writing poetry. Certainly, not like that poetry.

Jake was silent. He looked stunned. Helene looked pleased, proud, and just faintly mischievous. Peter Kipp was stamping up and down the room, declaiming that the magic fire of poetry should never be entombed within the magnificent trees of the forest, ground to pulp and rolled into sheets. "What is ink?" he demanded. "A rank poison."

"Especially this red ink," Malone muttered, emptying his glass and kicking it under the couch.

"Words have wings," Peter Kipp said. Inspired, he poured himself another glass of wine and went on.

"Words are winged things. O words! O wings! O things!" He was composing again.

Madame passed her plate to Zora for more spaghetti.

Jake was still silent and stunned, staring at Helene.

Malone had had enough. Besides, he was hungry. He rose, walked over to Wildavine, pulled her into a corner, and said, as lecherously as he could, "I want to speak to you. Alone."

Wildavine's eyes widened and brightened. She glanced around, everyone seemed to be busy. She led Malone through a door into the next room, a duplicate of the one they'd just left, save that the colors were brighter. She closed the door and bolted it.

"This is Zora's studio," she murmured. "But Zora won't mind." She lighted the candles on the table, and an incense burner. Malone sniffed and sneezed. She sprinkled a little perfume on the candles. Malone remembered he was a gentleman and muffled the next sneeze. "Glasses," he whispered, "bring me glasses!" She brought him two empty jelly tumblers as though they were chalices, and he pulled a half pint of rye he'd brought along for emergencies out of his left-hand pants pocket.

She coughed a little over the rye, and half knelt on the floor. "You said—you wanted to speak to me——"

"I want to ask you something," Malone said.

"Yes?" she breathed. "Ask me—anything."

Malone asked, "What the hell were you doing in the St. Jacques bar the night of the murder?"

She said, "*Oh*," and fled toward the door. Malone grabbed her by the wrist and dragged her back again. She curled up on the farthest corner of the couch, looking frightened and wild-eyed.

"Pull yourself together, baby," Malone said. He reached over, took one of her shivering hands, and warmed it between his own. "Because I'm your friend. I'm not going to tell the police anything, I'm not going to tell anybody anything, I promise." He began working on the other hand. "Please trust me. You'll tell me everything, won't you, baby?"

She nodded and said, "Bertha——"

Malone waited just long enough and then whispered, "Yes. Go on."

"I haven't any money," she whispered, "and there's always so many things. The rent and the grocery bill every month, and subway fares and stamps and things— a nickel here and a nickel there. I do a little typing, by the page, but I don't type very fast—though I'm very accurate—and I have about a hundred dollars a year from my grandmother's insurance. I was named for her. And

Bertha had so much money, and she liked me. You see," she paused a moment, "Bertha liked girls, not boys."

Malone said gently, "Go on, baby."

"Only I never—she never—well, we never——" She paused again. "You know what I mean."

"I do," Malone said, "and I'm not surprised at that."

"She admired my poems," Wildavine whispered. "I wrote a lot of them about her. And she kept lending me money and telling me I didn't ever need to pay it back. And—well, about other things—I always could find excuses. You know what I mean. I'd always have good excuses, too, for asking for loans, and she'd write back letters pretending to believe them, and then send my letter and a carbon copy of hers to her trustee. But she began to get terribly difficult. Insistent. You know. Or else, no more loans, and all the other ones paid back."

Malone lighted a cigarette, held it to her lips, and said, "And so?"

"She got this young man to marry her," Wildavine said, "so people wouldn't talk. Because they were talking, a little. I don't know where she found him. He was a professional dancing partner or something. I know she hired him to marry her. They were going to go on a big honeymoon tour. I was terribly broke, Mr. Malone. I had to borrow a hundred dollars. So I wrote her. She wrote back a letter, saying no. Then she called me up. It was the day she was married. She read me a copy of the letter over the phone—I hadn't received it then. Then she said she was sending the copy of it, with my letter, to her trustee, *unless*——" She paused. "You know what I mean. Unless."

"I know," Malone said.

"I didn't know what to do. I was desperate. Finally I

just said yes. She was very happy. She said she was going to cancel her reservations and spend her honeymoon here in New York, so she could see me every day. And she made a date for me to come up that night. She said she'd get rid of her new husband somehow. And she'd have the hundred dollars for me."

Malone said quietly, "And?"

"Well, I went there," Wildavine said. "I didn't know what else to do. I felt terribly scared, I thought about running away and all sorts of things. I called up from the lobby and there wasn't any answer. So I went into the bar and got a drink and waited. I kept calling and calling, but there still wasn't any answer. Finally I just gave up and came home. Of course, I never got the hundred dollars." She drew a long breath, and said, "That's all."

"It's enough," Malone said.

She looked up at him, expectantly and hopefully. "Was that all you asked me here for?"

Malone wanted to say, "Yes," and go away. His conscience objected, violently. He'd lured her in here under false pretenses. She had given him confidences which, while they might not be very helpful, had been interesting. Besides, she was damn near pretty, in the candle light. Malone whispered hoarsely, "No, it wasn't," and reached for her. She gave a pleased and muffled little scream.

Later, when he was leaving, he paused at the door. "I forgot to mention," he said, "don't tell anybody, but I'm a private detective working on this case for a client. I have a fat expense account, and I'm supposed to pay for any information I get. Your name won't ever be mentioned, and you can just forget the whole case, but your evidence has been very helpful and valuable. So, well, *here*——"

He shoved one of his remaining hundred-dollar bills

into her hand. "Good night, cutie," he said, turning the doorknob. "Maybe you'd better put on some more lipstick. Your friends may be wondering where you are."

He lurched down the stairs. Let Jake and Helene go home by themselves. Right now, there were just two things he wanted in the whole world. One was a steak. The other was a saloon.

Chapter Thirty

WHEN Jake finally put his arm around Helene, led her to the door, and said, "Well, we'd better be going," Peter Kipp was posing between the two lighted candles and declaiming something loud and furious, of which Jake could only catch the occasionally reiterated word "Helene" and "*Whither*." It was, Peter explained, a congratulatory poem. He was composing orally.

Madame looked up from a plate of bread and butter and gave out with her second remark of the evening. "Decomposing," she said.

Wildavine had been sitting on a corner of the couch, since her return to the room, pink-cheeked and silent. She looked a little surprised. Zora had been washing dishes in the hand basin. She came out to tell Jake and Helene good-by and come back soon. Wildavine rose.

"Thank you for a lovely evening," Helene said, clasping Wildavine's hand. "A wonderful evening. I've had such a nice time. And don't forget to keep that appointment with Mr. Zabel in the morning. Ten o'clock. Because he's looking forward to it so much."

Wildavine's eyes grew moist. "Oh, I love you both," she said, "you're both such marvelous people." Over her shoulder Jake could see Madame, otherwise unobserved, filching the last olive from the bowl on the table and shamelessly holding the jug of dago red to her lips. "Don't worry," Wildavine said, "I'll be there."

Peter Kipp swooped at the door, struck a pose, and said, "Good-by is good-by is farewell is farewell is good-by——"

Jake said, "Good night," loud, and all but threw Helene at the stairs.

He didn't speak again until they were safely in the taxi. Then he said, "Give me the lowdown. Has she really got an appointment with that guy?"

"Naturally," Helene said. "You don't think I'd lie about a thing like that?" She laid her head on his shoulder and said, "Jake, I wish I had a drink."

"There's liquor at home," Jake said sternly. He slid his arm around her. Temptation began to tickle him. Maybe Helene could make an appointment for him with Mr. Zabel of Zabel Publications. No! God forbid! He'd peddle his own canoodlings.

"Jake, there's the loveliest little bar, around the corner on Fourteenth Street. Oh!"

He kept on kissing her until they were well past Fourteenth Street. Then he said, "I'm very suspicious about that poem."

"It may be the only poem I ever wrote," she said indignantly, "but I'm very proud of it. Jake, darling, on Twenty-sixth Street——"

"—there's the loveliest little bar," Jake said. "We're going home, remember? Where did you steal that poem?"

"I didn't steal it," she said. "I took it out of a hat. Honest to goodness, I did. To be perfectly truthful, it was your hat."

"Not that poem," Jake said.

"That poem," she said. "I wrote all the words on little pieces of paper and put them in your old gray hat, and then I picked them out one at a time. I wrote the punctuation out in full, that's how it happened to get in. Jake, on Thirty-fourth Street——"

"We aren't going there," he said firmly. "Helene, how did you happen to pick the words you dropped in the hat?"

"Why," she said innocently, "I took them out of a quotation. 'Laugh and the world laughs with you, weep and you weep alone.' Jake, tell the driver to turn left on Forty-second and stop just past the——"

Jake did no such thing. He said hoarsely, "But the title?"

"Oh, that," Helene said. "It isn't a title, it's a dedication. To Ella. Ella Wheeler Wilcox. She wrote the quotation, only of course she couldn't have known it was going to be a quotation when she wrote it. Only I liked it better spelled the other way. Toella. I thought it was cute. Toella. A touch of the occult, and a nice feeling for movement."

For two cents, he would have smacked her.

She said, "Well, anyway, I sold Wildavine's poem for her. He's going to pay thirty dollars for it, he told me so. And she probably needs it. And he'll probably buy more of them. Jake, we might go to El Morocco."

Jake gave in. They settled for the Silver Dollar Bar, on Seventh Avenue.

He slid up on the barstool beside her and ordered two double ryes. Then he glanced at Helene. Funny that she was wearing that old blue dress and the polo coat. Hardly stepping-out clothes. He noticed too, seeing her for the first time in a bright light, that she wore practically no make-up. Oh, well, she'd probably had her reasons. You never could tell about Helene.

He reflected that she was the only woman in the world who could look so graceful perched on a bar stool. The only woman in the world who was so beautiful. The only woman in the world period.

"Helene," he said, "there's something I want to tell you——"

Not about the book, though, not yet. Not here in the Silver Dollar Bar. That had to wait till they were home.

"It's about murder," he said.

"Whose?" Helene asked. "Gloria Garden's? Bertha Morrison's? Or just any old murder that happens along?" She looked at him out of the corner of her eye. After all, Jake had things to explain. Maybe he was going to explain them now. "Go on, darling. Tell me."

"Not a real murder," Jake said, looking into his glass. "An abstract murder. Like this, Helene. A person murders another person. That's a terrible thing, for the person who gets murdered, and for his relatives and friends But it's more terrible for the person who does the murder. See? Because a person who murders another person usually does it for some specific gain, and the specific thing invariably turns out to be something else from what the person thought it was."

"You've had enough to drink," Helene said, a wifely gleam in her eye. "Let's go home."

He waved her away. "What I mean is this," he said. "In an abstract sense, of course. Suppose a person knows about a murder. Suppose he goes out to try and find the murderer, for some selfish reason of his own. He's making a murderer of himself, that's all. Maybe he's just curious and doesn't have any selfish motive. It's still all wrong. Because in the first place it isn't any of his business, and in the second—maybe you're right. Maybe we'd better go home."

Helene slid off the bar stool and said, "There's one damned good reason for finding a murderer, even if you're just an interested bystander. That's to keep him from murdering someone else." She waited until he'd paid the check, and then added, "You can do that two ways. One, by finding the murderer. Two, by finding his next intended victim and sticking around."

One of several million reasons why he was in love with Helene, Jake thought, was that she always knew what he was trying to say, even when it wasn't said very well. He tried to think of ways to tell her that, but none of them sounded convincing. "You're so understanding" didn't really cover the ground, and "I love you" was trite. He finally managed to explain what he meant by kissing her in the taxicab, from Forty-seventh Street to Fifty-first, through two stop lights.

They inquired at the hotel desk about Malone. He hadn't come in yet.

Malone was all right, Jake said firmly. Malone could take care of himself.

He closed the door to their suite and said, "Helene, I have a confession——"

She kissed him lightly on the forehead and said, "I'll be right back, darling. Make yourself a drink." She vanished into the bedroom.

Jake made himself a drink and then left it untouched

on the end table. He had to tell her the whole business, now. The book. His series of failures. Everything. What he'd learned about the murders, and what he hadn't succeeded in learning. Then they'd call up the Pennsylvania Railroad and make two reservations on a train for Chicago, and everything would be all right again.

Except for the thought Helene had planted in his mind. A reason for finding a murderer was to keep him from murdering someone else. It was a disquieting thought. Did he possibly know enough, in the confused and unmatched facts he'd stored up in his brain, to save another life? If he did—but he wasn't sure.

Helene came back into the room. She had on an ice-blue satin housecoat that rustled around her knees and left her pale shoulders bare. Her corn-silk hair was brushed out and hung, shining, showering over her shoulders. Her gold-colored ostrich mules appeared and disappeared at the hem of her skirt like kittens playing tag.

"You didn't finish your drink," she said reprovingly, picking it up.

"Helene, listen," Jake said, half desperately. "There's something I've got to tell you. It's that——"

The telephone rang. Jake swore and picked it up.

A female voice said, "Mr. Justus? Just a minute please." He waited, and Arthur Peterson's voice said, "Hello?"

"What the hell do you want," Jake snapped, "at this hour of the night?" It was only one o'clock, but still——

"Do you know where Dennis Morrison is?" Arthur Peterson demanded. "Is he with you?"

"No, and no," Jake said, looking at Helene. He hadn't noticed before that she'd put gold polish on the nails of her lovely toes. "Why?"

"He went back to the hotel from the hospital," Peterson said. "We put a cop in the lobby to watch out for him. But now he's gone. Somehow he slipped by the cop. I thought maybe you knew where he'd gone." He said, "The cop wasn't there to keep him from going away, he was there to keep him from being killed."

Jake said coldly, "I haven't seen him," and hung up. He looked at Helene.

Amateurs had no business mixing up in police affairs. Anyway, murder, like virtue, had its own reward.

Helene was beautiful, and he loved her.

And yet—"*a good reason for finding a murderer . . . to keep him from murdering someone else. . . .*"

At least, it wouldn't do any harm to ask a few questions of the elevator boy and the people down in the lobby. Jake said, "Helene, I'll be right back," and went out, fast.

Nobody had seen a thing. Not the desk clerk, nor the doorman, nor the cigarette girl, nor the head bellhop. And this time, he knew, it wasn't a conspiracy of silence. He wasn't a jealous husband, and he was backing up his questions with nice green folding money.

He asked one more elevator boy, who shook his head and said no, he hadn't seen anyone resembling Dennis Morrison. Jake got in the elevator to go home. He'd done his duty, and the hell with it.

"Sorry I can't help," the boy said, "but you could ride an ox down in one of these elevators and nobody'd notice. Or maybe he went down the freight elevator, or took the stairs. Poor guy, he sure must be nuts by now." He shook his head and sighed. "Awful thing." He grinned. "Too bad she didn't know she was gonna be murdered, or she wouldn't of called in a doctor."

"Doctor?" Jake said, his head spinning.

"Sure," the elevator boy said. "He said he was the

doctor she'd called. I knew he really was a doctor because he had his little black bag with him. I took him up. He asked me what Mrs. Morrison's room number was, and I told him. Oooops, sorry, Mr. Justus. I didn't mean to carry you past your floor."

"Never mind," Jake said. "Just take me back to the lobby. Thanks."

Dennis Morrison had gone out,

A doctor, with a little black bag.

If one could stop a murderer from murdering someone else——

He knew, suddenly, where Dennis Morrison was going, and why. He knew, too, that he had to follow him. To save Dennis Morrison's life.

Jake paused at the desk long enough to tell the desk clerk, "Please phone up to Mrs. Justus and tell her I've been suddenly called out on important business. And tell her to stay right there until I get back."

Chapter Thirty-One

"I AM *not* lost," Malone told himself firmly. "It's just that I don't know where I am."

He looked up again at the street sign, to make sure that he'd read it right. In spite of lack of sleep, brandy and Coca-Cola, red wine, rye, Scotch and soda, vodka, and beer, it was obviously a physical impossibility for Fourth Street to cross Eleventh Street. And yet, there it was, on the street sign. Maybe he ought to write a letter to Einstein about it, and at once.

He'd spent an hour trying to find a restaurant which didn't serve ravioli, curry, chow mein, or little hot biscuits. He'd succeeded in finding a number of bars, and he'd met a number of interesting people, all of whom he hoped he'd never see again.

He'd reached West Twelfth Street and then, going on, he'd reached Little West Twelfth Street. That had scared him and he'd turned back.

He'd found a bar run by an Armenian poet who charged a dollar for a drink, or gave you a drink free if you listened to his poems. Malone listened to one poem, paid a dollar for his next drink, and left.

Finally, he got back to Fourth Street. He followed it because it had a nice, substantial-sounding name. A street named that certainly ought to lead a person somewhere. To a taxi, and then to a hotel, and then to a ticket office, where he could get a train for Chicago.

Instead, Fourth Street had let him down. He'd followed it doggedly, and it had turned out to be a snare and a delusion. It had led him this far, and then abandoned him at a street intersection which obviously did not exist.

Malone stood considering the phenomenon for a long time, gazing thoughtfully at the street sign. To his surprise, it failed to disappear. He had a feeling that something ought to be done about it, immediately, but he wasn't quite sure what. Maybe he ought to phone the police.

No, the thing to do was to find his way back to the party he'd left so unceremoniously, and tell Jake and Helene. They would know what to do. He wouldn't have any trouble getting back there. It was somewhere south of here. Malone drew a long breath and plunged bravely in a direction he believed to be south.

Or was it south? After a few blocks he began to worry,

and finally tried a new direction, walked a few more blocks, and ended up on Fourth Street again. This was getting him nowhere.

A pedestrian came along at this moment. Malone swallowed his pride, stopped him and asked how to get to Morton Street.

The pedestrian thought it over. "Well," he said thoughtfully, "you go down this street." He pointed in the direction from which Malone had come. "At the next corner you turn left. Go a block, and turn right. Go another block, and turn left again. Then go two blocks and——"

"Never mind," Malone said hastily. "I'll find it myself."

Nevertheless, he attempted to follow the directions the stranger had given him. They landed him back on Fourth Street again.

Once he'd read a book about the big north woods that had contained directions on what to do when lost. Something about examining the bark of the trees. The problem, then, was to find a tree. He looked around hopefully.

A prim-looking, middle-aged woman was coming down the street. Malone stepped up to her, lifted his hat politely, and said, "Pardon me, madam, can you tell me where to find a tree?"

She screamed and fled.

The book had also advised building a small fire, sitting down, keeping calm, and waiting to be rescued. That sounded more reasonable. "Remember," the book had said, "if you are lost, people are looking for you." That was the most hopeful thought of all. "Most people, when lost, become panicky and start going around in circles." That had been his whole trouble, he'd been going around in circles.

There didn't seem to be anything with which to build

the small fire, however, and besides, Malone doubted if the police would approve.

He should have stuck to Fourth Street in the first place. Obviously he and Fourth Street were affinities. He started doggedly along Fourth Street, and got back to the corner of Fourth and Eleventh Streets again.

Malone was getting mad now. He was damned if he'd let Fourth Street fool him again. Eleventh Street looked more promising, anyway. He started off in a new direction with a feeling that now, perhaps, he was getting somewhere.

Ah! Waverly Place! That was a name he remembered. He was getting somewhere! He followed it with a growing feeling of confidence and reached a broad, well-lighted thoroughfare which looked vaguely familiar. Twenty-three Morton Street ought to be around here somewhere. He resolved to stick to Waverly Place, the only street he'd been able to trust so far. He sailed joyously on across the broad, lighted street and looked hopefully around for Waverly Place on the other side.

Just at that minute he remembered why he'd recognized its name. Once he'd known a chorus girl named Wanda Waverly. That discouraged him.

He walked the short distance to the next corner and looked around for the street sign. Waverly Place. He looked at the other angle of the sign. Waverly Place.

He pulled himself together and looked again at the sign, to make sure.

Reaching an intersection of Fourth and Eleventh Streets had been bad enough. But coming to the corner of Waverly Place and Waverly Place was the last straw.

A cruising Yellow, obviously sent by a merciful providence, came along just in time to save Malone from complete collapse. He sank back on the cushions and closed his eyes.

"Where d'ya want to go?" the driver asked.

"Chicago!" Malone said hoarsely. "And quick!"

He was still shuddering a little when he stepped into the lobby of the St. Jacques. The sooner he got out of this town, the better!

Helene stopped him in the middle of the lobby. She grabbed his arm and gasped, "Malone! I'm so glad you got here!"

"Out of my way," he said. "I've got to pack. The hell with Abner Proudfoot and his forty-five hundred bucks."

"Malone, listen to me!" She shook his arm. "Jake——"

He looked at her. She had on an ice-blue satin negligee, galoshes, and a fur coat. Her gleaming hair was down over her shoulders. It was pleasantly reminiscent of the first time he'd seen her.

"What's this about Jake?" he asked.

"He's gone." She caught her breath. "The police called. They said Dennis Morrison had disappeared again. Jake went downstairs to ask a few questions in the lobby. Then he sent me a message that he had to go out on important business. By the time I got my coat and galoshes on and came down here, he was gone."

Malone stared at her. Duty and temptation began to wrestle in his mind.

"Don't just stand there," she said. "Malone, *do* something."

"I'm thinking," he told her. "I'm between the devil and the sea-blue sheep."

She stamped her foot, said, "All right, I'll find him myself," and started to push past him. He caught her arm.

"Wait a minute," the little lawyer said.

They were beside the huge floral display where Jake and Helene had first met Dennis Morrison. If they'd only had sense enough to mind their own business then, all this wouldn't have happened. He stared at the flowers. Just one thing would fit the whole puzzle together.

"Helene, which flowers was Dennis Morrison stealing to take home to his bride?"

"Who cares?" She drew a long breath. "The lilies."

He nodded, and took her arm. "That's what I needed to know. Come on. We'll follow Jake."

"Follow him *where*?"

"I know where he's going," Malone said, "and why." He almost shoved her into the taxi. "Because even a drunk don't take lilies to a live girl."

Chapter Thirty-Two

"THERE HE IS!" Malone said. He started to hurry down the ramp toward the ferryboat. Helene caught his arm.

"No," she said. "Don't let him see us." She hesitated a moment. "Malone, he's doing something that—for some reason—he wants to do by himself. He doesn't want us to romp up and announce we're going along. We've got to let him do it his own way. But we've got to be there, in case—well, just in case."

Malone grumbled that Helene was obviously crazy, that it was two-thirty in the morning, and that he should have stayed in the hotel to do his packing. Jake was a full-grown man who could take care of himself, Helene ought to have sense enough to be home in bed at this hour, instead of riding around in ferryboats, wearing a negligee, and as far as Dennis Morrison, his missing bride, and the murder of Gloria Garden were concerned—the hell with it.

He ducked behind a pillar, pulling Helene with him, when Jake turned to look over his shoulder. Then he said, "Come on. He's out of sight. And we've got to catch the same boat."

"Malone, you're a very wonderful man," Helene said. She scampered down the ramp beside him.

Jake was up at the very prow of the boat, as though he couldn't wait for it to land. Helene and Malone paused halfway along the deck. The ferryboat gave a sudden quiver and started moving.

"Maybe we should have called up the cops," Malone said.

"Not necessary," Helene said. "Don't look now, but Birnbaum, O'Brien, and Schultz got on just behind us. They're trying to keep out of sight."

What had been a thin drizzle of rain, in mid-Manhattan, was a thick, smoky fog, here in the bay. The ferry moved slowly, the melancholy warnings of foghorns sounding from every direction. The few lights that showed were dim, misted blurs.

"This is my first ride on a boat," Malone complained, "and I can't see a damned thing. Not even the end of my cigar."

The fog was cold and wet on his face. He wished the ferry would be a little steadier.

"Malone, do you know where we're going?"

"Yes," Malone said, "but I don't know the address. That's why we've got to follow Jake." He decided to throw the cigar overboard.

"Malone, do you know where Bertha is?"

"Yes," Malone said tersely. "And don't bother me." He wondered if he could swim ashore, if he jumped overboard right here and now. He tightened his grip on the rail.

"That dinner jacket," she said.

Malone decided to jump overboard and take a chance on drowning.

"I wanted to wait until I could tell you and Jake at the same time," she said, "but——"

The little lawyer said, "*Shuddup!*"

"—since I did find out——"

He began to hope that he would drown.

"Malone!" She gasped. "Look, this is just a little ferryboat, just going over to Staten Island. Millions of people ride on it every day. You couldn't possibly be seasick on a ferryboat."

Malone said, "I'm unique," and was.

Fifteen awful minutes later he stumbled up the ramp, shamelessly leaning on her arm. "Thank heaven," he said. "Dry land." He paused for a minute until the dry land stopped spinning around. "Helene, isn't there some way of getting back to New York besides riding on that boat?"

"None," she said mercilessly. "And come on. Jake's headed toward something that looks like a streetcar."

Malone groaned, and followed her. "I'll have to spend the rest of my life on Staten Island," he said, "and I don't like it here."

There was a little three-car train waiting outside the ferry station. Jake got into the first car. Helene led Malone into the second. Malone hoped that Birnbaum, O'Brien, and Schultz were in the third.

He was beginning to feel better now, but he resolved not to tell Helene. He wondered what Staten Island looked like. All he could see was a gray-white wall of fog. It was a damp, unpleasant fog, one that hinted at the presence of things that could be imagined but not seen, horrors that couldn't be described in polite company. Malone shivered. Was that a banshee yodeling, or was it the wheels of the car as it went around a curve?

The cut over his eye began to itch. His stomach felt like a football that had gone through an Army-Navy game. He ached in every limb. And he was going to feel worse before the night was over. He knew it.

The little train stopped at a dozen stations. At every stop he bounded up to the door with Helene and looked out on the platform for Jake.

Then finally, there was a station where Jake got off. The fog was lighter here, but not much. Vague shapes loomed up through it that might have been houses, or trees, or prehistoric monsters. Helene held up the skirt of her negligee, and they waded through a patch of tall, wet weeds to what seemed to be a sidewalk. At least, Malone hoped they were weeds. A frog croaked suddenly, somewhere near his feet, and a cold sweat broke out all over his body.

"Don't let him get out of sight," Helene whispered.

Jake was moving slowly, pausing now and then, as though to make sure he knew his way. They followed at a discreet distance. Malone prayed silently that Birnbaum, O'Brien, and Schultz weren't too far behind. He glanced once, over his shoulder; they were nowhere in sight. He muffled a groan.

He was unhappy. He knew what they were going to find when Jake led them to their destination, and he suspected what was going to happen. It wasn't just a premonition, either. And he didn't like the prospect. He wished it weren't going to turn out that way.

A tiny street light flickered feebly and ineffectually in the fog. Beyond it, they passed four shadowy shapes of houses. The first three were unlighted. It might have been that their occupants were asleep, but Malone didn't think so. They had an empty look. A pale-yellow light showed dimly in the window of the fourth house. Then, beyond it——

Helene clutched Malone's arm. Jake was standing at the edge of what seemed to be a little open field, a tall, motionless, and silent figure. In the center of the field was another figure, on hands and knees. Helene and Malone crept up a bit closer.

Suddenly the door of the house opened, making a long, narrow panel of light. Old Dr. Puckett appeared in the doorway. He had a lantern in one hand, and an old-fashioned revolver in the other.

Malone had done his best to be quiet, but the fog had been too much for him. He sneezed, and loudly.

Jake wheeled around and stared at them. "What the hell are you doing here?"

"I might ask——" Malone began indignantly.

Helene gave a little gasp, pointed, and said, "What's *he* doing here?"

Malone looked at Dennis Morrison. He closed his eyes, quickly, but the image remained before them. A dead-white, desperate face, blotched with mud, and streaked with sweat, with damp, disheveled hair hanging over the forehead, and with burning eyes that stared out, wide with horror and a kind of madness. His hands were caked with mud, they were bruised and bleeding. A small trowel lay abandoned a little way behind him, for the last few feet he'd been digging, wildly, frantically, with his hands.

"Why, he's looking for Bertha Morrison's head," old Dr. Puckett said mildly, coming down the steps and into the garden. "Only he won't find it here. It's buried over there in the corner, by the crab-apple tree." He added in a tone of gentle reproof, "No sense in tearing up all those beets I just put in." Then he said, "You should have brought a shovel, son."

"I couldn't find one," Dennis Morrison said. He rose to his knees, with a sudden scream of terror. Then he was silent. The silence was more frightening than the scream had been.

Jake said, "Wait! Dr. Puckett——"

Dr. Puckett didn't seem to hear. He took a few more steps into the garden. Helene screamed, Jake reached for her and held her tight.

"You shouldn't have killed Hazel," Dr. Puckett said. His voice was quiet, too quiet. "Bertha was a bad woman, maybe she deserved to be killed, but Hazel'd done a lot for you. You shouldn't have killed her."

"I didn't want to kill her," Dennis screamed. "I didn't want to kill Bertha either. But I had to!" He tried to get up, and stumbled to his knees again.

Malone cried, "No!" and ran, not toward Dr. Puckett but toward Dennis Morrison.

"Please get away, Mr. Malone," Dr. Puckett said. "I'm not a very good shot and I don't want to hurt anybody."

Malone ran on anyway. He'd seen the move Dennis Morrison had made, toward his pocket. He wanted to call out a warning, but his voice seemed to have frozen.

Suddenly a big shape loomed up through the mist. A blow landed on his chin, a heavy body knocked him to the ground and held him there. He heard a shot, felt the bullet whiz past. Then there was another shot, from another direction, and he lifted his head just in time to see Dennis Morrison's eyes grow wide for a split second with terrible surprise, before he pitched, head forward, into the dirt, the automatic dropping from his hands.

Schultz helped Malone to his feet. "Hope I didn't hurt you," he said anxiously. Then, angrily, "You damn fool, don't you know any better than to do a thing like that?"

Malone didn't hear him. No one heard him. Everyone, even O'Brien and Birnbaum, was looking at Dr. Puckett.

Dr. Puckett was looking at his gun. He looked tired and, somehow, surprised.

"I guess I shouldn't have done that," he said. "Because now that makes me a murderer, doesn't it?"

Malone walked over to Dr. Puckett and took the old-fashioned revolver from his limp and unprotesting fingers. "Don't you worry," he said confidently. "The most beautiful case of self-defense I ever saw in my life, with plenty of witnesses. And besides, you've got the best damn lawyer in the whole wide world."

Chapter Thirty-Three

"THIS IS the sort of thing," Arthur Peterson said severely, "that invariably results when well-intentioned but untrained amateurs attempt to interfere with legitimate police activities."

Malone said, "Nuts." He finally got his cigar lighted. "We found Bertha Morrison's head, didn't we? And Gloria Garden's body. And the murderer."

O'Brien said, "You lay off him, Peterson. He's a cousin of mine."

"Mine too," Birnbaum put in. "On my mother's side."

Schultz said, "Unarmed, when he saw this guy he knew was a killer, he ran." He thought over the statement and added, "Not from him, at him."

"Nevertheless," Arthur Peterson said, "this interference brought about Dennis Morrison's death."

"Thereby saving the state the cost of a trial," Malone said, chewing on the cigar, "and the cost of a little electric current. You don't have any gratitude, that's all. Besides," he said, "you'll get the credit for tracking down the ruthless madman murderer of two helpless women." He was beginning to warm up to his courtroom manner now. "You caught him just when he'd returned to where he'd buried the head of one of his victims, and the body of another. Just when he was about to murder the aged father of one of his victims—who, luckily, shot first."

Arthur Peterson cleared his throat and said, "Of course, there's something in what you say."

"You're damned right," Malone said. He prayed that Dr. Puckett would keep his promise to shut up and let his lawyer do the talking.

Arthur Peterson's little office was full of people. Helene was there, her lovely face very pale, her gleaming hair tumbled over her shoulders, her blue satin negligee spattered with mud. Jake was there beside her, holding her hand tight. Dr. Puckett was sitting, silent and motionless, in a straight-backed chair. O'Brien, Birnbaum, and Schultz were ranged along the wall, looking admiringly at Helene. Standing near the door—he'd refused all offers of a chair —was Abner Proudfoot, looking annoyed.

Malone ached. Not anywhere in particular, he just ached. His suit was a mess, from his headlong fall into the mud. His jaw hurt, where Schultz had landed on it. The cut over his eye had reopened and was bleeding a little. The trip back on the ferry had been every bit as bad as he'd anticipated, even worse. And he'd have cheerfully given twenty years of his life for a drink. Yet, he was happy. He thought he saw a way out, if he could only put the story across now.

"But, Malone," Helene began. His eyes signaled her to silence.

"Morrison was a madman," Malone said thoughtfully. "Insane, and drunk. That explains everything." At least, he hoped that it would. He turned to Peterson. "You already know that he was behaving irrationally. That business of his riding back and forth on the ferryboats."

Arthur Peterson frowned. "Doc Grosher said he acted sane enough. Still, Doc Grosher has been known to be fooled before."

Jake coughed apologetically.

"But that business of switching the heads," Peterson said. "Dismembering Gloria Garden's body, and burying it, with Bertha Morrison's head, in her father's back yard."

"Her father's sister-in-law's back yard," Schultz said, with his passion for accuracy.

"Obviously, the act of a madman," Malone said. "And you'd better refer to her as Gloria Morrison, because she was married to him, too. Then he bigamously married another woman, Bertha, for her money, and murdered Gloria. When he truly realized the horror of his deed, in a mad and perverted attempt at retribution, he murdered Bertha, and switched the heads of the two unfortunate women. Why? An insane act, obviously. Yet, like all insane acts, with a certain twisted reasoning. The woman found murdered in the St. Jacques hotel would be recognized by the world as his wife. To him, however, Gloria, his secret bride, was his true wife. Therefore, he placed Gloria's head upon Bertha's shoulders."

"But, Mr. Malone," Dr. Puckett said, half hesitatingly.

Malone turned to him and said quickly, "I ask you, as a doctor." He glanced around the room. "I ask all of you, as reasonable, intelligent people. Was that the act of a sane man? I do not need to answer 'No,' I can see it written in your eyes." He paused and mopped his brow. "And why the midnight burial in that deserted corner of Staten Island? Why, you ask. Because his poor, mad brain demanded that, in some fashion, he return poor Gloria Garden to the aged father whom he had so cruelly and brutally wronged." He closed his eyes for a moment.

In another minute, Helene thought, he'll forget himself and demand that the judge instruct the jury to bring in a verdict of not guilty.

"Yes," O'Brien said, "but how about Gloria selling that other dame's jewels?"

Malone turned on him with a magnificent scowl. "Can you prove that was the case? Are you willing to take the word of a—a fence, instead of the word of a reputable lawyer?" He shook his head sadly. "Only heaven," he added piously, "will ever know who sold Mr. Prince those jewels."

"Yeah," Schultz said, blinking. "Only, then, how come somebody tried to murder him—Dennis Morrison?"

"Did anyone see an attempt at murder?" Malone demanded. "Were there any witnesses to the actual deed? Was the attacker ever found? The answer, ladies and gentlemen, is no. Poor boy," he sighed sonorously, "in his insanity, he attempted to do away with himself."

Arthur Peterson nodded and said, "Yes, that's possible. It all sounds reasonable. His going mad, committing the murders, switching the heads, and burying the head of one wife and the body of another in Dr. Puckett's yard."

"Sister-in-law's," Schultz muttered under his breath.

"But," Birnbaum said. "You'll excuse it, Mr. Malone." His brow wrinkled. "He buried them. So why did he go and try to dig them up again?"

"Who knows?" Malone said. "Who, now, will ever know?" He sighed again. "Perhaps," he whispered, "the man was a necrophiliac."

"Whatever the hell that is," O'Brien said, "you'd better leave it out of the report, Peterson. Just say the guy was a nut, all right, and it was a damn lucky thing that Dr. Puckett shot in time."

"A perfect case of self-defense," Malone said. He smiled reassuringly at Dr. Puckett. Dr. Puckett's tired old eyes smiled back. "I guess that takes care of everything."

"Except the letters," Arthur Peterson said. "Those letters that were received from Bertha Morrison. There still isn't any explanation for that."

"A mere trifle," Malone said, with a lordly gesture, but a worried frown wrinkled his forehead.

"A murdered woman writes letters, and he calls it a trifle," Birnbaum moaned.

"Why worry?" Malone said to Peterson. "Hell, you've got the whole case sewed up in a bag. You've got an explanation, a motive, and a dead murderer. If you ask me, the police did themselves proud in this case. You ought to get a promotion out of it." He began unwrapping a fresh cigar.

"Besides," Jake said, "I can explain about those letters." He gave Helene's hand a squeeze, and stood up. He might have been a miserable failure as an amateur detective, on his own, but there was one thing he could contribute.

"Bertha Morrison," he said, "was a very methodical

woman. She kept an address book with notes on the personal life of her friends. She kept a list of people to whom she owed letters, and of people who owed letters to her."

"We know that," Arthur Peterson said.

"Well," Jake went on, "she and her husband decided, for some reason, to spend a secret honeymoon in Manhattan, instead of going on the tour they'd planned. I know that, because while Dennis was out on his binge, she unpacked everything as though she were going to stay in the St. Jacques for a month. But she'd told all her girl friends that she was going on a honeymoon. So, she wrote all her thank-you notes and dated them ahead. She probably wrote postcards, too, and I'll make a small bet her friends will be receiving those postcards for the next couple of weeks.*

"In her typewriter there was a letter to her uncle George, dated three weeks ahead. And among her papers there was a receipt from the World-Wide Mailing Service."

"What in hell is that?" Malone asked.

"It's a letter service," Jake said. "I should have tumbled to the whole thing when I saw that receipt, but my mind was on something else. When I was a press agent and manager, I knew the World-Wide Mailing Service very well. They'll mail letters for you from any place in the country." He drew a long breath. "Say you're managing a radio tenor. You want him to get a fan letter from some certain part of Tennessee where response hasn't been so good. You write the letter, and the World-Wide Mailing Service mails it from whatever town you pick in Tennessee. Or suppose you want somebody to think you're in Florida, when you're really back home next to the radiator. The World-Wide Mailing Service mails a postcard

* Jake was right. They did.

for you. Bertha wanted her friends to think she was on a honeymoon tour, so she planted her letters with World-Wide Mailing Service."

"Well, I'm damned!" Malone said.

"Jake!" Helene said. "You're *wonderful!*"

Arthur Peterson said, "That's very interesting. And I guess that takes care of everything."

"I sincerely trust you are correct," Abner Proudfoot said. He'd been standing in his corner like a statue of gloom. "And now may I inform you that I have deeply resented being called from my bed and being brought down here at this hour of the night, for the purposes of listening to this explanation."

"Explanation hell," Malone said. "I had you brought down here to sign a check, chum." He pulled the crumpled, paper out of his wallet. "I, Abner Proudfoot, as trustee for Bertha Morrison, née Lutts, do promise to pay to John Joseph Malone the sum of four thousand five hundred dollars, in the event of the said Bertha Morrison, née Lutts, being found and proved innocent of the murder committed in suite 713 of the St. Jacques Hotel, on the night of April 9th." He read it out loud and then said, "Pull out your checkbook, chum. Because Bertha's been found, and because she sure as hell is proved innocent of that murder, since she was its victim."

"Nonsense," Abner Proudfoot said.

"It may be nonsense," Malone said, "but it's in your handwriting." He looked around the room. "Can someone here lend Mr. Proudfoot a fountain pen?"

Six fountain pens were offered, simultaneously and immediately.

"I did not come here to listen to any such ridiculous demands," Abner Proudfoot said. He started to put on his hat.

"If you owe my cousin Malone any money, you'd better pay it right here and now, buddy," O'Brien said, moving up a step.

"Or we'll collect it for him," Schultz said, moving up two steps.

"And if it should go into court," Birnbaum added, "I have an uncle, he's a judge."

"This is entirely out of my department," Arthur Peterson added, "but it does appear to me to be a legitimate claim."

Abner Proudfoot opened his mouth to speak, looked around him, and shut it again.

He took a step toward the door and said, "I shall take this up with my attorney. I refuse to be intimidated."

Schultz's eyes shone with the joy of impending battle. He turned back one cuff.

"Leave him alone," the little lawyer said. He doesn't like to be intimidated. You heard him." He took out a cigar and began slowly unwrapping it. "It's a good thing Dennis Morrison *was* mad. It's a good thing he didn't murder Bertha for her money. Because he'd have been so bitterly disappointed when he found out that he wouldn't get it."

"But he would have," Arthur Peterson said, a puzzled look on his face. "As her husband, he'd have inherited it."

"*If* there was anything to inherit," Malone said. "Maybe Bertha didn't know it, but maybe she didn't have any money. Maybe it had all been spent, gambled away." He looked at Abner Proudfoot and smiled amiably. "I might just happen to stumble on the evidence, and it would be interesting, all things considered."

Abner Proudfoot looked at him, at Arthur Peterson, and at the three cops. Then he took out his checkbook and his own fountain pen and made out the check, slowly and meticulously, dotting every *i*.

Malone watched him happily. Maybe, he told himself, he should have informed the police about Abner Proudfoot's embezzlements. About the well-dusted shabbiness of Abner Proudfoot's house and the disorganized and understaffed office that had tipped him off, about the evidence he'd been given by Charlie Firman. But frankly, he just didn't want to bother. Besides, Abner Proudfoot would get everything that was coming to him. In the first place, he was broke. In the second, Bertha's heirs, whoever they were, would undoubtedly investigate and bring charges, when they discovered that Bertha's fortune had all gone down a drain.

From the expression on Abner Proudfoot's face as he crossed the last *t*, the check was being written with his heart's blood.

"Thanks, pal," Malone said. He took the check, blew on it to dry the signature, folded it, and tucked it in his vest pocket. "I knew you'd be reasonable. And just to show you how reasonable I can be——" He took out the sheet of paper Charlie Firman had sent him, with all the facts and figures, and recklessly handed it to Abner Proudfoot. "Press that in your memory book, chum,"

Proudfoot looked at it. For a moment he looked frightened. Then he looked defeated, a man who knew when he was licked. And then he looked just plain mean-and-nasty vindictive.

"A clear case of blackmail," he said coldly. "I demand that this man be arrested. You saw him force me into giving him a check. You saw him, in return give me a paper full of—lying accusations." He tossed the paper on Arthur Peterson's desk. "I may have made some errors of judgment in regard to financial matters, and if it can be proven that I have done so, I will be glad to pay the penalty, but this—this extortionist!" He paused, as though speechless.

"Tt-tt-tt!" O'Brien said. "That's a very bad word."

Arthur Peterson glanced at the paper. He looked at Malone. Then he exchanged glances with O'Brien, Birnbaum, and Schultz.

He took off his glasses, folded them, and put them carefully away in their case. Then he launched into a little speech about the value to the police department of public-spirited citizens who did not hesitate to do their duty. He thanked Malone for his assistance in clearing up the murder, congratulated Jake for his brilliant deductions, and looked admiringly at Helene. He regretted the necessity for placing Dr. Puckett under arrest, even temporarily, since he had so obviously fired in self-defense and rid society of a dangerous madman. He hoped Dr. Puckett would be made as comfortable as possible during his brief incarceration. He praised O'Brien, Birnbaum, and Schultz for their untiring efforts, and added a pretty little phrase about departmental efficiency.

Under cover of the speech, Malone picked up the damning paper from the desk, and lit his cigar with it. The ashes fell, unnoticed, into Arthur Peterson's wastebasket.

"And as for you," Arthur Peterson said to Abner Proudfoot, "your accusations are obviously unfounded in fact. There is no evidence to substantiate your claims. And besides"—a thin but happy smile curved his lips—"that is not in my department."

Chapter Thirty-Four

JAKE YAWNED and stretched. "It's seven o'clock. Shall we send down for breakfast, or shall we all go to sleep and wait till we wake up to send down for breakfast."

Malone announced that he was going to stay awake until the banks opened, and then cash that check, fast. He looked at his watch and said, "It's time for breakfast, though."

"It's damned near time for supper," Jake said. He yawned again.

"What's more," Helene said coldly, "it's time for explanations. I'll order breakfast, while you two think them up."

Jake and Malone didn't bother thinking about explanations. Their eyes followed her as she went to the phone and called room service. She'd changed into a long, fluffy white robe that made her look like a Christmas-tree angel, washed her face and made it up again, and brushed out her shining hair. She said into the phone, "Send up six omelets with American-fried potatoes, hot biscuits, marmalade, and six pots of coffee."

"And a pint of gin and two quarts of beer," Malone said, signaling to her frantically. "And a piece of lemon-meringue pie."

She repeated it into the phone, hung up, and turned on him indignantly. "Now. What was the idea of all those outrageous lies you told poor, credulous Arther Peterson?"

"Now, look," Jake said. "It's late, and we're all tired."

"It may be late," she said stubbornly, "but we're not that tired. For that matter, you have some explanations of your own to make."

"I'll make them," Jake said, just as stubbornly, "when I've been fed, and not before."

"And while we're on the subject," Malone said, "how about that dinner jacket?"

Helene turned up her nose, folded her arms, and was resolutely silent until room service knocked at the door. She remained silent until half the gin and beer, all the food and all the coffee were gone. Then she poured out three more drinks and said to Malone, "Well? Why did you tell all that to Arthur Peterson?"

Malone said crossly, "Dr. Puckett was perfectly justified in what he did. You wouldn't like to see him stuck in jail, would you? I didn't think so. Well, he's safe with this self-defense setup. Only, I couldn't have fixed him up on a charge of mutilating a body and transporting a corpse without a permit."

"How did you know?" Helene asked.

"Because of the lilies," Malone said. "And why don't you go to sleep and leave me alone?"

"But, Jake," Helene said. "How did you know?"

"The little black bag," Jake mumbled. "And the elevator boy. Go 'way and let me sleep."

Helene poured three more drinks and said relentlessly, "You aren't going to sleep, either of you, until you've explained everything. Not if I have to light little bonfires under your pink toes. Maybe you ought to pool your information, and come up with a good story. And it had better be good, too."

Jake confessed to his bribery of the chambermaid, and his search of suite 713, and his deduction that Bertha had planned to stay, while Dennis had not. Malone came in with what Wildavine had confided to him, as Bertha's reason for staying. Jake apologized for his lapse in not recognizing, immediately, the significance of the receipt from the World-Wide Mailing Service, and Malone explained his relationship with Abner Proudfoot, omitting a few details which he considered entirely personal and nobody's damn business but his. Jake admitted his early suspicions of Wildavine, and Malone revealed that—probably as a matter of wish thinking—he'd pinned the whole affair on Abner Proudfoot.

Helene stated that all this autobiographical material was very interesting. She, however, would like to know exactly what had happened.

"From whose point of view?" Malone asked. "Dennis Morrison's? Well, the life story he gave us was true enough. Except, he left out a few things. He worked for an escort bureau, all right. But he left it when he married Gloria Garden, because she had a nice little income he could live on."

"He left it before he married her," Jake said. He brought the Gloria Garden-Dennis Morrison correspondence out of its hiding place to prove it.

"Well, anyway, he married her," Malone said. "But she didn't make enough money. He went back to the escort bureau in hopes of meeting a wealthy and foolish woman. Luck sent him Bertha Lutts. She was shrewd instead of foolish, but the result was the same, as far as Dennis was concerned. A marriage was arranged. He made careful plans. He'd go out and get drunk on their wedding night —a circumstance almost anyone could sympathize with. While he was away, she'd be brutally murdered, for her jewelry. He made plans for the disposal of the jewelry. But then he had to murder Gloria Garden, too, because she was threatening to give the whole show away. His alibi, of course, was to have been his getting drunk, and showing up at various nightclubs and bars, in various states of intoxication, and climaxing it by falling into the hands of some perfect strangers, in the lobby of the St. Jacques."

Helene said, "But, Malone——" He shushed her.

"Tell the story from Bertha Morrison's viewpoint," he said. "She had to have a lover or a husband, preferably the latter, to quiet certain unpleasant rumors that were going the rounds. She'd probably heard of the escort bureau through her cousin, she called up for a young man, and got Dennis Morrison. I've no doubt he told the truth, that she suggested the marriage. He certainly couldn't have known that she planned to spend her honeymoon in Manhattan, and not with him, or that she'd sent out those letters to be mailed. Or else, he would have arranged things differently

"Now, take Gloria Garden. She'd been in love with Dennis Morrison. He left her, to marry—bigamously— another woman. She wrote to her father about it, heart-broken. Then, the night of the murder, Dennis came back, with Bertha's jewels. Remember, he wouldn't have dared to dispose of them himself. He'd already given Gloria a long song and dance about selling the jewels for him, and running away with him, and she fell for it. Because she was in love with him and she didn't know he had mur-dered Bertha. Then, when she came back and met him, with the dough, he murdered her."

"He'd moved back in with her, too," Jake said, wide-awake now. "Because there were gaps in the closet where he'd taken his clothes away in a hurry. And there was a smell of shaving cream in the bathroom. But he was in such a hell of a hurry that he forgot to take his pipes along."

"A detail," Malone said. "It would never have been noticed, if he hadn't made another and more serious error. He had his plans very well made. Bertha would be found, brutally beaten and strangled, her jewels gone, the murder committed during the time when her bridegroom was out painting the town. Gloria Garden would be found, strangled, but there wouldn't seem to be any connection between the two crimes." The little lawyer paused long enough to drop his frayed cigar stub in the ash tray and went on. He would have established one of those imperfect alibis that can't be proved and must be believed. He had enough confidence in himself to get genuinely drunk and have a genuine hangover, in case the police got curious. It was a beautiful setup. Anguished young bridegroom. Slaughtered bride. Police looking for a robber-murderer. Time passes, the heat is off, Bertha is buried, and the young bridegroom inherits the dough."

"But why did he promote Gloria to sell the jewelry for him?" Jake asked. "Why didn't he just dump it in the river? It's being missing proved his point."

"Probably," Malone said, "he needed ready cash. It takes a little time for an estate to be settled, remember. And he had to murder Gloria, anyway. He wasn't safe as long as she was alive. With her dead, no one knew of his secret marriage to her. And how was he to know that Jake would go digging in Gloria's mattress and that Helene here would go out hell-raising.

"You can call it hell-raising," Helene said coldly. She

doled out the rest of the gin. "But I didn't have any fun. Or maybe I'm just the conservative type. What was the serious error Dennis Morrison made?"

"He underestimated old Dr. Puckett," Malone said. He lit a fresh cigar, and sipped his gin. Maybe, sometime, he'd get some sleep. "Maybe he didn't even know about old Dr. Puckett. But it must have been a nasty blow to Dennis when he walked in that room in suite 713 to identify his murdered bride and saw Gloria Garden's face."

"You are the longest-winded and most irritating man I ever knew," Helene said.

"And you are an impertinent young woman," Malone said. He rolled his cigar between his fingers. "Let's look at the story from Dr. Puckett's viewpoint. He's a country practitioner, and a shrewd guy. He knows about murder, and he knows about people. Gloria—or to him, Hazel—wrote all about her big love affair, and her secret marriage. She wrote him when Dennis deserted her, and he sent her a letter of sound advice, urging her to come home. I wish to heaven she had. Anyway, he got to thinking it over. Finally, he just packed up and came to New York. By the way, there aren't any lectures or any medical conventions going on right now. You'd think the police would have noticed that."

"The police didn't notice a lot of things," Jake said. "Go on, Malone."

"And by the way," Helene said, "how come you're so all-fired smart all of a sudden, Malone? How did you learn all this, anyway?"

"I didn't," Malone said promptly. "I'm making it all up as I go along. But from what I do know, and from what Dr. Puckett told me tonight, I'll bet you anything you'll care to name that I'm right."

He finished his gin, yawned, and knocked the ashes

from his cigar. "Gloria—or Hazel—didn't tell him Dennis Morrison's name. Not until he arrived here, the day of the murder. She told him everything she knew, then, about Dennis' marriage to Bertha, and their honeymoon at the St. Jacques."

"You mean he saw her," Jake said, "before she died?"

"He did," Malone said. "Thank God. They had dinner together, and she was happy. Dennis had planned to marry a rich and unattractive woman for her money. At the last minute, he'd decided he couldn't go through with it. He was going to steal her jewelry, Gloria would dispose of it for him, and they'd go away together, with a little stake, and start a wonderful new life together."

"And she actually fell for that?" Helene said incredulously.

"She was in love with him," Malone said; "she'd have fallen for anything. So much so, that when old Dr. Puckett realized he couldn't talk her out of it, she almost convinced him that it would work and she'd be happy." He closed his eyes for a moment. "They had dinner in a little French restaurant near where she lived. In spite of what she was telling him, he had a good dinner and a good time. She was more beautiful than he'd ever seen her before, and her eyes were shining with happiness. I'm giving you old Doc Puckett's own words. He never gave up trying to talk her out of it, but at last when he went away, he was ready to believe that it would turn out for the best. He left her, determined not to interfere."

"But he came back," Jake said.

Malone nodded. "Away from his daughter, away from the spell of her happy excitement, he thought it over. It wasn't just the little matter of jewel robbery that worried him, but his own private theory that crime brings its own punishment, one way or another. So he went back, to try to convince her that she must give it up, and come home with him. And he found her murdered."

He laid down the cigar. "He knew who'd killed her, and why. But he couldn't have proved it. He had one letter from her saying that the man she loved was leaving her for another woman, but it didn't mention that the other woman had money, and it didn't mention the man's name. He knew enough about murder and the law to realize that what Gloria had told him at dinner was the only evidence against Dennis Morrison, and that it wasn't enough to convict him. So, there was only one thing he could do."

"Plant some evidence that would convict him," Jake said. "I guessed that when the elevator boy said a doctor had come to see Bertha that night, carrying his little black bag."

Helene shuddered. "You mean he was carrying his daughter's head in that little black bag?"

"Can you think of a better way to get through a hotel lobby with a head?" Malone asked. "He knew he couldn't carry the whole body upstairs to room 713, and he was damn well going to leave some evidence there in Dennis Morrison's room."

"But how in blazes did he expect to get in?" Jake asked.

"He'd intended to stand around in front of the door for a couple of minutes," Malone said, "then send down for a passkey on the theory that the patient who had called him must be seriously ill. He thought Dennis and Bertha would be in the bedroom, and he could get in and out without disturbing them. Instead, he found the door unlocked. Bertha must have adjusted the spring lock so that Wildavine Williams could walk right in, and Dennis, after he'd murdered Bertha and gone away, didn't notice that the door didn't lock behind him."

"The poor old man," Helene said. "To walk in that way on two murders. But, Malone, why did he switch the heads?"

"To prevent the murderer from inheriting Bertha's money," Malone said. "He knew Dennis had murdered both those women, but he still couldn't *prove* it. But if he could keep Bertha from being identified, if he could make it appear that another woman had been murdered in suite 713 and that Bertha was just missing, then he would at least keep Dennis from attaining the object of his crimes for seven years." He paused, then added reflectively, "To say nothing of driving Dennis nuts in the meantime."

Jake said, "If we hadn't all been such dopes, we'd have realized right away that only a skilled doctor could have performed that decapitation, especially when we knew that the head and the body belonged to two different women, though they seemed to fit together perfectly."

"Sure," Malone said, "he was figuring on the police not being too bright. He even hoped they'd never catch on that the body and head didn't match. But even if the medical examiner did find out the truth, he knew they still couldn't identify Bertha's body without the rest of her. and he was right. It would have worked out that way, if I hadn't been so damned inquisitive." He puffed furiously at his cigar. "The old doc's pretty smart. He left a woman who seemed to be Gloria Garden in suite 713. Then he carried Bertha's head and his daughter's body over to Staten Island, in that same little black bag. He must have made a lot of trips."

Helene shivered. She walked to the window and looked out. The fog had been blown away, the sun had come out, and Fifth Avenue was bright and washed and new.

It was hard to believe that murders happened, in such a world.

"The next day he began putting in his sister-in-law's garden," Malone said, "to conceal the fact that digging had been going on. And then, just to clinch things, he turned up at police headquarters and identified the murdered woman."

"Dennis must have known all along," Helene said.

"Of course he did," Malone told her. "That's why he was riding back and forth on the ferry boats. He was trying to follow Dr. Puckett, learn where he lived and where he must have buried Bertha Morrison's head. He must have really gone nearly insane once or twice—as he actually did, I think, at the end—when he realized that his whole elaborate scheme had gone for nothing, unless Bertha's head could be found and identified. And Dr. Puckett learned that Dennis was following him, knew that sooner or later he'd find what he was looking for. That's why he tried to murder Dennis at the ferry station. And that's why he finally shot him, tonight. He was perfectly willing, after that, to tell the whole story and go to jail. Thank goodness I talked him out of it."

"We should have pooled our information," Jake said gloomily, "instead of fumbling around on our own. We'd have gotten this over a long time earlier. I tumbled to it tonight when I realized Dr. Puckett must have performed the two decapitations. I knew then that Dennis must be the murderer, and where he'd gone, and why."

"I tumbled to it," Malone said, "when I discovered how Dennis' subconscious had tripped him up. He'd intended to be picked up in the lobby, a harmless drunk, trying to steal flowers to take to his bride. Only, he tried to steal lilies, because he knew that she was dead. Once I could accept the premise that Dennis was the murderer, I knew

Dr. Puckett had done the monkey business with the heads."

"Let this be a lesson to all of us," Helene said. "Never keep secrets from each other."

Malone looked at her sternly. "And that reminds me," he said. "About that dinner jacket——"

"Oh, that," Helene said airily. "It had nothing to do with the case. It was just an accident that happened in the men's room of one of the night clubs Dennis visited while he was establishing his alibi between murders. The owner of the dinner jacket remembered it very well. It seems he loves champagne, but he's allergic to it or something. Anyway, he was ill. While he was holding his face under a cold-water faucet, the porter sponged and pressed his dinner jacket and hung it over a chair. There was a young man who seemed to be rather intoxicated at the next washbasin who also had his dinner jacket off. He was holding his handkerchief to his nose. The young man put on a dinner jacket, the porter folded the handkerchief for him and stuffed it in his pocket and the young man went staggering out. Mr. Zabel put on what he thought was his own dinner jacket, and he too staggered out. He hadn't had a handkerchief, he'd lost it somewhere. The next day when he realized there'd been a switch, he didn't say anything about it because it seems his wife didn't know he'd been out night-clubbing."

"Mr. who?" Jake said suspiciously.

"Zabel," Helene said in an innocent voice. "Owner of the Zabel Publishing Company. Only keep it to yourself, because nobody knows he was out that night."

Jake said, "I didn't think anybody would have bought that poem without being blackmailed. How did you find him?"

"Why," Helene said, "I told you, when we were at Wildavine's. I looked him up in the phone book and called for an appointment and went right over." She added, "I just said, 'Did you lose a dinner jacket?' and he said, 'Come right over.'"

"But how did you know who to call up?" Jake roared. "How did you know whose jacket it was?"

"Well," Helene said indignantly, "his initials were on the wallet. Q. P. Z. I knew there couldn't be many men whose last name began with Z who had those initials, and I didn't mind calling them all up until I got the right one. But there was only one. Quarles P. Zabel. And he's probably going to buy all of Wildavine's poems." She folded her hands in her lap and looked pleased.

Malone stared at her silently and reflected that every now and then, he underestimated Helene.

Jake stared at her, thinking the same thing. And adding to himself that, while he certainly didn't want *The Mongoose Murders*, by Jake Justus, to be published because of the little incident of the dinner jacket, still—he knew that if he could just talk with Quarles Zabel, he could talk him into reading and probably buying the book.

No! He didn't want it to happen that way. It was an almost unendurable temptation. Just to get an appointment with Quarles Zabel—*no!* Jake squelched the temptation once and for all. He'd worked long and hard on that book, and he wasn't going to have it published just because an absent-minded man had mislaid his dinner jacket in the men's room of a night club.

Furthermore, he wasn't going to capitalize on his part in finding the murderer of Bertha Morrison and Gloria Garden.

He'd take the book back to Chicago with him, that's

what he'd do! He'd rewrite it, page by page—already he had a new idea for it—and then send it back to the editor who had just turned it down. And *this* time——

But he still had to confess everything to Helene, and right now.

Malone rose, yawned, walked to the door, and said, "Well, good night. I'll see you at the train."

No one noticed him. He sighed, shook his head, and went out. Just as he closed the door he heard Jake saying, almost hoarsely, "Helene. I've got to tell you something——"

Chapter Thirty-Five

H E HATED traveling, but this time the sound of the wheels on the track was pleasant and reassuring. Every time they went around, he was a little nearer home.

Malone looked out the window. The train had come up out of the tunnel, but they were still in New York. Well, not for long. And in the morning he'd step off the train in Chicago. The streets would be dreary and dark under the el, there would be mud and slush underfoot, and it would probably be raining. He'd love it.

Everything had, he reflected, turned out well. He'd staggered off to bed, after leaving Jake and Helene, and when he'd waked, it had been four o'clock in the afternoon. Only, it had been the next afternoon.

And Jake had explained everything to Helene. It turned

out he'd been insane enough to write some fool book and he'd been trying, unsuccessfully, to sell it all this time. Now he was reading it to Helene. Malone couldn't understand why Jake would have done such a thing, or why Helene should be so pleased about it, but as long as they were happy, he was happy.

Abner Proudfoot was in jail. Embezzlement. Also, a couple of thugs had confessed to assaulting Malone, under orders from Proudfoot. Malone thought happily of his brief phone call to George Lutts, and purred a little over the fact that Proudfoot hadn't been able to raise his bail. Maybe, he reflected, he should have confided in the police about those cardsharps, too. No, he'd taken care of that matter himself.

Old Dr. Puckett would go home to Puckett's Mills, Ohio, and go on delivering babies, treating stomach-aches, gardening, and giving advice. Arthur Peterson and his three assistants had received high praise and moved a notch toward a promotion for the brilliant detective work displayed in solving the murders of Bertha Morrison and Gloria Garden. Malone was glad on both counts.

Finally, there was forty-five hundred dollars in cash folded in his wallet. Malone thanked providence he hadn't wasted any time cashing the check.

Yes, things had turned out surprisingly well. Maybe sometime he'd even go back to New York on a visit. He still hadn't seen Grant's Tomb and the Statue of Liberty.

But, meanwhile, he had a long train ride ahead of him. Jake and Helene were in their compartment, holding hands and looking starry-eyed. He didn't want to interrupt. He'd already gone through all the newspapers while waiting for the train to start moving. And he wasn't sleepy.

For just five minutes the little lawyer wrestled with temptation. Then he got up and started moving toward the club car.

Maybe, if he was lucky, he could find a friendly little poker game——